**Desire glowed in her ~~eyes~~ ~~...~~ ~~br~~eath of
cold air to clear his head and cool his untimely ardor.**

Unexpectedly, Lianna smiled and whispered, "I rather suspected you were a gentleman."

"Right-ho." His mouth twisted wryly. "You must know some deuced wicked fellows if, by any stretch of the imagination, you think what I just did was gentlemanly."

She rubbed her face against the front of his coat, laughing softly. "It wasn't what you did—it's what you didn't do."

"Ah yes." Cameron sucked in another cold breath of air. "Don't be so quick to give me virtues I don't have, sweeting. This damnable mist has the look of rain to it, and I've no desire to be flopping about in the mud."

"The skies are clearing." She skimmed her fingers down the edge of his open coat and smiled archly. "But protest if you wish. I know the truth."

If you did, he thought sourly, you would not be so damned jolly about it. But far be it for him to shatter any romantic illusions she might have with something as vulgar as carnal reality. That she would have to discover on her own.

"This is a book to be savored. Enjoy!"
—Janelle Taylor

ROMANCE FROM ROSANNE BITTNER

CARESS   (0-8217-3791-0, $5.99)

FULL CIRCLE   (0-8217-4711-8, $5.99)

SHAMELESS   (0-8217-4056-3, $5.99)

SIOUX SPLENDOR   (0-8217-5157-3, $4.99)

UNFORGETTABLE   (0-8217-4423-2, $5.50)

TEXAS EMBRACE   (0-8217-5625-7, $5.99)

UNTIL TOMORROW   (0-8217-5064-X, $5.99)

Available wherever paperbacks are sold, or order direct from the Publisher. Send cover price plus 50¢ per copy for mailing and handling to Penguin USA, P.O. Box 999, c/o Dept. 17109, Bergenfield, NJ 07621. Residents of New York and Tennessee must include sales tax. DO NOT SEND CASH.

HIGHLAND HEARTS

Virginia Brown

Zebra Books
Kensington Publishing Corp.

http://www.zebrabooks.com

ZEBRA BOOKS are published by

Kensington Publishing Corp.
850 Third Avenue
New York, NY 10022

First Printing: September, 1997
10 9 8 7 6 5 4 3 2 1

Printed in the United States of America

This book is dedicated to Rita Harris Burke, whose friend-ship Fate was kind enough to bestow upon me, and in whom I have found a kindred spirit. Only someone with a true Gaelic soul would join me in dancing around the well under a full moon. . . .

BALLAD OF GLENCOE

Oh cruel was the snow that raked Glencoe,
and covered the grave o' Donald.
Oh cruel was the foe that raped Glencoe,
and murthered the house o' MacDonald.

They came in the blizzard, we offered them heat,
A roof o'er their heads, dry shoes for their feet.
We wined them and dined them, they ate of our meat;
and they slept in the house o' MacDonald.

Oh cruel is the snow that raked Glencoe,
and covered the grave o' Donald.
Oh cruel was the foe that raped Glencoe,
and murthered the house o' MacDonald.

They came from Fort William with murder in mind.
The Campbell had orders King William had signed.
"Put all to the sword," these words underlined,
"and leave none alive called MacDonald."

Oh cruel is the snow that sweeps Glencoe,
and covers the grave o' Donald.
Oh cruel was the foe that raped Glencoe,
and murthered the house o' MacDonald.

They came in the night while our men were asleep,
This band of Argylls, through snow soft and deep.
Like murthering foxes among helpless sheep,
They butchered the house of MacDonald.

Oh cruel is the snow that sweeps Glencoe,
and covers the grave o' Donald.
Oh cruel was the foe that raped Glencoe,
and murthered the house o' MacDonald.

Some died in their beds at the hand of the foe.
Some fled in the night and were lost in the snow.
Some lived to accuse him, who struck the first blow,
but gone was the house o' MacDonald.

Oh cruel is the snow that sweeps Glencoe,
and covers the grave o' Donald.
Oh cruel was the foe that raped Glencoe,
and murthered the house o' MacDonald.

—Seventeenth Century Scottish Ballad

Letter that ordered the Massacre of Glencoe:

"You are hereby ordered to fall upon the rabelle, the Macdonalds of Glenco, and to putt all to the sword under seventy. You are to have a special care that the old fox and his sones doe not escape your hands. You are to secure all the avenues, that no man escape. This you are to putt in execution at five of the clock precisely. And by that time, or very shortly after it, I will strive to be at you with a stronger party. If I do not come to you at five, you are not to tarry for me but to fall on. This is by the King's special commands, for the good and safety of the countrie, that these miscreants be cutt off root and branch. See that this be put in execution, without fear of favour. Else you may expect to be dealt with as one not true to King nor countrie, nor a man fitt to carry a commission in the King's service. Expecting you will not faill in the fulfilling hereof, as you love yourselfe, I subscribe these with my hand."

—Robert Duncanson
Ballacholis, 12th February 1692

In memory of Sir Jerry Merritt, a gallant knight prone to rescuing damsels in distress. I'm confident he earned his wings and white charger long before he left this world.

Prologue

July 27, 1689—Killiecrankie, Scotland

On his knees, with blood streaming over his brows and into his eyes, Cameron MacKenzie drew in a painful breath as he fumbled for his sword. Victory felt very much like defeat, as far as he was concerned. Stupid of him to have forgotten that being a Conqueror and Defender of the Right could be uncomfortable to the point of pain. He wiped sweat and blood from his eyes with the back of one hand, grimacing at his sharp torment.

Dead and dying lay strewn all around him. Their pitiful sounds were rising into the evening air as he struggled to his feet. They may have won the battle, defeating William's forces in this narrow pass, but it was a minor detail, in his opinion. Staggering with exhaustion, he lurched across the littered battlefield, numb to the carnage. So many dead, so many mangled, and for what? A cause. A bloody, futile cause. Bile rose in his throat and he forced it back down. Patriotism and nobility be damned. He was sick of it already, sick of the sight and smell of blood and gunpowder, sick of the sounds of cannon and men and horses screaming. And it had not escaped his notice that the causes of this particular battle, the driving forces behind it, were conspicuously absent from the field and all possible danger and inconvenience.

Except, of course, for Bonnie Dundee, and that worthy's patriotism had earned him the dubious honor of bleeding to death on the battlefield.

At the very moment of victory, the vainglorious general and patriot Viscount Dundee had been killed, spoiling Scotland's hope of restoring the throne to King James. Cameron had the vicious thought that it served him right. They would be heroes, he'd told them, saving their country from the depredations of the English and William. Aye, but now their victory was barren. Now the loyal heroes lay in the pass of Killiecrankie alongside the dead villains of William's army. Heroes? Yes, but dead ones. Not much to recommend it, to his way of thinking.

Long shadows stretched across the rocks and slopes, and in the soft gloom Cameron stumbled over a dead horse and went down with a fierce crack. The jarring blow radiated pain from his knees to his neck. Snarling an oath, he used his sword to lever himself upright again, and pushed on. The rusty smell of blood filled the soft summer night; twilight would last until midnight, leaving enough light to hunt for his kin. His father and brothers had been beside him, fighting back to back in the comparative security of their clansmen until—seized by some Godawful notion of heroics—they had dashed into the very thick of the fighting. In an instant, they had been swallowed up by the savage battle, disappearing from his sight.

Finding them before dark looked hopeless, with all the clans widely scattered, heaps of corpses and blood running in rivulets to stain rock and ground—he steeled himself against the encroaching thought that surely he should have found them by now if they were still alive. Of course they were alive. It would be a cruel trick of fate for them to die now, when he had only just returned to the family fold after years away.

Not that fate had been especially kind to him of late. Circumstances—to wit, politics—had involved him in nasty situations not of his making. Boiling intrigue and false accusations had interrupted his studies at a Paris university, necessitating his return to Wester Ross and home to support his father in a feud that should have been settled long before he was born. Beastly things, politics and blood feuds. Pastimes for the terminally bored, in his opinion, who had nothing better to do than squabble over scraps of land and rock, or a real or imagined insult.

It was that way with Kenneth MacKenzie—laird of Kintroy, father of five sons, widowed husband, and testy old curmudgeon who was overfond of quarreling with neighbors. In one generation, he had managed, because of his quarrels, to lose near half the land handed down from the past six generations. It was, Cameron thought wearily as he stumbled along the rocky incline, an incredible waste of time and energy. Just like this battle. What had James ever done for Scotland? Not much that he could see. But then, this dispute was over what William intended to do *to* Scotland, which was apparently insupportable to his father. God, he just hoped Kenneth MacKenzie had enough sense to keep his petty feuds to himself before they lost Kintroy proper.

Looming just ahead he saw a familiar figure, and for a gratifying moment, his blurred vision tricked him into believing it was his father. His pace quickened, reproachful words already forming on the tip of his tongue, but when he drew closer, he saw with weary disappointment that it was not Kenneth MacKenzie who stood swaying in the gloaming, but his father's old friend and ally, the MacIan of Clan Donald.

"MacIan ... have you seen my father?" Cameron was vaguely surprised that his voice sounded like the rusty scratch of grating steel. His throat was raw and swollen, and he desperately needed something to drink that didn't smell of blood.

"Aye, lad." The MacIan's huge hand stretched out to rest on Cameron's shoulder. "I have seen him."

He tensed. Even in the dim twilight, the gleam of pity was easily seen in the old man's dark eyes. Cameron took a stumbling backward step. His guts began knotting as he flung up one hand to stave off the inevitable words.

But MacIan continued, softly relentless. "Your father lies by yon crag, I fear, and your brothers with him. It pains me to be the one to tell you of it, for you know I held him dear."

Cameron closed his eyes and swallowed hard; when he opened them again, the MacIan held out a flask. " 'Tis not much, Cam, but 'tis all I have to offer you now."

While the MacIan watched him silently, Cameron took the flask and drank deeply, his throat seared by the bite of the whisky. He wanted to howl his rage and anguish, but it would avail him little. It was done, and there was nothing that could be said, nothing that would bring them back. Fools that they were, chasing glory as they had, it would only prolong the inevitable even if he could somehow bring them back.

They were always too hot for battle—a bone of contention with Cameron, who thought there must be a less violent method of keeping political balance and peace between England and Scotland. This view had caused a rift with his father for years, with Kenneth MacKenzie accusing him of being cowardly, and his retort that it took more courage to face those pompous fools in Parliament than it did a loaded cannon.

Well, there would be no more lively discussions, no more disagreements.

He was all that was left now—save for sixteen-year-old Jamie safely at home in Wester Ross. Reminded of his younger brother, he lowered the flask and returned it to MacIan.

His words were a rasping burn in his throat. "I will take my father and brothers home."

The MacIan did not reply, but inhaled deeply, looking suddenly old. His broad shoulders were bowed, and he passed a hand over his eyes. "They were good men, lad."

"Aye. They were."

The old man put out a hand when Cameron turned away, and said softly, "There will always be a place for you in Glencoe should you ever need shelter. Do not forget."

"I won't forget." He took a deep breath, almost choking at the smell of death around him. "Nay, nor will I ever forget this day and what was lost here."

The MacIan's huge hand fell to his side, and he nodded. "None of us are likely to forget. 'Tis a bitter time for all."

It was, Cameron thought, an understatement. In the space of a single day, his life had been shattered beyond comprehension. Nothing would ever be the same.

Chapter 1

December 31, 1691—Fort William

Cold winds rattled the windows of the governor's room in the fort, and gusts of snow spit against the glass panes. In the hallway outside, footsteps sounded, then the door swung open and Major Forbes filled the opening.

"MacIan, chief of Clan MacDonald in Glencoe has come to swear his oath, Governor."

Colonel John Hill turned, erect and military despite the rheumatism that made his bones ache. His lean face broke into a smile, and he was unable to hide the relief in his tired eyes. "Show him in at once, Major. I have been thinking of him all this day. Praise God that he has finally come, for now bloodshed can be avoided."

Anxiety still tinged his satisfaction at MacIan's arrival, and Hill paced the room barely glancing at the traveling chests against one wall, a long table crowded with papers, and a few scattered chairs of untamed hide. Deerskins covered the wood floor in places, and the peat fire smoked badly, as it usually did in a northwest wind. Blue smoke lay in a thin haze in the room, heatless and stifling. Small windows were thick with snowdrifts, and the sky was dull and leaden, promising more heavy snow. Hill thought again how dreary it was to be stuck in such a place when he was well into his sixties and should be allowed some comfort in his old age.

But at least one of his worries might soon be alleviated, if MacIan had come to swear the king's oath, as ordered. King William had offered pardon to all those rebellious Highland clans whose chief would swear an oath of fealty to him before January 1, 1692, and here it was late December. Colonel Hill fretted. Politics, particularly Scottish policies, always caused him anxiety; it was enough to kill most men, and more then once he'd thought himself far too close to the grave. While he had come to like most of the gruff Highlanders he'd met in this Godforsaken country, he had little love for duplicity. That, he preferred leaving to devious men like Argyll and Breadalbane, both crafty foxes with little compunction in stealing from their own kith and kin.

In the past month, it had nagged at Hill that the MacDonald chief of Glencoe had not yet taken the king's oath, for the clan was a small one, and vulnerable. And now, devil take him, MacIan had waited far too long, and there was precious little time. Hill scowled. Curse the touchy Highland honor that would not allow any man to take the lead in renouncing those ancient loyalties, but must dawdle until the last possible moment before yielding to the inevitable. Now it was the end of December, and few clans had signed, especially in light of the rumors of French fleets on the sea and King James returning to Scotland and his own. . . .

That knowledge made Hill irritable, and he turned with a jerk when MacIan was ushered into the room, and raked the old man with an assessing stare. It had been thirty years since last he'd seen MacIan of Clan Donald, but Colonel John Hill reflected ruefully that time had dealt much more kindly with the Highland laird than it had him.

The chief of Clan Donald was six-and-a-half feet tall, but it was his massive shoulders that caught the eye first, giving him the appearance of a well-muscled bull. With dark, fierce eyes and a prominent nose that jutted out like the prow of a ship,

MacIan was an imposing figure. His white hair was worn so long as to brush against his broad shoulders, and two thick mustaches like staghorns draped down over his mouth. Atop his head a bonnet perched rakishly, adorned with a bunch of faded heather that was the MacDonald badge. MacIan wore trews of dark tartan and knee-high riding boots of untanned leather, and his broad belt bore a dirk, brace of pistols, and long sword.

Removing his bonnet, MacIan lifted a hand in greeting. His deep voice sounded like a young man's. "It is the MacIan, come to take the government's oath."

Rather testily, Hill retorted, "You've been a sight too long about it. You should be at Inverary, not Fort William."

"But you are the Governor of Inverlochy."

"True, but I am a soldier, and the law decreed that the oath must be taken before a civil officer—only a *civil officer* can accept your oath, MacIan. You must know that. In May, you were willing to go to Argyll at Inverary—"

"That was in May." MacIan's soft English held a lilting Gaelic accent as he lowered it to a rough growl. "Since that time, I am not liking the name of Campbell. In June, I had ill words from the fox of Breadalbane."

Hill nodded dryly. "I was informed of your disagreement at Achallader with Lord Breadalbane—something about cattle-lifting, I understand."

Drawing himself up, MacIan's bushy white brows lifted. "There was mention of that, but it was a lawful act of war after Killiecrankie."

"And was not the first time you've given offense to my lord Breadalbane."

MacIan grinned now. " 'Tis true, Governor, that Glencoe has never loved Glenorchy or Glenlyon. And maybe 'tis true that their cattle have ofttimes found themselves in Glencoe, and even true that there has been some dirking of Campbells by MacIans. Gentlefolk often quarrel if they live too near one another. But 'tis also true that the MacIans have never wronged another man as Breadalbane has done."

There was no argument to that, and Hill nodded. "True

enough, but let us talk now of the oath—the king offered you a way of peace, but you have come to the wrong place. I can do nothing for you, MacIan. In one day's time it will be the New Year, and the period of mercy will be ended. What possessed you to come here instead of Inverary?''

"I did only as many others have done. Glengarry has not sworn."

"Yes, but he has a strong castle and is situated so that he is difficult to get at. You in Glencoe are only a few, two hundred or less, and you've no friends nearby. Worse, you have made powerful enemies."

MacIan's eyes grew troubled, but his lilting English was proud and defiant. "I will tell you the truth, Colonel—I could not give my oath to your government until I was assured that a certain hope was useless. Aye, 'tis true enough that Glencoe has few, but we've no traitors among us. Our men have the same blood as Angus Og in their veins, the MacDonald who sheltered King Robert the Bruce so long ago in his castle of Dunaverty. Our heritage and faith keep us true to the lawful line of kings, so that nothing can make us forswear allegiance save by our rightful king's order."

Hill regarded him for a long moment of silence, then coughed slightly at the sharp tang of smoke from the peat fire. "Am I to understand that order has come to you?"

"Aye, it has."

Stubborn old patriot. Even across the water, the exiled King James still exerted much influence over his followers, the faithful Jacobites.

After a moment of thought, Hill rubbed his aching temples with both hands. " 'Tis almost too late. Argyll is not in town at the moment, but that is most likely the better for you. In his absence, Sir Colin Campbell of Ardkinglas is sheriff-depute."

MacIan nodded. "Ardkinglas may be a Campbell, but he is an honest man."

"Aye, so he is. I will write a letter for you to give him, but go straight and swiftly to Ardkinglas."

Shoving aside a stack of papers, Hill sat down at his table and took up his pen. With quick strokes, he penned a plea to

Sir Colin of Ardkinglas to allow MacIan to swear the oath, saying that he had sought peace in the wrong quarter, and because the weather in Lochaber was severe, he was late in coming to take the oath. God knew, it was true enough, for the recent blizzard had clogged the mountain passes and made the roads nearly impassable. And it was eighty miles to Inverary.

When MacIan left Fort William and Inverlochy behind at three of the next morning, it had begun to snow again. Hill stood in his greatcoat and nightcap, watching the MacDonald chieftain mount his sheltie. Four bare-legged gillies ran alongside their mounted laird, and they all turned down the Loch Linnhe road and disappeared into the swirling white.

"God help him," Hill muttered with the icy taste of snowflakes on his tongue, "for he will be a week late in swearing. . . ."

The second week in January, Colonel Hill received a letter from Sir Colin Campbell announcing that he had accepted MacIan's oath of fealty on the sixth of January. He asked the governor to give Glencoe protection in the interim, until the certificate could be presented to the Council.

Immediately, Hill sent out the letters of protection, and smiled with relief. Seated before his peat fire, he reflected that perhaps now peace could settle on the Highlands. There was no reason that MacIan's oath of submission to King William should be refused. No good reason at all.

"You took your bloody time answering my summons, Cameron MacKenzie. I thought you valued your head more than that."

For a moment, Cameron did not reply to the earl's comment. Bloody bastard. It would give him no end of satisfaction to see just how insulting Breadalbane could be with a dagger in his throat, but of course, that would only earn him a lively jig at the looped end of a long rope, compliments of the earl's next of kin. No point in tweaking the old boy's nose too hard, not when the bleeding sod was waiting like a hungry fox for him to make a mistake. So he returned the earl of Breadalbane's gaze coolly and said, "I value it well enough."

Breadalbane grunted an inarticulate reply that quite successfully conveyed his skepticism. Cameron's hands curled into fists behind his back. Be damned to him. He set his jaw and waited.

A cheery fire blazed on the hearth, and wine stood in a pewter cup atop his desk as John Campbell, earl of Breadalbane, regarded Cameron with slumberous, hooded eyes. The lazy posture would not have deceived a child. Behind those sleepy eyes was a devious brain that spun constantly, always seeking new lands and goods, new methods of thievery. A most enterprising fellow. For a Highland man, Breadalbane bore all the sins and none of the virtues . . . as Cameron knew quite well.

He decided to abandon diplomacy. "Colonel Hill informed me that you wish to speak with me before I leave, my lord. I am in a hurry, so state your business."

Cameron's curt words brought Breadalbane's brows up, and he leaned forward to clasp his hands atop his desk, the chair creaking beneath his ample weight. "Insolent lot, you MacKenzies. Tell me—how is your brother?"

"You would know that better than I, my lord." Cameron did not allow an eyelash to flicker, though he briefly envisioned his dirk in Campbell's throat. He allowed himself only a moment of indulgence in the fantasy before he acknowledged that such an act would sign Jamie's death warrant were he to yield to the temptation. His own life, he might risk with such madness, but not his brother's.

"Aye, so I would know, MacKenzie." Campbell smirked. "Your brother is alive, if that's any comfort to you. Your continued cooperation will of course keep him that way. It amazes me the lengths some men will go to in order to avoid serving their betters, but then, that's the reason I learned long ago how to curb the more barbaric impulses of men such as yourself. Aye, taking Jamie MacKenzie has served me well, for all that he is such a trivial prisoner to anyone else. . . ."

"Did you call me here to boast? A pity I've no stomach for

it.'' Some of his self-control wavered slightly, so that his words came out in a snarling purr though the pleasant smile on his face did not falter. ''If you did not have my brother in your prison, 'tis unlikely I would be available to listen. Say what you want with me and be done with it. I've a long road ahead of me, and snow lies deep in the passes.''

''Ah, that is what I want with you, MacKenzie. You know the path well, whether it's deep in snow or muck. I would have you accompany a troop from Fort William into the glen beyond Loch Leven.''

Cameron stared at him. ''You want to march men down the Devil's Staircase in late January?''

''No, I want you to take the ferry and go by way of the coast road beyond Ballachulish.'' The earl made a steeple of his fingers, and rested his hands against his mouth as he studied Cameron. ''You will report to Robert Campbell of Glenlyon, and are under his command until further notice.''

''Glenlyon—you must be daft. It was Glenlyon who brought false charges against my brother. I'd as soon dirk him as not.''

''Aye, but you won't. Unless you wish to meet your brother on that low road that leads to the grave. For that is what will happen, Cameron MacKenzie, and you know it. All that stands between your brother and the hangman is your conduct—or surrender of the papers you hold. What is your choice?''

There was no choice. Breadalbane knew it and Cameron knew it. If he was fool enough to surrender the only evidence against Breadalbane that could convict him of conspiring with the Jacobites, he and Jamie both would die. No, those papers were safely hidden, and would not be used until there was no other way to stay alive. Once they were given to Breadalbane, his life would be worthless. Damn the scoundrel—he could not kill Jamie outright or Cameron would promptly expose him. And if Breadalbane murdered Cameron, then the sealed papers were to be delivered from a Glasgow barrister straightaway to King William. No, the earl was as trapped as was Cameron, but with more devious methods of torture at his disposal. Cameron sucked in a deep breath that tasted of peat smoke and bitterness.

"When do I join Glenlyon?"

The earl smiled—a thin, cruel curving of his mouth as he reached for his wine and took a sip. When he lowered the pewter cup, red droplets misted his upper lip. "At once. Glenlyon has taken some Argyll men and gone out against clan MacDonald of Glengarry. You are to march with them, but not in uniform. As you are not a conscripted soldier, I also thought it best that you not be issued government arms."

Cameron's mouth twisted wryly. "You must have taken a sudden liking to me, my lord, for I can think of few things more useless than government-issued muskets. They have such a nasty habit of misfiring, or even worse—exploding in some hapless recruit's hands so that he is forced to depend upon a beggar's cup for sustenance the rest of his days."

"Your levity is out of place, MacKenzie." Breadalbane's eyelids drooped even more, and his mouth twisted into a snarl. "Your only duty is to accompany the troops into the glen beyond Loch Leven."

Cameron frowned. "Into Glencoe?"

"Aye. You will stay there until further orders are given. Are you familiar with MacIan of Glencoe?"

"You know I am. He and my father were friends."

"Then it should comfort you to spend some time with such boon companions." Breadalbane's smile did not reach his eyes. "But see that you do not forget those you have left behind, MacKenzie."

"It is quite unnecessary to remind me of that. And while we are being so civil, you might recall that it was my father's clan who fought against the clans of Lochaber for you. Your lands would not be vast enough to fit into a cracked teacup if not for Kenneth MacKenzie's fighting men."

"Aye, but neither would I have been accused of siding with Jacobites if not for a loose-tongued MacKenzie." He waved a negligent hand. "You tarry too long, and there is much to be done."

"Precisely what are my orders, if I am not to be in uniform? I'm certain even the redoubtable Glenlyon can find Glencoe without me."

Breadalbane rustled some papers on his desk, and his voice was sharp. "You will be given your orders by Glenlyon when it is time for them. Do not fail me, MacKenzie, or it will go badly for your brother. I will be certain of it. Shut the door behind you, for the wind is cold."

Cameron left without another word, not trusting himself to keep his temper. It wasn't until he stepped outside into the cold wind that he took a deep breath of air untainted by Breadalbane. Curse the bloody sod. He hated feeling helpless, hated this feeling of impotent fury. At some moments he seriously considered exposing the earl, handing over the papers and be damned to it all. But now that Jamie was in the earl's power, he could not. He could do nothing but act as Breadalbane's gillie.

A few flakes of snow fluttered down, lightly powdering his black hair with white. He looked up into the fading light of day, and saw Ben Nevis in the distance, the high mountain peak almost obscured by heavy gray clouds. More snow. The Glengarry MacDonalds would have gone to ground by now, tucked snugly into warm quarters to wait out the cold. Military action in the very heart of a Highland winter was uncommon, unless there had been an uprising or rebellion. What then, could Breadalbane have planned? More evil, no doubt. Whatever was afoot, it would bear trouble for someone, of that he was certain.

He had no love for the Glengarry MacDonalds, indeed, had crossed swords with them on more than one occasion, and had no objection to Glenlyon pursuing them to the ends of hell if he desired. After all, the rebellious nodcocks had not even bothered to take King William's oath. Yet he did not understand why Glenlyon was even going to the valley of Glencoe, for he knew that the MacIan had taken William's oath and bided by the terms.

If it was not the Glengarry MacDonalds they were to pursue, then what could Breadalbane have planned?

Chapter 2

February 1, 1692—Glencoe

Lianna Fraser grabbed her cousin's arm, alarmed at the sight
of so many soldiers flowing down the Loch Leven shore road
into the glen. "Who are they, Mary?"

"Red coats and gray breeks mean William's men, most like.
But the man in front wears a sprig of bog-myrtle in his bonnet—
which Campbell is he, Robbie?"

Robbie MacDonald squinted through the trees, one arm holding back his sister Mary and his young cousin. He was big and
brawny like many of his clan MacDonald kin, with his light
hair worn long to brush against his shoulders. His voice was
low and rough with contempt, the reply flung over one shoulder.

"Robert Campbell—the Glenlyon devil."

Lianna's fingers dug more tightly into Mary's arm at Robbie's ominous tone. "Does he mean trouble, Robbie?"

"Ah, tha' I canna say, lass. No' until he tells the reason he's
come to Glencoe with so many men. Mary, stay here with
Lianna until I see if 'tis safe for ye to be seen. And here—
hide my musket in the peat stacks. I willna risk it with William's
men." He looked troubled for a moment, then grinned. "No'

unless the MacIan gives word tha' we can use fire and sword against the bloody swine.''

"The MacIan would never do that,'' Mary said sharply. "He took William's oath and swore all to it. So dinna think you'll get a chance to act the fool, Robbie lad.''

Robbie laughed softly, and there was a reckless light in his dark eyes. "This would no' be the first time I have dirked a Campbell, or tha' the heather has overcome the gale.''

"Robbie, no!'' Mary swiped at her brother, but he eluded her with easy grace and stepped from the concealing brush into the open, where he joined the twenty MacDonald men moving forward to meet the soldiers. She stood there a moment, indecision on her round face, then looked down at the musket Robbie had left leaning against a rock. When she looked up at Lianna, her eyes were strained.

"I'll hide the gun in the peat. You wait here for me.''

Lianna would have protested, but the expression on Mary's face stopped her. She nodded, holding her cloak tight around her. "I'll call out if there's need.'' In only a few moments, Mary returned without the weapon, brushing dirt from her palms. She looked grim and troubled, and Lianna frowned.

"Do the soldiers mean trouble for us, Mary?''

Mary's voice was taut with apprehension. "Soldiers always mean trouble. William's soldiers, anyway. Perhaps we should go back to the cottage.''

But Mary didn't move, and Lianna realized how frightened she was. For an instant, she thought of her mother's dark words about William, though Papa had said irritably not to frighten the child—but then, Papa was far across the channel in France now, because of this same king and his soldiers. Yet up here in the remote Highlands, it was supposed to be safer. Wasn't that why Mama had sent her to her family? Never mind that Lianna had been too frightened to cross the Channel, terrified of the vast body of water that seemed endless. It was safer here than on a flimsy wooden craft at the mercy of the wind and sea, and so Mama had said it was best she come to Glencoe, because France was so full of foreign enemies anyway.

"Don't worry, Mary. There must be a good reason for them

coming here. Let's go back to the cottage. Robbie will discover their purpose and tell us, I'm certain.''

Mary looked up, biting her lower lip. "I canna go without knowing what is afoot—let's wait and watch.''

Lianna followed Mary into the rough brush of the thicket, where they peered out through the tangle of bare branches. Funny Mary, she thought, slanting her cousin a glance. So practical most of the time, with her no-nonsense ways, while beneath that pragmatic exterior lurked the heart and soul of a romantic dreamer. A glance at Mary MacDonald provided the idle observer only the most cursory of information: soft dark hair, warm brown eyes, and a sturdy little body that looked capable without a hint of grace. But despite this modest veneer, Mary was possessed of an inner beauty that the more discerning viewer would notice at once. At eighteen, two years younger than Lianna, Mary was years ahead of her in many ways. While she tended to be impulsive, Mary was more deliberate and cautious, and always willing to say something kind about others. There was a sweet pathos about her at times that was heart-tugging.

Mary might enviously remark on Lianna's thick red-gold hair and green eyes, or say wistfully that even if she had pretty gowns of fine material they would not look the same on her sturdy figure as they did on Lianna's slender frame, but there was no denying that in terms of capabilities, Mary far outstripped her. Though obviously shocked at Lianna's inability to bake bread, or dress out a deer, Mary was kind enough not to comment on her defects. And they had worked out a satisfying trade, in that Lianna was teaching Mary to read, while her cousin was teaching her to cook and spin wool.

There was something to be said, Lianna reflected as she peered through the bushes at the men below, for knowing more than could be found in books. Brisk air seeped through the open front of the garment to chill her, and she shivered. Mary was right. She should have worn something more practical than this thin linen gown. Her eyes narrowed against the light when she looked up. Snow lay thick in the mountain passes above them, and though no snow lay in the valley, the wind was icy at times, chilling her exposed flesh without mercy. Another shiver made her cling tightly to the edges of the cloak.

Mary must have felt her shiver, for she glanced around, her dark eyes narrowing slightly with amusement. "Tha' green linen gown is bonny, but not so very warm for you, I think."

"No." Lianna's smile was wry. "When I was sitting by the fire, I thought the weather would be fairer outside. I forgot that everyone else here seems not to mind the cold as much as I do. I should have taken your advice."

"Aye, but 'tis your first winter in the Highlands. Next year, you'll know better, I ken."

Next year? Dismay filled Lianna. No, she wanted to be home soon, back in Edinburgh where it was warmer, back with her parents and brothers, back at her studies—oh, why had everything changed so? A rhetorical question only, for she knew full well why her life had been turned upside down in a short space of time: Papa and her brothers had gone into exile with King James to France, and now Mama had gone to join them.

A foolish, noble cause, in her opinion. Why must Papa always be a hero? And her brothers were just as foolish, prattling of glory and honor when it all came down to the greed and vanity of kings. But of course, she would never express such radical views aloud, for it would cause no end of argument.

And it wasn't that she was unhappy with Mama's Highland family, but it was all so different, everything so foreign to her. Even the language was alien, the Gaelic tongue confusing most of the time. She knew a few words and phrases, of course, for Catriona MacDonald Fraser had used her native tongue on occasion, but for the most part, she spoke proper English like the other Lowland families.

Lianna sighed. But for Mary, who was cheerful and amusing, she would have been miserable here.

"Whsst! Lianna—do look there at the Campbell. Does he seem friendly to you?" Mary's knuckles were white where her fingers were curled tightly around a branch of the small tree hiding them, and her eyes were anxious.

Dutifully, Lianna moved aside a barren tree branch and peered through the tangle at Glenlyon. He was tall, almost as tall as her cousin Robbie, with a long thin face, hooked nose, and lips that looked petulant. His hair was flaxen with no gray that she could see, though he looked to be well past fifty. At first glance, he seemed almost handsome, but when Lianna looked more closely, she saw lines of dissipation around his eyes, and deep grooves on each side of his mouth. She shivered suddenly, but tried to be reassuring.

"He's smiling. That's a good sign."

"Perhaps. Ah, we need to be closer so we can better hear wha' is being said."

"Robbie told us to wait here—"

"Aye, but Robbie is down there and we are not. We can lie in the rocks above them, and no one will be the wiser. Are you coming with me?"

"I'm not a sure-footed goat like you," Lianna muttered, and Mary laughed softly. When they were sprawled on their stomachs atop a level rock slightly above the road, Mary motioned Lianna closer as they peered over the ledge.

"Move closer so we can hear, Lianna."

"Any closer, and I'll be atop their heads!"

Cautiously, Lianna edged forward a little more, until she could hear them as well as see the men below. Pale light glinted from musket barrels and buckles. So many of them, over a hundred, she thought, forming rank in the narrow pass between rugged rocks and brush. What did they want?

The MacIan's eldest son John stepped out to speak with Glenlyon, courteously inquiring the reason for their arrival at Glencoe. Tall and lean, John's face was grave as he regarded the soldiers.

Glenlyon smiled, and gave a congenial explanation that they were on their way to Inverary to collect cess and hearth-money for the government. "It was Colonel Hill's command that we bide in Glencoe a week or two. No doing of mine, John, but soldiers must obey their orders, heh? As the weather is unchancy, Hill called a halt to our march. Inverlochy is crowded as a cried fair, with no room for my lads to bunk, so here we are. The Candlemas rents are due, and with the grim duty of collecting taxes for Parliament from us poor Highlandmen—

well, nothing for it but the colonel decided we must pack off to Glencoe.'' Campbell shook his head, still smiling. '' 'Tis a heavy affliction, I know, but I will see that it's made as light as possible on you. After all, 'tis better that a friend and kinsman should be a burden than strangers, heh? And how is my nevoy Sandy? Fit and fine, I trust, and making my niece happy. . . .''

Mary nudged Lianna and whispered, ''Glenlyon is kin to the MacIan by way of marriage, as his niece is Alasdair's wife, so is daughter-in-law to the MacIan. He claims kinship to Alasdair as a nephew. Aye, he is a kinsman, but not one that is well-trusted.''

''He certainly behaves as if he is.''

''Aye, but John and Sandy see through him well enough, I warrant.''

Lianna turned back to listen, digging her fingers into a crease in the rock to hold on. John was nodding slowly.

''You and your lads are welcome here, Glenlyon. While Glencoe has not much to offer, what we have is yours for the taking.''

''I never doubted it.'' Glenlyon's teeth flashed in a hearty grin. ''I look forward to a family gathering, though 'tis a month too late for Hogmanay. Here, lad, let me introduce you to two of my officers, Lieutenant Lindsay and Ensign Lindsay. . . .''

''Come on,'' Mary whispered, and started to slide back down off the rock. '' 'Tis best no one sees us up here.''

Clad in her bulky garments, it was more difficult for Lianna than for Mary, and she wriggled backward along the rough slope, scraping her bare palms painfully. Tiny pebbles loosened and bounced, and she lost her grip and started to slip. Grabbing at a jagged edge, Lianna held tight to keep from falling.

Below, soldiers were filing past, headed down into the valley. Gray light gleamed on musket barrels, and she had a dizzying view of a sea of three-cornered hats bobbing in synchronized motion. Her fingers cramped, but she could not move backward without falling, nor forward without being seen, so she clung there, praying the men would soon pass so she could move.

''Lianna—put your feet against the rock behind you and ease down slow,'' Mary called softly.

Lianna felt blindly for the rock, and when her foot brushed against it, she levered herself upward a bit. Praise God—support! Now she could move, and she began to inch her way to one side to join Mary. *Blast all this wool*—Her legs tangled in the bulky folds of her cloak, and her gown wadded up between her knees, impeding her progress. More irritated than cautious, she reached down to snatch her cloak out of the way. The rock that supported her foot gave way suddenly, and sent her careening sideways along the steep slope of the boulder.

Lianna clutched frantically at thin air and rock sliding swiftly past her hands, then plummeted over the side and toward the road ten feet below. To her horror, she saw one of William's men below and knew that she could not avoid hitting him.

There was only time to scream a warning. She had a brief impression of dark hair and startled eyes looking up, then the jarring blow of her body against his as she descended on him like a sack of stones. A muffled curse sounded in her ear, but she was saved from striking the ground by a pair of strong arms around her. The force of her descent made him stagger, but he did not fall or drop her, instead held her against his hard chest.

Breathless and appalled, Lianna dared a quick glance upward. "I-I beg your pardon, sir!" Her heart was thudding, and her insides knotted. She twisted in his embrace, expecting him to release her. When he did not, but continued to hold her, she put a hand against his chest and frowned. "You may put me down. At once, if you please. . . ."

But his arms only tightened. Lianna looked up again, this time studying him. Something fluttered deep in the pit of her stomach, and her breath caught. Saints above, this was not at all what she expected from one of William's men. Horns and a forked tail, perhaps, but not this seductive insolence.

The clear gray eyes regarding her were coolly intelligent and fringed with dark lashes half-lowered in suspicion. His face could have belonged in an artist's rendition of a sullen archangel, with boldly sculpted lines of cheek and jaw, and a mouth set into a faintly sulky line. Gray morning light lent a diffused glow to his black hair and tangled in the ebony strands with

the subtle illumination of a tarnished halo. Like a fallen angel
. . . Oh dear. He was, Lianna thought with a hint of panic, as
beautiful and cold as a marble statue.

And his cupped hands were touching her in places only her
mother had seen. She squirmed.

"A most novel way of greeting the enemy, lass."

His voice held only a faint burr of the Highlands, deep and
richly textured, velvet over steel. Lianna took a deep breath of
cold air, her voice sharp. "And are you?"

"Am I what?"

"The enemy." She squirmed in his embrace again, this time
shoving the heels of her palms hard against his chest.

"No." He swung her down in an abrupt motion to set her
on her feet. "I consider those in Glencoe as my friends, not
my enemies."

Unconvinced, Lianna crossed her arms over her chest to still
their trembling. "So you say, but friends do not usually arrive
bearing arms, sir."

Glancing past her at the armed soldiers trailing into the valley,
his eyes narrowed slightly. "Glenlyon gave his explanation for
being here." His brow lifted mockingly when he turned back
to her. "But I am sure you heard all that from your hiding
place."

She flushed, but managed a casual shrug. "I heard some of
it, enough to know that he claims to mean us no harm."

"Aye. So he says."

Lianna frowned. "Sir, do you mean—"

"Oh no, don't be putting words in my mouth. I mean only
that he has distinctly given a reason why we are here."

Lianna stared up at him with a frown. He was so tall, his
frame a solid presence towering over her, dark and slightly
menacing. He stepped back to survey her with a raking glance
from head to toe, and his mouth twisted. "You're shivering
with cold. You should be by a warm fire instead of lurking in
the rocks to leap atop unwary strangers."

"Soldiers are supposed to always be alert. And anyway,
when we saw you coming, we had to find out if there was
danger, so we climbed up—"

"We?" His gaze swept past her to the high ledge of rock overhead, and this time when he looked back at her, amusement lit his eyes to the color of pale smoke. "Should I be chary of another angel falling from heaven?"

Heat warmed Lianna's cheeks at his obvious mockery. Annoyed, she tilted her head, weaving as much scorn as possible into her voice. "If I were you, I would be more wary of being left behind by your comrades."

"Nay, they are no comrades of mine. Being left behind would be a blessing instead of a curse."

There was such venom in his tone that any retort Lianna might have made stilled on her tongue. Confused suddenly, she fumbled with the hood of her cloak. Maddeningly, it defied her efforts to draw it over her head, the heavy cloth eluding her grasp. He reached out, his hands swift and competent as he pulled the fold of wool over her head and tucked her loose curls inside. The brush of his fingers against her cheek made her skin tingle, and she drew in a sharply audible breath that stilled his movement.

Unexpectedly, he smiled. She was transfixed by the change in his face. His features rearranged, becoming no longer coldly forbidding, but warm, Apollo come to life, imbued with a vibrant intensity that sent shivers up her spine. Slowly, she exhaled, and her breath formed a frosty cloud between them.

He studied her a moment, lashes half-lowered over his eyes, the faint smile still tilting his mouth. This time, there was no mockery in his tone, just a husky softness that sent a shiver up her spine.

"Such lovely hair. Bright as a candle flame." He lifted an escaped strand and rubbed it gently between his thumb and fingers. "And soft as copper silk. *Cáite an robh thu an dè?*" When she just stared at him blankly, his mouth crooked into a slight smile. "Just as I thought. You're no Highland lass. What is your name?"

"Lianna Fraser. Of Edinburgh."

She could have bitten her tongue immediately. Why should she give him her name—or any other information that might be used against her? But there was a strange tension simmering inside her, an invisible cord that seemed to be working her jaw, opening her mouth to blurt out details that he had no need to know.

"Edinburgh? You're a long way from home, then. Rather unexpected, finding so fair a Lowland flower blooming in the winter Highlands."

"I've been told that I frequently do the unexpected."

She pulled her hair from his hand and tucked it beneath the hood of her cloak. Her fingers shook slightly, and she knotted them into a fist and shoved them into the loose folds of wool cloak so that he would not see and think—or know—she was uneasy. It had grown quiet, and she glanced past him to see that they were all alone on the road now, as the soldiers and Glencoe men had disappeared from sight down the road and around a bend. Only the sound of the wind could be heard whining through the rocks. Her heart lurched. Had Mary fled, or did she still lurk in the rocks and trees?

As if reading her mind, he gestured to the empty road. "It seems that we have been forgotten. While I don't mind, it's probably best if you aren't found alone with me. Somehow, I don't imagine that your father would accept the unlikely explanation that is the truth."

"As he's far away, my father isn't likely to hear about it." She dug her nails into her palms when his brow rose, cursing herself for once more blurting out facts he need not know. What should it matter to him where her father was?—but it very well might, if he suspected that her father was the same Dallas Fraser said to be in exile with King James.

"Far away, is he? What a provocative thought."

His eyes sharpened, and the suggestion of a smile flickered at one corner of his mouth. She held her breath—did he guess? Would he make his suspicions known to Glenlyon and endanger them all? After all, being a Jacobite was a serious offense against the Crown, and the MacIan had sworn an oath of loyalty to William for all Glencoe. It could well be treason if they were accused of harboring a suspected Jacobite's daughter. There seemed no way to undo the damage she might have just done, nothing to do but pray he would not guess the truth behind her careless words.

A long moment of silence passed before he gave a casual shrug and said "How fortunate for me that your father is far away, little beauty," and she breathed a grateful prayer.

"So it is." A gust of wind scoured the rocks and lifted the hem of her skirts, and she put a hand down to keep them from whipping up around her knees. "While my father may be absent, my cousins are very protective of me, however. If I don't join them soon, they may very well come looking for me."

"Ah, that wouldn't be your cousin coming up the road now, would it? The fierce-looking chap with a long stave in one hand?"

Robbie . . . Lianna dared a glance, and was dismayed to see Robbie storming up the sloping road toward them. His hair glinted pale in the light, fluttering around his shoulders, and in one hand he did, indeed, carry a stout stick. Mary trailed behind him, her shorter legs struggling to keep up.

Whirling back around, she said urgently, "You'd best join the others quickly, sir. Robbie has a dreadful temper, and he doesn't always pause to ask questions before he acts."

"It must be a family trait."

The obvious amusement in his face made Lianna's voice sharp. "You might very well jest, but 'tis true, I assure you."

"Oh, I've no doubt of that, little beauty. But I think I can handle your cousin Robbie well enough."

Robbie was close enough now that Lianna could see the gleam in his pale eyes, and she turned back almost desperately. "Please sir—do not make me beg you. If you provoke Robbie into a fight, your captain will no doubt deal with us all harshly—"

"*Caileag górach* . . . I must seem a grim fellow, if you think I would risk starting a war. Do I really look that villainous? Or as if I'm one of William's men?"

"Aye, you look as if you have seen a fight or two."

"It's a far cry from a fight to a slaughter, and that's what it would be, Lianna Fraser, were I to fight Robbie MacDonald."

"Robbie's quite capable—"

He sounded impatient now. "Foolish girl, he's unarmed save for a wooden staff. I may not carry a government musket, but I've weapons enough to do damage to a brace of wild boars, in case you haven't noticed."

He stared at her, frowning, the wind tugging at his hair, and she suddenly realized that he was not wearing the red coat and gray breeches of the king's men, but tartan trews, knee-high leather boots, and a buff greatcoat. His head was bare, dark hair brushing over his collar in the back. A broad leather belt around his waist bore a brace of pistols, dirk, and a sword that dangled against his left leg. He looked competent and dangerous.

Though he spoke with a distinctive accent, his English was much more intelligible than that of some of her cousins. His words blurred only on certain syllables, with the lilt characteristic of the Scottish Highlands. And he made the name Fraser sound like a soft snarl.

"Run along to Mary while I properly greet Robbie, Miss Fraser."

It did not at first occur to Lianna to wonder how he knew Mary's name, not until Robbie reached them, a grin wide on his face. He halted only a foot away, eying the man up and down, his dark gaze raking over him with insolent thoroughness. They were of like height, but Robbie was fair and brawny, where the stranger was dark and lean as a weapon, looking as dangerous to Lianna as a wolf lurking in the rocks.

It was Robbie who spoke first, his rough Highland burr reproachful. "Plague take ye, Cameron, for no' coming down into the glen with the others. Until Mary told me 'twas you, I thought my wee cousin might be in trouble up here with one of William's bloody men—but wha' in God's name is a Mac-Kenzie doing with the fox of Glenlyon?"

"It's not by choice, Robbie, I'll tell you that much. Breadalbane can be—persuasive. Deadly persuasive."

Lianna looked from her cousin to Cameron and back again. Robbie swore in sympathy, clapping Cameron on the back in comradely fashion as they started down the steep slope into the valley, and both men seemed to have completely forgotten her.

When Mary reached her, her round face was flushed with exertion. "Are you all right? I saw you fall, and when I saw 'twas Cameron who caught you, I ran to fetch Robbie. If Glenlyon means trouble, I thought 'twould be best to hear it in private from a friend, so—"

"Do you know him well? This Cameron MacKenzie?"

"Aye. What did you think—? That I would leave you up here with a man who might harm you? Och, cousin, 'tis little you maun think of me if you think I would do such as that."

"That's not what I meant." Tugging irritably at the edges of her cloak where it flew open under the press of wind, Lianna stomped past Mary. She trudged down the steep slope between rocks, thinking furiously that her attempts to stave off a fight must have been greatly amusing. No doubt he thought her a foolish girl—indeed, he had probably known her MacDonald cousins longer than she had, for in truth, she'd met most of them only a few months before. Vile man—but would he inform Glenlyon if he suspected her father of Jacobite leanings? Men had been hanged and worse for being accused of Jacobite sympathies, and she shuddered to think she might have unwittingly endangered her kin.

Oh, this was all so confusing, the convoluted politics of the Highlands. No wonder Papa had frequently muttered that the clan system had a good premise, but a suicidal resolution. He'd spent the last five years trying to consolidate Scotland under one leader, and for his pains, was called Jacobite by some, Royalist by others. Yet Papa had managed to straddle the political fence quite efficiently. Apparently, she had none of Dallas Fraser's facile abilities, for every time she'd opened her mouth to Cameron MacKenzie, she had blundered badly.

"Lianna, Lianna—what is it? Cameron didna insult you, did he?" Mary's short legs pumped hard to keep up with Lianna's swifter pace and longer legs, and she sounded so anxious that Lianna jerked to a halt and turned on her.

"He's insufferable, rude, arrogant, and—" She took a deep breath, "—and I do not know if he can be trusted."

"Saints above—did he touch you?" Mary grabbed her arm when she started walking again, whirling her around. "Did he? Tell me the truth, or so help me, I will tell my father and you know what that will do—"

"No. Do not do that." Lianna met her worried gaze. Mary's honest brown eyes were indignant, outraged that her cousin might have been compromised or harmed in any way, and suddenly Lianna could not say aloud what she feared she had done. She managed a semblance of a smile, fully aware of the way her mouth didn't quite manage reassurance. "It's not that at all, Mary, I swear it. He did not touch me except when he broke my fall."

"Oh. But you said he insulted you, and you know tha' Robbie would—"

"I meant that he ... embarrassed me. He allowed me to make a complete goose of myself—is he trustworthy, Mary?" She glanced down the road again, frowning. "After all, he is William's man, and he's with Glenlyon. Can you trust him not to be here for villainous reasons? Peace is so uncertain right now, even with the pardon offered by William."

Mirth danced in Mary's dark eyes, and she tucked her hand into Lianna's arm and gave it a squeeze. "No one ever died of embarrassment, I ken. And you need not worry about Cameron MacKenzie. He is familiar to Glencoe. His father—slain at Killiecrankie, God rest his soul—was good friends with the MacIan. Cameron would never offer us harm."

Still clutching the edges of her cloak, Lianna did not reply. She looked ahead, watching MacKenzie's tall, lithe form stride beside Robbie down the narrow winding road through the glen. They were deep in conversation, apparently having forgotten the two women behind them. Then Cameron MacKenzie glanced back, and grinned when he saw her looking at him. The rogue. She turned her head away, and heard him laugh.

For an instant, she recalled the strange expression on his face when she had asked if he was the enemy. She'd had the oddest impression of doubt in his eyes, as if he wondered that himself, but then, she was always being told she had an overactive imagination. Should she mention it to Mary? It was entirely possible she was only being foolish again, as she had been earlier when she'd assumed he meant Robbie some harm, but she could not escape the disquiet that seized her. Maybe it was only the fact that soldiers had come to Glencoe, when the little valley had been so peaceful since she'd arrived this past summer. All this talk of loyalties, wars, and rightful kings was beginning to wear on her. She should ignore it all, as she usually did Papa's political diatribes.

Yes, it must be her foolish apprehension again, that was all. Nothing ever came of such vague, unfounded fears.

Chapter 3

It took all day to quarter Glenlyon's men among the cottages scattered through the glen, three here, five there, until they were all assigned places to eat and sleep. Officers, of course, were given their choice of dwellings, and the MacIan gravely offered his own principal residence as a courtesy. Glenlyon leaped at the chance, his bluff, hearty manner wearing thin on Cameron's temper, but apparently well-accepted by MacIan.

It occurred to Cameron that the laird's high sense of honor precluded his judging Glenlyon harshly. Noble, but foolhardy, just like his own father had been. It was akin to inviting a fox into the henhouse, in his opinion. But then, in the last few years he had become a cynical fellow, in any case. And if MacIan wanted to welcome Campbell to Glencoe, there was very little he could do about it.

Only John and Alasdair, MacIan's sons, seemed suspicious, and Sandy more so than his brother.

"I canna like it," he muttered to Cameron. "Glenlyon has not come to Glencoe for Glencoe's good. He may be a hearty fellow, but beneath those fine manners and cheery countenance is a heart as rotten as peat."

Cameron kept his opinion to himself, even though he heartily agreed with Sandy. But then, he had never trusted Robert Campbell. In his youth, Campbell had made ducks and drakes of his inheritance, gambling and drinking it all away, until poverty reduced him to taking the position of a captain in Argyll's regiment. After the defeat at Killiecrankie, Campbell had lost cattle to MacIan in the raids against his land—acts of war, certainly, but viewed with bitterness by not only Glenlyon, but Breadalbane, who had confronted the MacIan with his losses at a meeting of the clans in June. The Achallader confrontation must have been a lively encounter, and Cameron rather regretted that he had missed it.

He wondered what MacIan would say if he knew it had been the earl of Breadalbane who had sent Glenlyon here, not Colonel Hill as Campbell claimed. Glenlyon's assertion that the Governor had sent them was completely false. At the Ballachulish ferry above Glencoe, Colonel Hill's major had come across them on his return from London, and expressed surprise at seeing Argyll's troops. Major Forbes looked troubled upon learning they were to lodge in Glencoe—a fact that had not escaped Cameron's notice. But why would Glenlyon lie about it now, other than the fact that the Campbell preferred to lie even when the truth would serve him better? It made him uneasy, and someone should take MacIan aside and tell him that Colonel Hill, a rather kindly if ineffective fellow, had nothing to do with their presence in Glencoe.

But not him. What could he say? That Forbes was surprised to see them so Glenlyon must have lied? The lie would be easily explained away by that silver-tongued devil, no doubt, and then there would be billy-hell to pay. No, he could not risk repercussions against his brother Jamie. If he were to arouse suspicions that turned out to be false, he could do as much harm as if he had done nothing.

Lord knows, he was certainly no crusader, and he hated Glenlyon enough to do him an ill if he could—but he liked the MacDonalds enough to do them a good turn if he could. Discretion seemed the order of the day, though he fully intended to keep his eye on Glenlyon.

It was near the end of the day before all the baggage was

stored and men were billeted through the glen among the cottages strewn in copses or atop hillsides. Families tended to
build close to one another in small clusters of stone cottages
and outbuildings. Peat stacks were shared, as were stores, and
life was communal and content for the most part.

"So how d'ye find Glencoe, Cam? No' muckle changed
since yer last visit, I warrant," Robbie said, pausing beside
Cameron where he stood waiting for Glenlyon's order to be
given as to his lodging.

"No, not much changed at all since last I was here."

It was the truth. Glencoe was still as Cameron remembered
from a summer spent here when he was a boy; he'd fished in
the river Coe that snaked through the valley between craggy
buttresses. Midway through the glen, the river formed a shallow,
boggy loch. On the north shelf of the loch stood the village of
Achtriachtan, housing one of the gentry of the clan. The river
Coe wound through woodlands, its banks often swollen due to
the main tributary that drained from the corries of Bidean nam
Bian. Perched just north of this junction of waterways was the
village of Achnacon, and not far from it, the hamlet and farm
of Inverrigan. From there, the sea could be seen as a thin blue
haze on the horizon, and the MacIan's house of Carnoch was
nestled among the misty dunes and woodlands that stretched
toward the sea. Except for scattered shepherds' bothies and the
remote shielings that were used in summer, most of the clan
lived around Carnoch, or in the three clachans nearby.

Glencoe was a beautiful place, warmer in the winter, pro-
tected by the high crags around it, watered by the river and
lush with tall grasses for livestock. From Loch Leven and Loch
Linnhe came fresh herring and salmon, and the Coe abounded
with sea-trout. Oats and corn grew thick in the summers, the
hills were dense with red deer and roebuck, and the ancient
Royal Forest of Dalness was tenanted by MacIan's clansmen.
It was a snug, fertile valley, a garden of plenty amidst the stony
fortresses of mountains surrounding it.

Cameron had pleasant memories of it, of long days spent
fishing and hunting with his brothers while his father visited
the MacIan, of supping on foamy milk, hot bread, and rich

cheese in the evening while tales of valor were told around the fire. Pipers would play, up in the hills at the shepherds' crofts, and the haunting tunes of ballads and rousing war songs would fill the air of a long twilit eve.

And it painfully reminded Cameron of all that he had lost—of his own home and the king's justice. Justice—a regal name for thievery these days, he thought with admitted cynicism. But why shouldn't he be bitter? His fathers and brothers were hardly in their graves before the king's clerics and constables had come calling with eviction notices, and as a thoughtful touch, made certain that Cameron and Jamie left with only the clothes on their backs. Mercy was extended, however, and they were allowed to leave with heads still firmly attached to necks, but it had been close.

And now Jamie was bound in a cold prison by Breadalbane's order and Glenlyon's treachery.

Jamie—young, hot-tempered, too quick to retaliate and too slow to recognize danger. It could yet cost him dear, if Cameron could not convince the earl to release him. Breadalbane might hold him, but it was Glenlyon he held responsible for Jamie's imprisonment.

A lively burst of laughter caught his attention, and Cameron turned. He watched with interest as a group of young women emerged from a cottage, chattering like magpies. It was a touch of normalcy, sweeping out the sordid mess of his brooding thoughts like a gust of fresh wind through a cow byre. Lianna Fraser stood out from the others, her coppery mane of hair shining in the fading light.

How the devil had she come to be in Glencoe? Naturally, if her father was in exile with King James across the water, it was certainly reason enough for her to be anywhere else but with that worthy individual—kings having a lamentable tendency to draw trouble. But why come here, of all the Godforsaken spots in Scotland? With all the recent troubles, couldn't she have gone somewhere safer—Denmark, perhaps? Lord knows, it was the safest spot he could think of, and there were moments he wished he was there instead of here, having to stomach men like Breadalbane and Glenlyon.

It was Robbie who solved the mystery for him, his light brows lifting a little when he saw where Cameron was looking. "So ye have noticed our Lianna, have ye? Aye, she's a bonny lassock, for all tha' she isna from Glencoe. Her mother was the MacIan's niece by marriage, but was taken to wed against her will by a Borderer. But tha' was near twenty-five years ago, forgiven for the most part now, as he has been good to her, they say." Grinning, Robbie leaned close, his voice lowering as he nudged Cameron with his elbow. "But dinna think to do the same with Lianna, lad, for her father is privy to James and a formidable foe. 'Tis said he once fought seven men alone, and came out the victor."

Amused, Cameron eyed Robbie. "I assure you that I am not looking for a wife, Robbie. I've troubles enough as it is, God knows."

Robbie howled with laughter. "Aye, 'tis said tha' he tha' has a wife has a master." He rubbed his chin, still grinning. "But 'tis also said tha' lassies are like lamb-legs, they'll neither saut nor keep."

Withholding comment on that piece of proverbial wisdom, Cameron pointed toward the group of young women. "And what are the lamb-legs up to now?"

"Have ye forgotten? 'Tis St. Bride's Day. With the soldiers all settled, the lasses have decided to bed the Brideag as planned."

February 1—St. Bride's Day, celebrated in honor of St. Brigit. He'd not remembered; indeed, had not even contemplated the date until now. It hadn't seemed important. All his days seemed to blend together in a blur of waiting and watching. Half to himself, Cameron muttered, "I wonder if anyone has bothered to mention that St. Bride's day is really a pagan festival?"

Pagan or not, he watched with mounting interest as twelve maidens in white paraded around the glen with a straw figure festooned in flowers and shells, chanting, "O Bride, Brideag, come with the wand, To this wintry land. And breathe with the breath of Spring so bland, Bride, Bride, Little Bride. . . ."

As dusk neared, the straw figure was ceremoniously bedded

in an empty cradle. It was an old custom, and familiar one, for all that he had forgotten it. Those ancient pagans had bequeathed many intriguing customs, most of which he ignored. This ritual, he decided, had a certain charm to it, for all that it smacked of druids and sorcery.

Cameron didn't bother to point out to anyone that the original participants had most likely worn little more than the flowers, but settled back to enjoy the spectacle. Garbed in a white tunic, with winter flowers woven into her flowing copper hair, Lianna Fraser solemnly participated in the rite with the others. The thin tunic swayed temptingly around her legs and ankles, providing pleasant glimpses of bare skin but very little warmth, he was sure. It was quite likely that she was freezing, but would turn to ice before she mentioned it. He remembered how cold she had been earlier, garbed from neck to feet in a linen gown and wool cloak. Females could be exceedingly inconsistent.

Of course, there was always hazard involved in pointing that out to them, especially when in the awkward state of arousal— as he had unexpectedly found himself when the delectable creature now prancing about in flowers and gooseflesh had plummeted into his arms. It had been as startling as it was embarrassing.

It didn't help that she had also made him remember things he had no business remembering, long-gone emotions that could never be again. All those dreams had disappeared along with his ancestral lands, swallowed up by the crushing annihilation after Killiecrankie.

Depressing thoughts. He looked at Robbie, who never seemed to be depressed about anything. "Who did you say her father is?"

"Dallas Fraser. D'ye know him?"

Dallas Fraser. "Not the Dallas Fraser who has gone into exile with James as a mediator, the same Dallas Fraser who has been welcomed at William's court as well—and the Dallas Fraser who is said to wield almost as much power as does the king's advisor? *That* Dallas Fraser?"

"Aye," Robbie said cheerfully, "tha' is the same one."

Bloody hell—he would have to be mad or suicidal to pursue an idle affair in *that* direction.

"Come with me, lad," Robbie was saying cheerfully, ignoring the fact that at twenty-six, Cameron was a good five years older than he was, "for I have seen to it tha' ye'll be lodging wi' us while ye're here."

"Really. I'd be interested in knowing how you got Glenlyon to agree to that. If he thought I wanted to be quartered here, I'd be lodged in a peat stack instead."

Robbie grinned. "I ken tha' much, so I told him tha' I'd had a fight with ye when we were but lads, and thought ye needed close watch. He agreed, and suggested tha' I be the one to watch ye close, as yer temper is no' always reliable and I am."

Cameron had to laugh at that. "Ah, you're a canny lad. I should watch myself with you, Robbie."

"Aye. Now come along, for I smell a haunch of venison roasting. Our sup will soon be to table, and I've no' muckle left in my belly from morn. Of course, my father claims tha' I'm no sooner up of a morn than my head is in the aumrie."

"With strapping lads like yourself to feed, 'tis a wonder Colin has any food at all left in the cupboard of a morn."

"No truer words have ever been spoke, but there's no' a one of us as don't know how to hunt and fish for our keep. Aye, the larder is always full enough."

Glenlyon approached as they reached the cottage door; his face was reddened from cold and whisky, and his mouth twisted into a petulant smile. "MacKenzie. A word with you 'ere you take lodging with Colin's family. Alone, if you don't mind, Robbie lad. You know that a soldier's day is long."

Cameron stiffened, and heard Robbie mutter something under his breath before he went inside and left them standing at the open door. It creaked slightly on its hinges, a welcome and a refuge if need be, a reminder that he was with friends. Cameron turned to face Glenlyon.

"I have assigned two Lowland men to lodge here with you, MacKenzie. To keep you honest." Campbell studied him with a lazy smile that did not reach his eyes, and when Cameron did not reply, he shrugged. "See that you mind your manners among our hosts. If you do not, I will soon know about it."

Only great restraint kept Cameron from telling Glenlyon that he did not need an honorless man to lesson him about honesty.

A cold wind whipped down the valley, bending clutches of grass, tugging at Glenlyon's tartan. He put a hand to his head to hold down his bonnet, gave Cameron another long, narrow look, then turned on his heel and continued on to Carnoch, where he and the Lindsays were to take supper with MacIan.

Cameron watched silently. The bloody ass—did he think that his deeds had been forgotten? They had not, nor would they be until Jamie was free again. Slowly, he unclenched his aching fists and went into the cottage, nodding pleasantly at the two soldiers assigned to be his "guards."

"Sit down, lad." Robbie grinned at him from across a table set with haunches of fresh venison, mutton-ham, and hot oat-cakes cooked on the griddle. A decanter of French brandy sat in the midst of the feast, proudly placed there by Colin.

" 'Tis to celebrate St. Bride's Day and our guests," Colin said, sending a sly glance toward his daughter and niece. " 'Twas the lassies' notion tha' ye might enjoy a drop or two."

Cameron followed his gaze, not at all surprised when Lianna Fraser stuck her chin in the air and looked away. She'd avoided him all day, skittering away if he came anywhere near her. He found it as annoying as he did amusing. Did she think he would betray her father's identity to Glenlyon? Here, in this glen where every resident was a Jacobite? Silly little goose. He didn't suppose it had occurred to her that it would hardly avail him anything to cry foul. Glenlyon was not the sort of man to reward informers. But then, perhaps she didn't realize that yet. She would not be the first person deceived by Campbell's bluff heartiness.

Now, welcomed by old friends, his strange, bitter mood began to ease. There was only Colin, his wife Morag, Robbie, Mary and Lianna at home this eve, as Colin's other sons had gone hunting into the hills. The cottage was warm and cozy, with well-built furniture in the main room, generous kettles over the fire, and pewter dishes proudly lined along a wall shelf. Small touches, like cloth at the windows, gave it a comfortable feel, and the chairs were well-worn from many winter nights before the fire. All contributed to a sense of home and comfort.

The Lowlanders seemed to prefer keeping to themselves, and Colin slyly gave them places of "honor" by the fire to eat their evening meal, seating the two men on sturdy wooden stools next to the hearth. Tactfully, he indicated that his family was to speak English instead of the Gaelic that came much more readily to their Highland tongues, so that the Lowland soldiers would not feel alienated, or think they were plotting against them.

After the evening meal was finished and the young women began to clear the table, Colin lit his pipe and smiled expansively at his guests and family. "Come, Morag, tell the tale of St. Bride. We've a warm fire, gude company, and willing ears."

Morag, a stout pleasant woman with a cheerful smile and easy way, did not need to be asked twice. She smiled at her husband and settled herself in a chair by the fire. Care had been taken not to bring up an offensive subject, and the tale of St. Bride was a topic none could fault. Morag cleared her throat. She had a fine voice for story-telling, and it filled the comfortable room as densely as the peat smoke.

Even the Lowland soldiers were spellbound as Morag wove the tale of how Brigit, the Celtic goddess of fire, hearth, marriage and childbirth had been captured by the Blue Hag, who destroyed everything on earth and summoned darkness to descend upon the land, then forced Brigit to spend the winter imprisoned inside the rocky walls of Ben Nevis.

"In time, Brigit's name was changed to Bride, and the festival in her honor became Day of Bride." Morag paused for effect, glancing at Mary and Lianna, who sat on small stools nearby. "There wa' a strong, handsome god named Angus, who volunteered to rescue Bride. Great storms and snow and ice filled the land, but eventually, Angus and Bride were able to vanquish the Cailleach wha' had held the land in her icy grip since All Hallow's Eve. And now, every year on February first, we celebrate the Day of Bride to remember her battle to bring fair skies and warm days to the land.''

As her voice faded, a birch log popped in the fire, sending up a shower of sparks. Colin leaned out and thrust the brandy decanter toward one of the Lowland soldiers. ''Have a dram, Armstrong, you and Elliot. Mary, get another cup for our guests. Lianna, lass, isna there a platter of scones in the cupboard?''

''Yes, uncle.'' Lianna brought the plate of pastry from the cupboard, and came to stand by the fire, holding it out to the soldiers. She did not even glance at Cameron. Just as well. He had nothing to offer her but a few kisses stolen behind a hay rick or under the moonlight.

Her attention riveted on one of the Lowland men, and she smiled brightly when the lout gazed up at her with obvious appreciation.

''My thanks to a very lovely lady,'' Elliot said grandly as he took the proffered treat. ''Your hospitality is most welcome to us poor soldiers. Times are grim at Fort William, with meager rations, I fear.''

''No man who asks is denied roof or meat in Glencoe,'' Colin spoke up quietly. ''Highland tradition holds tha' all who ask are given shelter.''

A noble sentiment, Cameron thought cynically, but one that was likely to end up starving them before winter loosened its grip on the land. Especially with men who ate like Armstrong and Elliot, both wolfing down food as if there was no tomorrow. Few rations had been brought by the troops, for Glenlyon had known that those in Glencoe ate well if not lavishly. Kippered salmon and salted beef would be the worst they would get, and that only if no game could be hunted in the hills. Was that Breadalbane's intention?—to starve them? If so, he'd chosen the wrong year and glen, for the harvest had been good this year, and game abounded in the Glencoe hills.

Lianna paused in front of Cameron finally, and held out the platter of scones. She averted her eyes, turning her face toward the fire as if fascinated by the blaze, clearly avoiding him. He supposed he should commend her on her shrewd judge of character, but instead he found it irritating that she had taken him in such great dislike—especially as he was certain he had felt her response to his touch earlier. Absurdly, he was goaded into provoking her attention.

When he reached for a scone he deliberately tilted the platter, so that the remaining pastries skidded toward the edge with alarming speed. It had the desired effect of jerking her attention to the platter, and then to him as she righted it. "Do be careful, sir!"

"My apologies, Miss Fraser." He met her startled gaze with a bland smile that sparked angry glints in her eyes. He fought the impulse to laugh. Anger did wonders for the female complexion. She had a lovely glow. He blinked at her in feigned innocence, and took a bite of the scone. Her eyes narrowed with suspicion, but of course, she would not be rude to a guest in her uncle's home.

Lianna snatched back the platter and moved past him in a huff of indignation and rustling skirts. His admiring gaze followed the enticing flow of gown about her legs; no simple saffron tunic such as the other women in Glencoe wore, but made of fine linen and cinched with a jeweled belt at the waist. It was a charming gown with full, flowing sleeves cuffed at the elbows, and belling skirts that swayed enticingly with each step. Though Cameron was no authority on female fashions, he had traveled enough to recognize expensive feminine attire when he saw it.

But then, Lianna Fraser didn't look the type to reside in a stone cottage, snug as this one may be. No, she had the look of a young woman more accustomed to carpeted drawing rooms, the tinkle of china and silverplate, and fires that did not smoke or smell of peat. It would not surprise him in the least if she had never slept on anything but a feather bed, and was accustomed to soft hot rolls for breakfast every morning.

Again and again during the evening, while tales of Scottish valor were told and songs sung of ancient days, he found his gaze straying back to Lianna. By the time the fire was low and the last song being sung—the sweet strains of *Crodh Chailean* filling the cottage with the tale of how the fairies had come to Coire Gabhail and whispered the melody to a herd-girl—

Cameron was determined to speak to Lianna Fraser alone. When the last notes of the lullaby faded away, he stood up from his place by the fire and stretched.

Robbie blinked sleepily at him, and grinned a little. "There is a pallet by yon wall for ye, Cameron. The blankets are of our best wool, so ye'll be warm enough this night."

Shadows lined the far wall, and beyond a door lay the family sleeping quarters, with a separate loft reached by a steep ladder. This cottage was larger than many in Glencoe, and as Colin had so many children, divided into rooms. Instead of hard-packed dirt, rough wooden planks were notched together to form a floor.

"A better bed than I'm used to, Robbie, and that's a fact." Cameron glanced toward Lianna, who had scooped up a furry kitten from the floor and cradled it beneath her chin. The tiny creature meowed, a thin wail like a squeaky hinge.

Lianna whispered something to the kitten that elicited another squeak. When Cameron laughed at the ridiculous sound, she looked up with a slightly wary smile. "She's young yet, and has lost her mother, so I have been feeding her warm milk. I've been trying to wean her to chopped fish."

" 'Tis bad luck to have a cat in the house, ye know." Robbie's disgusted snort was evidence enough of his opinion, but he added loudly, "And a waste of good milk for a cat tha' will never catch mice, I warrant."

Lianna looked affronted. "When she's big enough, she'll catch mice."

" 'Tis no' even a bonny cat, but a useless, ugly beastie. Ye should have let me drown it instead of waste food for a creature tha' will most like die anyway."

Lianna's eyes flashed angrily, and Cameron saw her temper rise. Before she could retort, he stepped close to her and stroked the kitten's furry head with one finger. The orange ball of fluff squinted up at him and squeaked again. Though he privately agreed with Robbie, he saw a way to smooth his path.

"Robbie lad, how can you say this animal is ugly? It's but a wee thing, and too early to tell. I've heard it said, that when you were born you were so ugly your mother took you to the linn at dusk to toss you into the water as a changeling.''

His immediate reward was Lianna's soft laugh of appreciation and Robbie's indignant protest. "Ye should be muckle shamed for telling such a black lie, Cameron! I was so fair a bairn tha' all came from as far away as Inverness just to watch me sleep. . . .''

"Whsst," Morag said tartly, "'tis you who should be shamed, telling such a tale. The hour is late, and morning comes early, with tasks to be done whether we've had our sleep or not. Lianna, a pallet has been laid for Cameron by the weaving bin, if you will please show him to it while Mary makes certain our other guests are tended. You, Robbie, put tha' great back of yours to work at something besides leaning against a wall, and fill the kettle with water for the morning.''

Grumbling, Robbie went to lift the huge cauldron from over the fire, swinging it out to be filled with buckets of water. Cameron watched Lianna, and saw the quick, frowning glance she gave her aunt as Morag banked the hearth fire and Mary showed the soldiers to their pallets at the far end of the room. Apparently, escorting him to the weaving bin involved being alone with him.

"You don't have to show me my pallet if it makes you uneasy," Cameron said quietly, and she looked back at him. Her brow lifted.

"Why should it make me uneasy?''

"There is no reason at all.'' He paused, then said so softly only she could hear, "I am not a traitor.''

He paused to let her absorb the implications behind his comment. Robbie banged the heavy metal cauldron against the stone hearth, swore in Gaelic, then left the cottage with two big buckets. Cold air swept in the open door and made the fire dance, illuminating Lianna's oval face.

The thick coppery mane of her hair was caught back in a snood on the nape of her neck, heavy and luxuriant, the severe style framing her features. Short, straight nose, high cheekbones, pale skin—only a faint spray of freckles across the bridge of her nose and her cheeks saved her from the cold perfection of a porcelain doll. Her lashes cast long shadows on her cheeks, and her gaze turned troubled. He smiled slightly.

Foolish, suspicious little goose, to worry so that he would betray them all with the news that her father was a famous Jacobite. It was unlikely that Glenlyon would take *his* word for anything, and even more unlikely that the king would harm Dallas Fraser's daughter.

Of course, there was the off-chance William would not pass up an opportunity to wreak vengeance on those left behind, especially if it could be done under pretext of a mistake. It was the kind of thing devious men were prone to do, with kings the worst of all.

If she knew him better, she would know how he detested the insidious sins of politics. But she did not know him, and it was increasingly obvious that this lovely girl with the great green eyes like forest pools still fretted senselessly about the threat of exposure. He would set her mind at ease.

He leaned forward under the guise of stroking the kitten, until his mouth was close to Lianna's cheek. "Silly sprite, save for yon Lowlanders, every man in this cottage is for James."

Her breath caught, a soft, audible sound. *"Every* man?"

"Aye, lass." Personally, he reserved judgement on James's ability as a king, but she needn't know that. It would only worry her. "All of us."

"Then why—?"

"Am I with William's men? 'Tis a long tale that only worsens with the telling of it. It's not by my free choice, as even Glenlyon would be happy to tell you. So do not worry that I will tell what should not be told."

Lianna's fingers stroked the kitten's head and she looked down at it for a long moment, then up again, smiling this time. "Mary said I could trust you."

"Did she?" They were so close he could count her eyelashes, breathe in the scent of her, almost hear her heart beat beneath the pretty green linen gown. "Mary is a very discerning young woman. If I were you, I would respect her opinion." He had an excellent view of the sweet temptation of firm breasts beneath the snug bodice. Most enticing. A French fashion, with a low, straight bodice that barely covered her breasts. Bless the French, who celebrated a woman's figure instead of hiding it beneath yards and yards of material. The kitten nestled into the shadowed cleft between her breasts and yawned. Lucky beast, to be cradled in such beguiling luxury. His gaze shifted again, to find Lianna watching him. Unabashed, he shrugged. "Of course, Mary meant 'trust' as it pertains to national security, I am sure."

"I realized that fact very quickly, sir." She shifted the kitten to cover the entrancing view. "You could have *told* me that you knew my cousins, you know."

He drew back—regretful at the loss of charming view—to laugh softly. "And miss the expression on your face when Robbie greeted me as friend instead of enemy? My pleasures are too few to deny myself when I can."

"Mary told me about your father. I understand."

Appalled, he stared at her. There was sympathy in her words and tone, swift and devastating. He didn't want pity. Not from anyone. Never from her.

"No," he said roughly, "I don't think you do understand."

She fell silent again, and he heard the kitten begin to purr, a soft rattling contentment. Peat hissed in the fire with a crackling sound. The aroma of roast meat still hung in the air, mingling with peat smoke and Colin's tobacco. The sympathetic smile lingered on Lianna's lips, and he was suddenly uncomfortable and uncertain. He must look a fool, gaping at her like a lackwit, stealing peeks down her bodice as if he was a green youth who'd never done more than dream about a woman. Good God, what a vision he must present.

It was embarrassing. What was it about this girl that made him forget caution and common sense? It certainly wasn't her looks, though she could definitely claim beauty. This was different. There was something else that lured him, had kept him lurking about all day for a glimpse of her. It could just be her air of elegance, so unusual in this rural setting. No. He would have noticed her even had she not tumbled into his arms like a baby sparrow from the sky.

That much admitted, he examined his motives—What did

he want from her? With her father being Dallas Fraser, anything other than a chaste conversation would most likely earn him a swift and painful demise. He might be a fool, but he'd never considered himself so rash as to risk death for a tumble in the hay. Yet, improbably enough, he suspected it wasn't just a prurient interest that drew him. How intriguing—and amazing.

To cover his damnable confusion, he leaned close again to stroke the kitten, and caught a faint flowery fragrance. Elusive, sweet . . . A woman's perfume. His belly clenched in involuntary remembrance. God . . . For a moment, a fragment of time, he had a flash of what his life might have been.

But not now.

He drew back abruptly, his hand falling away from the kitten. "Robbie is right, you know. It is a wee ugly beastie."

"Oh no. You've already committed yourself otherwise. You cannot change your mind now, Cameron MacKenzie. It's too late." She held up the kitten. "Here. Take Maggie."

"Maggie?"

"A grand name for a regal cat, don't you think?"

"Aye. A grand name, but I'm not so sure the cat has earned it yet."

"She will." Lianna smiled, and her earlier caution seemed to have melted away. "There, you see?" she said when he gingerly allowed the kitten to be placed in his hands and the tiny creature yawned and nestled trustingly in his palms, "she trusts you, so I shall also."

Watching her face, the teasing lights in her eyes and the way her mouth curved so winsomely into a smile, he decided to allow himself a brief moment of fantasy. The warmth of the fire, the sweet scent of perfume, even the purring kitten—all combined to remind him that these moments were precious few and not to be wasted. So he smiled back at her, ignoring the harsh realities, content for this moment to indulge himself. He thought he rather deserved contentment, brief as it may be.

It was a peaceful moment, as nourishing as the meal he had eaten earlier but far more lasting. Not even Robbie's noisy return a few moments later ruined it. Gently, Lianna retrieved her kitten from him.

"It's late. Shall I show you to your pallet now?"

"No, I can find the weaving bin and my blankets. You'd best go on to bed. Maggie looks too sleepy to stay awake much longer."

She laughed softly. "Good night then."

"Good night, beauty."

A dimple flashed in her cheek, and nuzzling the kitten close, she disappeared up the ladder to the sleeping loft. He watched until her kid slippers left the highest rung—and surprising himself—not with any lurid hope of glimpsing an ankle, but just to be certain she was safely up.

It was the damndest thing: he'd grown accustomed to discomfort and frustration, indeed, had begun to welcome the sharp edge it gave him. He'd changed. He was no longer the idealistic dreamer he had been for so long. Too much had happened since Killiecrankie. Life had taught him how little tolerance it had for fools, a lesson he'd learned swiftly and well in a very short time. Survival wasn't always what it was cracked up to be.

But, with a sense of amazement, he felt for the first time in over two years, that survival wasn't as bad as he'd begun to believe.

Chapter 4

Fort William, Inverlochy

Colonel Hill stared at Major Forbes in consternation. A cold chill ran up his spine, and his hands knotted into fists atop the documents strewn on the table. "You say that *Glenlyon* has an Argyll regiment of Breadalbane's men headed for Glencoe? Did he say why, for God's sake?"

Forbes shook his head, looking worried. "Not to me, sir." A short pause fell, then Forbes blurted, "Over a fortnight ago I sent out the orders that the MacIans should be considered loyal subjects and not molested in any way, sir, just as Ardkinglas instructed. But now—"

"Aye. *Now* . . ." Hill took a deep breath to still the nausea churning in his belly. His mouth twisted bitterly. "It's true then. The insolent Glengarry MacDonalds run amok, and refuse to take the oath, yet MacIan has made an honest effort to comply. For that his clan is to be rooted out like rats in a nest. 'Tis plain that my sworn word to him carries no weight, that it has been dismissed out of hand—and I gave MacIan my protection." He surged to his feet, unable to sit still, aware of

Forbes still staring at him with grim apprehension, as if waiting for a denial of the facts.

Forbes cleared his throat. "Sir, the letter from the Master of Stair demands I lead a detachment from this garrison to block possible escape from Glencoe by way of Moor of Rannoch. Am I to follow those orders?"

Hill closed his eyes, sick and furious. "Aye. It seems that we have little choice but to obey, as King William has signed the papers. I do not understand why, but it is not my place to question our king. The devil take them for treating me as if am of no account. Livingstone has sent Hamilton detailed instructions instead of me—*Hamilton!* My second-in-command, yet he is to manage this affair. Ah, I should be grateful, I suppose, for having such a distasteful task taken from me, but am not unaware of the insult to my integrity and ability." He shoved angrily at the letters on his desk, and one of them fluttered to the floor. "A rum lot, those earls of Argyll and Breadalbane, and the Master of Stair worse than all."

When Forbes hesitated, Hill looked up; his shoulders bowed with fatigue and distress. "Aye, give the orders, Major Forbes. But I fear we shall all rue the day such treachery against an honest man was done. If not for my daughters and hopes for a pension . . . but I am old, and there is nothing I can do but wash my hands of it. I have been given my orders, and have always obeyed, God help me."

Hill waved a hand in dismissal, not even noticing when Forbes left and closed the door behind him. He sank back into his chair, staring dully at the peat fire. Smoke curled up, and in the wisps he could almost see a heavy-jowled face framed by a periwig, mocking and intelligent and manipulative—Sir John Dalrymple, the Master of Stair. A complex man, and above even Breadalbane when it came to intrigue. He would not doubt at all if this whole affair was not due to Stair's manipulations. It was just the thing for a man of his caliber to concoct, for whatever reason he might have. Dear God, the man was a piece of work. Even his wife had been accused of dabbling in the forbidden arts, and he was of a mind to think Stair was involved as well. Ah, but what could he do? It was

out of his hands now. From Argyll and Breadalbane had come
orders to deliver "letters of fire and sword," and not to trouble
the government with any prisoners.

God, it was a sick, ghastly business.

Mary nudged Lianna with her elbow, and when she looked
up, tilted her head toward the grassy haugh in the midst of the
cottages. "He's a fine, braw callant, don't you think?"

Lianna didn't have to look; she knew who Mary meant
Cameron MacKenzie. As if she hadn't noticed him herself
hadn't watched him from under her lashes of an afternoon wher
he joined the other men playing at wrestling or tests of strength
Bare-chested at times, his muscled skin tawny and smooth ir
the winter light, he would be impossible to ignore. Despite her
sternest vow, every time she looked at him her heart gave a
peculiar thump. It was very annoying. As if she needed another
hotheaded hero in her life, someone likely at any moment to
rush off to some war and leave her behind to wait and worry
and then return quite gaily and rattle on about what fun it had
been, shooting and being shot—oh no. Not for her. Hadn't she
had enough of that? Hadn't she watched her mother agonize
enough to know what it was like? Oh yes, she certainly had.

She had no intention of having anything to do with Cameron
MacKenzie. Not that she refused to be polite to him. She was
very polite. After all, she had been taught manners, hadn't she'
She spoke to him, always a neutral topic, about the kitten, or
the weather, or some other trivial matter.

And it had not escaped her notice that he did the same.

His comments were always polite and distant, pointless ques
tions about the card game the night before, or if Maggie had
liked the day's catch of fresh herring. Never more than that
Never a hint that he thought of her as anything more than Mary
and Robbie's Lowland cousin. And after that first night when
he had all but declared for King James, never a hint that he
was anything other than Glenlyon's loyal soldier. It was a
troubling question in her mind, the nagging worry that he might
somehow betray her mother's family.

But this morning, she tried not to think of all that, but sat with Mary outside the cottage carding wool. It was a soft day, with fitful light and temperate weather, the wind blowing softly down from the mountains and the sun flirting with clouds. For the past two mornings, the soldiers had been drilling in the grassy heath between the cottages, their muskets gleaming in the rare sunlight as they wheeled, pivoted, and thrust at invisible enemies with imaginary bayonets fixed to their weapons.

Lianna had already noticed that Cameron did not join them in their maneuvers, though he usually lounged nearby, watching. Most of the time, he wore his trews and shirt, with a plaid slung carelessly over one shoulder. Today, the wind picked at the ends of the plaid, lifting it to flap against his broad back as he leaned against a cottage wall to watch them drill.

Sergeant Barber was attempting to train the newer recruits, with increasing frustration as they moved slowly and clumsily. It could not have escaped his notice that some of the Glencoe men watched with gleeful interest when one of the recruits stumbled, knocking down the two men next to him. Muffled laughter blended with the wind, carrying to Barber's ears. He came to an abrupt halt only a few feet from the cottage, glaring at Cameron MacKenzie.

"Here, you—MacKenzie. Fall into rank."

Cameron shook his head. "I am not a recruit, Sergeant. I was not even issued a proper weapon, in case that fact has escaped your notice."

Furious, Sergeant Barber opened and shut his mouth like a landed fish for a moment. His face reddened. "You do not need a weapon to follow orders, MacKenzie. Do as you're told, or it will go hardly with you."

Unfolding his lean body, Cameron straightened to his full height, which was considerably more than Barber's, and a trace of hostility edged his words and his eyes as he gazed at the sergeant. "I think not. I take my orders from Glenlyon, distasteful as that may be."

Lianna's heart thumped with alarm as Barber's mouth curled into a snarl. "You bloody well take your orders from an officer, MacKenzie, whether you like it or not."

"Aye, true enough—but not from you."

Tension hovered between the two men, and Lianna bit her lower lip anxiously. Was he mad? Military insubordination was not tolerated. Even in the quiet life of the glen, all men were expected to obey their laird. Refusal was dealt with harshly, for laws were laws, whether of the glen or king.

Two officers stepped close to listen, and one of them was a Lindsay, the brutish one, who always looked at her with thin, hot eyes that made her uncomfortable. Beside her, Mary muttered something beneath her breath about distracting them, and put down her wool to move forward with a bright smile.

"Captain Lindsay, would you be kind enough to settle a quarrel for me? My cousin and I disagree as to whether King William is in Flanders or France fighting the enemy—I say Flanders."

Lindsay, who had started toward Barber and Cameron, paused a moment, flicking Mary a quick glance. "Flanders, the last I heard. Why would you want to know?"

Mary put a hand on his sleeve, fingers curling around his arm as she smiled and shrugged. "I was only saying tha' I'm glad we have such brave soldiers here to guard us, instead of risking them in Flanders, 'tis all."

Lindsay frowned impatiently. His attention swerved back to the sergeant and Cameron, and an ugly expression formed on his face. He shook loose Mary's grasp with a polite but impatient comment, and moved toward Cameron and Barber.

Anxiously, Mary glanced at Lianna, then up the glen, where light picked out the gilt braid on a red coat. Glenlyon. The captain strode beside the MacIan, and despite his tall frame, he looked small next to the huge Glencoe laird. His attention was snared by the knot of angry men, and he changed direction to approach.

"Are we having troubles, Sergeant Barber?" Glenlyon's smile was smooth, but his eyes were narrowed and hard when he looked at Cameron.

"Aye, sir. This Highland rogue refuses to drill with the others."

Glenlyon's smile thinned into a smirk. "Does he now. How unwise of you, MacKenzie. May I ask why you refuse?"

"I've no desire to be a hero, Captain." Cameron shrugged carelessly. "But don't let my convictions prejudice your men. By all means, drill away."

It sounded insolent, reckless, and Lianna held her breath. The great fool—did he not think what Glenlyon might do? And what did he mean about not wanting to be a hero? It was a novel comment, unexpected and totally alien to her opinion of him. With his devil-may-care attitude, he seemed just the sort to swagger about taking all kinds of risks. What a charlatan.

"Am I to understand that you are refusing to obey my order, MacKenzie?" Glenlyon's brows rose.

"I was unaware you had given me one. Do you order me to drill with your soldiers? Keep in mind that I've no military training, unlike these proficient gentlemen I've been watching. My weapon of choice is a sharp word or an insult, not a musket and bayonet, but I will do my best not to accidentally gut the man next to me if you insist that I join your men in maneuvers."

After a fleeting glance at the MacIan and a brief hesitation, Glenlyon pursed his lips thoughtfully. "Aye, you have a point, MacKenzie. I had forgotten that you are only with us by courtesy of my lord Breadalbane. The earl stressed that you were selected especially by him, and I am afraid that I have misused you. Your help has been invaluable to us of late."

Cameron stiffened. Behind Glenlyon's amiable comments lurked a wealth of spite, for the MacIan had tensed at Breadalbane's name, and looked now at Cameron with troubled eyes. A distinct coolness shrouded the laird when he regarded Cameron, and Lianna recalled that Mary had told her MacIan had quarreled hotly with the earl of Breadalbane.

"You've taken up arms with Breadalbane, have you, lad?" the MacIan said after a moment, and his tone was carefully neutral. "I didna know."

After a moment of strained silence, Cameron nodded shortly. "Aye. It seems that ofttimes a man must choose the lesser devil."

It was a noncommittal reply, one that could be taken either

way, as the MacDonalds bitterly opposed the Campbells as well as the king whose oath had been taken. The MacIan's dark eyes fixed on Cameron's face as if searching for something, then he shrugged. "All men must make difficult choices."

"I've not forgotten Killiecrankie."

Glenlyon frowned at that. "None of us have. It was a hollow victory for James, I fear, but God smiled on William that day. And now we are all abiding under our rightful king's rule, as good citizens should. Sergeant—" He turned to Barber. "MacKenzie has no musket, and no need of formal drill. At such time as we need him, I am certain that he will do his sworn duty and uphold the king's commands, as well as those of Lord Breadalbane."

With a resentful glance at Cameron, Barber jerked his head in a respectful nod. When Glenlyon ambled away with the MacIan, the sergeant exchanged a glance with Lindsay before looking menacingly at Cameron.

"Don't think I'll forget this, MacKenzie."

"I'm certain you will not." A faint smile played at one corner of Cameron's mouth.

Lianna didn't realize she'd been holding her breath until both Barber and Lindsay walked away. Then the tension that had coiled tightly in her began to unravel, and she exhaled deeply.

Cameron turned, his eyes meeting hers, traces of the hostile smile still on his mouth. It was as if they were the only two there, as the world narrowed between them. His smoky eyes were challenging, holding hers until she felt she should look away; only stubbornness made her resist.

"You great bloody fool," she said softly, and saw the quick flare of light in his eyes before he hid it with a lowering shift of his lashes.

"I've been called that many times before, *caileag.*"

"No doubt. And deserved it every time, I'll warrant. Have you run mad, defying Glenlyon like that? Robbie told me that the man is more powerful than he has a right to be—and a Campbell enemy of the MacDonalds, at that." When he looked up again, demon-smoke in his eyes, she hissed, "If you do not care for your own safety, then think of the others here who might suffer!''

Tension flared between them, sizzling as hot as the last drops of boiling water in a tea kettle, then Mary laughed shakily. ''Cam, what made you tweak his nose like tha'? Is it not chancy to make him your enemy?''

The demon-smoke dissipated, and his eyes were cold steel again, sharp and gray and brittle. ''It would be more chancy to have him as friend. An enemy makes his intent plain.''

''Aye, but not always in time,'' Lianna said bluntly, and when his gaze shifted back to her, she refused to retreat. ''Why must men always think themselves invincible? You're like a great brawling bull run amok in the market, this way and that, until in the end you still must be brought to heel.''

Mary looked appalled. Her cheeks reddened, and she made a peculiar noise like a deflated bagpipe. Lianna ignored her. She was too painfully reminded of her father and brothers, and how they must always be heroes, never content to just be alive and at peace . . . but why let her personal grievances transfer to others? If the man wanted to snipe at his officers, it was of no consequence to her. If they took him behind a peat stack and executed him, it would make no difference to her.

Except that she remembered how tenderly he had cradled her kitten in his huge palms, as gentle as a mother, his mouth twisting with wry humor. She puffed out her cheeks, then exhaled slowly. ''Ah, forgive me my bad temper, sir. 'Tis my worst fault.''

''The cow may want her tail yet, lass.''

Lianna flushed at the implied rebuke. ''I didn't mean to be unkind. It's just that . . . that men never seem to think of consequences.''

''Don't lump me in with all the rest.'' His voice roughened to a low growl. ''I know full well the consequences that come with my actions—what of you?''

''I didn't deliberately taunt a man more powerful than I am—''

''Did you not?'' In a move so quick she didn't anticipate it, he had her by the wrists, jerking her so hard against him she could feel his belt buckle press into her stomach. He held her tightly, ignoring her angry demand to be released, and there was a thin smile on his face that was not reflected in his eyes. "Perhaps you'd best reconsider that hasty remark."

"I take your point," she said tightly after a moment, and he released her so abruptly she staggered. He put a hand on her shoulder to steady her, and she shrugged it away. His action had been more unsettling than she wanted to admit. For an instant, there had been a fluttering response to his grip, a brief thought that he intended to kiss her. Ridiculous, of course. He was only sulky that she had pointed out the flaw in his actions. Rubbing her chafed wrists, she looked angrily up at him. "What would you have done if Glenlyon grabbed you like this?"

Surprisingly, he grinned. "I would not have been tempted to kiss him as I was you, that much is for certain."

Mary laughed, a low, soft hoot. After an instant's startled surprise, Lianna launched—as she usually did when flustered— into attack. "I still say you're a great blundering idiot to challenge Glenlyon."

"I did not expect you to change your mind. And I can't say I disagree with you. But there are things I will do because I must, and things I refuse to do because I can."

"How academic. What courses of philosophy did you study?"

"Survival."

The simple answer took her back; she should be ashamed of her ill-temper and pique. It was obvious this Highland rogue had not had an opportunity for an education, and just as obvious he was years ahead of her in practical experience. Mary was looking at her oddly, lower lip caught between her teeth, and she knew she had disgraced the family by being discourteous to a guest. It was the very height of rudeness, and Aunt Morag would be extremely upset when she learned of it. *If* she learned of it. Perhaps this arrogant rascal could be persuaded to forget her lapse of good manners. But how did she manage it? Especially when he made her so uncertain of herself?

Fortunately, Mary stepped into the breach again, her voice calm. "It's a fine day, and Robbie has gone to meet Alex and

Ian. You remember them, don't you, Cam? My oldest brothers are nearer you in age, I think.''

"Aye. We used to fish Loch Triachtan when we were lads.'' Cameron's reply was quiet, his eyes wary now when he glanced her way.

Lianna's chin came up. Mary's tact only made her own rudeness seem worse by comparison, so she drew in a deep breath and forced a polite smile.

"I used to fish with my brothers, but it has been a long time since I've had the opportunity.'' When he said nothing, she flushed a little, but forged ahead, determined to make amends as best she could for speaking her mind so harshly. "Perhaps I could go with you the next time you go down to the loch to fish.''

Silence fell. Then a dog barked, and some children ran past, voices raised in excitement as they chased a wooden hoop that rolled through the grass. Sergeant Barber barked an order to the drilling soldiers, and they broke ranks in dismissal.

Cameron's attention focused on Lianna. A quiver hovered at the corners of her mouth, as if she wanted to say something else. No doubt, another scathing appraisal of his character or intelligence. It would probably do no good to tell her quite truthfully that he had studied at a Paris university for three years before returning home to help his father and brothers fight for their lands. Another futile act. His life was full of them.

And if he had any sense, he would run from the wide green eyes gazing at him so critically. Futility was inherent in any personal relationship for him. Hadn't he discovered that at great cost? All he had loved, he had lost. His father, brothers, lands— even what reputation he'd once had. Gone. As distant and extinct as yesterday's shadows. As inaccessible as the lovely girl gazing at him now.

Knowing that, he was amazed at the words that popped uninvited from his mouth: "Aye. If you insist upon feeding fish to that ridiculous cat of yours, you might as well come along and be of some use in catching them, Miss Fraser.''

That was how he found himself nudging a small boat into

the dry, rustling reeds that lined the loch, dumping netted fish into a large woven basket of river reeds, accompanied by Lianna Fraser and a thousand doubts as to his sanity.

Lianna was dressed warmly, for the wind down by the loch was cold as it swept over the water, riffling the reeds in a melodic whisper. He was disappointed at her choice of garments; he'd liked her pagan attire much better.

Her face was flushed slightly, from excitement at how many fish he was netting or from the wind, he wasn't certain. What he was certain about, was that he was treading dangerously near lunacy. It could be described as nothing else. Save for lunatic motives, why else would he be down here alone with her? It was too tempting, and he was positive that Mary suspected his motives were not at all inspired by fishing.

He pulled the small boat up onto the shore to keep it from drifting away, then splashed through the reeds to where Lianna had perched atop a rock to gaze with intense satisfaction at their catch. She looked up when he reached her, a smile curving her mouth.

"What a lovely catch. Many more than I thought you'd manage."

A gust of wind caught one of her curls, lifting it in an idle drift to waft across her face, and she gracefully brushed it aside. A dimple flashed in one cheek, and in the diffused light of sun and cloud, the scattering of freckles across the bridge of her nose and across her cheeks glittered like a sprinkling of gold dust.

"I'm gratified that you approve, Miss Fraser." Reeds crushed beneath his high boots made a faint popping sound, and he shifted, kneeling down by the basket to fasten the leather clasp. The ripe smell of fish mingled with the fresh wind and sharp tang of loch and reeds. At eye-level with Lianna, he glanced at her face. It was shining with pleasure, flushed from the wind and radiant. He couldn't help returning her smile. His hand stilled on the leather clasp. He watched in smiling silence when she bent to scoop up a rock from the boggy shore and toss it into the water. It made a plunking sound, and ripples billowed outward in ever-widening circles. A bird swooped and soared, then dropped low to skim over the surface of the loch before coming up with a tasty meal of fish. Snow-capped peaks cast shimmering reflections in the waters of the loch.

It was one of those moments of vibrating intensity, of sudden clarity when surroundings seemed more brilliant, with vivid color and texture—a moment that he instinctively knew would remain forever in his memory. And a moment that he suspected would alter everything that came after it.

He was sharply aware of a high bank of clouds overhead, gray with fading sunlight behind them, gold-rimmed and glowing with spears of light fanning out; of Lianna's rusty-gold hair that had come loose from the neat knot on the nape of her neck to straggle in endearing wisps on each side of her face; and he was stingingly aware of how much he had missed just this sort of moment. The simplicity of it, the serenity, caught him with all the force of a plank across his chest, stunning him. Did she feel the same need? The vital necessity that made him snatch at rare moments as if starved for them? He wanted it so badly— but dared not leave himself vulnerable. It was too dangerous.

He buckled the catch on the basket, then stood up, hefting it in one hand. Lianna rose with him, straightening her skirts as primly as if she was in a Glasgow drawing room. "This has been a lovely afternoon, Mr. MacKenzie. I think we have enough fish now to feed a round dozen Maggies, don't you?"

"Maggie-cats big as tigers, I'd say." He smiled lazily, and put out a hand to help her down from the rock. "Watch your feet."

She laughed. "Do I look that dainty?"

"Aye. You do, Miss Fraser. As fragile as one of these reeds."

"Really." She allowed him to help her step over the marshy ground to solid footing, then released his hand. "But reeds aren't that fragile, Mr. MacKenzie."

"Are they not?"

"No." She turned to meet his gaze, a faint smile curving her lips. "See?" One foot pressed down on a clump of reeds, bending them to the ground. When she stepped back, the reeds began to slowly rise again. "Reeds are hardly as fragile as people think. In fact, I'd say they are quite pliable at times."

Amused, he gazed down at her. Then, deliberately, he reached out to snap a reed stalk in two. He held up the broken end. "Not so very pliable at other times."

She shrugged. "Disaster can always befall, whether 'tis reeds or people. But the reeds that stay whole are the ones that bend before the wind instead of break."

"And which kind of reed are you, Miss Fraser?"

"I'd like to think I'm pliable." Her brows knotted into a frown over the bridge of her nose. "But then, I've not been tested by strong winds. You have. I think you must have learned at an early age to bend, Mr. MacKenzie."

"Ah, so we're talking about me now. You should have told me where this conversation was leading, Miss Fraser. I could have saved you some time. Be direct. Exactly what is it you want to know?"

A rosy flush stained her cheeks and made her eyes look very green. Ah, she looked so young, so naïve. So self-possessed at the same time. His earlier assessment had been the most accurate, he thought, watching her. She was little more than a spoiled child, cosseted and petted, and probably quite vain to boot. He'd bet a guinea on it.

He set the basket down among the reeds. She looked a bit flustered, chewing on her bottom lip like a small child, lashes lowered to hide her eyes. Apparently, her composure was fading. Amusement fought with irritation.

"Well, Miss Fraser? What is it you want to ask me?"

"If you are truly one of William's men. Oh, I mean—I know that you came to Glencoe with them, but today I heard you say you are not a soldier." Her lashes lifted, eyes gazing into his as if searching out the truth.

"Aye. That is what I said. Your powers of observation are very keen."

"Robbie said—not to me, but I heard him talking to Uncle Colin—that Glenlyon is not to be trusted. If you are with him . . ." Her voice trailed into silence.

If she had slapped him in the face with one of the fish, it could not have shattered his brief contentment more effectively. He looked away. Water sloshed around the reeds, and the sun was hidden by the clouds as it dropped behind mountain peaks. A thick mist began to lower, shrouding hills and water. It grew cold quickly without the sun to warm the air, and Cameron bent to pick up the basket of fish before looking at her again.

"Finish the sentence: If I am with him, I am not to be trusted as well. Say it. You will feel much better if you voice your prejudices, Miss Fraser."

Ominous light sparked in her eyes. Hands on her hips, she bristled like an angry cat. " 'Tis not prejudice to wonder about a man's motives, Mr. MacKenzie. You've not fully explained your intentions, you know."

"I'm well aware of that." He was angry now, too. Why must she nettle him? "Has it occurred to you that it would be dangerous for me to admit to being against Glenlyon? And dangerous to you if I admitted anything else? No, don't answer. I can see from your expression that you haven't thought of that. Worry about your wee kitten, girl, and don't be bothering a man with things you do not understand."

His voice had grown rough, and he saw from her eyes that his reply had done nothing to weaken her determination. He dropped the basket again, and reached out for her before he realized what he was doing, dragging her to him. He had no idea what he intended—to shake her, perhaps, as he would have a stubborn child—but her unexpected reaction shattered his intentions.

"Bloody hell—" His oath hung in the air between them when she leaned into him and tilted up her face as if for a kiss. Caught between astonishment and desire, he found himself bending to graze her parted lips with his. The first, feathery contact sent spears of need shooting through him, and he swallowed a groan. Her arms came up to wind around his neck, and her firm young body pressed against his as she closed her eyes and pursed her mouth. This action caught him by surprise as well, and he smiled wryly. She was just a girl playing at passion, and did not realize how long it had been for him, how near the brink he stood.

Cupping her chin in his palm, he grasped her face with his fingers and held her, staring down at her until she opened her

eyes. He started to tell her to go back to the clachan, to her
cousins and safety, and not to be out alone with a man like
him, tempting him with dreams and kisses. But there was a
soft haze in the wide green eyes gazing up at him, and a winsome
curve to her sweet mouth that lured him. He swallowed hard
and pressed his forehead against hers.

"You obviously don't know what you're doing."

"You're not the first man I've kissed, Cameron MacKenzie."

Her soft whisper dispelled the imaginary fabric of sweetness
he'd woven around her. He was tempted to call her a meddle-
some little jade; that would certainly send her off in a temper.
But as badly as he wanted distance, he didn't want to hurt her.
He straightened, his voice brisk.

"I'm quite pleased to hear it. Is this in the nature of an
experiment, perhaps? A comparison between us?"

"No." She spread her fingers through the hair on the back
of his neck, tugging lightly. "Curiosity, I think. And—oh, I'm
not quite certain what else."

"Are you not? I would enlighten you, but that would most
likely get us both into trouble." He reached up to pull her arms
from around his neck but she rose to her toes, capturing his
mouth, and instead he pulled her hard against him again. This
time he kissed her thoroughly, ruthlessly, his mouth plundering
hers until he heard her soft whimper against his lips. Even then,
he did not release her, but took advantage of her parted lips to
slip his tongue between them. She opened willingly, almost
eagerly, though he heard the quick little intake of her breath
that signified her surprise.

It occurred to him that this was a trap of some kind, devised
by Glenlyon perhaps, or even Breadalbane. The chit was a
Lowlander; how well did her MacDonald kin know her? Anything could be possible. Visions of outraged officials, a weeping
girl claiming violation, and a gallows flashed before him in a
blur. Then she moved against him, her hands sliding from his
neck to move around his waist, and he lost that important thread
of thought. For the moment, it was paramount that he hold this
soft, perfumed creature in his arms, taste her sweetness before
it was taken away.

It was a moment of scalding illumination.

And all too brief.

Lianna pulled away. A faint mysterious smile curved her lips. The only indication she was affected, was the rapid rise and fall of her chest. She gazed up at him in the low misty light, her mouth still moist from his kiss. And there in the face he had foolishly thought of as childish, was a female wisdom and knowledge staring back at him, an awareness that made him despair.

In a voice that sounded rusty, he said: "Go away."

And she laughed.

Chapter 5

"He *kissed* you?" Mary's dark eyes widened, glistening in the faint light of a lamp that barely illuminated their tiny cubicle. Drawing her knees up to her chest, she wrapped her arms around her legs and rocked forward, staring at Lianna with such fascination and envy that she was moved to elaborate.

"Twice. And he used his tongue."

Clapping one hand over her mouth to stifle a sudden squeal, Mary put the other on her cousin's arm. "The rogue! Ah, I knew Cameron MacKenzie was a braw man, but I had no idea he was so wanton—did you kiss him back?"

"Of course." She paused, worrying a long strand of her hair between her fingers for a moment. Honesty demanded she tell the entire truth, but confessing that she had practically thrown herself at him sounded so—sordid. So she compromised. "I was quite willing. Actually, I wanted him to kiss me."

She had no intention of admitting that she had been as shocked by her action as he had, and shivered as she reached for the coverlet to draw over her bare toes peeking out from beneath her nightdress. Wind whipped around the corners of the cottage with a thin wail, and it was cold as usual in the sleeping quarters up above the main room. The kitten had burrowed into a mound of coverlet until all that could be seen was the orange tips of pointed ears.

"Did he—?" Mary paused for a moment before finishing in a rush ". . . do anything else? Like—touch you?"

"Only when he put his arms around me."

"If Robbie knew, there would be a fight for certain," Mary said with a shake of her head. "No man should take liberties, unless he intends to wed the lass."

"Oh, 'twas only a kiss, Mary. That's all. Just a kiss." Her eyes narrowed. It might not have been such a good notion to allow Mary to badger a confession from her, but the truth was, Cameron MacKenzie was the first man other than her father or brothers that she had kissed, and of course, there was a vast difference.

The actuality of the difference still had the power to leave her insides knotted and her lungs strangely depleted of air. How did she explain the intensity of her reaction when he had brushed his mouth over hers, when he had held her hard against him and she had felt his muscles quiver with strain, heard his rough groan and knew that she had affected him as well? She could not form the words, and would not have tried if she could. That part of the kiss she wanted to hold to herself, like a precious jewel to be kept hidden for only her inspection and admiration.

Why had she done it? Seized by some kind of madness, she had boldly flirted with him, practically daring him to kiss her, and when he had, had not thought twice about yielding. It had been a most enlightening discovery.

She'd thought of little else since the afternoon when he had walked her back to the clachan and left her at the cottage door, glancing at her, the very devil in his gray eyes and the sulky downward tilt of his mouth. After unceremoniously dumping the basket of fish by the door, he'd pivoted on a booted heel and stalked away.

Familiar with her brothers' reactions when bested at something, Lianna understood that Cameron felt himself the loser in whatever kind of contest he considered had been waged. That suited her quite well, for it removed the entire burden of responsibility for her actions from her shoulders. Now, she felt only partially at fault for the kiss—if fault could be claimed at all.

Still, if he didn't recover from his sulks soon, she might be forced into initiating another confrontation, which she feared would definitely be too forward. She had made the first move— if there was to be a second, it must come from him. Hadn't she watched and listened to her brothers often enough to know that? Surely, she had learned something about how men viewed females intrepid enough to pursue them. There was a fine line between showing interest and being too available. And she already balanced much too precariously on the edge.

How frustrating, to be forced to wait for him to decide the inevitable. Mama was right: Men were dreadfully stubborn.

She stretched, yawning. It had been a long day that had seemed to drag on endlessly.

"Lianna?" Mary murmured from under the soft wool quilt, "do you think I will ever be kissed?"

"Of course you will. Didn't you tell me that Hugh MacEwen once tried to kiss you when you met up with him in Kinloch-leven?" She settled beneath the quilts, gently situating the grumpy kitten in a woolly hillock where she would not be squashed. "If you had let him, I've a notion Hugh would have already come courting."

Mary laughed drowsily. "Aye, 'tis true enough, I warrant. He was always after me, Hugh was, asking for a kiss and a cuddle."

"Then he will be again. Mama has told me many a time that men usually don't know what they want until we tell them. Papa, of course, takes exception when he hears her say it, but I've watched them carefully and have decided that Mama is right. All you have to do, Mary, is allow Hugh to realize that you are willing. You are, aren't you?"

"Aye. If he hadna caught me by surprise, and with my brothers just around the corner, I would have let him kiss me then."

Lianna smiled. "There's always next time."

"Robbie has planned a trip to Kinlochleven next month, to barter for goods. He might agree to take me with him."

"You should go."

"Aye. It would be good to see Hugh again."

When Mary's voice drifted into sleepy silence, Lianna fell silent, blinking drowsily up at the bare eaves darkened by night's shadows. Occasionally, insects fell from the thatch that worked its way through the framed roof. For a moment, she longed for her own home, where there were proper ceilings and fireplaces in all the rooms, and planked floors with nice carpets laid atop them, and frame beds instead of stuffed mattresses on the bare floor. How had Mama endured this primitive way of life? But hard on the heels of that thought, she recalled the breathtaking view of the sun rising above the towering crag of Bidean nam Bian, and the melodic sound of water against the shores of Loch Leven, and the bright green of summer slopes that were thickly carpeted with wildflowers and grass.

Glencoe possessed a wild beauty that she had not considered when first told she would be staying a while, and she winced at the memory of the royal fuss she had made when informed of her parents' plan.

"Stay *here?* I refuse. Mama—say you are jesting."

Catriona MacDonald Fraser's green eyes had cooled, a certain sign that she was angry. " 'Tis no jest, Lianna. I grew up here. These are good people, strong people, and loyal. They will protect you as I am not certain I can at the moment."

Fear spiked her then, and she stared at her mother with horror. "Are you in danger, Mama?"

The green eyes thawed, and Catriona hugged her only daughter. "No, not really. Neither is your father, so don't look at me like that. But France is no place for you right now, and since William has offered the olive branch of peace to those lairds who will take it, I canna see a reason in risking you."

The soft Highland burr she had retained over the years blurred her words when emotional, and Catriona's voice thickened. "Ah, dinna greet, lass. Tears will no' help ye now—'tis only for a short time. By spring, you'll be back in Edinburgh, I warrant."

Lianna had held tightly to that implied promise, and though she had slowly come to love her cousins and settle into life in the glen, she always felt as if she did not belong. She didn't understand the Gaelic, save for a few words here and there, and no one made an attempt to pretend an interest in the books and studies that engrossed her. The books she had brought with her were too familiar by now, and she longed for springtime and the return home. It wasn't that she was unhappy; she was restless, unsettled, and yearning for familiar surroundings. Until Cameron MacKenzie had arrived in the glen, she had been very discontented.

Now, she worried that he would leave before she was ready for him to go, and she didn't quite understand how she had become involved with him so quickly. It was a mystery to her why he had the ability to intrigue her so; none of her brothers' friends had ever elicited more than a mild interest from her, and none of the radical young gentlemen who visited her father had engendered anything but a raging desire to escape their political fervor. She certainly had no intention of associating herself with men who fancied themselves heroes. But not even the young men at the college where she took classes from a tutor had earned more than a mild flirtation on her part, and certainly no longing to be closer.

Yet Cameron MacKenzie could, with a glance from his smoky eyes and a twist of his sulky mouth, exude such immense attraction for her that she came fairly close to making a fool of herself just to catch his notice.

Yes, it was a complete mystery.

He was everything she disliked in a man: uneducated, sardonic, reckless, probably prone to heroics despite his protests, but worst of all—fraudulent. He came to Glencoe as King William's man, yet secretly swore to favor another king. Could she trust a man like that?

She closed her eyes. Impossible. She couldn't even trust herself. How could she ever trust him?

The kitten squeaked, then padded softly across the lumpy coverlet to reach Lianna's face, and she gently drew it beneath the covers. Soft fur brushed against her cheek, and as it settled, a steady purring rattled the tiny feline frame. She cradled it close, fingers stroking the fur until she fell asleep.

It was hardly the sort of emotion he would cultivate, given the choice, but Cameron reflected darkly that much as he had tried to avoid it, he was given to long periods of reflection about Lianna Fraser. Not just reflection—active lust, to label it correctly. Damnably inconvenient. He could hardly afford to go about mooning over some young woman who had so far managed to twist his guts into such a knot he doubted he'd ever be able to comfortably eat a full meal again.

It was the damned kiss that had done it, relegating the safe emotion of indulgent amusement to extinction. Replacing detached tolerance with raging lust was not a beneficial arrangement in this instance. This was a situation he had never thought would happen to *him*. Through his life, he'd observed from a safe distance the tangled mess other men had made of their lives over a woman, and it was hardly comforting to realize that he had even the slightest inclination to follow in their less than stellar footsteps.

Even more amazing, was that the woman happened to be the daughter of one of the most discreet Jacobites in existence, the redoubtable Dallas Fraser, scion of a long line of radical activists, and no doubt a genuine hero to boot. Hardly the sort of family he wanted to be aligned with, in any case, especially not in the dubious aspect of ravisher of said hero's daughter. Suicidal, he might at times be, but surely he knew better than to tempt fate so foolishly.

Yet, knowing all of that, he still found himself fighting the temptation to concoct some idiotic excuse to draw her away from the others, to seduce her with flattery and any other trick he could manage to devise. Given a few minutes alone with her, he was certain he could successfully ruin both their lives.

So, he was immensely grateful to be denied the opportunity to act on his inconvenient lust. It was much better this way, he consoled himself, and really, what did a few sleepless nights matter in the grand scheme of things?

Except that this night, tossing and turning on the hard pallet spread on the floor, he was having a particularly difficult time resigning himself to denial. Bluntly—he had developed a ferocious itch for Lianna Fraser. Hardly a confession he could make to Robbie. Or anyone else for that matter. Though he did suspect that Mary was speculating about his motives; it was evident in the sly glances she gave him, and in the cunning little way she seemed to contrive excuses to bring him into closer contact with the subject of this damnable itch. He couldn't help but wonder if she was being deliberately cruel, or accidentally Machiavellian. At moments, restraint was torture.

Knowing all that, he wasn't as surprised as he might have been by Mary's machinations the next morning, when she oh so innocently asked that he search for Lianna.

"Robbie said he thought she went up the glen a bit, to visit with Duncan's wife. I'm up to my elbows in bannock dough, or I'd go myself. You don't mind fetching her, do you, Cam?"

Of course he minded. For a brief—very brief—moment, he considered refusing. It was just the sort of situation he should avoid, as he was well aware that Duncan's cottage was removed from the others, and any fetching to be done would involve long stretches of empty road and far too much privacy. But he didn't refuse, nor did he point out the obvious fact that there were a round dozen children running about who would undertake the task.

Resigned to an imminent struggle with Moral Scruples over Pure Lust, he nodded a polite consent. "I don't mind at all."

She gravely accepted the lie, and he started out, his strides long over the rutted road that led up the glen. The wind had a bite to it, the mist was thick and heavy, and he reckoned that it wouldn't be long before a terrific storm blew down from the crags and enveloped Glencoe with snow. He was surprised they weren't already knee-deep in it. That was one of the things he detested about the Highlands, the way snow piled up in cracks and crevices, slipped in over thresholds and under window sills, determinedly seeping into the marrow of his bones at times. At least in Paris there had been relief. And black snow had its charms when it was piled up in the gutters instead of clogging carriage wheels and barring roads. He had fond memories of sitting in a coffee house involved in a lively discussion about art or philosophy while the snow piled up in the gutters and the streets took on the wet sheen of polished silver. Very satisfying.

But that was years ago. Another lifetime. This life had far less satisfying moments in it, save for the few he had gleaned since being in Glencoe. Oddly, the most gratifying times he had spent in the past two years had been in this little valley in the past week.

At the moment, the only thing marring his new-found contentment—other than the awakening of a conscience he was most dismayed to discover he possessed—was his recent meeting with MacIan. It would not have surprised him if the laird had been brusque to the point of rudeness, thinking as he did that Cameron had taken up arms for Breadalbane even knowing that worthy's reputation as thief, murderer and black villain, but MacIan had only briefly mentioned it.

"Aye, lad, Sandy told me the truth of it." A faint smile had curled MacIan's mouth under the thick white mustache. "After only a moment's thought, I knew you would not be so foolish as to trust Campbell of Breadalbane. But Glenlyon has a way of telling things that can lead a man's thinking down the wrong path at times."

"He does it deliberate," Cameron replied. "He knew what you would think, and so you did. A lesser man than you would hold it against me."

"Ah no, I loved your father, and his son has proven himself a fair and wise man as well."

Silent for a moment, Cameron wondered moodily what MacIan would say if he knew that Kenneth MacKenzie's son had no love for James, or William either. But of course, he had no intention of mentioning that.

"Cam, dinna be too hard on Glenlyon. I think he is in an awkward position, but he seems to be a just man. Ah, I know you think otherwise because of your brother, but hear me out. He has never been a match for the fox of Breadalbane, and now here he is, near sixty years old and naught but a gillie of the earl's. I think him more honest than is evidenced by his tartan and the man he serves.''

All Cameron could say was, ''I hope you are right.''

It had not been a satisfying meeting, and at the back of his mind was the worry that the MacIan trusted too much in Glenlyon's hearty manner, and not enough in the man's reputation. But then, there was little he could say without setting it all cock-eyed, so he kept his mouth shut and said nothing. It was generally safer most of the time, though deuced hard to do.

He was halfway to Duncan's house when he saw Lianna trudging along the road, her hair loose and flying about her shoulders in a shimmering red-gold cape. He stopped to wait for her, leaning back against the flat surface of a rock at the narrow track's edge and crossing his legs at the ankle.

He knew the exact moment she noticed him, because her chin tilted upward and even at a distance he could see the surprise in her face. Either this was all Mary's crack-brained notion, or Lianna was a devilishly good actress.

His suspicions were confirmed when she reached him, a little out of breath and her cheeks flushed with color from the brisk air. She pushed the hair from her face and eyed him with a lift of her brows.

''What are you doing here?''

''Mary sent me to fetch you.''

''Oh. She did? Are you certain?''

''Quite certain, thank you. I may have my fantasies, but plodding up a rocky track against a bracing wind is not one of them.''

''You needn't sound so defensive. I only asked because I told Mary quite clearly that I would be back in plenty of time to help boil the bannocks.'' She paused, frowning. ''Is she all right?''

''Quite all right, except for being immersed in bannock dough up to her elbows. Or so she put it. At the time, she was standing in the doorway, so I can't say what she was really doing in the kitchen.''

Lianna's mouth stretched into a tight line, and for a moment he thought she was about to berate him. But she shook her head, looking exasperated. "She doesn't want me to help. I knew she didn't, because I really can't cook or bake very well, but I did think I could be of some use, after all."

"If she didn't want you to help, Miss Fraser, I hardly think she would have sent me after you," he pointed out gently.

"Oh no, she has something else in mind besides bannocks, but I'm certain you have already guessed that."

He hadn't expected her to be so frank, and grinned. "Well, I must confess I had some notion that she was being sly. Shall we indulge her and take our time returning?"

"We might as well. If we don't, she'll only concoct some other situation, and it might be even worse." She cast him a slant-wise look from beneath her lashes, and tucked her hands into the loose edges of her cloak. "Unless you had rather go on, of course."

"Ah no, I'm game. A little romance is certainly more entertaining than listening to Robbie recount yet again how he met up with a Campbell below Kingshouse, and with great effort, bravery, and skill—"

"'. . . 'managed to best th' bluidy foe with a single sweep o' my axe—'" they chorused in unison, then laughed.

With laughter still filling his throat, he said to her, "I suppose you've heard that tale more times than I have of late."

"Precisely twenty-seven, unless you count this retelling, which would make it twenty-eight."

Laugh lines formed brackets around her mouth and at her eyes, endearing and fiercely seductive. The mist had draped glistening diamond dew in her hair and on her flushed cheeks. He was tempted to lean forward and kiss the tip of her nose, but could imagine how she might react to that. Rejection would be disappointing, and response would be deadly.

So he only straightened from his half-sprawl atop the rock to put a comradely arm around her shoulders, careful not to touch anything he shouldn't, and steered her toward the middle of the rutted track that passed for a road.

"There's a spot ahead that's sheltered from the wind, and

has an excellent view of the glen, if you care to see it. I noticed it yesterday, when I was scouting about.''

''I wondered where you went every day.'' Another slanted glance from her eyes that he could feel furtively searching his face, then she laughed softly. ''You don't drill with the soldiers, you haven't been joining the afternoon games or the evening card parties, and I thought perhaps you had decided to leave Glencoe.''

''It would be best if I did.'' He didn't elaborate. ''Blasted mist—it hangs about much too long for my comfort. Do you suppose the sun would melt the snow on the peaks if it stayed out longer than an hour or two at a time?''

''Most likely. It was nice this summer, though, when it was warm and the wind was soft. I liked going up to the shepherds' bothies with Mary, for it was so beautiful and we would stop to pick flowers, or listen to the pipes play.''

''But Glencoe is not your favorite place.''

She hesitated. He glanced down at her, and saw the conflicting emotions flit across her face.

''Not favorite, no, but I have grown more comfortable here than I first thought I would be.'' A slight smile curved her mouth. ''I admit that I went into a fit of the sulks when Mama informed me that I would be staying here with her kin for a while.''

''A scene I am most glad not to have witnessed,'' he said. ''If a fit of the sulks is anything similar to the foot stomping I saw you engage in the first day we met, I don't think I care to hear about it.''

''I did not stomp my feet.''

''Ah, but you did. I saw you. It was after Mary joined you, and Robbie and I had moved down the road a pace to have some private conversation. Definite foot-stomping.''

She bit her lower lip, glaring at him but unable to hide the slight quiver at the corners of her mouth. ''Only one stomp. Two at the most. And I was dreadfully upset with you for allowing me to think the worst.''

''So you have said.'' His arm fell away from her shoulders, and he reached for the hand she withdrew from the protective folds of her cloak, tucking it in his fist. "The mist has lifted. Just off the road a little farther up is the place I told you about. It has a splendid view of the glen."

She smiled. "Are you asking me to walk with you?"

"Aye, in my own charming fashion. It's only a little way, you understand."

Actually, it was farther than a little way, and involved climbing over some rocks and through brush, but despite the exertion, Lianna did not complain. Her cheeks were quite pink, and she was a little breathless when they reached the flat slab of rock he had in mind, so that she made no protest at all when he put his hands on her waist to lift her atop it.

To his consternation, Cameron discovered that she wore none of the female underpinnings beneath her dress that could so frustrate a man, for he felt only supple flesh and warmth when he put his hands under her cloak to grasp her waist. That first day when he had caught her, he had grasped only handfuls of thick wool, with no opportunity to determine anything other than the vague shape of her limbs beneath his palms. Even when he had kissed her, he'd felt more wool than woman beneath his hands. But today—he took a deep breath. Today, his fingers encountered warmth and pliable material. His imagination supplied the details that were denied him as his palms skimmed along the smooth seams of her dress as if seeking a firm grasp.

She grew still. The tension that had been coiling in him for almost a week drew taut, until he wondered if his face reflected the lust he felt for her. In one of those erratic tricks of fabric, the cloak had fallen completely open, lending him access to her body, to the heat radiating out, to the visual feast of the tops of her breasts that were visible above the lacy edge of her bodice. The neckline was narrow and cut straight across, apparently intended to bind, but Lianna's bosom refused to be so constrained, and the delectable swells beneath lace held him mesmerized.

After what seemed eternity, he dragged his gaze from that tempting view to her face, and found no help there. She looked dazed, her lips parted and moist, the bright pink of her cheeks making her eyes look very, very green beneath the fan of black lashes. Her breath came in little pants for air, pushing her breasts out with each inhalation, and he knew he was doomed. There was nothing for it—he had to kiss her, had to ease even a small bit this driving, fierce need that left him sleepless and aching.

His head bent, and her lashes drifted down. Deadly, deadly, deadly . . . his mouth claimed her soft lips, lightly at first, a gentle exploration that did nothing to relieve the throbbing heat in his groin. He hadn't really expected it to. There was only one thing that would provide relief for that, and he damned well wasn't going to give in to it.

But still, when she leaned against him and he could feel the soft press of her breasts against his chest, taste the sweet pressure of her mouth returning his kiss, he could not help the fleeting wish that he could lay her down on a cushion of grass and instruct her in some of the finer points of passion.

It was only a fleeting wish, however, for he knew that it would never do to deflower the virginal daughter of a radical hero like Dallas Fraser. It was a surer way to hasten death than even Breadalbane could conjure, and for all his mutterings about survival not being all it was cracked up to be, he still had Jamie to think about.

So he contented himself with another lingering kiss, a chaste embrace, and regretful withdrawal. It was the safest course he could manage, and he prayed that she didn't do as she had last time and fling herself against him. His manly resolve would ony stretch so far.

Fortunately, Lianna seemed to have no idea how close she had come to something a bit more carnal and much less romantic. She sighed when he drew back, and smiled up at him dreamily.

He cleared his throat and tried to focus on the reason he had brought her up here in the first place. Ah yes—the view. Putting his hands on her shoulders, he turned her around and in a voice that sounded strangled, said, ''Look west, beyond Ardgour. When the sun sets, it looks aflame, but now there's a deep purple haze lying like velvet around those rock formations.''

"It's beautiful. Almost like a fairy castle. If I half-close my eyes, I can see turrets, spires, all glittering as if shot with silver and gold."

"That's quartzite."

"Beast. Don't spoil the illusions."

"Ah yes, we must have our illusions, mustn't we. I always forget to use 'em, myself." He pulled her back against him so that her spine pressed from his chest to his waist and lower. God, the erotic sensation of her bottom against his groin made his fingers clutch the wool cloak and knot it in his fists. He was sweating. Every time she moved, pointing out another imaginary site, it sent shudders through him. He was a lecher and worse. This was torture. He made a mental note to have harsh words with Mary. She should have minded her own damn business.

He leaned forward; his breath stirred soft tendrils of Lianna's hair and made her shiver. He curved his arms around her to keep her warm, and when his forearms pressed just beneath the luscious swell of her breasts, the view was arousing. He stared. He couldn't help it. His mouth went dry, his good intentions dissipated like smoke, and before he knew exactly what he intended, he had turned her in his embrace.

She made a soft, breathy little sound but no protest, not even when he crushed her mouth beneath his, driven by the fierce desire to possess her, aching to press himself into her warm, willing body and forge toward mindless release. When she opened her mouth to gasp for air, he took advantage with his tongue. His hand slid under the heavy weight of her damp hair to cradle her neck in his palm, thumb rotating gently against the small spot beneath her ear. While he deepened his kiss, excitement swelling, his hand shifted lower to cup her breast, bunching the fabric of linen and lace. She shuddered and pushed against him, but feebly. His lips left her mouth and moved to her earlobe to blow softly.

Another shudder racked her body, and he took immediate advantage of her confusion to rotate his palm in a gentle exploration of her breast. Her muscles tightened, and he could feel her quivering confusion mixed with resistance, an irregularity he ignored. She began to breathe in soft little pants, erratic and labored. He smiled against the side of her neck, and when she murmured protest, a rather vague, halfhearted repetition of his name, he ignored that too.

The rich fullness of her breast against his palm left him lightheaded. Apparently, all his blood had rushed to another region of his body. This was going too far. He should stop. And he would, after one more kiss . . . just one more, a memory to take with him, something he could drag out from the dark recesses on those long cold nights when he was all alone in some dank cave or crowded inn, with the stench of unwashed bodies around him leaving him yearning for better days. This memory would be the best yet.

So he kissed her again, gently ruthless, not letting her retreat, determined to wring every last vestige of sensation he could manage before he must halt. But then she arched into him, dissolving any shreds of his restraint with her naïve response.

It was as if floodgates had been opened, and her kiss was hot and steamy and untutored, propelling him away from his gallant resolve into raw lust.

The softness of her breast, the urgency of her kiss and the violence of his need all fused into a mindless surge toward consummation. His thumb and finger closed on the tight bud of nipple pressing against the material of her gown. She made a small sound in the back of her throat, a blend of shock and excitement. His kiss deepened until her head fell back, giving him access to her bared throat, the sweet-scented pulse in the hollow, then lower to the quivering fullness that beckoned him. Lace scratched his mouth, and he tucked his fingers into the very edge of the bodice to hold it down, but somehow, he was tugging it lower.

Lianna made a sound now like a faint whimper, and the arm he'd put behind her to hold her against him tightened. It was insanity and he knew it, but for the moment, all common sense was suspended. Her hands were on his shoulders, fingers digging into him, but no protest emerged; nothing but a silent shudder that left him reeling with indecision. His body loudly demanded that he continue, but his brain—not always the most reliable or consistent organ he possessed—whispered caution.

And then she moaned slightly, a soft female sound that was infinitely seductive, and he lost all track of the importance of restraint. It was far too blissful to tug down the bodice and release the curving temptation of her breasts to his touch and taste and sight—much too pleasurable to rake his tongue over the sweet quivering mounds that beckoned him to explore even further. She shivered. A silk chemise still covered her breasts, sheer and sensual, an erotic barrier to the promised land. He moved it aside with one hand, his tongue following the slow path his fingers took, laving across skin that smelled of soap and perfume and everything in life he had missed. She clutched him more tightly, head back and her body a feathery weight in his arms. His mouth brushed over the taut rosette of her nipple, a creamy rose against ivory, and he drew it gently between his lips and heard her soft cry.

Excitement surged through him in a tidal wave. He thrust his hips against her, damning the cloth barrier even while the muffled contact sent exquisite tremors through his body and urged him to closer pleasures.

"Lianna . . ." His voice sounded husky and hoarse, and much much too intense. He closed his eyes, the taste of her on his tongue, while his body raged protest at the delay. She squirmed up against him, the little minx, her movements awkward and inexperienced as she clutched at him, her hands fluttering over his shoulders and arms, up to his face, then back again.

"Cameron . . . Cameron . . . please . . ."

He took a deep breath, and paused in his delectable exploration when he heard the faintly desperate note in her voice. She didn't know what she wanted, had probably never gone quite this far before, and wouldn't know how to handle the clamor of her body's response. While he could instruct her in the proper responses, it would be disastrous if he did. More than disastrous—fatal.

Lianna Fraser was from another world, one with soft white skin and expensive clothes, with French perfume and silk undergarments, and that world was no longer available to him. Once—so long ago now—he had lived in a similar world; then he might have had something to offer other than a satisfying tumble in the heather.

But not now.

Somehow, drawing from a reserve of control he hadn't known he could access, he kissed her gently and covered her bare breasts with chemise and bodice again, regretful and throbbing with fierce need.

She blinked up at him like a baby owl, confused and innocent, wiser than she should be with her lips all moist and swollen from his fervent kisses. Desire glowed in her eyes, a hazy sheen that he was certain was mirrored in his own, and he took a deep breath of cold air to clear his head and cool his untimely ardor.

Unexpectedly, she smiled and whispered, "I rather suspected you were a gentleman."

"Right-ho." His mouth twisted wryly. "You must know some deuced wicked fellows if, by any stretch of the imagination, you think what I just did was gentlemanly."

She rubbed her face against the front of his coat, laughing softly. "It wasn't what you did—it's what you didn't do."

"Ah yes." He sucked in another cold breath of air, thinking ruefully she wouldn't be so grateful if she knew it was thoughts of reprisal more than gallantry that kept him from tossing her expensive skirts over her head and taking her in the nearest patch of heather. "Don't be so quick to give me virtues I don't have, sweeting. This damnable mist has the look of rain to it, and I've no desire to be flopping about in the mud."

"The skies are clearing." She skimmed her fingers down the edge of his open coat and smiled archly. "But protest if you wish. I know the truth."

If you did, he thought sourly, you would not be so damned jolly about it. But far be it for him to shatter any romantic illusions she might have with something as vulgar as carnal reality. That she would have to discover on her own.

It seemed like hours before he got Lianna down off the crag, bitterly wondering why he was such a fool to have taken her up there in the first place, and infinitely relieved that he had not done anything too damaging to either of them.

All in all, leaving Glencoe behind would be the best thing to happen—provided the departure came quickly.

Chapter 6

A fire burned cheerily on the hearth, and Lianna huddled close to it, rubbing her hands together. In this clime her skin was dry and cracking, and she was almost out of the cream she had brought to keep it soft. It seemed the height of decadence at times to use the scented salve, especially when Mary looked at her so oddly and smiled a funny little smile, as if she thought her cousin pretentious to be using such beauty aids. Even the suggestion that chapped skin was painful did not alleviate Lianna's suspicion that Mary might be right. She did seem rather vain compared to her cousin.

And Mary—politely but still conveying her disdain for such things—always refused the offer to share Lianna's creams and perfumes. "Och," she'd said, "I dinna have no use for such things. 'Twould be like trying to hold back the sea with a spoon anyway."

A gentle reminder that once Lianna left, Mary's life would go on much the same as before. There would be no beauty aids, no cuddling in the loft at night to whisper secrets or confidences, or share the news of the day. Lianna realized with a pang that she would greatly miss Mary when she left Glencoe behind. Having a "sister" had been immensely satisfying.

Now, glancing up from the fire to Mary, she saw her cousin's sly smile and grimaced at her. Scheming little wretch that she was, sending Cameron up into the hills after her—and then, of course, wanting to know every detail when they had come down to the clachan again, all wind-blown and obviously disheveled, looking as if they had been doing exactly what they had been doing.

It was not at all comforting for Lianna to realize she was that transparent. Did it show so greatly that somehow she had tumbled head over heels in love with Cameron MacKenzie? Love could be the only thing to explain her inexplicable actions. It must be love, or she would not have allowed—nay, encouraged—him to kiss her, touch her intimately as he had, and of course—she would never have found such pleasure in it if she did not love him.

Once, she had assumed that when she fell in love, it would be a quiet, sedate emotion, slowly growing into a lasting affection for a man. She had no desire to be like her mother in that respect. Oh, no. Catriona Fraser swept tempestuously from sweetly affectionate to wildly raging when it came to her husband. And Dallas Fraser was just as bad. Their love was not at all calm. They seemed perfectly happy with the situation, but Lianna, as a child, had often feared her parents would do something dreadful in one of their stormy quarrels. Never to her or her brothers, but to each other. When she grew older, she finally understood that though her parents might bicker furiously on occasion, they were devoted to one another.

Outside, the melancholy strains of *Lament of Macruimen* filled the air, the pipe's mournful wail drifting on the wind. One man had started it, coaxing a melody from the *feadan,* and then another man joined in, using a full set of pipes that gave the tune substance. Being much too loud for indoors, the pipes were normally played outside in fine weather. At night, frequent *ceilidhs* were held around the fire, with harp and chanter providing instrumental melodies, and the *sesnachaidh,* or bard, reciting poetry or telling tales. Out of courtesy, no tribal songs were played to rouse enmities between clan Donald and clan Diarmaid, but the pieces chosen to be played were ballads familiar to all Scots, not just MacDonalds and Campbells.

The past week and a half had been, for the most part, pleasant in the glen, and Lianna wondered if she were the only one who dreaded seeing the soldiers leave. It was because of Cameron MacKenzie, of course. The afternoon atop the crag had left her caught between confusion and strange yearnings. At night, wrapped in warm blankets and lying beneath the eaves with Mary and the kitten, she thought of him as he had been then, recalled the urgent pressure of his body against hers and her own wild response. It had been unexpected, sweeping away all caution and restraint, and when he stopped she had been weakly glad as well as disappointed.

There was more to it, she knew. She wasn't entirely ignorant about what happened between a man and a woman, after all. But even after her mother's frank lecture, she hadn't expected to feel so—restless. As if there was more just beyond her reach, an empty need that needed to be satisfied.

She smiled, blinking at the flames dancing on the hearth. Cameron tried to be cynical, tried to pretend he wasn't gallant and kind, but she knew better. Despite his protests to the contrary, she thought him quite chivalrous. Voicing that opinion had wrung a deep groan from him.

"You think I'm gallant because I didn't toss you down on the heather? Good God, Lianna, you really have known some rum sorts, haven't you."

The bleak light in his eyes was still puzzling, and after that conversation, he seemed to avoid being alone with her. She knew why. He did not want to lose control again as they had that day. While she was grateful that he cared so much for her honor, it was frustrating. She wanted to be alone with him. Or alone enough to ask important questions about their future. He wasn't a soldier, but he was with Glenlyon. When the soldiers left, he would as well, she presumed. Did he intend to come back?

Mary left off gathering wool yarn from a basket and came to stand at the fire by Lianna. She put her hands out, smiling a little. "Where is Cam today?"

"Outside with the others, I think." Lianna slanted her an upward glance. "But you already knew that when you asked the question."

"Aye." Mary laughed softly. "He stayed behind while the others marched along the coast road toward Ballachulish. I dinna think he much likes being with the soldiers, d'you?"

"No. Understandable, I suppose, if he and Glenlyon are great enemies as you told me." She paused, frowning a little. "Why did Glenlyon have his brother arrested?"

" 'Twas false charges, I heard. Something about a stolen horse tha' was not really stolen, but was not found until after Jamie had been put into prison by Breadalbane. Cam has been trying to sort it all out and find the men who purchased the horse from Glenlyon, so it will clear Jamie of all the charges."

"Yet Cameron arrived here with Glenlyon."

"Aye. The earl of Breadalbane holds Jamie's life in his hands, and 'twas the earl who bade Cam join with Glenlyon to collect tax money and go along to convince the Glengarry MacDonalds to take the king's oath."

"I expect things will go badly for them if they don't take the oath." Lianna sighed and smoothed her skirts over her knees. The kitten meowed at her ankles, and she reached down to lift the orange creature onto her lap. It immediately began to purr and arch its back and tail. Stroking the soft fur, she looked up at her cousin. "I hope they take the oath. If not, there will be trouble for a certainty."

Mary looked glum. "Aye, trouble for all of us if they do not yield. Robbie says that Glengarry is not—"

The door swung open with a sudden crack, startling them both, and they turned to see Cameron step into the room. He paused just in the doorway, blinking at the change of light, until Mary said sharply to close the door before they all froze. "The old ones say that there will be snow before evening, filling the corries until they are flat with the braes," she added.

"I wouldn't doubt it." Cameron shut the door firmly. "The wind has shifted to the northeast. It sounds like a kelpie coming down through the gullies of Aonach Eagach."

"You have been up there on the crags?" Mary asked in surprise.

Cameron shrugged. "Just below. I rather fancied a stroll this morning, as the weather is so nice for it." His gaze shifted to Lianna and paused, and her cheeks grew warm at his steady regard. He grinned. "I hope I am forgiven for not inviting anyone along to hazard the winds, but it didn't seem like the thing to do on this raw day."

Mary laughed. "I've a notion you went just to avoid marching with the others. Armstrong and Elliot looked none too happy to be trudging up the road instead of just drilling in the haughs as usual."

"No." Cameron's gaze swung to Mary and lingered thoughtfully. "I don't imagine they were, poor sods. It's devilish cold out there. Did anyone ask for me?"

"Only Sandy, the MacIan's son. If you're thinking Glenlyon has missed you, he didn't come by way of here to find you."

Cameron came to stand by the fire. He locked his hands behind his back and rocked forward on his toes a moment. His mouth was slanted moodily, and his eyes were half hidden by his lashes. He looked brooding and sulky, and Lianna wondered what had been said to change his mood so quickly. The buff coat swung against his knees, and his black boots were scuffed and crusted with mud and frost, as if he had been climbing in the rocks.

"Did Alasdair mention what he wanted?" he asked after a moment, and when Mary shook her head, he muttered something under his breath. Then he straightened his shoulders and lifted them in a light shrug. " 'Twas probably to berate me for winning at cards again. He's a deuced bad player, and even worse loser."

"Robbie said you were all at the MacIan's house last night, until Lady Glencoe grew tired of your company."

"Aye, but she was much too polite to mention it, unlike some people I know." Smiling slightly, he reached out and tugged at one of Mary's dark curls. "But I forgive you."

Mary snorted with derision, though her cheeks were flushed a bright pink that was quite becoming. "I dinna ask for your forgiveness, Cameron MacKenzie. You're a rogue, you are, and deserve to be tossed out on your ear a time or two.''

Cameron was smiling, and when he looked up, his gaze caught Lianna's and made her heart lurch. ''I've no quarrel with that, bonny Mary. I'm a rogue through and through. It's one of my best virtues. In fact—it's my only virtue, despite rumors to the contrary. But being a rogue is a damned sight more rewarding than being a gentleman.''

Lianna leaned closer to the fire, to conceal the fact that her cheeks were flaming. Oh, he was a rogue indeed, to refer so slyly to that day on the crag when she had called him a gentleman for not taking advantage of her compliance. Of course, Mary didn't know what he meant, but she certainly did.

Maggie squeaked a protest when she set it on the floor and stood up, then with an indignant hiss, the kitten marched to a warm place on a stone by the fire and proceeded to wash. Lianna looked from Maggie to Cameron again. He was watching her with the smile still curving his mouth, but his eyes were dark-gray with uneasiness. She shivered suddenly, and didn't know why.

''Is something wrong, Cameron?''

He looked slightly startled. ''Now don't you start that as well. Sandy has complained that his wife has been as nervous as if she had seen a ghost, waking him up at all hours of the night. Why do you think something is wrong?''

''I . . . don't know. But there's something odd in the air today, hasn't anyone else noticed?''

Mary shrugged. ''Nay, I ha' not noticed, but then, I ha' been inside most of the day. After the soldiers left on their march, it was so quiet, I—'' She paused, brightening. ''Aye, it was that, I think. After hearing them about all this time, the sudden quiet must be what is odd.''

''That wasn't what I meant.'' Lianna shrugged. ''But you are probably right. They'll return soon, noisy and wanting to play at games as usual.''

But when the soldiers returned, there was little enthusiasm for the games usually played in the haugh of an afternoon. Instead, they seemed glum, and joined into the games with a desultory spirit. Then the air grew even colder, chilled by a sudden icy wind that swept down from the mountain crags and into the meadows by Carnoch. The sun had set when Lianna and Mary left for their cottage, scurrying through the grass toward the warmth of a fire.

"Did you hear the tale Alasdair's wife repeated?" Lianna asked Mary when they were before the fire again. Morag had prepared a kettle of stew, and the delicious odor filled the room with tempting anticipation.

"Aye, I heard it." Mary frowned, her movements slow as she glanced toward the far end of the room where Armstrong and Elliot sat on benches talking in low tones. She lowered her own voice. "D'you think it's true?"

Lianna hesitated. "I don't know," she said finally. "It was a child who brought her the tale, after all. Children are prone to exaggeration."

"Aye, but about something like this? I dinna think a bairn would invent such a grim tale."

"Perhaps he was mistaken."

Mary looked up, her eyes worried. "Why would he repeat it so carefully to her? And if 'tis true, why would an Argyll man be talking to a stone in Gaelic, telling the rock if it knew what would happen this night it would be up and away?"

"I don't know. That does sound dreadfully odd. What did Alasdair say to his wife about it?"

Mary snorted. "Sandy told her that all Argyllmen were full of nonsense and fond of making daft speeches. He thinks the soldier only means there will be snow."

"That is possible, of course. Well, I am certain that John and Alasdair will know if something is amiss, for they are to play cards with Glenlyon and the Lindsays tonight."

"Aye, they will know."

But Mary didn't look convinced, and Lianna still felt on edge and nervous. Normally, she wasn't sensitive. Her mother was uncannily so, but she always seemed to miss something important, or misread the obvious. Yet, this afternoon, she had felt the definite stirring of misgiving.

Armstrong and Elliot stayed to themselves instead of striking up conversation as they usually did, and none of the other soldiers who were prone to a bit of idle flirting had even glanced at her or Mary. And then there was Cameron: he had definitely been acting odd today, and she wondered if it was all connected.

At the games, he'd stayed apart, arms crossed over his chest as he observed the men playing. He did not attempt to join in, and he did not wander over to talk to anyone. Instead, he remained to one side, aloof and brooding. When he came back to the cottage, she intended to ask him bluntly what was wrong. He might tell her not to be prying into his business, but then again, he might divulge his reasons for acting so strangely.

But supper came and went, and Cameron did not appear. Armstrong and Elliot—who were supposed to be his guards— did not seem unduly worried about him, and shrugged when Lianna finally asked if they had seen him.

Armstrong replied, not quite looking at her as he shook his head. "He was called up by Glenlyon. Probably to play cards with the others tonight."

It was not at all the answer she wanted, and Lianna felt increasingly uneasy. It was hardly likely that Glenlyon and Cameron would sit down to a pleasant game of cards together. While Glenlyon might join MacIan or the Lindsays every night for cards, the men he invited to play with them were usually John and Alasdair.

Not even Robbie could ease her mind, and Uncle Colin gave him a sharp look when he muttered that the Campbell was a daft old drunkard who rarely did anything sensible.

"It's true," Robbie added defiantly, "for all tha' ye might want to ignore it. I don't trust him no more than does Sandy."

"Whsst!" Colin slanted a meaningful glance toward the Lowlanders in their corner, and Robbie lapsed into sullen silence. "Och," Colin said more loudly, "you younger men dinna know how much easier ye have it these days. Why, when I was a young man, we had no bannocks to greet us when we got home, for war had laid the land waste. Aye, 'tis much easier now, lad."

Robbie smiled a little, and Colin droned on, talking about the old days and ancient battles like Flodden Field, Bannockburn,

Sauchieburn, and the more recent ones of Bothwell Bridge, and
Claverhouse and the Covenanters. Glenlyon was not mentioned
again, but the tension was still there.

It was a most unsatisfactory evening, and when Lianna and
Mary went up to bed, by silent consent, they did not discuss
it. It was too unsettling. Both of them undressed only partially
because of the cold, wearing warm wool gowns to slide quickly
beneath the coverlets. Lianna pulled her kitten up close, snuggling it beneath her chin as she stared up at the eaves.

Why had Cameron not come back tonight? The last she had
seen of him, he was leaning against a rock with a scowl that
would frighten Lucifer, and had not even acknowledged her
tentative wave. Indeed, he had not seemed to know she had
been there or that she was leaving.

Whatever was he thinking?

Bloody hell, Cameron thought with sick fury rising in his
throat. Aloud he said calmly, ''You must be daft.''

''Hardly.'' Glenlyon smirked. ''But then, you would not
know the difference. What is it to be, MacKenzie? Your orders
from Breadalbane were to obey my commands. Do you now
defy me?''

''Let us suppose—just for the sake of discussion, of course—
that I choose to defy you. What are my options?''

''None. You will obey, or you will be shot.''

''I see.'' Cameron stared at Campbell for a long moment,
at the flushed complexion and red-rimmed eyes, the cruel slant
of his mouth and his obvious enjoyment. Oh aye, he was definitely savoring this moment, the bastard.

His gaze flicked to the men behind Glenlyon. The loutish
Lindsays and Sergeant Barber watched him closely. No help
there. Indeed, they would probably enjoy the night's work. . . .

He looked back at Glenlyon and shrugged his shoulders
carelessly, stalling for time while he tried to conceive a way
out of this dilemma. Rising fury threatened to tamp out caution,
and he held tight to his self-control. He needed all his wits
about him, by God; he didn't need to let his temper run amuck.

It didn't help that his brain was spinning in disbelief, or that his blood had turned to ice in his veins and his heart felt like a squeezed sponge.

After a polite cough to cover his seething anger, Cameron said, "It's not that I have anything against the murder of two hundred people, you understand, but don't you think the outcry will be too great to bear? It seems rather foolhardy to contemplate the destruction of an unarmed clan who has sworn loyalty to William, after all. And have you considered how your niece will feel when you kill her husband? It will hardly promote family affection, in my opinion."

"I don't need your opinion, MacKenzie, just your answer. What will it be? You might recall, by the by, that the earl still holds the key to your brother's prison cell, should you be tempted to do anything too foolish."

He was well aware of that, thank you, and while his mind was spinning from one possibility to another, he saw with sinking realization, that there would be no compromise. If he refused to join them, they would shoot him. If he gave a warning to the men of Glencoe, they would still shoot him. Of course, dead, he would be of little use to anyone. Alive, perhaps he could salvage this mess. God, he hated Glenlyon, hated Breadalbane almost as badly, and wondered bitterly how either man could actually conceive of rising up in the night to slaughter the men who had fed and housed them for almost two weeks. It was an incomprehensible act of heinous crime to the ethical mind, but therein lay the key—neither of these Campbells were ethical in the least. It was a depressing realization, but not surprising.

"Enough delay, MacKenzie." Glenlyon stood up, his gaze almost level with Cameron's. "Do you join us?"

He hedged. "I don't seem to have much choice. If I do not, I perceive that I will be shot out of hand."

"Aye, and if you are fool enough to attempt warning anyone, not only you but your brother will die. Keep that in mind."

Coldly he answered, "I assure you, I have already thought of that. It is hardly the kind of thing I would overlook when dealing with a man of such ruthless efficiency." When Glenlyon's eyes narrowed slightly, Cameron added with a shrug, "You could scarcely expect me to forget Jamie after you have gone to so much trouble to shower him with attention, could you? It would be unforgivable on my part."

"Don't be so cheeky, MacKenzie. It would give me great pleasure to take you to Inverlochy in chains."

"I am well aware of that, and intend to give you no reason to do so." The glib lie rolled smoothly from his tongue. He managed a smile, and hoped it didn't look too sick on his face. The urge to wrap his hands around Glenlyon's throat and squeeze the life from him was almost overpowering, and it was with great effort, that he restrained himself. "By the way," he asked casually, as if the answer did not matter, "do you intend to put all to the sword, or only the fighting men?"

"We are not butchers, MacKenzie, but soldiers. Only the fighting men, of course."

Lieutenant Lindsay laughed, and Sergeant Barber grinned, sending a cold chill down Cameron's spine. Cameron's hands knotted into fists, and he tucked them into his armpits to hide the involuntary reaction. He waited, silent while he struggled for control.

Glenlyon glanced toward the door of the empty cottage they were using as a guardhouse. "It's best that you remain here, I think, until the hour for assault. Oh, and Sergeant Barber will hold your weapons for you until time to use them. You understand, of course."

"Of course." He drew in a deep breath, but remained stock still while Barber relieved him of pistols, dirks and sword. He felt strangely naked without them, and much too vulnerable for comfort. He looked up at Glenlyon and managed a casual lift of his brow. "Do you suppose a fire would be out of the question? It's deuced cold in here."

"We do not wish to alert our hosts. Button your coat."

"It may have escaped your notice, but it's been snowing like blazes for the past hour. A small fire would hardly cause comment, I think."

"In an unused cottage? You're being rather obvious, Mac-

Kenzie. Remember what I said—one mistake, and the consequences will cost you dear. Think of your brother.''

There was an underlining mockery beneath his words, a derisive note that alerted Cameron to the truth: Glenlyon was waiting for him to blunder. It was what he wanted. It was probably what he was planning, and no matter what Cameron did, the outcome would be the same. If he erred or not, he would be dead. It struck him with grim irony that Breadalbane had managed with one stroke of genius to rid himself of two enemies at once—Glencoe and MacKenzie.

God, he had been so caught up in Lianna Fraser, that he had not focused on what he should. He'd ignored the little signs around him because his attention was on sweetly scented skin instead of what it should have been on. He should have remembered that it wasn't only his life at stake, but Jamie's. Now, because of his inattention, all their lives were in danger. There may have been nothing he could do about the king's orders to use fire and sword against the men of Glencoe, but he could have at least done something to warn the unsuspecting families of the glen before now.

Glenlyon left him in the guardhouse with Barber as his companion. Cameron sat on the cold floor, huddled into his greatcoat and wondering bitterly if he would have time to warn the glen before they killed him. He saw it now, the hideous reason for these orders: Slaughtering Glencoe would possibly bring the stronger, larger clan of Glengarry to heel, and even if it didn't, the act would serve as a daunting warning to any other clan who might choose to defy William. The fact that the MacIan had taken the king's oath would be suppressed, of course. And most likely, the shameful act by Glenlyon would be glossed over with the explanation that the men of Glencoe had provoked their own fate. The Highlands would be properly cowed, and Scotland under William's heel, giving free rein to the men bent on plundering the countryside in the king's name.

Oh, it was an evil, ingenious plan, and smacked of Breadalbane's fine hand.

A cold chill that had nothing to do with the frigid air inside the cottage ran through him. The desire to kill Glenlyon and

Breadalbane was strong enough to clog his throat and make him choke. He looked up, and met Barber's smirking gaze.

"Tell me, Sergeant, have you known what was intended all along?"

"Aye, from the first." Barber grinned. "Just me and Glenlyon knew. Sticks in your craw, don't it."

"Oh no. Rising in the night to slaughter one's hosts has been an unfulfilled dream of mine for some time."

"Insolent bastard. Since you're so squeamish, it might be best if you slipped out the back door."

"And make your job easier? I don't think so. Obviously, that's what you want me to do, and I'm not that obliging a fellow. If you want to kill me, you'll have to do it without being provoked, I fear." He smiled when Barber's grin vanished. "Would it be easier if I turned my back for you?"

Barber half rose from the upturned crate he was using as a chair, then slowly sat back down. His knuckles were white where he gripped the stock of his musket. "You won't be so cocky when it's time, MacKenzie, I promise you that."

"Never," Cameron said softly, "make promises you are unlikely to keep."

Silence fell. Barber was ruminating on Cameron's words like a milch cow, apparently mulling over his desire to kill him now or wait a little longer. He didn't see the point in delay, himself. Not that he wasn't grateful. It gave him some time to come up with something besides pointless sacrifice. It occurred to him that if he could arrange it, dying to save his brother and Glencoe would be a fairly good trade. After all, he hadn't been much of a hand at anything else. And it would be a worthwhile bargain, for Jamie was young and still had enough optimism to succeed where the rest of Kenneth MacKenzie's sons had not.

God, being heroes had doomed his father and older brothers, but being a rogue had the same consequences. If it wasn't so damnably infuriating, it would be amusing, he supposed.

It was after midnight before Glenlyon returned to the guardhouse, and with him was Lieutenant Lindsay. They paid little attention to Cameron after a cursory glance, but huddled across the room in low conversation. No effort was made to hide their plans, more evidence that Glenlyon did not intend Cameron to survive. Tucked into the folds of his greatcoat, he pretended to be asleep as he listened with mounting rage to the details.

Hamilton, Duncanson, and Drummond were bringing more troops. Over eight hundred soldiers were to descend upon the glen by seven of the next morning, armed with musket, sword and vengeance, while Glenlyon with his hundred men was to begin his assault at five. No men were to be spared, and all escape would be blocked. Troops were stationed at all likely routes with the orders to give no quarter.

It was a diabolical plan, designed to exterminate the entire MacIan clan. Cameron grew deadly calm. Any hope of bartering his life for his brother's was dashed. He thought of Jamie, locked in a cold prison cell with the threat of death hanging over him, and spared a brief prayer for his forgiveness. After all, Jamie's hot temper and foolhardiness had helped put him where he was, but the women and children of Glencoe did not deserve to be widowed and orphaned, then left homeless in a blizzard. It was a damnable position, made more so by the bitter knowledge that there was very little he could do for himself, and nothing he could do now for Jamie. Their fates were sealed. But if there was the slightest chance to warn Glencoe, he must take it.

It was near five before Cameron was kicked awake from his supposed sleep and ordered to join them. Barber had the look of blood lust in his eye, and it was all Cameron could do to remain comparatively calm at his taunts.

"Wake up, you bloody sod. It's time to show your friends how you really feel about them." Barber laughed. "You are to go with me and Lindsay to the MacIan's house. The old man trusts you, so it will be easy for you to distract him long enough for us to begin our work elsewhere."

"Jolly decent of you to think of me," Cameron said in an effort to keep a light tone but knowing he had missed by a mile. His smile felt more like a grimace. "But don't you think it would be a bit too obvious if I were to show up at his door at five of a morning?"

"Tell him you had a fight with your doxy, and can no longer stay in the same house." Barber's lips curled back from his teeth in a sneer. "Your activities with Miss Fraser have been reported, MacKenzie. Did you think you could hide it for long?"

Cameron's hands clenched and unclenched behind his back. "Doxy? A thought strong, to refer to her in that manner, don't you think? It's not as if I've spent much time with her."

"Aye, tell that to a man thick-headed enough to believe it."

"I thought that I just did." Cameron smiled at Barber's angry hiss. "At any rate, whether I have spoken more than a half-dozen words to her or not is not the issue here. You want me to awaken the MacIan at a time of morning guaranteed to make him suspicious. Why not wait until daylight has come? Any man woken at this hour would leap at once to the correct conclusion that trouble is afoot. I think—"

"It ain't up to you to do the thinking, MacKenzie."

It was on the tip of Cameron's tongue to tell him that someone other than the appointed lackwits ought to be doing it, but Lieutenant Lindsay chose that moment to bang on the door and slip inside the guardhouse. He looked sullen and impatient.

"We're to go now, Sergeant. What is the delay?"

"This bleedin' sod wants to try and talk his way out of joining us, I think. Maybe we should oblige him."

Cameron's insides froze at the implication. "You have misunderstood me, Sergeant. I merely mentioned that I thought it unwise to be too hasty, that's all." His gaze shifted to Lindsay and he shrugged. "If you want to warn the entire glen, arriving like thieves in the night is the most certain method I could recommend."

"It ain't up to you to recommend nothin'." Lindsay's youthfully petulant face creased into a scowl. "You're to follow orders or pay the price for disobeyin'."

"Yes, so Glenlyon has mentioned." Cameron stuck his hands deep into the pockets of his greatcoat. "Shall we go, then?"

Snow was whirling thickly through the glen, and the wind was an icy tempest that froze his lungs as he trudged through the drifts toward Carnoch and the MacIan. With the wind such

a loud howl coming down through the passes, it was unlikely
that anyone sleeping in the cottages would hear a shouted
warning. It was unlikely that they would hear the sounds of
murder until it was too late. Devil take Glenlyon, Barber and
the rest—what the blazes could he do to stop it?

Not much, with Barber on one side, Lindsay and a few
soldiers on the other, and the world a frozen hell around him.
But he knew, with a sense of rising futility and impending
doom, that he would attempt some kind of warning. It would
hardly make any difference to his fate anyway. He'd already
seen the looks passed between Barber and Lindsay, and knew
that when steel was drawn, he would be the first to feel it.

Odd, but he wasn't afraid. Regretful, perhaps, for his brother
and the copper-headed little minx who had provided such an
enchanting distraction, but no fear. In battle, he'd felt fear—
deep and quick, slicing through him as deeply as any sword
blade, but there had been no time to dwell on it. Then, there
had been time only for reaction, for survival. Fear was quickly
relegated to the back of his mind. This was different. Perhaps
he would feel fear at the last moment, when the inevitable
loomed before him and he poised on the brink, but now, all he
felt was disgust for his companions and sorrow for those of
Glencoe.

He wondered if Lianna Fraser would mourn him.

Then there was no time for speculation, no time for formulat-
ing a plan, no time for anything but grim vigilance as they
reached Carnoch and Lindsay banged on the door for admit-
tance. A sleepy-eyed servant opened the door after a moment
to peer at Lindsay in frowning surprise.

"Aye?"

"We've come to visit your chief on a pressing matter. May
we enter?"

The door swung open to admit them, and they filed inside,
Cameron neatly surrounded by soldiers. An Argyllman, tall
and narrow, with a pocked face and hooded eyes pressed into
him on one side, and a stout Lowlander nudged against his
back. He was completely boxed in.

The fire was banked, lending only a subtle glow to the main

room. Cameron heard the MacIan's servant wake him in the other room. MacIan gruffly shouted for a morning draught of hot whisky to be brought for his visitors as he dressed, and emerged looking rumpled and curious.

A tight knot burned Cameron's stomach as he tried to think of a way to warn MacIan without alerting Barber to his actions until it was too late. If he was to engage MacIan in conversation to provide a distraction while the soldiers began their dirty business, the least he could do was forewarn him of their intentions—bluntly, if necessary.

His mind whirled with possibilities, and he took a step forward, catching MacIan's attention. As the old man half-turned with a welcome on his lips and in his eyes, a shot rang out, loud and reverberating in the main room. MacIan stumbled a step, looking startled, and Cameron's muscles went paralytic with shock. *The bloody bastards—they intended to kill MacIan first all along. . . .*

"No!" he howled, desperation and rage filling his lungs and surging into his muscles as he lunged away from the Argyllman gripping his arm. "You treacherous bastards—!"

MacIan had half turned with a faintly puzzled expression on his face, when another musket shot shattered the air, smelling of heat and gunpowder. Now MacIan staggered and pitched forward to the floor with a sighing grunt. His large frame sprawled lifelessly, blood seeping from a hole in the back of his head.

Cameron had a vague image of smoke curling from musket barrels, of Lady Glencoe screaming as soldiers rushed her in a frenzy, clawing at her clothes and jewelry, swearing at her when she struggled. Wrenching away from his guard, he grabbed his musket, giving the man a vicious kick as he swung around with it. Another shrill scream filled the air, and he brought up the gun and emptied it. One of the soldiers pawing at Lady Glencoe spun around, clutching his shoulder. A low snarl at Cameron's side gave him brief warning, and he turned on the balls of his feet, slashing out with the gun barrel, catching the Lowlander on the point of his chin to send him stumbling backward. Fury filled Cameron and a red haze swam before his eyes as he used the empty musket like a club in an effort to reach Lady Glencoe.

Then Barber was in front of him, a wild light in his eyes, his teeth bared in a feral grin as he shoved the barrel of his musket hard against Cameron's chest. "You great bloody ass, did you think we would risk having you warn him? Glenlyon is not that big a fool. Duncanson and his four hundred will be here any moment, and we will finish what should have been done years ago."

Lindsay and the Argyllman grabbed Cameron's arms from behind to hold him. For a moment, he didn't resist, but it would have done no good anyway. The butt of the empty musket slammed against the side of his head, and blinding splinters of light sparked behind his eyes. Another blow, this one across the face, and a shooting pain radiated from his jaw to his neck. He lurched to one side, and was jerked upright. Blinking blood and pain from his eyes, he snarled an oath and lunged for Barber.

Lady Glencoe screamed again as Cameron twisted free from his captors. Two more soldiers grabbed him and shoved him hard against the wall, pinning him while Lindsay finished his work with Lady Glencoe. Hatred and nausea rose in Cameron's throat, and he briefly closed his eyes as MacIan's wife was stripped naked and men clawed viciously at the rings on her fingers. Several soldiers, incensed at the delay, used their teeth to gnaw at the rings until her fingers were mangled and bloody.

There was a commotion at the door, and three clansmen rushed inside, staring in horror at MacIan lying in his own blood on the floor. Muskets spewed shot, and two of the men fell at once, while the other sprawled groaning near the threshold. When he looked up, blinking with pain and confusion, Cameron recognized him. It was Duncan Don, who had arrived in Glencoe the night before with mail for MacIan.

Cameron shook his head slightly, hoping Duncan would get the message. Apparently he did, for he slumped limply to the floor and closed his eyes.

In only a few moments, it was over. Lindsay looked up, and

gave the order to drag out the corpses. The bodies of the three
men who had just rushed in were taken outside, Duncan Don
with them, no one save Cameron noticing that he was still alive.
Then Lindsay gestured to the MacIan's body. Lady Glencoe
trembled in the shadows, her chin lifted defiantly while her
chewed hands dripped blood. She did not speak, but watched
numbly as her husband's body was dragged from the room and
flung out into the snow. Cameron wondered if she was too
dazed to realize the enormity of the situation, for she did not
protest when Lindsay shoved her outside, sending her naked
into the blizzard.

Then he was being dragged outside as well, rough hands
slamming him painfully against the door frame. A fist plowed
into his stomach when he balked, then the barrel of a musket
crashed against his head. Reeling, he stumbled and went to his
knees. Snow struck him in the face, cold and wet and reviving
him a little. He had a brief view of the bodies lying in a snow
drift, then Lindsay was hauling him to his feet to shove him
forward. Another hand caught him, and he looked up through
the blood dripping into his eyes to see Sergeant Barber.

Barber's mouth was curled into a sneer. "You don't seem
to be following orders, MacKenzie. You were supposed to
distract MacIan, not shoot him in the back."

An inarticulate reply clogged Cameron's throat. He sagged
between the men holding him up, somehow getting his feet
under him to stand straight. Taking a deep, painful breath, he
forced out in a grating whisper, "You sorry bastard."

A musket barrel jabbed into his belly. Between waves of
pain, he heard Barber laugh softly. "Bloody fool. Too bad
you refused to take my orders. There were witnesses to your
defiance, and no one will doubt that you defied orders again."

Be damned to him. It wasn't as if he had a choice anyway.
It had been foreordained the moment Glenlyon and Breadalbane
conceived this unholy plan. When Barber took several steps
backward, lifting the musket, Cameron managed to straighten.
He stared at Barber steadily, and braced himself for the inevitable. A howling gust of wind spun a funnel of snow against his

face. He should say something profound, pray maybe, but all he could think was that it was a damn cold night to die.

Then came the expected explosion, the sharp smell of gunpowder and a bright burning pain before the blinding snow darkened with a swift, swooping sound to blot out the world.

Chapter 7

A low rattling like hail against window shutters woke Lianna. It was muffled, almost obliterated by the noise of the wind beating down the glen. Beside her, the kitten sat up with a jerk. Ears pricked forward, the gold eyes gleamed in the darkness, barely visible.

"It's only the wind, Maggie," she whispered, and tried to stroke the soft fur. But Maggie eluded her, leaping up and padding swiftly across the coverlet and across the loft to disappear from sight.

Lianna blinked sleepily, frowning. Aunt Morag would be displeased if Maggie got into anything, fussing that cats should stay in the stables and eat mice instead of sleeping in a bed and eating fresh fish. And Lord help her if Robbie overheard, for he would be certain to tease her most unmercifully. She should retrieve the kitten. But it was so cold, and she dreaded leaving the warm spot beneath the coverlet. She stole a glance at Mary, but all she could see was a mass of dark curls peeping out from the very edge of the covers.

After a moment of indecision, Lianna sighed and slipped from beneath the coverlet. She shivered at the icy chill, and felt her way to the ladder. Halfway down, she heard the strange popping sound again, louder this time. Blinking in the gloom, she glanced toward the end of the room where Armstrong and Elliot slept. They were gone. Only empty blankets could be seen next to the chimney wall. The blankets Cameron was to use still lay folded neatly atop a stool.

While she hesitated, she heard Robbie's gruff voice. He sounded sleepy and angry, and she moved the rest of the way down the ladder. In a moment, he and Colin appeared in the room, silhouetted against the sullen glow of the embers on the hearth.

"Wha' are ye doing up, lass?" Robbie belted his plaid around his waist and shrugged into a shirt before pulling on his boots and looking up at her with a tight frown.

"Something woke me. I think it must be hail against the windows."

" 'Tis no' hail tha' makes tha' sound," Colin said, and now Lianna noticed that he too was dressed, wearing trews and a thick wool shirt. "Wake Mary and dress."

Apprehension filled her, and she nodded shortly and climbed the ladder again to shake her cousin. Mary was already awake, jerking on her stockings with shaking hands. They dressed silently and quickly, not daring to say aloud what they feared. When they came back down, Robbie and Colin were gone.

In the main room, Morag was peering out the window. She was fully dressed, her hands pressed against her mouth. Mary went to her side. "What is it?"

Morag shook her head. "I am no' certain. But be ready to hide if need be."

Lianna cleared her throat. "Who would we hide from, Aunt?"

Her aunt turned from the window, and a thin white glow slanting through the open shutters revealed how worried she was. She shook her head. " 'Tis probably nothing. The wind, or tree limbs snapping under ice."

"But Robbie doesna think so," Mary said in a quavering voice, and Morag turned back to the window without replying.

Lianna shivered. She tucked her hands beneath the edges of her cloak. Maggie. She had to find her kitten. If there was trouble, the tiny thing might easily be crushed in the dark. Quietly, she searched beneath the table, under stools and chairs, and among the empty wool blankets still spread on the floor for Armstrong and Elliot. There was no sign of her, and when she called softly, there was no answering squeak.

Mary knelt on the hearth and stirred the embers into a small fire. When Lianna joined her, she looked up, her face strained in the flickering glow. Fear shadowed her big dark eyes, and she caught at her lower lip with her teeth to still its betraying quiver.

"I'm frightened," she whispered. "A while back, a spae-wife prophesied that the MacIan would be murdered in his own home. D'you suppose that 'tis true? D'you think that trouble has come to Glencoe?"

"If it has, there are enough soldiers here to help ward off an enemy, I would think." Lianna paused, frowning. Shadows of doubt nagged her, but she resolutely shoved away any dark suspicions in the face of Mary's fear, and managed a reassuring smile. "Prophecies rarely come true, I've found."

"Aye, you are most like right on that, though I—"

"Listen." Morag tensed, putting up a hand, her body stiffening at the window. Then she turned, urgency in her tone. "Out the back way, hurry!"

"What is it?" Lianna surged to her feet, clumsy and awkward in her haste. A low rumble could be heard, then shouts and erratic pops. The wind was a dull keening, but even above it, she made out the distinct sounds of angry men and outraged howls.

Mary fumbled at the latch on the back door, her hands shaking so badly she could scarce manage it. Blown snow clogged the opening so that she had to lean heavily against the door to press it open. With a soft grating sound and Lianna's weight combined with hers, they swung open the door. A bitterly cold blast of air swept over them, while behind them, Morag was urging them outside.

"Hurry, hurry. . . ."

A loud crack split the night, and Lianna saw a yellow-orange spurt like a flame visible in the blowing snow. She blinked,

uncertain what she had just seen. Mary grabbed her arm to pull
her forward, and then Morag screamed.

She was crying out in Gaelic, and Lianna caught only a few
words she knew, but they were enough to warn her: *"Cunnart
... Sasannuch ... ruith...."*

One word stood out: *Sasannuch*—Englishmen? In Glencoe?
Dark shapes swarmed toward the cottage, and in the murky
light she made out the gleam of musket barrels and red coats.
For an instant, she didn't understand. Weren't these the same
soldiers who were their guests?

Then, as more men streamed around them and she heard
Robbie snarling curses, she realized that none of these faces
were familiar. Among the Lowland accents, she detected a few
distinct notes of English. Chaos erupted, and in the confusion,
Lianna was shoved to the ground. She peered up through the
loose tangle of her hair, scrambling to her knees as she looked
around for Mary. Someone was screaming. Men were shouting,
and the echoing roll of musket fire was deafening.

It had grown lighter, and in the gloom, she could see Robbie
silhouetted against a white drift sloping up the stable wall. He
swung a stave, connecting with a sharp crack against a soldier's
head to send him sprawling backward. Robbie's pale head was
uncovered, and his plaid swung against bare legs as he turned
to strike out at another redcoated enemy. Howling defiance and
curses, he leaped forward, stave lifted high over his head.

As if in a dream, Lianna saw the soldier lift his musket and
aim, saw the yellow spurt of flame at the end of the long
barrel, and watched in horror as Robbie fell backward into the
snowdrift. He didn't move, but lay as if flung by a giant's hand,
a red stain blossoming on his shirt.

While Lianna stared in horror and disbelief, the soldier
lunged forward with glittering bayonet, and Robbie's body
jerked at the impact. Someone was screaming. Snow pelted her
face and into her open mouth, and she realized it must be her.
But she was not the only one.

Mary floundered through the snow toward her brother, wail-
ing his name, fighting the redcoat who tried to stop her. Still
crouched in the snow outside the cottage's back door, Lianna

struggled to her feet and lurched through the deepening drifts toward her cousin. The soldier holding Mary turned, and in a trick of light, she saw his face: Elliot. The man who had lodged with them these past eleven days, who had sat at their table and eaten their food—Elliot, who had a bayonet fixed to the barrel of his musket and was cursing Mary as he tried to hold her. With chilling clarity, Lianna knew that Glencoe had been betrayed.

Urgency gripped her, and fear for her cousin, who was lashing out at Elliot with bared teeth and clawing hands, screaming at him in Gaelic. She mustn't . . . oh no, she mustn't for he would have little compunction about killing her as well. . . .

"No, Mary! Oh stop Mary please no . . ."

She tried, dear God she did her best, but her arms and legs would not obey her command to move more swiftly, and when she saw Elliot turn with a snarl on his face and his musket flashing, she knew she would not make it in time. Pale light glittered briefly on the wicked tip of the bayonet, then winked and disappeared, and Mary crumpled to the ground.

Elliot stood over her for an instant, then looked up and saw Lianna. He looked dazed in the gray light, and his hands were shaking. "I didn't mean . . . she wouldn't stop. It's not my fault. D'you hear? Not my fault."

Ignoring him, Lianna flung herself toward Mary's still form huddled in the snow. Tears scalded paths down Lianna's frozen cheeks, and she pulled frantically at her cousin. Soft dark curls tumbled across pale cheeks as she turned her over, and then Mary's lashes fluttered and she moaned.

"Robbie . . ."

"Hush. There's nothing to be done for him now, and we must see to you." Slightly amazed at how calm she sounded, Lianna gently examined Mary. There was a nasty wound spurting blood in her side that must be tended quickly. But not here, not now. She dared not linger, when all around them men were shouting and firing weapons, and ominous red stains streaked the snow banks.

Snow was driving harder now, slashing sideways in blinding curtains, and urgently, Lianna tugged Mary to her feet. "We must escape. No, do not think of that now . . . come on, Mary, or we will die as well.''

Bearing most of Mary's weight against her, Lianna looked up to see Elliot staring at them. Blood still stained his bayonet, and he held his musket loosely in his hands.

Lianna met his gaze steadily. ''We are leaving. If you mean to shoot us as well, do it now. Look into my face and pull the trigger, if that is what you intend.''

The wind whipped her words away, but he must have heard them, for he jerked his head. ''Go while you've the chance. Hide well. I cannot be responsible for Drummond's men.''

Slowly, she moved past him, almost carrying a sobbing Mary. At any moment, she half expected a musket blast and impact of a lead ball in her back or head. But there were only shouts of excitement as men emerged from the cottage with pewter dishes, cups, trinkets, and other treasures. She thought briefly of her kitten, and hoped that the tiny creature would stay hidden until she could return for it.

With the snow dragging at their feet and the wind a bruising pressure against them, Lianna and Mary left the cottage behind and moved into the teeth of the storm. Only scant traces of road remained visible, and Mary had to point the way though she was staggering and barely able to remain on her feet. Lianna half carried her, bearing the weight with Mary's arm thrown around her neck and her own arm around her cousin's back. She glimpsed others fleeing into the gray-white blankness, and the sound of crying children was barely heard over the shriek of the wind.

Morag, Colin. Where were they? After Robbie's fall, she had not seen her aunt and uncle. Everything had narrowed to the painfully clear horror in front of her, with the edges mercifully blurred. It had all the elements of a nightmare now, a haze of images that didn't seem quite real but could still inspire driving panic, the kind that should jerk her awake in the safety of her own warm bed.

Mary slipped, dragging her sharply down with her, reminding her this was no nightmare but too terribly real, and Lianna caught back a sob. No time for tears, no time for terror, no time for anything but flight. She gently pulled Mary up again, and struggled onward, not daring to stop. Snow kept coming, hiding everything from sight only a few feet away. Her breath was a painful drag of air in lungs that felt frozen, and the tears had long since become ice on her cheeks. She bent her head, plodding forward, pressed onward by a sense of urgency so sharp it was like a physical pain. Her cloak was gone, lost somehow in the snow outside the cottage.

She tried not to think of her aunt and uncle, or of poor Robbie lying dead in the snowbank. Yet she could not help but wonder about Cameron MacKenzie, and if he had been among the soldiers who had attacked the cottage. The assault certainly explained why he had not come back for the night, and she thought bitterly that she had never been so wrong about anyone.

It was obvious that for some inexplicable reason the soldiers had risen against them, but the reasons weren't important right now. Nothing mattered but that she get Mary to warmth and security before she bled to death from the gaping wound in her side.

"Whsst, man, get up or die here."

Cameron's eyes jerked open. Dull pain like a dozen hammers pounded in his head. Slowly, he put up a hand to touch the source of the pain, and his fingers smeared something wet and warm. Blood, no doubt. But he was alive. Partially.

He squinted up through whirling snow, and saw Duncan Don tugging at him imperatively. "Get up, or I canna help ye!"

Groaning, Cameron rolled to his side. The least movement was agony. "Where . . ."

When he couldn't finish the question, Duncan jerked his head impatiently. "No' tha' far away. I dinna want to leave ye to die in the snow, but ye canna lie here longer. They will come back."

Cameron pushed to his knees, wavered there a moment, then accepted Duncan's hand to lurch to his feet. "You look bloody healthy for a man who was just shot," he muttered.

Duncan shrugged. "Better than you, I warrant. Here. Take this. 'Tis the best I can do."

Something cold was shoved into his hand and Cameron looked down. It was a dirk, the long blade lethal and promising. His fingers curled around it. Some of the haze was clearing from his head, and he shivered at the icy bite of wind.

When he took a step, Duncan put out a hand. "Dinna go tha' way. They're doing their bloody work there, and ye're likely to be caught. Come up into the hills wi' me."

Cameron's head lifted, and he saw a rosy glow illuminate the gray sky and pinken the falling snow. Fire. Of course, they would burn everything. He staggered another step, and Duncan caught his arm.

"Dinna ye hear me? 'Tis dangerous tha' way."

"I know." Cameron smiled slightly. "But that is the way I must go. Yes, well you might look at me like that. But I have to know if she is all right."

Duncan gave him a long look, then glanced behind him. "I canna stay. Women ha' a better chance than a fighting man, ye know."

"Not in this storm. They'll burn every cottage and hovel and drive out all the cattle. There will be nothing left when they're through. I've seen it before, and I am quite familiar with the thorough methods William's men employ. But my thanks for saving me from freezing to death."

" 'Twill be a waste if ye follow tha' path." Duncan nodded briefly, and a spasm of pain creased his face. "God speed to ye."

"And to you." Cameron tucked the dirk into his belt as he leaned into the wind. Damn the throbbing ache in his head. Even his vision was blurred, and the snow only made things worse. He could scarcely see, and it hurt to think. Only instinct drove him now, so that when he reached the cottage, he was at a loss.

Flames engulfed it, the wet thatch burning fiercely and the timbers groaning. Numb, he stood there, not caring if he was seen. Nothing moved. The only movement was the dancing light across the snow, the licking flames that rose into the sky like greedy fingers.

When he finally brought himself to move closer, he saw the awkwardly sprawled bodies in the snow. Robbie. Colin. Ian from the cottage down the glen—all dead. Barber's taunting laugh haunted him, and he fully expected at any moment to stumble over Lianna or Mary. Discarded items from the cottage lay scattered about, a broken piece of crockery, a torn shirt, a blanket, but no more bodies. No soft female forms frozen in the grim posture of death.

His foot caught on something and he looked down to see an abandoned cloak. It was a dark splotch against white, half covered now by snow, trampled by boots. He recognized the crumpled cloak as Lianna's, and knelt to lift it, wadding the soft wool in his fist and pressing it against his mouth. Helpless rage welled in him.

Had they suffered the same humiliation and indignities that Lady Glencoe had endured? God, he hoped not. His hands curled into impotent fists. Lianna was so thin-skinned, always cold even when everyone else went about in shirtsleeves. Did she have clothing? Shelter? Protection? Damn the bloody bastards to hell and back, she would quickly freeze to death in this fierce weather. He had to find her.

Cameron surged to his feet, tossing down the ruined cloak and stepping over a broken stave lying on the ground. The roof beam collapsed in the flames, and the fire rose higher, a gnawing hungry beast devouring wood and snow. Heat danced across him, a strange contrast to the icy blast of the wind and snow. His head ached, and blood trickled into his eyes from the burn of musket ball. He knelt for a moment to scoop up a handful of snow to press against the wound. It should slow the bleeding for now.

While he knelt there, he heard a strange, squeaky sound and glanced up, tensing. His hand went to the dirk in his belt, fingers closing around the hilt. The squeak sounded again, a faintly familiar tremor that was barely discernible above the whine of wind and crackle of flames. Nothing moved save for the fire-shadows, and he frowned. Then he saw it, a slight wobbly shadow that shot out from beneath the shelter of a smoldering peat stack.

Maggie. The kitten dashed toward him, spraddle-legged and emitting that strange squeak as he scooped it up. The orange fur was slightly singed in places, and the tiny animal was trembling violently. He cradled it in his palm as he rose to his feet, wondering what the devil he would do with the thing. He couldn't leave it here. It would die in the storm. After an instant's hesitation, he slid the kitten into the huge warmth of his greatcoat pocket, where it immediately huddled in a shivering ball. If nothing else, Lianna Fraser would be glad to see it.

A shout penetrated the swirling fog and snow, and he turned. Glenlyon's men were returning, no doubt to check for survivors. His future would be extremely short if they found him here, and he turned up the glen. One brush with death was enough for the night, and he had no intention of giving Barber or Glenlyon the satisfaction of killing him again.

Ducking behind a lopsided pile of rocks, he made his way up behind the cottage to the ridge above it. Just that effort left him breathless and aching, and he paused to drag in air and survey the glen for the best route of escape. From that vantage point, he saw soldiers spreading out across the glen, more cottages and stables on fire, and heard the lowing of hungry cattle and sheep. Letters of fire and sword, sealed and delivered in ruthless annihilation, just as Glenlyon and Barber had said. The bastards.

He thought of their chagrin when they realized he was still alive. Glenlyon would most likely have a raving fit when he learned that his tidy little plan had miscarried. It would give Cameron great satisfaction to get a glimpse of that illuminating moment, but he supposed he should just be grateful he was still alive to enjoy wistful thoughts of it.

A howling gust of wind swept from a ridge downward, spitting snow against his face in stinging pellets. The main roof beam of the cottage collapsed in a grinding shower of sparks that outshone the gray light of dawn. He certainly didn't need to linger, not when soldiers still clogged the glen and might at any moment see him standing atop the rocks. It was too dangerous here, and most probably fatal in the treacherous snow of the mountain passes, yet there was no choice.

He had to find Lianna.

Chapter 8

"Appin . . ." Mary shivered, then wheezed, "We must . . . get to Appin. Shore . . . road . . ."

Lianna squeezed her hand tightly and shook her head. "Not the shore road. It is the most likely to have soldiers patrolling it. Is there another way?"

Wind buffeted them, and Mary shivered again. Lianna moved closer, wrapping her arms around her cousin, praying for an end to the snow. They huddled next to a rock for shelter from the wind, but would freeze if forced to remain long. They needed decent shelter, needed food and care for Mary. She wanted to cry but didn't dare. That would hardly help Mary.

Still shivering, Mary raked her clenched hand across her chin and shook her head. "So . . . hard to think. Dalness. Lairig Gartain . . . pass between . . . the Shepherds. . . ."

Lianna stared at her, flinching a little at the brisk bite of wind that dried her eyes and chilled her face so that it felt like a block of ice. "Shepherds? Who are the shepherds you mean?"

Mary feebly waved one hand. "No. Shepherds—of Etive."

"Ah." Dismayed, Lianna nodded. They would never make it through such rugged country. The Shepherds were two huge promontories like sentinels, southeast of Glencoe and at the west end of Rannoch Moor, where in the summer black cattle grazed on the steep rock shelves. But to get there in winter, even through the pass, was daunting. "Is there another way?"

"Buidhe Glen."

That was worse. Rugged even in fair weather and good health. She inhaled, feeling lightheaded. She wished she had her cloak, but it had slipped off when she had rushed to Mary, and was lying somewhere in the snow by the cottage.

The cottage . . . a glance back had shown her that there would be no going back, for flames painted the sky and dawning light with searing crimson. All of Glencoe looked to be on fire, and there would be no going home for any of them.

"Dalness it is, Mary. Come along, then. If we linger much longer we are likely to freeze."

Heaving Mary up with her, Lianna stepped gingerly from behind the rock, and sucked in a sharp breath at the icy blast of wind that struck them. She staggered a little, then righted herself and Mary, and bent into the wind.

In the blowing snow, landmarks were blurred or invisible. She lost the road several times, and once almost stumbled over the edge of a precipice. It was Mary who stopped them in time, putting out a hand with a sharp warning. She was growing weaker.

Lianna pressed on desperately. The cold was taking a toll on both of them. Snow crunched underfoot, the keening wind burning cold on unprotected skin. Every breath was an icy struggle, searing her lungs. Her hair was wet and hung in matted snarls down her back and in her eyes, and now her feet were soaked as well. She could barely feel them, or her hands, and thought of frostbite. Each step became an agony, every attempt to use her hands a trial. And she could not imagine what it must be like for Mary, who, though more accustomed to the bitter cold of the Highlands, was injured so badly and losing blood.

The world narrowed to a continuous haze of blinding white snow, wind, and misery. Trees were little more than stark, twisted black shapes against white. Rocks towered on each side or across the path, forming slick, dangerous barriers that were difficult to navigate. Lianna was too miserable to even worry about pursuit. If Glenlyon's soldiers pursued them into the teeth of this gale, she would surrender. Gladly, if only they would tend Mary and give them food and warmth. But of course, it was doubtful such gentle mercies would be offered if they were pursued this far.

"There," Mary said finally, her voice so faint Lianna had to struggle to hear, "the pass . . ."

The opening of the Lairig Gartain was across the glen from the deep slash of the Devil's Staircase that ascended the northern wall toward Kinlochleven, and Lianna remembered that it was the military road frequently used. In daylight, they could be seen by soldiers using that road. She quickened her pace, fear lending her strength.

Now they came upon more fugitives, all fleeing from Glencoe. Mostly women and children, old men and women, had chosen this route, it seemed. Only a few younger men were among them. The whimpering of frightened, bewildered children had ceased, dwindling into numb apathy.

Lianna fell into step with them, forcing Mary along as best she could, and when a young man stepped forward and wordlessly lifted her cousin into his strong arms, she wept with relief. Perhaps they would make it.

The snow had stopped finally, though the wind still blew drifts against rock and tree and the walls of the shepherd's bothie where they found refuge. Lianna huddled next to Mary, grateful and exhausted. The roof leaked, wind and snow blew through cracks in the walls, and the floor was hard-packed and icy, but it was better than being at the mercy of the waning storm. Eleven people filled the tiny shack, and the whimpering of the children had faded into exhausted slumber at last. The smell of wet wool, fear, and bewilderment permeated the small square room.

Mary's breath came in short, labored pants for air, and even though she had stopped bleeding, she was too weak to do more than open her eyes when Lianna spoke to her. Now she slept, her erratic breathing rattling in her throat.

"Is she no better, lass?"

Lianna looked up at the young man who had carried Mary the last mile through the snow and shook her head. "No. If she can't get warmth and food soon . . ." Her voice trailed into a thick whisper. There was no point putting into words what all knew. Mary would die if no help was found for her.

He put his hand on Lianna's shoulder, and his face was grim. "We canna risk a fire right now. Duncanson patrols the glen, while bloody Hamilton ha' butchered an old man by the river." His mouth twisted with hatred. "The murderin' foxes ha' even killed bairns, one no more than five. I saw it—I saw wi' my own eyes tha' devil Drummond pistol a child when Glenlyon lost the stomach for it."

Helpless rage filled his eyes, and Lianna looked away. She couldn't face the horrors anymore. What she had witnessed was bad enough, but what she had heard of the atrocities committed pierced her to the very marrow. How could men do such barbaric things to their own countrymen? And it was not the English as Morag thought, but Scots who turned on them in the night, though they had done it in the English king's name.

Sickened, Lianna concentrated on Mary, smoothing her brow, wiping her pale cheeks and holding her hand, murmuring comfort to her. The day dragged on, and two of the men left to survey the area for signs of soldiers. Lianna wet Mary's dry, cracked lips with melted snow and dragged a damp cloth over her face again. She was weaker. The fever was fading, but the pallor of her face and chilled flesh was even more frightening.

As night drew near, coming swiftly with the gray winter skies, Mary awoke finally. Her lashes flickered, and she opened her eyes to gaze up at Lianna. Gray light revealed the distant shadows in her dark eyes.

"Lianna? Are ye there?"

"Yes, yes, Mary. Right here beside you." She curled her fingers around Mary's sturdy little hand. It was limp now, the small calluses rough against her palm. She swallowed a raking sob to say, "I haven't left you. Soon, we will be able to get to a safe place where there will be food and a fire, and someone to tend you better than I can.'' Her throat thickened when Mary managed a wan smile. God, her hand was so cold, her fingers lying slack instead of holding . . . *please God give her strength* . . .

"It's so dark . . . I can barely see ye for th' shadows . . .'' Mary drew in a rattling breath and let it out again. "I dinna know why . . . why did they do it? Ah God, Robbie. Robbie.''

"Hush now, don't talk.'' Lianna swallowed hard. "Save your strength. When Donald and Calum return, they will take us to safety and you will get well, but you must reserve your strength now. Your wound may reopen.''

"It doesna hurt . . . anymore.'' Mary inhaled sharply, and her hand trembled in Lianna's clasp. "But now . . . I am so cold . . . canna we ha' a fire?''

"Not yet, dear one, but soon.'' She closed her teeth on that lie, and smoothed back damp strands of dark hair from Mary's forehead. "Alex and Ian will find us soon, I warrant. They must have heard the shooting or seen the fire by now, and will come down from the hills to help.''

She hoped it was true, that Mary's older brothers would learn of the slaughter and come to look for them. They had been expected back from hunting for the past fortnight, but had not come. A thought struck: Had Glenlyon somehow come across them as well? Was that why they had not returned yet to Glencoe? They were Mary's best hope for survival now, and if they were already captured or killed—

Abandoning that thought, she held Mary's hand and looked up at the small window over them. Gray light was fading. It would be dark shortly, and no one had come. Calum and Donald may have been caught. How long could they linger here waiting? They would die, all of them, if they did not get food and warmth soon.

She half turned, glancing at the others in the tiny bothie. One of the children was sobbing softly, and a baby wailed its misery. A woman returned her gaze numbly, and Lianna glanced at the silent infant in her arms. There was no movement.

"He wa' all tha' I ha' left,'' the woman said, startling her with the calmness of her tone. "They killed th' others. My husband, my older bairns—dead. Sword and musket took them awa', and now bitter cold ha' taken my babby. I am alone."

Lianna couldn't reply. No one else spoke, and the sobbing child snuffled and hushed. The wind rattled through a broken window shutter. Mary squeezed her hand, and she turned back to her, bending to hear the barely perceptible words:

"Ha' ye seen my parents? Did they flee?"

"Yes, they fled." Lianna hoped Mary would forgive her for the lie, but she had no idea what had happened to Morag or Colin. Events had moved so swiftly, with no time for anything but flight. The last she had seen of her aunt was just outside the cottage, when Robbie had been killed.

Mary's eyes closed again, and after a moment she looked up with a faint smile. "I never got to kiss Hugh MacEwen. It would ha' been nice, I think."

Lianna held tightly to her hand, rubbing it between both of hers to warm it, and managed a bright smile. "Oh, you will get to kiss your Hugh yet, Mary MacDonald, don't you worry about that. Just think now about resting, so that when—"

"Nay. It willna . . . happen now." Mary shuddered, then drew in another labored breath. "Dinna . . . greet . . . for me. I dinna . . . mind . . . so much. But I canna . . . understand why. Why wa'd our own . . ."

Her voice drifted into a faint wheeze, and she shivered again, so that Lianna leaned over her, sharing body heat. Her throat ached. She wanted to scream, but instead she murmured soft words of comfort, stroking Mary's face, telling her she would be all right, that soon she would be warm again. The lies stuck in her throat, sharp and hurting, and still she forced them out, willing them to be true.

Dark fell, leaving the interior of the bothie in black shadows. Muffled sounds and an occasional whimper broke the silence inside, while outside the wind had lessened to a low moan. Lianna dozed at last, fitfully, waking every time Mary moved or groaned.

When morning came, Mary was still clinging to life. During the long night, Calum and Donald had returned, and said it

was best to leave before first light, for Hamilton had arrived
with more men and they were scouring the glen.

Kneeling beside them, Calum looked meaningfully at Mary
and said, "It willna be long now. D'ye come?"

Lianna did not hesitate. "No. I cannot."

Calum nodded understanding. He glanced behind him, then
back to her.' 'We mustna stay, for if the soldiers find us . . ."

"Yes, I know. You have a family to think of. I understand,
but I must stay with Mary."

Rising to his feet, Calum paused, a frown creasing his brow.
"I dinna like leaving ye. Wha' if the soldiers come?"

"I don't know. If they come, I will do what I must then. I
only know I cannot leave her now."

"I will send someone back to help ye as soon as we get to
Glen Etive, lass."

"Thank you." Lianna pressed her lips tightly together to
keep from blurting out a plea not to be left behind. As the
others gathered themselves up, she watched silently, managing
a calm smile as they left. When the door swung shut behind
them, it was deathly quiet.

"Ye shouldna stay."

Mary's weak voice quavered on the last word, and Lianna
turned to her. "Don't be silly. When I leave, it will be with
you."

Grasping her cousin's hand, Mary's lips moved soundlessly
as she formed the word, "No."

"Yes, of course we will. Someone will come soon. And you
heard Calum. He will send someone for us as soon as they
make it to Glen Etive. That's not so very far, you know, only
a few miles, and the snow has stopped and even the wind is
not so hard now." She heard herself chattering, sounding like
the rattle of a boiling pot lid, but could not stop. She must
fill up the silence, must fortify them both with courage and
determination, or all would be lost.

Drawing her knees up to her chest, she sat close to Mary,
draping her damp skirts over her cousin for added warmth,
talking quietly to keep up her spirits. She chafed Mary's hands
between her own, then removed her leather shoes and rubbed

her icy feet to warm them, telling her about the parties she had attended in Edinburgh, and the huge spires that jutted above the city like mountain crags.

Lianna was telling her about the quaint little inn she had visited that kept live ducks in a wooden tub in the common room when she heard a thump at the bothie door. She paused in midsentence, heart racing, and surged to her feet. It was still light enough that she could see through the cracks in the door, and the movement outside was a quick blur but recognizable as a man. Few women would be that tall or broad.

"Wha' is't?" Mary mumbled, and Lianna quickly knelt beside her and put a finger over her lips.

"Shh. Wait."

Tense, knowing there would be nothing she could do if the soldiers had found them, Lianna watched with agonizing apprehension as the door began to open. It hung crookedly on leather hinges, one of which was broken, and creaked as it was pushed back.

She blinked. With the light behind the intruder, she could not make out the features for a moment, not until he stepped inside and the gray light from the broken window fell across his face.

Cameron MacKenzie.

"Thank God," he said, his voice familiar and husky as he moved toward her. "I thought—"

"Murderer!"

He stopped, eyes suddenly wary.

Rage and pain and anguish welled up in Lianna until she could not think past the images burned into her brain of Robbie lying dead in the snow, of the bodies she had seen, and the tales repeated, and before she realized that she had even moved, she'd flung herself at him with bared teeth and raking fingers, clawing at him. Panting, hitting him with her fists, she kicked him, calling him the worst names she could utter.

After the first blow, he did not try to defend himself, except to turn to one side so that her fists landed on his shoulder and back. He stood there, not moving until she finally collapsed into a heap on the cold floor at his feet, panting for breath and exhausted.

"Are you through, *caileag?*"

"No." She stared up at him through the mat of her hair, hating him at that moment, wondering bitterly how she had ever been so foolish as to think he would not betray them. "Traitor."

"No matter what else you may think of me in all truth, I am not a traitor. I was not part of that slaughter."

He spoke quietly, staring down at her, and she shook her head. It hurt to think. He was only lying again, and she would not be fooled this time. Besides, there was Mary to think of, lying on the bare floor and whimpering with distress.

Cameron pulled something out of his coat pocket and moved to Lianna, bending slightly as he held it out. "I found this at your cottage."

She glared up at him, wishing she had the energy to slap him. "Loot? Why offer me your ill-gotten spoils? None of the other traitors were so foolish—" A faint squeaking sound stopped her, and she pushed the hair from her eyes to look at his hands. A small ball of orange fur peeped over Cameron's broad palms, and Lianna reached out with shaking hands to take her kitten.

"Maggie. Ah, Maggie . . ." She cradled the tiny protesting creature against her cheek. An ache clogged her throat, and she dared not look at him or say anything for fear of bursting into tears. She could not weep, could not lose control or she would never stop. Still, she held Maggie hard against her, burying her face in the matted fur that smelled of peat and singed hair.

Cameron straightened, then went to kneel beside Mary. More gently than Lianna could have imagined, he examined the wound in her side, then slid his greatcoat from his shoulders and tucked it around her.

"This should keep you warm a while, bonny Mary. Lazy lass, lying about when you should be out trekking in the cold with the rest of us." His teasing words brought a faint smile to Mary's mouth, and Lianna watched silently as he removed his plaid and folded it to place under Mary's head. Hardly much of a sacrifice, to her mind. After all, he still wore his wool shirt and trews, and the hilt of a dirk jutted from his belt.

As much as she distrusted him, she wanted to hear him say that Mary would be fine, that he would help them get to Glen Etive or Appin and safety. But could she trust him? She thought of him as she had seen him that first day, tall and dark and dangerous, a reckless, competent soldier. It was at odds with the way she viewed him now: contemptible, cowardly, given to occasional moments of generosity, but only for his own gain, she suspected. Why else would he be here?

"Why are you here?" she asked bluntly, and he turned to look at her.

"For the same reason as you, I expect. My welcome in Glencoe was terminated rather abruptly."

"Don't be flippant. You know what I mean."

"Yes," he said, "I suppose I do. You want to know if I was part of that rabble down there, if I plotted with them to fall upon my hosts and friends and slaughter them. While I appreciate your keen interest in my motives, I'm afraid that no matter what I may say, you will think what you wish to think. You've made that quite apparent, so be damned to you."

"I'm not surprised that you would deny it."

"No, I suppose you aren't." His gaze was darkly brooding, but he shrugged and looked back at Mary. Bending close, he said something to her in Gaelic that made her smile. He gripped her hands and held tightly, whispering to her.

Lianna stroked Maggie's fur, cuddling the kitten with a rising sense of isolation and despair. She tried not to think, tried not to ponder the reality that she could not escape. Mary was dying. She could not escape that fact, but could not yet face it. God, she wished she were brave, wished she could be like her mother, who had never seemed afraid of anything.

All her life, she had been afraid. Oh, she'd tried not to show it, for her brothers would have been even worse if she had let them know how she felt, that heights frightened her, and the thought of Papa fighting frightened her, and just thinking of losing Mama made her insides squeeze together so tightly it left no room for breathing. But of course, she'd never say it aloud, never admit to it. How could she? Everyone in her family was brave. She was the only sniveling little coward in the bunch.

It would never do to let them know, for they would be so disappointed, though they may not tell her. Logan and Morgan would have no compunction about telling her, perhaps, but she could not bear to disappoint Papa or Mama.

Maggie squeaked, and she realized she'd been squeezing the kitten much too tightly. Whispering apology, she rose to her knees, then to her feet. Cameron still held Mary's hands, still spoke softly to her in Gaelic, and she caught a few familiar words and phrases as he told her how lovely she was, and how sweet, and how brave.

A low rattle sounded deep in Mary's throat, and Cameron turned to look at Lianna. "I think you need to come say your farewells, *caileag.*"

Lianna couldn't move for a moment. Not yet. Not right now. Oh God, not Mary who had never been kissed, who had so much life in her and was scared of nothing.

But then she jerked forward, releasing the kitten as she leaned toward Mary and took her cold hand. A distant glow lit Mary's dark eyes. Her lips moved, barely forming words. "I'll miss ye. . . ."

"Oh Mary, Mary . . ."

"Tell . . . Hugh . . . MacEwen . . . wha' he missed. . . ."

Lianna laughed, a painfully hollow sound. "I will. I will tell him for you, Mary. Oh, I love you . . . I do. . . ."

"I . . . know."

A shudder racked her, and Mary's hand convulsed in Lianna's, then went limp. She sighed, a long soft sound, and was still. Lianna gazed at her numbly. Mary's eyes were still open, and Cameron reached out to gently close them. Then he turned to look at Lianna.

"I'm sorry."

She met his gaze, knowing she should react, but could find nothing inside her to use, nothing. Not even the fear was there at this moment, only a frozen wasteland as wide and icy as the snow-covered Highlands.

   Rising to her feet, she scooped up the kitten and crossed the tiny room, putting as much distance between them as possible. She leaned back against the wall and closed her eyes, and tried to think of nothing.

Chapter 9

"Lianna—bloody hell. I realize it's upsetting, but we don'
have a choice. We must leave her."

"She needs a proper burial." Lianna's jaw was set, and ther
was an obdurate gleam in her eyes that he'd already come t
recognize. "We cannot just leave her here. It's not fitting."

"I suppose it's more fitting to end up dead ourselves. Tha
is what will happen, you know, if you insist upon being s
damned stubborn."

"Men always seem to confuse stubbornness with resolve."

"I've told you before—don't lump me in with the lot yo
must have known." He raked a hand through his hair and stare
at her through narrowed eyes. Stubborn little chit. He had
mind to just leave her here, if that was what she insisted upor
except that—improper rogue that he was—he could not stom
ach the notion of Drummond's men getting hold of her. He'
already run across too many of their victims to risk anothe
And the worst of this was, she suspected him of being one o
them. It was in her eyes, her voice, her words. If his ow
obstinate nature had not surfaced, he might have taken the tim
to convince her that he would rather be skinned alive than b
one of those stalwart fellows capable of murdering their hosts

ut of course, he refused now to even attempt it. Let her think hat she will.

"Very well," he said after a moment, and slid the dirk from is belt to toss at her feet. "Have a go at it. Try digging a rave with that. It's the only tool we have, other than bare ands or teeth, and if you've a mind to utilize those, use your wn."

She looked down at the dirk, then up at him. There was a eculiar flatness to her expression, a numb resignation that rmented him. So much for shocking her from apathy. This uicidal insistence about burying Mary was the only sign of notion she had shown since her cousin's death. Now he was : a loss what to do, if indeed, there was anything he could ay or do that would make a difference to her.

After a moment she said dully, "I would like a moment one with her, please."

Relief flooded him. He managed to nod his head gravely. Don't take long. Drummond or Hamilton is likely to remember this little hut any time now. It's too close to Glencoe to gnore for long."

He scooped up his dirk and stepped outside to leave her one with Mary. It wasn't long before she emerged from the ut. A brief glance at her face showed no sign of emotion on er features, nothing but the blank apathy that made him shiver very time he looked at her. It wasn't natural. Not for anyone, nd especially not for Lianna Fraser, who had an opinion about verything whether it was right or wrong.

Ice and snow crunched underfoot, and he said nothing as he ent to her and pulled his buff greatcoat around her. She ccepted it silently, holding that damned kitten up to her chest s if it was made of precious glass. Ridiculous, to be jealous f a cat. But he was. Maybe not jealous, but envious that the at enjoyed her affections while he was treated like Attila the un. It seemed to make no difference to her that he had risked lot to come after her, when he could have already been safely ucked into a cozy crofter's cottage where Glenlyon's dirty ork could not reach. After all, he was quite capable of making across the mountain pass north and to safety, despite his head

njury. The wound wasn't as serious as it looked—not that she
ad bothered to notice or comment. Or care.

It was petty and he knew it, but he retreated into sullen
ilence. They struggled through the snow without speaking for
ome time. Lianna plodded at his side, his greatcoat dragging
hrough the snow behind her to leave a wake like a waddling
now. He grimaced. Anyone attempting to follow them would
ave no trouble. From other tracks left by fleeing refugees, he
urmised many were headed for Appin and the well-armed
tewart clans. But Lianna was in no condition to make that
ourney, and he had a closer destination in mind.

Dark came early in the winter, and as the gray light faded
nto deep shadows, Lianna roused from her lethargy to ask
where they were going.

He hesitated before replying. In her present mood of indiffer-
nce, any answer would no doubt be accepted, so he opted for
he truth. "I've friends nearby who will take us in a while."
t was best not to mention that these friends were Campbells.
Not from the same Campbell clan as Glenlyon or Breadalbane,
ut Campbells nonetheless.

She nodded, bending into the wind, and he moved closer to
rovide a buffer from its force. She didn't even seem to notice,
ut only cuddled the kitten more closely against her chest,
rotecting it with the greatcoat. Cameron watched enviously.
t must be true that cats had nine lives. This one had certainly
lready used a fair share of 'em, and looked to have an unending
upply. He could only hope that such good fortune would rub
ff, for they were going to damn well need it.

Lianna was only vaguely aware when Cameron lifted her in
is arms to carry her. She was so cold. Though the storm had
bated, drifts still blew before the force of the wind, stinging
er face and wetting her so that she held more tightly to Maggie
nd the coat for protection. At one point—she wasn't quite
ertain when—Cameron had paused behind a pile of rocks,
ug them a sheltered spot in the snow, then let them rest for
while. He kept talking to her, telling her that she would be

all right, and that they would soon be warm and fed, but it didn't really seem to matter. She recalled asking once where they were going, but she hadn't bothered to listen to his reply. That didn't matter either. Why must he talk to her?

He seemed to think she should be grateful for his help, but all she felt was a kind of dull awareness. Mary was dead. Robbie was dead. Uncle Colin and Aunt Morag—God, she didn't even know if they were dead or alive. It was vaguely surprising that she didn't feel more sorrow or pain. She should. She knew she should. Yet it was like a dream, a walking nightmare that went on and on, with piercing cold to remind her that she was alive and awake.

Maggie mewed pitifully, and Lianna roused enough to cuddle her close. The kitten became the focus of her concern. She had to keep her alive. Mary had brought her the kitten from the stables on Christmas Eve, saying matter-of-factly that it would die if it wasn't tended. Mary knew how distanced she felt living in the Highlands. Practical Mary. Sturdy, laughing Mary, so like Robbie at times, teasing and—but they were both dead. All she had left was Maggie.

And Cameron MacKenzie.

It was growing dark again, and in the fading light and stark white surroundings, his face was clearly etched: compelling and handsome, with cuts and bruises marring his beard-stubbled jaw and mouth. As usual, his mouth was turned down in a brooding slant, and when he looked at her—as he seemed to do frequently—it grew even more sullen. He expected something of her, obviously, but she didn't know what. Didn't want to know. It hurt to think, hurt to remember, and she wanted peace. Forgetfulness.

If she focused on drawing gulps of searing cold air into her lungs, she didn't have to think. She didn't have to wonder if Cameron was responsible for the killing, for the looting and burning, if she thought only of survival.

''Ah, it's still here.'' Cameron paused, and his arms tightened briefly around her before he swung her to her feet, one arm around her shoulders to brace her. ''Let me check it out first. If it's all right, we'll have some shelter for tonight, anyway.''

Lianna stood where he left her, not moving as Cameron cautiously approached what appeared to be a grove of trees and evergreens. Bare tree limbs mingled with feathered green branches bristling with needles, and rocks tumbled beneath in a haphazard pile. Snow covered it all, frosting trees and rocks with thick powdery white, beautiful and deadly. She stood still, Maggie under her chin, and waited.

"Empty as Job's cupboard right now," he said when he returned. "Which should suit very well."

She blinked at him, having no idea what he was talking about. There appeared to be nothing there but trees and rocks. Perhaps he had gone mad as well as the rest of the world. Nothing seemed impossible now.

But he was taking her by the hand and leading her as if she was a child, telling her to duck her head or risk snow down her collar, then preceding her inside a narrow tunnel formed by tree branches and twisted rock. Gray light filtered through the branches to light a tiny cubicle. It smelled dank, musty, and cold, and reminded her of a grave. She drew back, but his grip on her was firm, and he pulled her inexorably forward, his voice reassuring.

"It's not so bad, and we can have a fire if I can find some dry wood. Don't look at me like that. If I were going to do you harm, all I had to do was leave you behind."

Now he sounded cross; his brows were drawn down over his eyes and he was blinking snow from his lashes. "Deuced late to think of caution, isn't it? Of course it is. You're stuck with me now, so might as well make the best of it. For a while anyway."

"Yes." She moved forward, the greatcoat dragging over rock and cold ground. "A fire would be nice."

Cameron shivered, and she noticed that all he wore against the cold was his plaid wrapped around waist and broad shoulders, and tucked into the belt holding up his trews. His wool shirt was wet and clinging to his body, and his lips looked purple. A cut was dark crimson on his temple, and his hair was matted together. The purple and blue bruises looked recent. She blinked.

"You have bruises on your face."

"Do I? I didn't notice. Sit down there on that rock. A fire first, then we'll take stock of the rest. I don't suppose you'd part with the coat for a little while, would you? No, I didn't think so. Never mind. Wait here for me."

Her head ached. She sat down on the rock, slowly digesting his rapid-fire comments. One had seemed to meld into the other, all indistinguishable from the rest, and no sooner had she understood one remark, than he'd gone on to the next. He must have an inexhaustible supply of energy.

Shivering, she drew the coat more tightly around her. Maggie made a funny noise, and she peered inside the leather garment to see if she was all right. A pink nose twitched, followed by a faint rattling purr. The triangular little face was wet, the whiskers flat against her head, but she was alive. Lianna stroked her, then closed the coat again to keep her warm.

The gray light had faded before Cameron returned, but he brought wood with him. She could hear his muttered curses, sounding breathless, and then he was near, kneeling on the hard-packed dirt. He swore again, this time in Gaelic, a phrase she had heard Robbie use more than once, and there was a clicking sound that was familiar—flint against steel. A spark briefly lit the interior. Again the strike, more Gaelic curses, a few more sparks, and finally, a tiny ellipse of light. It caught, and there was the smell of burning leaves and twigs.

Lianna held her breath. The tantalizing promise of warmth brought her forward on the rock, until she was next to Cameron. He smelled of wet wool. As the flames ignited into a tidy blaze, he looked up at her. Light flickered over his face, and the bruises stood out in stark relief. They looked painful. Just what he deserved.

Rather gingerly, she opened her coat and drew out the kitten. It squeaked, a weak sound, and she held it on her lap as the fire grew into enough heat to warm the stone cubicle.

"Maggie needs to eat."

"I daresay." A dark brow rose at her comment. "It might have escaped your notice, but we haven't eaten in quite a while either, you know."

"I noticed. Where are you going to get some food?"

His mouth turned sulky again. "There's a charming little inn on the Rue de Seine that I favor, but unfortunately, it's a bit far away."

She stared at him until he looked away, into the fire as he fed it some more dry twigs and branches. In the same sulky tone, he muttered, "I suppose since I'm already cold and wet, I might as well see what I can do. If it's not too much trouble, while I'm gone, please see that the fire does not go out."

After he ducked back out the entrance, cursing when snow from the tree branches above fell on his head, Lianna began the painful process of thawing out. It hurt. Even with her hands tucked inside the coat all day, they had turned to icy, numb blocks at the end of her arms. Her feet were even worse. She fully expected them to turn black and fall off.

When Cameron returned, he was empty-handed. He met her stare defiantly. "It's not as if I have anything other than my dirk with me, and any sensible rabbit or deer has holed up for the night. Besides, it's dark. I can't see past my hand."

"Maggie will starve."

"Then she can feast on our corpses, because we'll probably die first, by God. Thank your stars that she's so damned scrawny, or I'd have her skinned and roasting on a spit over the fire by now." When Lianna gasped in outrage, he glared at her. "Don't think it hasn't occurred to me."

"Depraved monster."

"And worse. If I wasn't such a monster, I certainly wouldn't have come looking for you, nor would I be sitting in this damned dank box arguing with a woman about a cat. Christ. I should have stayed in Paris and drank myself to death. It would be infinitely more amusing than coming back to Scotland to watch grown men play at stupid heroics."

She studied him when he lapsed into silence again. Some of the daze began to fade, though his comments were, for the most part, beyond her. Paris? What did he have to do with Paris and heroics? *He* certainly wasn't a hero. She knew that well enough. Stupid heroics, he'd called it. He would not know a real hero if he rubbed elbows with one.

Dallas Fraser was a hero, and for the first time that she could remember, Lianna thought a hero would be very useful. A hero would provide food, shelter, and safety. A hero would not have let Mary die. A hero would not have let the soldiers kill her kin or burn their home. . . .

She looked away from him, back down at the kitten. "What about food? Maggie can't go long without eating."

There was a long pause, and she looked up again. Resentment simmered in his eyes, turning them to slate gray. In the flickering, erratic light, he looked hellish with his beautiful battered face, a demon conjured up by hell-fire and evil spirits. She shivered. Maggie squirmed, and she clutched her protectively to her chest, staring back at Cameron.

He looked away, and broke a slender branch between his hands with a brittle pop. "I set a trap. Maybe there will be something in it in the morning. It's the best I can do with such limited resources. And don't look at me as if I intend to slaughter your kitten. God. What you must think of me. I suppose I should be outraged, but somehow, I'm not. The whole damn thing is too outrageous. I might believe it of me myself, given the same circumstances."

He lowered himself to a sprawl on the hard dirt floor, wincing. The resentment in his eyes faded into fatigue as he gazed into the low flames. Thin curls of smoke drifted up to flatten against the low ceiling. Lianna looked away and murmured to the kitten.

After a moment, Cameron rose, went outside, and in a short time, returned with pine boughs. Traces of snow still clung to pungent needles and branches, wetting the floor as he dragged the boughs inside, and Lianna frowned.

"What are you doing?"

"Making our bed. Unless you fancy sleeping on the cold, hard ground. I don't."

"You prefer sleeping on wet trees instead."

"Before you leap to conclusions, Miss Fraser, you might give me a few moments to manage this." He looked sulky again, and she lapsed into silence.

The fragrance of pine filled the entire rock cavity, smelling clean and sharp and fresh. Cameron arranged the boughs against one wall, then unwound his plaid from around his waist and shoulder. He held it out over the fire, shaking it a little so the smell of wet wool mixed with pine scent. After a few moments, he covered the pine boughs with the plaid, then stepped back to survey his handiwork. He could not stand up straight, as he was so tall and the rock ceiling low, but bent his head and nodded with satisfaction.

"That should do. With my coat as a blanket, we should rub along quite well for the night." He turned to Lianna. "I have a notion that what I am about to suggest may seem outrageous at first, but think a moment about it, and you will see that I am right."

She stared at him, eyes narrowing a little in suspicion as he began to unbutton his wool shirt. He paused, muttered something under his breath, then winced as he unfastened the last button and began to shrug it over his shoulders. There was a muffled curse from beneath the wool, a groan, and she sat up straight, stiffening.

"What are you doing!"

The wool slowly slid over his head and hung for a moment on his wrists, and he looked up at her with pain in his eyes. "Self . . . flagellation. Oh don't look so shocked." He drew in a breath, then let it out slowly. "I only meant that some movements are sheer torture." As he peeled away the shirt and began to arrange it on a rock near the fire, he glanced up at her moodily. "Compliments of a nasty-tempered individual, but then, you wouldn't care to hear about that, I'm sure."

"You are quite right."

She sat stiffly, trying not to look at him, though it would have been impossible not to notice the horrendous array of black and purple bruises on his chest and ribs. He had taken a beating from someone, that much was apparent. While she could not help feeling that he deserved it, at the back of her mind was the niggling worry that he was truly injured. She surveyed his face as he knelt by the fire spreading his shirt to dry. Along with the assortment of bruises and raw, red scrapes, a matted clump of hair above his left ear barely covered a deep gash. It was crusted with dried blood, and looked nasty.

"Who hurt you?"

He looked up, his hands stilling on the wool. "Nice of you to care, but it really doesn't matter now."

"It does to me." She drew in a deep breath that tasted of pine smoke and scent. "Was it—"

"Was it friend or foe, you mean? That would depend on your point of view, now wouldn't it." He sounded angry, his motions jerky as he flopped a damp sleeve over the edge of the rock and jerked at the wool hems. "As you seem to think me a fiend incarnate, capable of murdering those who have befriended me, I'm not sure I want to answer your question."

"Don't sulk. It's childish."

"Is it, now." His upward glance through thick lashes was sullen, and mature enough to almost frighten her. "If anyone should know about being childish, I suppose it's you, Miss Fraser, but let's not quibble about semantics at this point. I'm tired, cold, and hungry. I don't want to quarrel, nor do I want to dredge up unpleasant memories. There will be time and enough for that before we're through, I think. I prefer concentrating on survival, if you don't mind. And as part of survival, heat is vital."

He stood up, dark, dangerous and bruised, staring down at her with an almost hostile gaze. She sat quite still, holding Maggie, looking up at him with growing apprehension.

Holding out a hand, he said, "My coat, if you please."

Slowly, she slid the greatcoat from her shoulders and held it out wordlessly, shivering at the onslaught of chill air whisking over her. He gave the coat a shake that dispelled drifts of smoke.

"Now undress."

Lianna blinked. "I beg your pardon?"

"Undress. Disrobe. Divest yourself of your garments. You are familiar with one of those terms, I hope."

"Of course I am." She inhaled sharply. "But I have no intention of—"

"Spare me the protests, if you please. While I do confess

to a less-than-detached interest in your charming little body, I am in no condition to do anything about it at this time, if indeed, I could summon up a more than remote desire. Your clothes are wet, and need to dry. While I hold up the coat, you undress and spread them out by the fire, then go lie down on the pine boughs. I will cover you with the coat. We don't have enough wood to last all night, and it's going to get deuced cold before morning. Does anything I've said convince you to stop staring at me like that and cooperate?''

Numbly, she nodded.

"Good. Then be kind enough to do it before I collapse with fatigue.''

Lianna set Maggie down carefully on the floor. The kitten made no protest, but sat listlessly. It had been two days since there had been anything but melted snow to ease thirst and hunger, and that only sparingly. Now, perhaps, with a fire and promise of food, the kitten would rouse.

She tugged at her laces with clumsy fingers that still felt the effects of the cold, fumbling at them until Cameron swore and knelt beside her. Pushing aside her hands, he swiftly untied her laces. Balefully, she regarded his efficient movements while she wondered why he wasn't as affected by the cold as she. She had heard it said many times—always by Lowlanders— that Highlanders were clean-fleshed and recovered quickly from gaping wounds that would kill another, but Robbie and Mary were proof that was not always true.

"Turn around now, while I finish,'' she said when he had the laces undone. "Put the coat on the pallet and don't turn back until I tell you.''

"God forbid that I should be tempted,'' Cameron muttered, but rose to his feet and turned his back.

Shakily, she removed her shoes, gown and drenched stockings, then hesitated before removing her shift. It would be nice to have it dry as well, but she had no desire to lie naked in the same vicinity as Cameron MacKenzie. It was disturbing enough that he was stripped down to his trews, unsettling that she would even care. A brief memory flashed into her mind, of purple shadows misting the crags and lying in the hollows below Ardgour, of Cameron MacKenzie's hands on her with such tantalizing sweetness. She blinked away the memory, hands knotting into painful fists.

As her hands and feet thawed, the frozen part of her brain seemed to dissolve as well, melding into raw images that she wanted to thrust to the back of her mind. Resolutely, she shoved them away, thinking instead of the kitten and the gnawing hunger in her stomach. Nothing else should matter. Nothing.

Lianna slipped out of her soggy shift and arranged it atop the rock, then—with a glance at Cameron's back—moved to the pallet of pine boughs and slipped under the coat. The frozen leather had thawed into a more pliable covering, and she pulled it up to her chin.

"Hand me Maggie, if you please."

Cameron said something in Gaelic, then scooped up the kitten and brought it to her, bending to place the animal lightly on her chest. He was frowning. "It might help if you kept her warm. She doesn't seem to be doing well."

"She'll be fine." Lianna drew Maggie to her, and tucked her tenderly beneath the coat. "Once you find food, she will be just fine."

On one knee, he gazed down at her. Lianna didn't want to look at him. He was too close, and she felt too vulnerable. She could feel the heat from his body despite the chill air. His hand dropped to rest on the coat, nudging the lump that was Maggie.

"Lianna."

She looked up at the subtle change in his voice. Her breath caught. Withdrawing, she looked away, her voice a sullen mutter. "Leave me alone. I'm tired and want to sleep."

"No doubt. I wouldn't mind it myself." He sounded the same again, tart and mocking, and she looked up. His long lashes were tangled, wet from the snow, half lowered over his eyes. "I hate being the one to bring this up, but you do realize that you're going to have to share, I hope."

"Share what?"

"Bed and blanket, sweeting. Ah, don't look so shocked. You didn't really think me noble enough to freeze just to protect your modesty, did you?"

"I didn't think about it at all. Put more wood on the fire. You can't truly mean to—"

"Ah, but I do. Unless you prefer sleeping on the bare floor in the rather underdressed state in which you arrived into this world, you will agree. That is your other option. I'm afraid that I must insist you share."

"I will not!" Outraged, clutching the coat to her chin, she glared at him. "You are the most outrageous—"

"Outrageous or not, I intend to be warm tonight. Or as warm as I can get in this brutal cold. As you might recall, that is my coat. And I brought in the wood. And the pine boughs. So, actually, you see, I am the one sharing with you. No thanks are needed. Just move over."

Horrified, she watched in numb silence as he began to untie the flap to his trews, releasing the cord with deft fingers. She pulled the coat up to cover her eyes, and heard his soft, mocking laughter.

She heard his boots scuff across the floor, then the sound of them dropping to the floor, then what must be the sound of his trews being laid over a rock to dry. It made sense that he be dry as well, of course, and warm. But she had not thought—not considered that they would be forced to share bed and blanket in this manner. She should have kept on her shift. But already she was so much warmer, with the bleak comfort of the fire and the warmth of plaid beneath and greatcoat atop . . .

"If you touch me, I will kill you," she said into the soft gloom of the greatcoat, and apparently he heard her, for he replied in a strangely soft voice.

"There's been enough death lately, I think."

Lianna closed her eyes tightly, willing herself to think of nothing, even when Cameron slid beneath the coat next to her and she felt the searing heat of his body brush against her quaking limbs. She turned to one side, the kitten nestled close to her, agonizingly aware of Cameron.

Stiffly, her muscles aching with the strain, she lay quite still so as not to accidentally touch him. But there was nothing she could do about his proximity, and no matter how hard she tried, nothing she could do about the wayward drift of her thoughts.

It was impossible to ignore him. She wanted to. Oh yes, she wanted to. She wanted to pretend he didn't exist. She wanted an end to the agony of indecision as well; was he the kind of man to toss in his lot with Glenlyon? After all, he'd said quite plainly he wasn't a hero, and there certainly didn't seem to be a shred of decency or nobility in him. She knew all about heroes, after all. Papa was a sterling example, all noble and expounding on causes like Liberty, Justice, Truth, and Right. Not once had she heard Cameron refer to those values with anything other than mockery. Perhaps she'd been hasty about detesting heroes. One certainly would be useful right now. A real hero. Not a fraud like Cameron MacKenzie, who had shown himself capable of finding a warm shelter and starting a fire, but had provided no other necessities.

The blaze dwindled, and Cameron leaned from beneath the greatcoat to feed another piece of wood into the fire. Lianna peeked warily from beneath the coat. Light played over his dark hair and strong shoulders, gleaming on the smooth muscles of his back. Her gaze traced the strong line downward, to his lean waist and hips, visible as he leaned forward, and she flushed.

It was disturbing to be so close to him, to be totally naked and lying next to him like this, when the memory of their kisses intruded at the most inconvenient moment. She shut her eyes, squeezing them tightly together, and her fingers curled around the kitten's tiny frame. Maggie stirred, but didn't respond except to snuggle more closely to her, and Lianna thought desperately that she had to get away from Cameron MacKenzie. She had to.

Oh, if only her parents were in Scotland. They would find her. Then she could leave all this behind and go home.

Chapter 10

"Try chewing it up for her." Cameron's suggestion was acknowledged by a quick upward flash of Lianna's eyes, then she went back to coaxing the kitten to eat. With a growing sense of futility, he watched her struggle to feed the kitten. Maggie lay limp and listless, eyes screwed into narrow slits. The only sign of life was an occasional brave purr. The bloody cat was dying, poor creature. Better off for it, probably, but how to tell Lianna? She'd lost so much. Losing the kitten would not be easy for her.

He began to wish for some kind of reaction from her, other than indifferent irritation. Even hysteria would be better than the cold, icy detachment of the past days, in his opinion. It wasn't like Lianna to be so unemotional, so numb to even his most provoking comments. He was near his wit's end how to deal with her. This stoic dry-eyed response to Mary's death and the massacre wasn't in keeping with Lianna's character. From what he'd observed, she was more the kind to throw herself into grief, weep and rail against Fate, then sit up and wipe her eyes and go on with life. It was a natural reaction for her. Not this dull acceptance.

She glanced up, a faint frown puckering her brows into a knot. "Maggie likes rabbit. Why won't she eat?"

"Maybe she's waiting for fish. Herring. Mackerel. Sea-trout. Roast goose. I know I wouldn't mind a bit of that myself, but rabbit was all I could manage this time. I fully intend to lodge my complaints with Management." Bloody hell, couldn't she even smile? No, she looked so damned serious, so wrapped up in the kitten that nothing else mattered. He blew out a heavy sigh. Enough of this nonsense. She had to come round, or they would both be in the soup. If redcoats stumbled over them in this tiny shelter, they were finished. It was well hidden, but some of the soldiers were familiar with this area and might recall that there was a shelter used by hunters on occasion. Or, they might feel they'd made their point and go back to Fort William. He fervently hoped for the latter. There was enough to cope with, just trying to survive. He gravely regarded the kitten.

"She's weak, Lianna. After all, she's so tiny, and there was the fire, the cold, nothing to eat for almost three days—it might be best to let her go."

Rage flashed in Lianna's eyes, surprising him at the show of emotion. "How dare you even suggest that I give up! Oh, that would be your answer, I'm certain, but I won't give up. Do you hear me? I refuse to let her die!"

Cameron sat back. He watched silently as Lianna tried to coax Maggie with the choicest bits of rabbit—not that there were many choice bits on the scrawny meal. But it would keep them alive, he supposed. If he didn't suspect there was a great deal more behind Lianna's desperation to keep the kitten alive than even she knew, he might have been more vocal about giving up the tastiest tidbits to a cat.

But he kept quiet and let her tempt the listless kitten with cooked bits of rabbit, raw bits of rabbit, even minced rabbit. Nothing seemed to matter. Maggie lay quietly, responding to Lianna's voice or touch with only a faint, rattling purr.

If the kitten was going to die, he hoped it would not linger. It was too painful to watch, and too dangerous to wait.

It was almost dark when Maggie died, a soft, faint mew and

rough scrape of her tongue over Lianna's hand giving her brief hope before she grew still. Lianna held her, whispering to the tiny creature, stroking her singed fur and pleading with her to live. For a while after Maggie stopped breathing, she kept talking to her, until finally Cameron couldn't stand it any more.

"She's dead, Lianna. Let her rest now."

Wheeling on him, her eyes bright with a fierce light, Lianna spat, "Go to the devil!"

"I probably shall, but you better hope it's not today. We still have a long way to go, and I don't think you can manage it alone." He rose to his feet, wanting to tell her that he was sorry about Maggie, but not knowing if it would help. She certainly didn't seem to want to hear anything from him.

She sat still, gazing at the kitten and stroking it, until he knelt beside her. "Give me the kitten."

"No. She's just resting."

"Dammit, Lianna, she's dead. Can't you see that?"

When Lianna turned, he saw the tears that silvered her eyes and streaked over her cheeks. "I don't want her to be dead, Cameron. She's all I have left of . . . of Mary. She was a gift. On Christmas Eve, Mary brought her to me, and I was supposed to keep her safe. Don't you understand that? I was supposed to make her well and keep her safe, and if she dies, I failed. I couldn't keep Mary from being hurt, and I couldn't save Robbie, and I can't even save . . . a . . . cat. Oh, God, I tried so hard . . . so hard!"

Sobs tore at her, racking and harsh, and Cameron stared in appalled silence as she lifted the lifeless little bundle of fur in her hands and held it to her cheek, rocking back and forth with grief-stricken sobs. He'd never heard anyone cry like that, as if her heart had been torn in two, as if her very body was ripping apart, and it left him awkwardly helpless. Well, he'd wanted emotion from her, and now he had it. He just hadn't expected it to be quite so heartrending, hadn't expected her sorrow to affect him like this, make him feel strange to himself, and useless. His usual glib comments stuck in his throat only half formed, and all he could do was stare at her, wondering how to ease the pain that he understood.

Aye, he understood it well, this helpless frustration of futility. He hadn't helped his father and brothers, and nothing he'd done had swayed them from rushing headlong to their fate. Nothing Lianna could have done would have changed anything either, for Mary, Robbie, or Maggie, but she wouldn't want to hear that right now.

Awkwardly, he reached out, and to his vague surprise, she did not resist when he took her into his arms and held her against his chest, rocking her as she'd rocked the kitten, holding them both against him while his throat tightened and unshed tears burned his eyes.

Lianna wept, great tearing sobs that shook her slender frame, until only dry, hacking coughs emerged. It was a relief, a torrent of tears for Mary and Robbie as well as the tiny kitten, and despite the violence of her reaction, he welcomed the release. Now, perhaps, she could go on.

After a while, when the sobs had lessened to faint whimpers, he stroked back the damp hair from Lianna's face. Gently, he took the kitten from her and placed it on the pine boughs before using the hem of his shirt to wipe Lianna's teary face. "There's a place not far from here that we can bury Maggie, if you like. And stones we can place over her so no wild animals will be able to get to her."

It was atonement for not being able to bury Mary, an offering he wasn't certain would be accepted, but Lianna nodded, her body still shaking. She clung to him, leaning into him as trustingly as a child, and he held her, one hand tangled in her hair to press her head against him while he just held her. Oddly, it eased him as well to hold her like that, to sit in silent grief for all those that had died, for the treachery he had not been able to halt, for the loss of friends.

They buried Maggie in a piece of Cameron's shirt, wrapping her in the material and covering the spot with stones. Lianna stood for a moment, then looked up at him.

"I'm ready now."

He nodded. They still had a long way to go before reaching safety. And he had no idea what Glenlyon and Breadalbane intended to do next.

* * *

olonel Hill listened with growing horror. Glenlyon had
ved at Inverlochy to report, along with Hamilton and Dun-
on. And Major John Forbes.

was the latter who told him the truth of it once they
e alone, of how the plan had been bungled and innocents
hered. " 'Twas not warfare, but a massacre,'' Forbes said
rly, looking sick, and Hill shook his head.

Dear God. Women and children as well?''

Aye.'' Forbes drew in a deep breath. ''Drummond was the
st, and Barber. Drummond had orders to let none escape,
he meant to obey, 'twas plain. Ah, the bloody fools! They
l muskets instead of cold steel, which set up the alarm.
t of the men escaped, save for old men and youths who
never seen battle.'' He swallowed hard, looking away from
into the fire. ''We were late arriving, and Hamilton was
ible to block the main exit. But I went down into the glen,
saw children lying dead in the snow, what the kites and
s had not already devoured. All that was left of one was
. hand. A child's hand.'' He closed his eyes and shuddered,
voice lowering to a whisper. ''It is ruined, for certain, for
glen is a charred, barren place now. And I wish to God I
never seen some of the things I saw. . . .''

olonel Hill briefly closed his eyes. He must make his report
e Master of Stair, and there would be an uproar over this.
the affair had been bungled was bad enough, but for
nen and children to be slaughtered . . . any who had escaped
the raging blizzard were likely dead as well. He prayed
the truth of it did not escape, for there would be an outcry
ver Scotland if it did.

anna stared into the flames, holding her hands palms-out
arm them. It had been over two weeks since Glencoe's
ghter. Two weeks, and they were still in hiding. Different
s had given them shelter, but only for a short time. It was
gerous shielding those the king's men sought, and Cameron

was reluctant to risk others. Many nights were like this c
sheltered in an abandoned shepherd's bothie, with only a
and a few blankets to warm them.

She slanted him a glance. He sat across from her, sharpen
his dirk against a whetting stone, his attention focused on
blade's edge. Firelight glanced off his dark, gleaming hair
the sharp bones of his face. Beard-stubble darkened his j
giving him a piratical appearance. His lashes made long sh
ows on his cheeks, and when he glanced up and saw her look
at him, he lifted his brows quizzically.

"Are you all right?"

"Yes. Just . . . sleepy."

He nodded, one side of his mouth quirking up in a b
smile, and went back to work on his dirk. It was only a h
lie. After eating, the warmth of the fire and late hour left
eyes itching for sleep. At least they had food now, and w:
clothing. Cameron had seen to that. The generosity of th
who gave them refuge was given to not only one of MacIa
but to the MacKenzie, she was surprised to learn.

He was a man of many surprises, she was discovering.

Losing the kitten had been devastating on top of everyth
else, but it had been Cameron who kept her from sinking
bitter despair. At first he had been comforting, holding
murmuring to her that it would be all right, the kind of thi
one said when one didn't know what else to say. She'd rec
nized the phrases, because she'd used them herself on occas
Meaningless, for the most part, and awkward, said to com
a friend in their grief, even when there was little that cc
help. But that he cared enough to say them, meant a great d

And then, there were the nights they'd spent together, sr
gled beneath the greatcoat, sharing body heat to keep f
freezing. Not naked again, as that first time, but somehow n
intimate with their clothes on. Maybe it was because she
differently about him now. The barrier she'd erected was g
having been banished by necessity and the struggle for survi

And, despite all odds, she began to think of Cameron N
Kenzie as something of a hero. Not like her father and broth
who seemed to her to take extraordinarily unnecessary ri

t quiet, steady heroism. The kind that kept them alive with
le fanfare or shouting. She thought she must be falling in
·e with him again.

lt bothered her, for though she was almost certain now that
d had nothing to do with the horrors in Glencoe, there was
l that tiny shred of doubt lingering, cropping up at the most
onvenient times to make her say something sharp. And then
would give her that sulky, brooding look, his eyes gray
·entment, his mouth turned down, and she would look away.

Now, she stood up and yawned, then moved toward the pallet
pine boughs and wool blankets, the last donated by a crofter's
nily who looked as if they could spare little. Yet all had
·en generously of what they had, sharing winter provender
l stores with the stragglers fleeing Glencoe. What would
y have done if not for those brave souls? She shuddered at
thought.

''You're going to bed, then.''

She turned back to look at Cameron, who was gazing at her
h an odd expression. ''Yes. Did you need something?''

For a moment he stared at her, eyes the color of dark gray
oke, then he looked down at his dirk and whetstone and
ok his head. ''No.'' The blade scraped over the stone a few
es before he said softly, ''Nothing at all.''

Already on the pallet with a blanket over her, Lianna
lressed beneath the covers, leaving on just her shift, as usual.
en she slid her dress from beneath the blanket to the floor,
: took note of the tension in the set of his shoulders and
sture. ''Cameron—what is it?''

He flashed her another glance, then shrugged lightly.
'omorrow we go to a village in a nearby glen. It's been a
tnight, time and enough for Glenlyon and any of his villains
have vacated Glencoe. No one has seen sign of them for a
ile, anyway, so I thought it was time we test the waters.''

She froze. This was not the first time he'd made this sugges-
n, but the very thought of encountering more trouble made
· blood freeze in her veins and her insides quake with terror.
o. Not yet. They may—''

''Christ, Lianna.'' He sounded exasperated, and his hands

stilled on the dirk and whetstone. ''We can't hide in the hi
forever. Lord knows, I've been tempted to stay hidden mc
than once in my life, but it only prolongs the inevitable.''

''Maybe it will be all right for you. After all, you're no
MacDonald of Glencoe.'' Her hands tightly clenched the wo
and it was hard forcing words past the tight lump in her thrc
''But I am. My mother is a MacDonald, and Glenlyon has n
me. He knows who I am, and if—''

''If he wants to kill you, hiding in caves and endangeri
other clans will only delay it. Do you think I would risk y
if I thought he wanted to kill you?'' He raked a hand throu
his hair, leaving finger-tracks through the dark strands. ''If i
anyone he's after, it's me. By now, I'm certain he realizes I
not among the dead. He may think I've wandered off into
hills to die, or he may be still looking for me. Whichever it
I need to go back.'' He set aside the dirk and stone and ca
to kneel beside her on the pallet. Firelight flickered over c
side of his face, leaving half in shadow as he took her reluct.
hand in his. ''I have to think of my brother. Jamie is be
held by Breadalbane, and if there's a chance I can help him
have to take it.''

She withdrew her hand in a jerk. ''There's nothing you c
do to help Jamie if Breadalbane and Glenlyon want you de
He may already be—'' She halted, the word trembling on
tip of her tongue at the sudden flare of angry light in Camero
eyes.

''Aye, well you should pause,'' he said softly, soundi
dangerous and bitter. ''Just so your skin is saved, you do
care about anyone else, is that it? Well, my sweet, you do
have a choice this time. I must go where I can find out ab
Jamie, and if you prefer hiding up here in a cave, be my gues

She looked away, shame mixing with fear. ''I . . . I'm so
for being so cowardly, Cameron. And I didn't really mean t
you should forget about your brother. I understand, truly I
it's just that . . . that I'm afraid.'' Biting her lower lip, she lif
her gaze to his. ''I've never been very brave. There are
many things that frighten me, and even though I have tried
times not to be so timid, I can't help it.''

"Timid? You?'' An amused smile slanted his mouth, and
reached out to cup her chin in his palm. "Ah, sweeting,
it is the last word I would use to describe you. Do you think
have forgotten how brave you were to rescue Mary as you
d? And how you got her away from the soldiers, then up into
e hills? You did that on your own, with no help from me or
yone else. You were very brave, *caileag,* and don't deny it.''

"Brave.'' The word tasted sour on her tongue. She jerked
ay from his hand to stare down at the blanket. "It was hardly
ave when I was so terrified I could barely speak, hardly brave
en I stood and watched instead of doing something to help
bbie . . . brave? Oh no, Cameron MacKenzie, I was anything
t brave.''

"And just what would you have done to help Robbie? Taken
bayonet in the belly like Mary did? That would not have
lped anything, only left four of you dead instead of three.''
Her head came up at that, and her eyes narrowed. "Three?
ho besides Mary and Robbie died that night? Tell me, Cam-
n, because I can see in your eyes that you know—Morag.
d she die as well? Did the soldiers kill her, too?''

He swore softly, and gripped her trembling hand in both of
. "No, I did not see Morag. I meant your uncle.''

"Uncle Colin.'' Tears filled her eyes, and she blinked them
ay. She seemed to cry at everything lately, weeping at the
st little thing. But her tears had done nothing to help, except
rhaps ease her grief a small bit.

Drawing in a steadying breath, she looked away from Cam-
n to stare at the fire. She wiped at the tears, and cleared her
oat. The words came out in a rushing tumble, a eulogy of
rts for her uncle: "Colin was a good man, a kind man for
his blustering ways at times. He always claimed Mama was
favorite sister. Of course, she is his only sister, and that
s the joke, you see. When they were children, they were
ry close. Then Papa came to the Highlands and saw Mama,
d even though Uncle Colin tried to get her back . . . well, it
rked out well, I suppose. And Mama came back for visits,
ugh Uncle Colin never quite liked Papa.'' She smiled wryly.

"My father stole my mother away, you see, and it was a gre uproar."

"Ah yes. Robbie told me a little about that. Your fath sounds like quite the dashing hero. Most admirable, I'm c tain."

Her smile faded. "Quite. If you admire heroes, he would the one to admire."

"So I understand." Cameron released her hand and sat ba on his heels, one side of his mouth tucked into a faint smi "Of course, we villains have our good points as well."

Amusement tempered her sorrow, and she regarded him wi a lifted brow. "Really? Name them. I seem to have momentar forgotten the virtues of being a villain."

"Oh, they are quite numerous. For one thing, we are nev called upon to risk life and limb. We are rarely expected collect bruises in the line of duty, and no one asks us for c opinion on politics. It's just naturally expected, you see, t villains will do foolish things like remaining safely out of line of fire, away from battles, and out of the political fray except when it is personally advantageous, of course."

"Of course. But that would not explain how you came be enemies with Glenlyon or Breadalbane, or how your brot came to be taken prisoner, then. If you are as villainous as y claim, it seems to me you would still be sitting in Paris as y say you want to be."

Some of the humor faded from Cameron's face, and his l thinned into a tight line. "Ah yes, but you see, my father a brothers had a penchant for heroism. God only knows wh but there you have it. Foolish of them, for it earned them dea while I was unfortunate enough to remain alive to deal w Breadalbane and Glenlyon. Another of my misjudgments the side of safety that had appalling consequences, I fear should have known better."

The familiar mockery was back in his voice, the wry derisi in his comments again. She wasn't too surprised. And she did blame him. It was much easier now to understand why Camer viewed the world with such cynicism. How could he not, wh the world that had always seemed safe, if rather unpredicta

times, had gone completely out of control for him as it had
r her?

She was only just beginning to understand the emotions that
ove him, and the events that shaped those emotions.

"Yes," she said bitterly, "you should have known better.
o one is ever safe from treachery."

"Ah, I note that you are learning one of life's more painful
ssons. A pity. I rather enjoyed your innocence."

"Did you?" Her smile felt tight. "You equate innocence
ith stupidity. I pray to God I am never innocent again."

"No doubt, but you might consider that the antithesis of
nocence is guilt. Rather staggering supposition, isn't it."

Lianna studied him, the dark angles and planes of his face,
e way his dark hair fell to his shoulders in thick gleaming
rands instead of neatly tied back. His garments were not those
a gentleman, but perhaps Highland gentry, with the wool
nic, tartan trews, knee-high boots and a plaid that was slung
relessly over one shoulder reminding her of the men of Glen-
e. Cameron looked rough, and unsophisticated, a Highlander
ith only a faint burr to his speech. Yet his phrases were often
oquent and erudite, certainly not the kind of language learned
a bog.

"Why were you in France?" she asked, picking with one
nd at balls of wool lint on the blanket.

"Delightful notion, changing the subject." His mouth
isted with wry humor. "France. Ah . . . Paris in the springtime
most delightful. Wine, women, that sort of thing. A young
an's interests stray to the more mundane and carnal pleasures
life at certain times, you know. Or maybe you don't know.
ust me on that one."

"Trust is hardly applicable when it comes to you." She
imaced at a tiny ball of lint she rolled between her fingers.
But, as I see you have no intention of telling me the truth
it, I suppose I'll be forced to accept that rather frivolous
planation."

"Yes, well. So you must. Pardon, but not everything in my
e is open to discussion."

"Why not?"

He looked faintly surprised, then shrugged. "Shabby bus ness, some of it, too depressing to relate. Don't you have thin in your life you'd as soon not remember?"

She drew in a shaky breath and nodded. "Of course. B only recently."

He didn't reply, and for a moment there was only the sou of the fire crackling to break the silence. Lianna surveyed hi through her lashes. He put a hand atop hers, his thumb id caressing her skin, dragging over the small knuckles at the cre of her fingers in a slow drift. She almost snatched her ha from his—then didn't, but kept it still and quivering benea his much larger one. His hands were dark, like the rest of hi broad and capable—much more capable than she ever wou have thought. She had a brief recollection of his hands wieldi a dirk, cutting tree branches to form a shelter, ice coating fingers so thickly he could scarcely bend them. The same han had torn strips of his own shirt into a shroud, then tende wrapped a dead kitten in the cloth for burial.

Perhaps he wasn't a hero, but he was no rogue, either.

Unbidden, came the memory of the night spent uncloth beneath the greatcoat, when his every movement had be imprinted on her mind as well as body. The abrasive scrape his leg next to hers, the searing heat of his body so close, t solid muscle of him a lean promise and threat at the sa time—and even in her distress, she had quivered with a respon that was vaguely frightening.

There was a terrible strangeness in her that none of h mother's lectures had prepared her for, the heated, pecul rush that washed through her at times when Cameron glanc up and caught her eyes; sometimes it sent a jolt through h entire body. At other times, when he was undressing befc slipping into his own pallet by the fire and she stole peeks him—wicked, certainly, but irresistible—she had experienc the same heated rush like liquid fire in her belly and lower

Oh, why Cameron, of all men? She'd never experienced t kind of response before, certainly with none of her brothe friends, or the other young men she'd met. Even those Glencoe, who had made excuses to visit her, bringing her sm

4 FREE BOOKS

These books worth almost $20, are yours without cost or obligation
when you fill out and mail this certificate.
*(If the certificate is missing below, write to: Zebra Home Subscription Service, Inc.,
120 Brighton Road, P.O. Box 5214, Clifton, New Jersey 07015-5214)*

Complete and mail this card to receive 4 Free books!

YES! Please send me 4 Zebra Lovegram Historical Romances without cost or obligation. I understand that each month thereafter I will be able to preview 4 new Zebra Lovegram Historical Romances FREE for 10 days. Then if I decide to keep them, I will pay the money-saving preferred publisher's price of just $4.00 each...a total of $16. That's almost $4 less than the regular publisher's price, and there is never any additional charge for shipping and handling. I may return any shipment within 10 days and owe nothing, and I may cancel this subscription at any time. The 4 FREE books will be mine to keep in any case.

Name _____

Address _____ Apt. _____

City_____ State_____ Zip _____

Telephone ( )_____

Signature _____ LF0997
(If under 18, parent or guardian must sign.)

Terms, offer and prices subject to change without notice. Subscription subject to acceptance by Zebra Home Subscription Service, Inc.. Zebra Home Subscription Service, Inc. reserves the right to reject any order or cancel any subscription.

ZEBRA HOME SUBSCRIPTION SERVICE, INC.

120 BRIGHTON ROAD

P.O. BOX 5214

CLIFTON, NEW JERSEY 07015-5214

gifts of carvings or flowers, had not interested her, and finally they had stopped.

But Cameron ... oh, God, Cameron. He was different from anyone else she had ever met, with his lazy mockery and smoky eyes that seemed to see far too much and too clearly. At times she even felt herself agreeing with him, and that was probably the worst of all. Papa would be horrified at some of Cameron's opinions of King James, while he would most likely agree with the tart observations about William.

But it was not his difference that intrigued her most about Cameron MacKenzie. Oh no. It wasn't even his handsome face, with its irregular, rugged features that were somehow in marvelous proportion and breathtakingly masculine.

It was his masquerade. She saw through it.

She was certain he didn't realize it, but beneath the sarcasm and indifference, was someone very much like herself. He felt things deeply, but instead of talking about them, and exploring his emotions, he made light of them, dismissed them, ignored them. And felt them all the more keenly for trying to pretend they didn't exist.

And somehow, it was endearing.

It changed the way she viewed him, for now that she understood, she could forgive much; overlook the outwardly heartless comments he might make on occasion, to see the truth beneath. Didn't she hide her real feelings as well? Oh yes, she certainly did. When frightened, or feeling awkward and uncertain, she masked the fear and clumsiness with bravado, very much like Cameron did.

But she still felt uneasy with him at times, the knowledge that he could make her feel like that, make her remember things she should have forgotten, and kept them sharp in her mind.

Cameron lifted his head and smiled at her, a faint smile, eyes beneath his twisted lashes a hot, smoky haze. There was warmth and intimacy in the smile, in the touch of his hand on hers, where his thumb rubbed lazily across the sensitive cup of her palm. She held her breath, feeling a bit lightheaded.

If he had gripped her too firmly, or even spoken, she would

have resisted. But he didn't, and the soft silence shrouding them created an air of seclusion that was intimate.

Lianna smiled back at him, a little breathless, and he opened his hand to tuck his fingers into hers where they pressed against her palm. Slowly, holding her gaze, he brought her hand up to his face and pressed it against his cheek. The rough stubble of two days beard scratched the back of her hand. His face was warm, heated from the fire, a contrast of smooth and rough.

Still holding her hand, he drew it upward, uncurling her fingers to trace them over his face, his brows, his cheek, the tiny scar at the left corner of his mouth, then over his lips. He nipped lightly at the tips of her fingers, and she caught her breath when he pressed a kiss into her open palm.

It was dangerous, and she knew it, yet she could not help the fatal fascination that drew her to caress his cheek, the chiseled outline of his lips, and his strong, square jaw. The attraction that had been between them since the first moment she'd fallen from the rock into his arms was still there, despite past suspicions. It lay like a sleeping tiger beneath his words, his glances, even his subtle and brazen mockery at times.

And she felt the same irresistible temptation.

It was foolish—fatal. Yet she could not resist the lure that drew her to him, the lure of mystery and knowledge that he held in his hands, the sweet power of his touch and kiss. She'd felt it that day on the crag above Glencoe, and she felt it still.

He looked up at her, a flashing glance full of gray hope and speculation, and she knew he fought the same restless need that was curling inside her. Smoke curled behind him from the fire, a wispy haze and flickering light that gave the impression of the devil's own, and she almost told him, but then he was leaning forward, and there was no time.

His mouth brushed across her parted lips, tongue flicking out to tease the corners, trace the curve of her lower lip then the top before stealing inside. She closed her eyes. It had grown so warm, but she was shivering, the blankets still clutched to her chin. Cameron's hand laced with hers as he gently, slowly pressed her back into the pallet of pine boughs.

Sharp scent from crushed needles wafted around her, mingling with the acrid drift of smoke. Cameron's weight shifted, and she felt the heavy constraint of his frame bearing her against the unyielding boughs and wool. He released her hand to brace himself and ease his weight, still kissing her gently.

Lianna spread her hands under his shirt and across his bare back, testing the smooth, hard skin with her fingertips in light strokes. Heat radiated outward as she held him; everywhere he touched her, she blazed with an aching need that left her trembling. The need soared, spread through her in a burning tide, then seemed to coalesce between her thighs, making her throb.

"Cameron . . ." His name came out in a faint moan when he lifted his head, and she blinked up at him. With the light behind, his face was shadowed, but there was a hard edge to his features, and his eyes glittered in the dim light.

"We don't need to be doing this, you know."

He sounded practical, and if not for the little break in his voice, she might have thought he was unaffected. But white lines bracketed his mouth on both sides, and there was a tension in him that made his arms vibrate.

"I know . . . I know." She swallowed hard. "We should . . . stop."

"Yes." His head bent and he kissed her again, hard and fierce, his mouth a savage, bruising pressure. He moved to kiss her throat, his hands tunneling into her loose hair, closing into fists as he held her. "We should . . . definitely . . . stop. . . ."

When she washed her tongue over the column of his throat, she heard him groan. Tensing, his muscles contracted beneath her palms and he pushed himself up, bracing his body on his hands, staring down at her. His breath was coming in harsh gusts of air between his teeth, and there was a wild, fierce light in his eyes.

Drawn by the need to feel him next to her, to have him hold her, she moved her hands from his back to his chest, still under his shirt, her fingers trailing over his ribs. He sucked in a sharp breath, and emboldened, she slid her palms down to his waist.

Cursing softly, Cameron bent in a swift motion that took her by surprise, pushing her backward as he bent to kiss her mouth, throat, the bare skin above the blanket's edge. Then the blanket slipped lower, and his fingers were curled into the ragged edge of her chemise, pulling it free. His breath heated her skin as he tugged at the flimsy fabric with rough moves. Cool air whispered over her bared breast, the exquisite contrast making her nipple harden into a tight knot. With an excited, hoarse sound, Cameron kissed her breast, drawing the nipple against his teeth until she was shivering and arching upward into the sweet pleasure.

Tugging at her nipple with his mouth, he curled his fist on the blanket and pulled it away. She was aflame with need, wanting an end to the restless, aching throb between her thighs, faint whimpers catching in the back of her throat.

Then—shocking her—his other hand was between her thighs, stroking upward with shuddering ecstasy, sending the world into a spinning whirl as his fingers slid inside her. She moaned, arched upward into his hand, her fingers sliding over him with fluttering, aimless motions. Aware only of Cameron's dark face above her, his intent expression and the fervent demands of her body, she clutched at him wildly.

"Cam . . . eron. Oh . . . I don't know . . . what . . ."

He shushed her gently, his mouth moving from one breast to the other, his hand sending shivering ripples through her body. He bent his head until all she could see of him was his tangled black hair and taut sweep of his shoulders. His hand moved between her thighs again, thumb raking over the aching center of her until she was arching upward and crying out his name, quivering with excitement and growing tension. She heard him groan, then she convulsed into shuddering release that was unexpected and shattering.

Whimpering his name, she clung to him and he held her as the spasms faded. His heart was an erratic thud against her cheek, his wool shirt damp and sliding to one side to bare a muscled arm. Slightly dazed, Lianna pressed her face into his chest.

After a moment, Cameron pushed her away and sat up, pushing his hand through his hair. There was a tight, tense look about him, and she felt suddenly shy.

As if sensing it, he reached for the blanket and drew it up and over her, then looked away into the fire.

"It might be best," he said in a low voice, "if you take my dirk."

Blinking in confusion, she stared at him. "Why?"

"Because, if I come near you again, you'll have to use it on me. Next time, I won't stop until it's too late."

There was a note of controlled violence in his words and as he turned to look at her, she saw the raging frustration in his eyes. She nodded mutely. Her face flamed. He was right, of course. What was she thinking? How had she let herself forget everything she'd been told all her life? He would never respect her if she made it so easy for him. She had observed her brothers enough to know how they felt about over-bold females.

"Cameron—"

"No. Don't say anything. Please." He dragged in a harsh breath. "I'm reminding myself that your father is Dallas Fraser, and unlikely to appreciate any explanation I might make for your condition were we to ... consummate. So please, make it easy on me. I shall endeavor to forget what just happened, and will do my utmost not to lose control again. Just keep your damned clothes on, will you?"

Lianna watched as he shot to his feet and stalked to his own pallet, hugging the blanket to her. A faint smile tugged at her mouth. Oh no. He wasn't going to get off that easy. Not after what had just happened between them. He may not want to admit it, but he cared a lot more for her than he pretended. If he did not, he would never have been gallant enough to stop when he did.

Snuggling down into her blankets, Lianna listened to Cameron's frustrated snarls and bad-tempered mutters until she grew sleepy. Oh yes, Cameron MacKenzie was not as immune to her as he imagined he was.

Chapter 11

A wet rain was falling in the French countryside, one of those dismal drizzles that could seem interminable. Catriona Fraser turned away from the window when she heard her husband's voice downstairs, and smoothed her bright hair. Even after so many years, every time she heard Dallas arrive home her blood quickened.

She met him in the parlor, where he was shrugging out of his wet coat and staring into the fire. Dallas looked up when she entered, and there was such a grave expression on his handsome face that Catriona's heart skipped a beat. She crossed to him swiftly, and he reached for her.

"Dallas, what is it?"

"Bad news, Cat. Sit down."

"No. I never have been one to take bad news sitting down and you know it. Tell me now, and be quick about it."

Rain had dampened his blond hair in darker streaks, and he pushed it from his forehead with one hand, inhaling sharply. "There is news just come from London about a massacre in Scotland. The MacIans of Glencoe. 'Tis rumored that the entire clan was slaughtered in their beds."

Catriona swayed slightly, but her chin came up and she held

ast to her courage. "Lianna? Oh God, Dallas—our daughter, oo?"

"I don't know. I only just heard the news myself from one of our couriers, who brought it posthaste."

Already Catriona had turned on her heel and started for the door, and Dallas caught her as she reached for her cloak hanging rom a hook. "Cat, what are you doing?"

"I must get passage to Scotland. Logan and Morgan—where re they?"

"On their way home from booking passage on the next ship o Dundee." Dallas's mouth twisted. "Did you think I would tay here when my daughter may need me? God, if anything as happened to her . . ."

He shoved his fist into his open palm and turned away to ace back and forth in the parlor. Catriona went to him. "You lon't blame me for sending her there, do you? I thought . . . I ust thought she would be safer than here."

"God no." Dallas turned, reaching out for her and pulling er into the safe haven of his arms. His hand stroked her bright urls, so like Lianna's, that red-gold tint that had drawn him o her so long ago. He sighed against her cheek. "I would never lame you for that, Cat. You should know better. I allowed her o go, and thought it was best. Now . . . now, we'll go after er." His voice hardened, chilled to that steely softness that lways made his wife shudder as he added softly, "And if they ave hurt her, I will see to it that those responsible pay with heir lives."

Catriona clung to him fiercely. "Good."

Lianna looked uncertain. Her mouth turned down at the orners. "Yes, they seem nice enough."

"Jolly good of you to recollect that, as this is not the first ime they have fed us." Exasperated, Cameron nudged her lightly. "Be a good lass and remember your manners, will ou?"

She gave him a quick, fierce glance. Her voice was a low,

venomous hiss. "They are *Campbells* . . . what do you expect from me?"

"I told you—good manners. Keep in mind these Campbells have given freely of food and supplies, and more importantly— they are not the same Campbells responsible for Glencoe."

"Their name is Campbell. Robbie was right. Any Campbell is a MacDonald enemy."

Irritated now, Cameron put his mouth close to her ear and leaned against her as if whispering sweet words. He felt anything but sweet, with Malcolm Campbell just across the room and probably wondering why his guests were being so rude. "Since when did you become a MacDonald," he half snarled in her ear, "and not a Fraser?"

"You know very well—"

"That your mother is a MacDonald. Aye. But you are also a Fraser, and if what I've heard about your father is true, he has sense enough to be diplomatic to even his enemies. I would imagine that's how he's kept his head all these years. There's a lesson in that if you care to take time to learn it."

"I've learned a very harsh lesson recently, thank you." She shrugged away the restraining hand he held on her shoulder, though she did lower her voice so that only he could hear. "Since when did *you* become so trusting?"

She was right, of course. But he had already told her that he'd known Malcolm Campbell almost as long as he had known the MacIan, and there shouldn't be any questions about it. Malcolm was risking his own safety by sheltering them, if she would only stop to think about that instead of dredge up clan rivalry. God, he was sick of it, the constant quarrels, wars, the risks men took just to survive.

"Whatever happened to the notion of the lamb lying down with the lion?" he muttered, more to himself than her. She shot him a frowning glance and he shrugged. "Never mind. I guess we know how that turned out. Lamb stew, or at the least a very sleepless lamb."

"Yes, I would say the results of such trust were less than satisfactory."

He couldn't blame her, he supposed, but it made it devilish

difficult to remain in Rannoch Moor with her so on edge. Perhaps he should have taken her to the Stewarts in Appin, where others from Glencoe had gone. This had just seemed closer and easier, and since they were on Breadalbane lands, he was pretty certain Glenlyon and the earl wouldn't think to look for him here. Who would think that the prey would take refuge in the hunter's lair? No one with any sense. He was vaguely amazed himself that he dared it. If not for clan lairds like Malcolm, he would not have attempted such a foolhardy feat.

What he hadn't considered was that Lianna would hold the clan name against them. Foolish of him. After all, this was Scotland. Names were everything. Hadn't the MacGregors learned that almost a half-century before? Aye, and lost their name because of the trouble, turned out into the world landless and nameless, and to a Scot, that was a fate worse than death.

In theory, this had seemed like the perfect solution. He could leave Lianna here in safe hands, and go on his way. If Breadalbane thought him dead, he might very well hang Jamie without delay. It would be too much to hope that he would release him out of hand. That would be too humane. As yet, there had been no public hanging. Jamie was still alive, and he needed to set about freeing him before it was too late.

So he tried to jolly her into a better humor, but Lianna was having none of it. Feeling misunderstood and quite out of sorts, he got up and walked across the room to join Malcolm Campbell. Leave her to her sulks, by God. He'd had enough for the moment. Hadn't he kept her alive? Aye, and gotten no thanks for it. He hadn't even taken her damned virginity when he'd the chance, though it had cost him a sleepless night and enough discomfort to last a lifetime. By the time morning light brightened their little shelter, he'd been feeling very sorry for himself—and sorrier still that he had not taken advantage of the opportunity.

Best in the end, though. Facing Dallas Fraser with his daughter's belly swollen through Cameron's manful efforts would not be a feat for a coward. No, he had done the right thing, even if it wasn't for the right reasons.

"Greetings to ye, Cameron MacKenzie," Campbell said when Cameron sat beside him. A slight smile curled the old gentleman's mouth. "I take it yer lady is no' pleased tae be stayin' wi' us."

Cameron briefly considered lying, but realized the futility. He shrugged. "It's difficult for her to trust in the name Campbell after what happened at Glencoe."

"Aye, 'tis easy to understand. And I canna say I blame her. But no' all Campbells are like the earl and Glenlyon."

"No, and not all MacDonalds are like the MacIans of Glencoe."

Malcolm nodded slowly, his gaze drifting back to the fire. "Aye. But ye're welcome to stay here as long as ye need. I dinna like what Breadalbane or Glenlyon ha' done, and willna refuse shelter to any man wha' comes to my door. I knew your father well, ye ken, and he wa' of the same mold. No man wa' ever turned from Kenneth MacKenzie's door, nor refused meat at his table."

It was true, but Cameron did not think it wise to point out how being so generous and open had ended up costing Kenneth MacKenzie his life. Along with his notion of heroics, of course. But those ideals had all been so intertwined it would have been useless trying to untangle one from the other. It was a miracle his father had survived as long as he had.

Just as it was a miracle he had survived this long.

"I don't suppose you've any more news from Inverlochy," he asked Malcolm at last, and the old man eyed him for a brief moment before nodding.

"Aye, news enough. Your brother is still being held by Breadalbane. Drummond and Glenlyon ha' made their report at Fort William. 'Tis said tha' Glenlyon was in Edinburgh bragging at the coffee-houses tha' he would be given a promotion for his work at Glencoe." Malcolm paused to suck on his pipe for a moment, his eyes narrowed against the curl of tobacco smoke. "And 'tis also said that he is like a wild man, with the look of Glencoe hanging aboot his face like the deil's own mark on him."

"Well it should." Cameron leaned forward to frown into the fire. "He did the devil's own work that day."

"Aye, and Drummond as well, I ken."

"There were more than a few who should live long enough to regret it." Cameron sat back again. "What news of Breadalbane? I know he collects your rents and you are kin to him by way of marriage, but I know too that you've no liking for him. Have there been accusations against him as well?"

Malcolm grunted. "Ye should know well enough that the fox of Breadalbane is too canny tae put to paper any words tha' can be used against him later. There ha' been no word against him, nor Colonel Hill of Fort William. Indeed, there has been no word against any of them for the bloody work they did against MacIan's clan. 'Tis said tha' if he had taken the king's oath—"

"MacIan took the oath." Cameron smiled tightly at Malcolm's surprise. "Aye, he took the oath and Hill will verify it. They used MacIan as a warning to all in the Highlands what can happen if there is thought of rebellion."

Malcolm swore harshly, and his hand tightened around the stem of his pipe. "Tha' has no' been told, Cameron."

"No, it wouldn't be told by the men who did the killing."

For a long moment, Malcolm Campbell stared at Cameron, then he shook his head. "There will be an outcry o'er all o' Scotland when the truth is known."

"I hope so." Cameron's eyes narrowed. "I hope so."

Catriona Fraser stared out the window of the Dundee Inn at the wet streets for a long moment. Then she turned, slowly, to gaze at her husband. It was incredible—unbelievable. In a voice that was remarkably steady, she said, "I take it you want me to believe tha' my daughter is missing, aye, e'en dead."

"It's a possibility, Cat." Dallas sounded grim, and his blue eyes were cold. "We must face it."

"Nay, ye can face it if ye maun, but I willna!" As always when distressed, Catriona's Highland burr intruded into her usually careful speech. Tears blurred her vision, and she glared at her husband with angry pain. "She isna dead, and dinna ye say it tae me ever again."

Dallas Fraser reached out in a swift motion, his hand grasping his wife's wrist firmly to pull her to him even when she resisted. "Cat, Cat—I don't want to believe it either. Do you think I do? But until we find her, we must be prepared."

"Deil take ye for e'en saying it," Catriona mumbled against his chest. "Wha' ha' ye heard?"

His arm tightened briefly, and she stiffened. Then he released her, and taking her by one hand, led her to a chair in front of the inn window. "Sit down, Cat. I have learned something— no, not about Lianna, though it does indirectly affect her, devil take it." He inhaled deeply, blue eyes fixed on her face with a steady gaze. "Dalrymple—Master of Stair, you might recall—has expressed public regret that any of the MacIans escaped. So, 'tis obvious that some did manage to flee the glen. Unfortunately, he has also said that he intends to prosecute them to the utmost, and intends that others than MacDonalds inhabit Glencoe. Some of the soldiers there that day have begun to talk, and though 'tis denied that MacIan took the oath, 'tis generally agreed that they were murdered in their beds."

Catriona shuddered, and jerked her hands from his to surge to her feet. "The pawkie bastards!"

Dallas did not bat an eye at his wife's curse. After more than twenty-five years, he had become well-accustomed to her fiery nature. Indeed, it was what had drawn him to her so long ago, had made him risk everything to wed her. Now all he could do was watch helplessly as she raged, threatening all manner of vile retribution against Stair, Glenlyon, and of course, Breadalbane, her old enemy.

When she grew calmer, he smiled slightly, locking his hands behind his back as he stood in front of the fire. "I am prepared to do what is necessary to get our daughter back, you know."

Catriona paused, her face flushed with fright and fury, and nodded. "I know. I never doubted it for a moment, Dallas. But wha' can be done?"

"I have my methods. Arrangements have been made, and I leave in an hour for Fort William. No, do not even ask. 'Tis best I go alone. You'll frighten old Hill half to death, and nothing will be learned.''

"Oh aye, and you won't scare him, I suppose.'' She eyed him with a lifted brow. "I know you, Dallas Fraser. You'll have Colonel Hill quaking in his boots before you even walk into the fort. I must go. I can find out things in ways you cannot.''

Dallas scowled. "No, Cat. I take Logan and Morgan with me, and that is all. You will remain here in Dundee and wait for us. I won't risk you if there's danger.''

Her chin lifted, and Dallas recognized the sign of stubborn refusal, to his great chagrin. "Dammit, Cat, I mean it! Do you think Breadalbane would stop at hurting you? He won't, and you know it. Look what he's already done—dammit, listen to me.''

Crossing to her in two long strides, he grabbed her when she turned away, whirling her around and jerking her up against him. His hands were tight on her upper arms, but in the hot green eyes blazing up at him was the familiar light of willful intention, and he knew it would be useless to argue further. Long years of frustrating experience had taught him that much.

"What do you intend to do?'' he asked resignedly.

"I don't know yet.'' She shook her head when he frowned again. "I won't be in danger, I swear it, Dallas. I wouldn't risk Lianna that way. Now come, if you are leaving in an hour I need to be certain that you have what you need for the journey. Are Logan and Morgan in the common room waiting, or must I prepare for them as well?''

Dallas Fraser stared after his wife with narrowed eyes when she pulled away to begin packing his clothes in a leather pouch. He knew better than to trust her not to react with her heart instead of her head, but God help him, he didn't have time to lose if he wanted to find Lianna.

"Cat—'' She turned, eyes wide and brows lifted in inquiring innocence, and he groaned. "Cat, remember that I cannot be in two places at once. If you get into trouble, it will not help Lianna.''

"I have no intention of getting into trouble, Dallas. And

believe me, I want nothing to distract you from finding our daughter. But I canna wait here with nothing to do but sit and stare at four walls, and you must know that. I would go mad waiting and worrying."

He sighed. "I know that. Just remember that Breadalbane will stop at nothing to get what he wants. He's capable of anything, as this Glencoe massacre proves."

A fierce light gleamed in Catriona's eyes. "Aye, 'tis true tha' the old fox is wicked enough to dance with the deil, but I ha' known him long enough to learn some of his weaknesses."

"Cat—"

"Nay, dinna tell me not to risk our daughter again. She is alive, Dallas, and we will find her. Then I will deal with John Campbell as he should ha' been dealt with long ago."

It was the best he could hope for, the half-promise that she would wait, and when Dallas joined his sons in the common room of the inn, he was not at all surprised by their skeptical reactions to their mother's being left behind.

"She won't stay," Morgan said frankly, and smiled a little when Dallas nodded glumly. "But you obviously know that."

"Aye, but there's nothing I can do about it. Your mother has a mind of her own, as she has always had."

Dallas said nothing when Catriona came down to bid them farewell, lifting to her toes to kiss her tall sons on their cheeks, her hair a bright copper gleam against Logan and Morgan's fair heads. His sons resembled him, with pale hair and eyes, while Lianna had her mother's red-gold hair and green eyes. It had always amused him how it had worked out, for he'd half expected his children to inherit Catriona's wild temper and blazing hair. Thank God they had not, but were more even-tempered. The Highland blood ran in their veins, but was mellowed by his calmer temperament, and kept them out of trouble.

Not so with Catriona, whose quick temper had caused him no end of trouble at times. He could only pray that she would not do anything foolish or impulsive while he was gone. Breadalbane was dangerous.

Chapter 12

"For the last damn time, Lianna—these Campbells are not the same as Glenlyon and Breadalbane. Can't you see that?"

Denial quivered on the tip of her tongue. She looked away, twisting her hands in front of her, agitated that he would risk them this way. Couldn't he understand how she felt? Logic told her that Malcolm Campbell was not like Glenlyon, but there was a certain resemblance in the tall frames, and they bore the same name. And after all, Malcolm and his clan lived on Breadalbane lands, did they not? They were on the earl's rent rolls, so their first loyalty would be to him or even their own welfare instead of to a hunted fugitive. She took a deep breath.

"I see it. But I'm not staying behind. I intend to go with you."

"Snow is up to our asses, and you want to trek off into it. Christ." Cameron shot her a furious glance, shaking his head, and moved to stand at the small window.

Malcolm had lent them an empty crofter's cottage not far from his own. It was small, but adequate, and certainly better than sleeping in the snow, but she could not feel easy. The window shutters were open, and a cold wind swept into the tiny room, chilling her even in front of the fire. Shivering, she pulled the edges of the blanket more tightly around her and kept her gaze on the leaping flames. ''I'll go alone, then, since you don't want to take me with you.''

Cameron made a rude sound. ''Right-ho. And get how far before you tumble down a corrie or off a precipice? I shudder to think.''

''That shouldn't matter to you.''

''Aye, you're right. It shouldn't. But it does, devil take you.'' He sounded sullen, and he banged shut the wooden shutter. His boots scraped across the dirt floor as he came back to the fire and knelt in front of it.

She stole a glance at him. Light glimmered on his black hair and profile, illuminating the stark set of his cheekbones and straight, narrow nose. The faint scar at the corner of his mouth grew taut as his jaw tightened, and she looked away again.

''I will not stay here, Cameron. Especially not without you. I feel as if every eye is on me, as if I can make no move that is not watched and reported.'' She stopped, swallowing the surge of fear that rose in her, the inexplicable, mindless fear that had driven her since February thirteenth. Since her secure world had been shattered by unexpected horror and death. She didn't expect him to understand. She didn't understand it herself. It was illogical, and she knew it, knew that Cameron trusted Malcolm Campbell and so should she.

But she couldn't. She could not bring herself to feel at ease in this remote glen filled with Campbell kin. Memory of Robbie's distrust of all Campbells was too recent, too painful and sharp, and she could not ignore it.

''Christ.'' Cameron shook his head. He put a hand to his eyes and pressed his fingertips against his closed lids as if in pain. After a moment, he lowered his hand and looked up at her, and there was the ghost of a smile on his lips. ''I might feel the same if I were in your place, but I could wish you would trust me more.''

''It's not that I distrust *you,* but—''

''Aye, so you've said. It's anyone with the name of Campbell. I could tell you tales that would explode any myths you may have heard, but there are just as many true tales to match, so I won't. And I've sad experience with the earl and Glenlyon, both bloody bad Campbells and a dark blot on the clan name, so I can quite truthfully say that I understand." He reached for a poker, and dug at the burning peat for a moment until it flamed higher, then slanted her a glance.

"We've rogues in the MacKenzie clan as well, you know. And I am not referring to myself, but to a kinsman—distant, by some miracle—who not so long ago earned a curse from the Brahan Seer. By all accounts, it was well deserved, as Roderick MacKenzie was said to be quite maliciously making sport of a young lass picking herbs on Fairburn Muir. The soothsayer halted Lord Roderick's amusement at the girl's expense, and when my gallant kinsman made threats he could well execute—having the power of pit and gallows at his disposal—the seer quite indignantly prophesied the end of his line of MacKenzies. There were dire predictions about his descendants vanishing not only from Fairburn but the face of the earth, and some ridiculous twaddle about a cow giving birth in the topmost chamber of the tower, but the upshot was, that those with him—all MacKenzie lairds—would also meet grim ends."

"And—have they?"

"It's a bit too early to tell."

"Really, then, what is the point of this absurd tale?"

Cameron smiled slightly. "That not all men of the same name behave the same. My father and brothers would never have molested a young girl, nor did they earn a curse on them from a soothsayer. Yet their last name is the same as the men who did earn the curse, Lord Roderick of Fairburn, and Sir George of Avoch—known by some as Bluidy MacKenzie, if that tells you anything. Do you by chance see my point?"

"By more than chance. A hammer would be more subtle." Crossly, she looked away from him back at the flames of the fire. "It's nice to know that MacKenzies are villainous as well as Campbells. And I still want to leave."

"Of course. Why stay where you're safe? Meander on off into the snow and cold. You might even meet up with more

Campbells, who will be a sight more glad to have you, I warrant, though not for the reasons you might expect."

He sounded mad and disgusted, and she frowned. "I want to go to the MacDonalds of Glengarry. It has been said that they are too powerful for Breadalbane to persecute."

"Oh aye, and too bloody mean to part with food or shelter, I'll tell you that much. I've some experience with them, and none of it pleasant."

"But my mother is a MacDonald, so we are distant kin. And Robbie didn't have anything wicked to say about them."

"Then Robbie was lying through his teeth to you. He had plenty to say to me about them, and I don't recall any passing pleasantries." He shot her a brooding glance from beneath his lashes. "There was bad blood between them, y'see."

"No, I don't see. And I don't mean to call you a liar, but I am certain if Robbie had bad words to say about them, I would have heard."

"I doubt it." Cameron stretched to his full height, leaned a shoulder against the wall, and smiled sardonically. "Unless Robbie was in the habit of confessing his carnal offenses to you, I find it extremely doubtful that he mentioned his running feud with clan MacDonald of Glengarry."

"I can't listen to any more you have to say." She surged to her feet in agitation. "You aren't always right. And I don't want to stay here. My mother's clan was murdered in their beds by Campbells, and I won't stay. Do you hear me? I won't stay!"

Her voice had risen shrilly, and Cameron straightened. He put a hand on her shoulder, his fingers digging in. "Blast you, be quiet! I have no intention of alarming or insulting our hosts, since you seem to have forgotten any manners you might have once been taught. They can probably hear you all the way to Inverness." His hand dropped from her shoulder when she grew quiet. "You want to seek refuge only with MacDonalds? Fine. I'll take you—but not to Glengarry. It's too far. I just hope you and your bloody borrowed loyalties live long enough for me to say 'I told you so,' for I assure you, I will."

She shrugged carelessly though her throat ached with uncertainty and distress. What if he was right? Oh, her head hurt so badly, and it was so difficult to know who to trust anymore. But she trusted Cameron, even if only so far. After all, he had been with Glenlyon, hadn't he? That was hardly in his favor. What if he was wrong about the Campbells?

"Cameron ... you needn't be angry with me. I just can't stay here any longer feeling the way I do. You see that, don't you?"

He blew out a harsh breath, and this time the hand he put on her shoulder was gentle. A faint, wry smile tilted his mouth, and he drew a finger along the line of her cheek. "Aye, lass. I see that you are too distraught to stay here. No sense in forcing you, I suppose, though I do think going to the MacDonalds is unnecessary. And possibly dangerous, depending upon the king's mood. Why not the Stewarts of Appin?"

"No. The MacDonalds. I trust that name."

"Yes, I suspected logic would have no place in your decision." He drew her to him. His hand spread over the back of her head to press her face against his shoulder when she commented angrily on his remark. "Hush. I don't think I can listen to any more of your badgering. You have become a terrible shrew, and we're not even wed. I rather thought nagging came after the wedding vows, not before, but that only goes to show you that I have no notion of women's true nature as I once thought I did."

Because he was holding her against him, his hand tangled in her loose hair and his arms gentle around her, she did not take exception to his comments about being a shrew. Indeed, she ignored them. It was his casual reference to wedding vows that struck her. Surely, he did not think—but perhaps he did.

Drawing back, she surveyed him with a faint frown. "What do you mean about wedding vows?"

"Don't come all prim and proper with me, sweeting. I told Malcolm that we were handfasted. It saves your good reputation, y'see."

"Handfasted!" She stared at him in shock and outrage. "How dare you! Why, I never agreed to such a thing and you know it!"

"Oh aye, but no one else does. And being handfasted is hardly like being married, though if you prove out barren, I may send you back to your parents." He grinned, a mocking grin that made her eyes narrow suspiciously.

"To be handfasted, I have to agree," she pointed out in a tight voice. "And there were no words said between us."

"Yes, well, you would quibble about details." His brows lowered slightly. "Circumstances being what they are, I thought it was the best thing at the moment."

"But to be handfasted—that means that we are considered joined as husband and wife for the space of an entire year. You will just have to tell Malcolm Campbell that you lied, that—"

"A year and a day." When she blinked in angry confusion, he smiled. "Handfasting is for a year and a day. Of course, at the end of that time, both parties are free to go their own ways if it hasn't worked out as hoped."

"You are completely mad. We are *not* handfasted, nor did I agree to anything of the kind. What if my parents should hear of this before I can explain? And anyway—"

"Lianna, you are taking this much too seriously. I only said it to protect you, not bind you. Believe me, marriage or any form of it is *not* in my plans for the future."

That took her back. "Ever?"

"Quarrelsome creature." He looked down at her oddly. "Can you not be satisfied with anything I do or say? No, don't answer that." He put his hand beneath her chin to lift her face. Firelight was reflected in his eyes, and he had an oddly wistful expression that made her catch her breath as she gazed up at him. "Would it be so dreadful to be handfasted with me, Lianna? Or even wed to me? I'm a rum sort, I know, but I do have a few good points."

"You . . . hide them well." She could not let him know how just his touch affected her, and how the light in his eyes made her remember things best forgotten. He would be the ruin of her if she allowed it, and she could not . . . but oh, how he made her feel when he looked at her with that funny twisted

smile, with his lashes half lowered and a gleam turning his
eyes all hot and smoky. . . .

"I would never wed you," she said almost desperately,
looking away from the heady allure of his gaze, "never. While
I may have—experimented—with you a time or two, that was
all it was. An experiment. Nothing serious, no matter what I
may have led you to believe. You are not at all the type of
man I would ever marry, even for only a year and a day."

It was a lie, and she knew it. But how could she admit to
what she felt when every instinct warned against it? He had
just made it quite plain that he did not intend to wed her, that
he considered her a temporary diversion. What a fool she had
been to think he cared. . . .

His hand tightened on her chin. One of his brows lifted in
a subtle curve, and his mouth twisted into the moody smile
that she had come to recognize. "Yes, I do hide my virtues
well, I suppose. Since I am so fraught with bad habits, and
obviously completely unredeemable, it shouldn't matter what
I do, should it?"

She would have said yes, but his mouth came down over
hers in a swift, bruising kiss. She should have expected it. The
flash of sullen mockery in his eyes should have warned her,
but it hadn't. She was too slow to read the signs when they
argued, it seemed, too foolish to stop before she pushed him
too far.

But this was danger. Her every nerve quivered with the
promise of disaster, her senses susceptible to his touch and his
mockery, the temptations in his hands on her, his mouth on
hers . . . destruction loomed, and she eagerly embraced it.

Her hands came up of their own volition, as if pulled by
invisible cords to clasp him by the shoulders. In the back of
her mind, danger was shrieking a warning, but the urgent needs
of her body worked quickly to suppress common sense.

And Cameron obviously recognized that.

Instead of holding her gently against him, his arm was a
hard pressure at her back, his other hand moving to tangle in
her hair and hold her, while his mouth crushed against her

lips with searing force. Her head reeled. She couldn't breathe, couldn't think, could only react.

Her scalp tingled at the inexorable tug of his fingers in her hair. The fierce pressure of his mouth on hers tasted of desire more than anger, painful and rousing. When his hand slipped through the loose strands of her hair and down her back, spreading over her spine just above her hips, he held her that way, pressing her against him. Her breasts flattened against his chest, and she felt the heat of him even through his wool shirt and her dress and chemise.

He groaned, a muffled sound against her lips. For a moment, she thought he meant to stop, but he only muttered something in Gaelic, sounding almost desperate, and captured her mouth again, his tongue darting between her lips.

Cameron's touch and kiss consumed her; his hands shifted as he explored her body. Slowly, feeling awkward and uncertain, her fingers crept up the strong line of his neck and under his hair, then smoothed down over his broad shoulders, knotting wool shirt into her fists, clenching and unclenching her hands as he tugged at the laces of her gown. Heat and intense longing made her burn for him, yearn for his hands on her, strive for release from the coiling tension inside her. The hot ache surged through her to focus between her thighs, a throbbing pleasure that had her molding her body to his as if trying to be a part of him.

Then her laces were undone and his mouth was on the bare skin of her breast, searching and finding the taut, aching peak to nuzzle until she moaned. Her eyes closed. She leaned back, offering herself blindly, feeling wild excitement at his tongue moving over her. The heat between her thighs grew hotter.

Vaguely, as if in a dream, she was aware that he was lifting her in his arms, crossing to the pallets spread on the floor, then dropping to his knees. He held her against him briefly, his mouth caressing her skin from throat to lips. Then he lay her back and leaned over her, his body a heavy weight pressing her into the wool blankets. She felt him groan, a rumble deep inside his chest. Her hands slid under his shirt to caress the bare skin of his back, fingers sliding over the powerful muscles n an exploring glide. Still braced on his forearms, he hung over her a moment; his head bent to kiss the line of her throat, the bare skin of her breast, then her mouth again while his weight pressed her down into the mounded wool pallet.

Then his hands were tugging at her opened gown, pulling it away, and cool air washed over the bared skin of her breasts, belly, and thighs. She should have protested, but she was beyond it. At this moment, all she wanted was release from the tightening urgency inside her, the release that she knew he could give her. Vanished were thoughts of propriety and morality, of possible consequences.

Cameron sat up, shrugged out of his shirt and tossed it aside. Firelight glowed on the curves of his chest and shoulders with golden color, played over the faint splotches of faded bruises. Hard bands of muscle roped his abdomen, intimidating and intriguing. She looked up at his face. His features were sharp with desire, the motion of his hands swift and efficient as he tugged at the waist-cord of his trews. She closed her eyes.

Then he was lying over her again, and his skin was hot where he pressed against her, the smooth span of his chest a firm pressure on her bare breasts. She shivered. He kissed her again, more gently this time, though she could feel him quiver with strain. He moved down, his mouth trailing kisses from her lips to her breast before his tongue flicked out in tiny, heated darts against her nipple. She moaned softly, and reached for him. Her hands traced up his muscled arms to his shoulders, then down over his chest in shy exploration, fingers sliding over the ridges of his belly and lower.

A rough, hoarse note sounded deep in Cameron's throat when she touched him. He grabbed her wrist to hold her hand still. "Not . . . now. God. Not now." He bent. His lips closed over her nipple and drew it against his teeth in a gentle inhalation. When she writhed beneath him, gasping and clutching wildly at him, he moved to her other breast, teasing it as well. She arched upward, mindlessly seeking relief.

Cameron groaned against her breast. His hand moved down over the small mound of her belly and lower, fingers brushing through the tight nest of curls there to slip into the moist, hot crevice between her thighs.

"Oh Yoy." The words exploded from him in a husky moan. He drew in a deep breath, and paused. She looked up at him, holding her breath, feeling dizzy and daring and as if she poised on the brink of discovery. Then, slowly, she arched upward into his hand. Cameron closed his eyes. Corded muscles stood out on his throat as he swallowed, and then he muttered, "I should know better, but God help me . . . God help me, I just . . . can't . . . stop. . . ." He bent and kissed her again, fiercely, taking her breath away.

His hand moved, sliding deeper inside, and Lianna arched upward. His fingers explored the hidden recess, and her legs closed convulsively around his hand. His mouth tugged at her nipple while his thumb raked across the top of her sex in an erotic move that made her cry out. She burned all over, ached for something that eluded her, the sweet release that he had given her once before . . . she curved her hips upward, head tossing against the blankets while she pushed into his hand. It felt as if her entire body was aflame with need and detached embarrassment; a vague sense of shame that she was so abandoned simmered beneath the desire urging her on. She should stop him, should stop herself. Yet she could not, even when he paused, swearing under his breath and shuddering.

"Cameron . . ." His name came out in a whimper, soft and urgent, and he groaned.

"You're . . . killing me . . . Lianna. God. I want to, I swear I do, but . . . I might . . . go too . . . far."

"I don't care." She didn't. Not now. Maybe not ever. All that mattered was the sweet sensations he was creating with his hand and mouth. "Please . . . oh Cameron please don't stop. . . ."

He sat back, legs bent under him, his hand caressing her thighs. "Christ . . . you don't know what you're saying. You're so bloody beautiful . . ." He spread his fingers across her, thumb still on that achingly sensitive peak between her thighs. For a moment he watched his hand, and despite the chill air around them, his face was damp and misted. "So damn beautiful

... especially here. Copper silk ... pink satin ..." He tugged at the nest of curls gently, and drew in an unsteady breath. "So damn beautiful, *eudail.*"

The Gaelic endearment trailed into a fervent sound. Lianna twisted beneath his hand, saw his upward glance like demon-smoke through his lashes, then they lowered to hide his eyes. His knees spread, pushing her thighs apart, and then he was leaning forward again. His breath came in rapid pants for air; bronze light gleamed over his shoulders. She pressed forward again, up into his caressing hand, moaning.

Again he glanced up at her, fierce light in his eyes, and then he moved his hand. She cried out softly and reached for him, but he was moving between her thighs. A new pressure nudged against her, soft and hard and heated, and she inhaled sharply.

Silent, he took her hand and drew it between their bodies to touch him. Her fingers trembled over the solid length of him, skimmed over heated skin that was hard and soft at the same time. She drew in another sharp breath, and curled her fingers around his length. He shuddered, groaned, and after a moment, gently pulled her hand away.

Braced on his arms, he pushed forward, his length gliding over the moist heat between her legs, producing shivering sparks that radiated up and through her, sending her blood pounding through her veins in liquid heat. She gasped his name, glancing up at his face, and he held her gaze as he pushed forward again in a heavy slow thrust. Feeling uncertain, breathless and aroused, she closed her eyes and heard his mutter of excitement. His body slipped over the focus of fiery agitation in a long glide, then back. She twisted under him, pushing her hips up to meet his thrusts, and suddenly he slid downward.

This time there was a sharp ache just at her entrance, startling her. Her eyes flew open to stare up at him. He wasn't looking at her, but his face was turned toward the fire, his features intent and hard, shadowed on one side and illuminated on the other. Even the tiny scar at the corner of his mouth was taut with strain. She quivered under his weight and this new, peculiar sensation. After the first sharp pain, her body stretched slightly to accept his invasion. He moved only a little forward, then stopped before full penetration. She felt his arms vibrate with tension, and moved her hips slowly to encourage him forward to ease this aching need deep inside. He jerked his gaze back to her, his hands moving to pin her shoulders back into the blankets.

"Be still . . . I don't know how long I can . . . hold back." He closed his eyes and groaned, head tilted back, and his hips moved slowly against her, sliding inside just a tiny bit more, until she could feel her body stretch almost to the point of pain. Then he withdrew completely and moved forward in a long glide across her cleft that summoned sweet ecstasy and shuddering response.

"Cameron . . . oh God Cameron . . . it feels so good, please don't . . . please . . ." Incoherent pleas rose between them, and she didn't know if she was asking him to stop or continue. Her hands fluttered up, touched his chest, his jaw, then clutched aimlessly at the blankets as the tension coiled in her higher and higher, until she felt as if she would explode with it. He moved against her steadily, masculine hardness raking over that sensitive peak in searing strokes that made her arch blindly upward.

Heated waves shuddered through her, and Cameron muttered softly and went still. But she couldn't stop, could not halt the surge of frenzied response that made her cling to him, gasping his name as her body jerked with ecstasy.

Cameron remained still until the spasms faded. When she grew still, he bent and kissed her with fierce intensity before taking her hand in his and guiding it to him. Her fingers curled around him and he strained against her, his hand teaching her the motion. His head was bent, his dark hair tangled over his forehead, his face intense. After a moment, he groaned and caught her wrist, pulling her hand away as he flung himself to one side atop the blankets. He shuddered, made a harsh guttural sound, then his entire body grew rigid.

Cameron lay still with his face pressed into the angle of his arm and blanket. After a few minutes, he looked up at her through his lashes, a smoky glance. A wry smile tucked in one corner of his mouth, and his voice was husky. "My own little experiment. A rather powerful lesson in restraint, I think, though I did not do as well as I had hoped.''

She found her voice after a moment. ''Cameron, I didn't mean that about you being only an experiment.''

''Didn't you? No matter. I would relish the idea of explaining my lack of restraint to your father, should I ever meet him.'' He rolled to his side, flinging an arm across his eyes. His trews were still open, exposing that part of him that had been so hot and hard just a few moments before.

Lianna looked away, vaguely unsettled by his partial nudity even after what they had just done. She flushed slightly and bit her lower lip. She told herself this was Cameron, the man who had come after her, followed her from Glencoe when he could have gone his own way. Yet, despite knowing that, a part of her still yearned to hear him confirm his feelings, tell her that he cared about her, wanted more than just these intimate moments.

Drawing in a deep breath, she looked back at him. He had rolled to his side, and the blanket hid his body from view, making it easier for her to face him. ''Did you mean what you said about handfasting?''

''What did I say?'' His brow lifted, and there was a lazy drift to his lashes now. ''Something about it not being binding, I hope.''

She paused. Carefully picking her way through this conversational maze, she managed a casual shrug. ''Yes, that part is quite plain. No, I meant what you said about telling Malcolm Campbell we were handfasted. Does that make it definite?''

He yawned and stretched, gave her a sleepy smile and shook his head. ''No, beauty. Not at all. As you so correctly pointed out, both of us have to say the words. I just thought it best if no one knew we are traveling in sin together.'' The sleepy smile wavered a bit, and he shrugged. ''I just hope your father doesn't hear about it before you can tell him the truth. I don't fancy having him look for me. From what I've heard he is a most formidable foe.''

''I think,'' she said slowly, ''that you are very much like Papa in some ways.''

"Good God. Don't share that opinion with him until I'm far away, if you please. It will be much safer for me."

She smiled slightly. It had occurred to her on more than one occasion that Cameron MacKenzie had similar traits to Dallas Fraser. Resolute determination was the one that came most frequently to mind. When Papa made up his mind about something, it was almost impossible to change his view. She had observed that it was very much the same with Cameron. Right or wrong, he doggedly pursued his course despite any proof to the contrary. She sighed. Perhaps she should reconsider her decision to leave Rannoch Moor. Despite their name, these Campbells did not seem like malicious people. They had been only kind to her, and she was grateful for their generosity. Perhaps Breadalbane would not look for her here. But did she really want to take that risk?

That was not the only concern, of course. If she convinced Cameron to take her with him, along the way he might decide he wanted to stay with her. After what had just happened between them, he might deny wanting her, but she knew better. He just needed the time to realize it himself.

Chapter 13

"Dallas Fraser? Here at Fort William?" Colonel Hill rose to his feet, flustered at this bit of information. "So soon? Dear God. Whatever does he—"

"His daughter was at Glencoe."

Hill swallowed hard. He felt lightheaded. His hand shook. "At . . . Glencoe, you say."

"Aye." Forbes grimaced. "It seems her mother is Catriona MacDonald. Perhaps you would remember her? Angus Mac-Donald's daughter."

Hill collapsed into his chair and fumbled for a piece of linen to wipe his brow. He had dreaded this possibility from the moment Ensign Elliot had informed him that Dallas Fraser's daughter was among those in Glencoe. Bungling fools, to have involved the daughter of a powerful man in their depredations . . . but there was nothing to do but brazen it out now, and hope that Fraser would not bring hell down upon all their heads.

"Yes, yes, of course I remember Angus's daughter," he said to Forbes. "But that was so long ago that—I mean, she has been gone so long from Glencoe . . ."

"Aye, 'twas before my time. I understand she left when she wed Dallas Fraser. It was a bit of scandal back then, wasn't it? The earl of Breadalbane was involved, though no one seems to remember quite how.'' John Forbes shrugged, and his gaze said plainly that it could hardly matter now. He was wrong, of course.

Hill nodded agreement, delaying the inevitable. ''Give me a moment before showing Fraser in. There are things I would like to—''

''Colonel Hill, I'll be talking to you now instead of later.'' Dallas Fraser suddenly filled the opening of the door, tall and brawny and dangerous.

Lurching to his feet, Colonel Hill stammered out an apology, feeling like ten kinds of a fool as he did. ''Beg pardon, Fraser, but I wanted to review—''

''Never mind.'' Fraser indicated the open door with a jerk of his head, and Major Forbes took the blatant hint and opportunity to escape. Steel-blue eyes swung back to Hill. ''My daughter was at Glencoe, as Forbes just told you. I want to know where she is now.''

''Good God, man, it's not as if I was able to keep track of survivors, or even all those inhabiting Glencoe.'' Hill paused, realizing he was blundering badly, and cleared his throat. ''There are survivors, of course. Many of them. In terms of military precision, the affair was bungled.'' He could not keep the bitterness from his voice when he added, ''Of course, I was not informed of the plans beforehand, nor even afterward, though the Master did send me a letter.''

''Stair.'' Fraser nodded. His keen eyes swept over Hill, then shifted to the fire on the hearth before returning. ''What of Glenlyon and Breadalbane? Their parts in this were not small, I understand.''

''Really, I can hardly discuss government affairs with you,'' Hill began, but Fraser cut him off with an oath.

''Don't try to deceive me with that bunk, Colonel. Do you think soldiers don't talk? They do. I know more of it than you are obviously prepared to admit to, but by God, I want to know what you've heard of the survivors, and if Stair means to persecute them.'' He leaned forward, fists pressed against the top of Hill's desk, his voice soft and menacing. "I want my daughter."

Intimidated despite his resolve not to be, Hill found himself relating the events that led up to the massacre, and even the way he had been betrayed by his superiors.

" 'Twas as if they consider me a doddering old fool," he added glumly. "Although Stair did promise me my pension and perhaps a knighthood."

"The price of silence comes cheap."

Dallas Fraser's soft comment hung in the air between them for a moment, then Colonel Hill rose stiffly from his chair. He paced in front of the fire, his hands locked behind his back, sorrow and rage weighing heavily on him. Finally he turned to face Fraser, and saw not only a powerful man, but a tormented father. He thought of his own daughters in London, and that decided him.

"Your daughter is alive, if my information can be trusted, Fraser. She was seen leaving the glen with her cousin."

"Are you certain it was my daughter?"

Hill hesitated. It would be much safer to pretend ignorance, and let Breadalbane deal with the repercussions. But that was not only cowardly, but cruel. He sucked in a sharp breath that tasted of peat smoke and nodded. "It was your daughter. One of the soldiers from this garrison knew her. He was quartered with the family, you see."

"Aye, 'tis easy to see the extent of the treachery involved." Fraser raked him with a scrutinizing glance that seeped into his soul, and Hill found himself flushing with shame.

"I had no part in this campaign, Sir Dallas, none at all."

"Did you not? I understood you sent a garrison to accompany Glenlyon to Glencoe."

The soft reminder made him look away. "Aye, 'tis true. But those were my orders. You must know how it is when one is commanded to obey. I am a soldier still, and had little choice in the matter."

Heavy silence fell, and after a moment, he glanced up. Dallas Fraser was staring into the fire, eyes narrowed in thought. Then he swung his gaze back to Hill, pinioning him like a helpless insect. "Where is Lianna? You have heard something, and I would know the truth whether 'tis what I wish to hear or not."

Hill hesitated, painfully aware that Dallas Fraser was fully capable of creating much more trouble than even the ruthless earl of Breadalbane could imagine. But to tell what he knew would only cause more chaos, add more fuel to the fire, and so he weighed his answer carefully. If he revealed that Lianna Fraser was in the company of a man named Cameron Mac-Kenzie—outlaw, rogue, hunted by law and lawless alike—he might very well see the Highlands turned upside down with fire and sword. And despite rumor to the contrary, he was not at all certain MacKenzie deserved what had been said about him. He remembered him, and had liked him.

As Fraser's eyes narrowed angrily, Hill shook his head and said, "It was reported that she was last seen in a shepherd's bothie beyond the sentinel crags of Glencoe."

"Probably fleeing to Glen Etive." Apparently satisfied, Dallas took a step back toward the door, then turned again to look at Hill. "I will find her. When I do, any man who has dared to harm her will find himself wishing for death long before it comes. You might pass along that information, Colonel Hill. It could be useful."

His voice trailed into silence, and Hill shuddered. There was a fierce look on Dallas Fraser's face, and he was suddenly glad he was not Cameron MacKenzie.

"There are MacDonalds at Loch Treig, you know." Cameron squinted into the sunlight. It had grown much warmer, though snow still lay thick on the high crags, and even in some of the glens. Tiny flowers thrust fragile blossoms up through snowdrifts and on bare patches of ground. Spring would come to the Highlands soon, but at the rocky edge of Loch Ericht, patches of ice still floated on the water.

"Are there? I thought you had decided upon going to Glen Nevis." Lianna tugged at her hair, frowning when the plait she had wound came loose in her hand. She sighed impatiently.

Cameron studied her in the light, watching the play of sun

on the red-gold gleam of her hair. After a moment, he looked away. Watching her fuss with her hair reminded him of the intimacies they had shared. It would be best if he could just forget about it, but that was unlikely.

At night, curled in blankets next to her, it was all he could think about. At those times, he often tried to think of anything but the woman next to him, think of anything but her mouth, her breasts, her flat belly and rounded thighs . . . God, he could make himself crazy just lying next to her and not touching her. He must have been insane to have ever yielded to the temptation to touch her that first time. It had been impossible to resist since then, and damn her, she made it far too easy for him. That she was still a virgin was a bloody miracle. He had turned himself inside out to keep her that way, but there were moments when he'd almost lost control. It would be so easy to just slip inside her a little farther, so easy and so satisfying . . .

Tension made his voice rougher than normal, so that she looked up with vague surprise when he told her it was time to move on. He scowled. "Loch Treig is between here and Glen Nevis. It's closer, but not as close as Rannoch Moor was before you insisted upon leaving. Malcolm considers us both daft, you know."

"It's just that Robbie said—"

"Robbie. The authority on clan rivalry and who to trust." He raked a hand through his hair, exasperated with her. If he had any sense at all, he would have just abandoned her without a qualm. It would save them both a great deal of trouble, and she would be safe enough if she learned to keep her opinions to herself.

Lianna was staring at him, eyes shadowed by her lashes, and he had the absurd desire to kiss the tip of her freckled nose. Instead he said, "Fort William is not far from Loch Treig. Close enough to be dangerous to the wrong people."

"I know."

"Yet you prefer it to Rannoch Moor just because 'tis a Campbell who offers food and shelter."

"No, that is not it at all." She paused. Ducking her head, she focused all her attention on the loose end of her braid. Her cheeks were pink, and her lower lip trembled slightly. "I was afraid to stay without you."

"Good God, must you pretend to be helpless? I know better. You're as defenseless as a she-wolf."

"You needn't sound so cross." She tied a strip of cloth around the end of her plait, and tucked it under the hood of her cloak before frowning up at him. "I offered to go on alone. In front of witnesses, even."

"Yes, I recall that idiocy. I thought Malcolm Campbell was going to fall down in a fit of apoplexy. Please be good enough in future to save your most foolish suggestions for the young and strong."

Lianna looked up when he rose to his feet, shading her eyes with a cupped palm. "Yes, he did seem rather upset by the idea. Perhaps he's not as dishonorable as I thought."

"Ah no, you're not switching loyalties on me now. We're too far from Rannoch Moor to go back. Loch Treig is closer, and that is where I intend to take you. No, don't look at me like that. I told you there are MacDonalds there. I will not risk taking you farther."

She considered it, and after a few moments, nodded. "Yes, that sounds reasonable."

"Then I'm amazed you agree." Disgruntled, he stared past her. Snow-capped peaks made pale streaks on the horizon, miles and miles to be crossed yet before he could see her safe. Clouds hid the top of Ben Alder, a blue haze on the horizon. Green folded hills, misty lochs, and more mountains lay between him and Fort William, but that was his ultimate destination. Hill had not seemed adverse to him the last time they'd met. Perhaps the governor would give him aid in freeing Jamie without turning him over to the earl of Breadalbane. It was worth the risk. He had heard that Hill was distressed over the massacre, and indeed, all news about the fate of Glencoe had Scotland in an uproar. In the past month since, word had apparently traveled far.

Four weeks. He winced at the thought that Breadalbane might very well have done away with Jamie by now. It was possible, despite the fact that his brother was said to be still alive. Perhaps killing him outright would be too much coming so hard on the heels of the massacre, or it could always be that Breadalbane knew he was still alive and planned to use Jamie against him.

The latter was the most likely.

Which made it all the more imperative that he be cautious. He looked back at Lianna.

"If you are through resting, my lady, your entourage is ready to depart."

She was surveying her sturdy shoes with something like dismay. They were ugly, clunky things, looking more like boxes on her slender feet. He couldn't really blame her, but at least she had protection. Malcolm's wife had given the footwear to her before they'd left Rannoch Moor, seeing that Lianna's shoes were worn through. Now she looked up at him, a faint smile on her mouth.

"I shouldn't complain, but these shoes are not the most comfortable I've ever owned."

"No doubt, but a damned sight more comfortable than bare feet on the rocks, I imagine."

"Yes, you are always so practical." She smoothed her skirts down over her legs and stood up. "I'm ready. Do you think we will get there soon?"

"By tomorrow night, at the earliest. Barring another snow storm or fit of fatigue."

Sounding slightly shy, she turned her face away and asked, "Will I . . . see you again after we arrive?"

"I imagine. It would be impolite to just leave you at their door, I think."

When she didn't look at him, but stood twisting her hands in front of her, he sighed and reached for her. He turned her to him and she came willingly, burying her face against his chest in that curiously vulnerable way she had, making him feel like slaying dragons for her. Unfortunately, he was just the kind of dragon he should be keeping away from her, so it was definitely a conflict of interests to even think along that line.

As always, the pressure of her breasts against him produced an immediate response, and he could tell that she was fully aware of it. Damnable male urges. There was very little he could hide from her in that respect.

"Lianna—" He tilted her face up to his, frowning a little. "It would be best if you didn't mention some things to anyone once you are with your family. Do you understand what I mean?"

"Of course." Her brow arched slightly. "You don't want me to tell Papa what we do at night under the blankets."

"Christ. You don't have to be so bloody blunt about it."

Laughing, she put her arms around his waist and held him when he would have pushed her away. "Don't be so sulky, Cameron. I'm not as big a fool as you obviously think. Papa would be outraged, and even if we haven't . . . haven't done anything to actually spoil me—"

"Must you make sex sound like an overripe vegetable?" He pushed her away despite her grip, shaking his head. "You've no notion whatsoever of the strain my efforts at not *spoiling* you has caused me. It has been damned hard at times. No, don't say what I see you mean to say—I'm in no mood for that kind of talk."

Lianna laughed again, softly this time. "Are you not? I daresay it's the first time. You are usually full of that kind of talk, even when I don't want to hear it."

"It's only because you were obviously filled full of nonsense about certain bodily functions which are quite normal. Until I told you differently, I am certain you were convinced that babies are found under cabbage leaves instead of produced by the more conventional method."

Her face altered a bit, some of the light dying from her eyes. "No, I was taught correctly, though not in as much detail, of course. Mary told me a lot, some of which I admit is questionable. But Mama saw to it that I knew . . . the basic things."

"Yes. Very basic, if what you've exhibited is any indication." He looked away from her, focusing instead on the sharp edge of the sword Malcolm had been generous enough to give him. It was an old weapon, but serviceable if needed, he supposed. Damn good thing. He wasn't at all certain how long it would be before they were seen by troops still in the area.

When he glanced up, he saw Lianna looking at him with a deep flush on her cheeks and outrage in her eyes. He tried to remember what he'd said, then smiled a little. "Don't be offended, angel. Being innocent is not a particularly virulent disease, and actually quite endearing. I would have been appalled to find you as knowledgeable as a Liverpool drab, I assure you."

"I never know when you're serious."

"I'm serious now, sweeting." He slid the sword back into its sheath and reached for her, sighing a little at how easily she came into his arms. Aye, she made it much too easy for him to hold her, much too easy for him to corrupt her. It was his lamentable lack of character that made him do the things he did, made him take advantage of her innocence, though God knew, she certainly had her own share of guilt in the process.

"Cameron—must you leave when we reach Loch Treig?"

His hand fisted in her thick hair, gently tugging until her face was tilted up to his. "We've discussed this subject to the point of exhaustion. My answer is the same. I must find out about my brother."

"Yes, I know. And I want you to discover what you can, of course." She drew her finger over the angle of his bearded jaw with a slight rasping sound. "But you said I will be close to Fort William. You can come back for me, can you not? It will be much safer than waiting for word to get to Mama and Papa where I am, don't you think?"

"Why must females always ask questions that have been answered? No, Lianna. I cannot come back for you."

For a moment she didn't respond, then said so softly he almost didn't hear, "Then we've only tonight left to us."

His arm tightened briefly, then he pushed her back a step. There was no point in replying to that; it was better pretending he hadn't heard. After all, he had no idea what the future held, no idea if he would be able to leave Fort William once he'd arrived. Circumstances changed in the blink of an eye when political issues were involved.

"Come along, Miss Fraser. We've got a deuced lot of territory to cover before dark. I know of a shepherd's bothie not far away, and we can stay the night there. Much better than last night's accommodations, I think.''

''You know a lot about this area, it seems.'' She gave him an odd, slanted glance from beneath the furry brush of her lashes. ''Have you spent a lot of time here?''

''More than I care to remember at the moment, thank you.''

''Have you ever been happy?''

The question took him back. He had been about to wrap her cloak more tightly around her before they started down the slope, but his hands stilled on the wool edges. ''Happy?''

''Yes. You know—content. Lighthearted. Happy.''

''I am acquainted with the definition, little goose. But I admit to curiosity as to why you would want to know such a thing.''

She ducked her head. ''Because . . . you always seem so bitter and cynical. And I wondered if you had ever been happy or were always this way.''

''Ah.'' He was caught between amusement and irritation. And for the life of him, he could not answer the question. After a moment, he shrugged. ''I've never thought about it before. There have been times in my life I've been content enough, I suppose.''

''When?''

''Devil take you. Is this a subject to discuss while trekking down a blasted mountainside? I don't think so. Come along.'' He snapped the edges of her cloak together and turned her around with a determined thrust. ''This is a fascinating topic, but it can wait.''

Apparently, it was a topic intriguing enough to her to bring it up again once they were cozily ensconced in the rather shabby shepherd's bothie tucked beneath a grove of towering evergreens. When he had a fire going, and their meal of bread and cheese carefully portioned out, she looked up at him over the flames with renewed determination.

''Did you have a happy childhood, Cameron?''

The glance he gave her should have withered any further curiosity on her part, but it obviously missed. When he didn't reply, she asked again, and he gave an impatient poke to the fire with a stick.

"Blast you, must you keep on about it? I don't know. It was ueventful for the most part, save those times my father took in his head to play hero and run off to fight some idiotic ar, or start a feud somewhere." He scowled at her through e orange and yellow flames. "Why so intent upon knowing?"

"Because I had a quite happy childhood, and I hoped that ou did as well."

She sounded so sincere, that for a moment he could only are at her. There was no point in telling her that the most emorable events in his life had been the death of his mother, ad the deaths of his father and brothers. In between, had been ars of occasional pleasures, such as the time he had spent at niversity before being called home to participate in a war that e didn't condone. But why depress her with the truth? He would have just made up some edifying tale that would satisfy er, and let it be.

"Angel, the most pleasant event in my life has been meeting ou," he said, and meant it, to his chagrin.

"Really, Cameron, you needn't be mean about it. I only anted to know because I'm interested in everything about ou. I care about you. A lot. How could I not? After all, you ave saved my life, and ... and I lo—"

"And you want to show your gratitude by badgering me." e tossed the stick into the fire, amused and dismayed by her ushed, trembling face. "Dear child, do you fancy yourself ifatuated with me? That will end quickly enough once you e back with your family. Besides, you don't really know nything about love. It's only our intimacy that misleads you that conclusion, I am certain. Not to mention the illuminating tle facts I've shown you about your charming body and its apabilities, for which I will pay dearly, I assure you."

She looked away, biting her lower lip, but he had seen the ash of hurt resentment in her eyes. It was better this way, of ourse: A small prick now rather than a sharper jab later. omorrow he would deliver her to the MacDonalds and be on s way. It was unlikely that he would ever see her again, and ointless to attempt it. He was just an interlude in her life,

though she would probably always remember him as the ma
who had educated her in certain pleasantries.

So why did the thought of never seeing her again distur
him so? There should be no end of young men just waiting t
court her, and he found to his annoyance that the very thougt
of that infuriated him.

To dispel the unsettling and irrational reaction to that cor
cern, he said curtly, "Don't fall in love with me, Lianna. You'
be a widow before you were long a wife, I promise you."

"You've a most agile imagination." She leaned forward t
put a slender branch into the fire, and when she glanced up
her eyes were green flames. "Is it so unreasonable to wonde
why you are as cynical and embittered as you are? It is not a
if we have not spent a great deal of time together, and I'r
curious, that's all."

"Curious." Disgruntled, he studied her face in the flickerin
light. Her hair had come all loose and waved about her shou
ders, a coppery mass that framed her face. In the past week
she'd lost weight, and the bones of her face were sharper, mor
defined than when he'd first met her. She looked older, wise
and infinitely more desirable than even the first time he'd see
her. He looked away, stared down at his hands where they wer
knotted around a pine branch. It snapped in two with a brittl
pop, and he tossed it into the flames. Leaning back, he stretche
out his legs and crossed them at the ankle. "Beg pardon fc
being impertinent enough to think you might actually care abou
me."

"Don't come the aggrieved party with me, Cameron Mac
Kenzie." She sounded indignant, and he lifted a brow in su
prise when she waggled a finger at him. "You know very we
that I care about you. If I didn't, I certainly would not allo\
you the liberties I do, nor would I . . . I—"

"Enjoy them?" he supplied helpfully. "Don't be shy. I ca
tell you do, you know."

"I don't deny it," she said, though her cheeks were a ros
color that had little to do with the fire.

He snorted. "Little good it would do you to try. Don't glare at me like that. Why should I play the gallant and pretend that I haven't noticed? Is it because it's not something that would be discussed in polite company? In case you haven't noticed, m'dear, we ain't in polite company. And I am not one of the men you must be used to keeping company with, all presentable and mannerly, shipshape and Bristol-fashion. I'm a rogue through and through, just as you have said more than once, and you're right about almost every other thing you've said about me, save that I would betray my friends. I draw the line at that. Anything else is fair game. So don't be making sheep's eyes at me, and thinking that anything will come of our little sojourn together, because it won't. What we've had between us is all we'll ever have, and even if you hoped there would be more, your precious papa would put an end to it quickly enough."

He didn't know why he'd said all that, save that she seemed to think they had a future together when he knew damn good and well his days were numbered. Even without Breadalbane's enmity, there were too many other axes waiting to fall. He knew that. If not for his very limited expectations, he would have already taken her maidenhead, put a child in her and wed her by now.

But that was impossible.

Lianna Fraser had nothing in common with him, and he recognized that even if she didn't. Other than the fact they had shared the same tragedy, their interests were wildly diverse. And other than the fact he had introduced her to a few fleshly delights—mostly to her advantage—there was nothing between them. He couldn't allow it, even when he had those wild, brief moments of fantasy that gave him glimpses into what might once have been.

He wanted her, and he couldn't have her. She wanted him, and she couldn't have him. But that was the very devil of it. If it wasn't so bloody pathetic, he would have laughed at the irony.

And it didn't help when she lifted wet lashes to gaze at him, and he heard himself groan a surrender and take her into his arms to kiss away doubts and dreams. If this last night of unconsummated love was all he was to have with her, he would grab at it while he could, devil take the consequences.

Chapter 14

"Lady Fraser, come this way, please."

Catriona followed the servant into the earl of Breadalbane's wood-paneled study, and managed a decent smile when he stood to greet her.

"It has been a long time," he said gravely, and she nodded.

"Aye, it has, my lord."

"Please be seated. I find myself quite curious as to your reason for this visit." He waved an expansive hand at a stuffed chair in front of his desk, and she sat down in a rustle of silk skirts and nervous aplomb.

Folding her hands in her lap, she began without delay. "It is a matter of extreme importance to me, my lord, or I would not have bothered you with it." She paused, studying his fleshy face for some hint that he would help. There was none. His heavy-lidded eyes regarded her with polite attention when she said, "As you know, there has been a matter of unrest in Glencoe."

"Ah yes, the MacIan tragedy. Pity. The old laird should have taken the oath, and avoided that disaster." Breadalbane made a steeple of his hands, smiling at her over his fingertips. "The affair has caused talk all over Scotland, I understand.

But surely you have not come to me on behalf of your relatives there, Lady Fraser. Your husband is well known in many circles, and much more acquainted with methods of gathering information and aid.''

It was a sly dig at Dallas and his connections, but she refused to take the bait. ''My husband's resources are much more limited than yours, my lord, as he is so involved with parliamentary matters of state. And anyway, since you are much closer to those involved, I hoped that you could give me word of my daughter. She was staying with my brother and his family in Glencoe when the tragedy occurred.''

''Was she?'' His brows rose. ''How troublesome. Whyever would she be there in the savage environs of the Highlands of a winter, when she could be in France with her family?''

''France? Oh no. I'm afraid you have been misinformed, my lord. My oldest son has been ill, and we had to take him to Italy for his health.'' She stressed *Italy,* smiling at him. ''Lianna preferred remaining in Scotland, and so I allowed it. After all, as you are aware, I did spend the first years of my life in the Highlands.''

''And have obviously polished up your rough edges, I see.'' Breadalbane's bland smile did not reach his eyes. ''I seem to recall a wild young lady with flaming temper to match her hair.''

''That was a long time ago.''

''So it was. So it was.'' He studied her, the smile still on his mouth. ''And now you have a daughter. And a son.''

''Two sons. My daughter is near twenty now, and I am very worried about her. Have you any word of the survivors of that ... trouble?'' It had been on the tip of her tongue to say massacre, but she caught it in time. He would hardly appreciate being reminded that the military action was considered a crime by most of Scotland.

''Not being involved with it, I have received only scant bits of information, of course. There were survivors of that campaign, mostly women and children, of course, who were allowed to leave Glencoe unmolested. The operation was aimed at the rebellious men of Glencoe, not innocent citizens.''

Catriona's hands tightened on the folds of her skirt, and she strove for calm. "So I understand. My concern, you see, is mostly for my daughter and relatives. Would it be possible for you to discover their fate?"

Breadalbane's eyelids lowered slightly, and his crooked mouth pursed into a knot. "Perhaps. I shall summon my steward, and see if he had the latest reports. You must know that I cannot be aware of the fates of all those in Glencoe, but of necessity, reports were written and filed about the campaign."

"Campaign." She drew in a deep breath at the careless term for horrible slaughter, but managed a calm smile. "I would greatly appreciate your aid, my lord."

There was a heavy pause while he studied her with hooded eyes, then Breadalbane called in his steward. "Lady Fraser wishes to know the fates of her Glencoe kinsmen, and especially her daughter. Find the information for her, and bring it to me."

"Aye, my lord." The steward hesitated a moment, then nodded and left the room, shutting the door behind him.

Catriona sat tensely, hoping that her hatred and dread did not show. She knew from past experience that to show any sign of weakness could be fatal with this man, and if she were not so desperate to find Lianna, she would not be here.

Rising to his feet, Breadalbane glanced at her with sly speculation as he crossed to an inlaid liquor cabinet against the far wall. "Sherry, Lady Fraser?"

"Yes, please." Catriona sat coolly, but wondered if John Campbell remembered the past as well as she did. Most likely, but with a different perspective, she was certain. In his later years he had grown stouter, but still bore the dignified air of an earl. That he had been involved in blackmail, money-lending, and oppression, and was fully given to moments of violence and murder was well known, yet he still had power. Not even his involvement in intrigue the past summer with the Highland chiefs favoring James had brought him down, when indeed, it certainly should have done. But when the news came out, he was able to divert the brunt of it, escaping unscathed for lack of solid evidence. So like Campbell, so like the man who had almost ruined her life years ago, and would have killed Dallas Fraser if he'd been able to manage it.

But that was then, and now she had come to him because she knew he was behind the Glencoe massacre, knew that he would know of Lianna's fate if any man did, and nothing mattered but her daughter.

"Your sherry, Lady Fraser."

"Thank you." She accepted the tiny glass, remaining poised as she sipped daintily. Campbell smiled, a lazy smile that sent shivers of apprehension along her spine.

"You are as lovely as ever, if I may be so bold as to comment, Lady Fraser. I see you do not paint or powder. An affectation. It proves you have changed a great deal."

The sherry was dry, tasting tart on her tongue. She frowned at the crystal glass, and her fingers tightened on the slender stem. "Aye, my lord. We have all changed in many ways, but time has not altered some things."

"No, of course not. Your . . . husband . . . remains as fierce an adversary as ever, though he has managed to gain a great deal more power. I commend him on his choices in life."

She lifted her eyes to his, swallowing the surge of rage that rose in her. "My husband has his enemies, as do all men of position and power, yet he has never struck a man from behind, nor avenged himself on their family."

Breadalbane's brow lifted. "My dear Lady Fraser, do you suggest that I have committed such depredations?"

" 'Tis said that you are behind the recent activities at Glencoe, my lord, so I did wonder if 'twas your clever hand I saw in the manipulations."

"Ah, blunt as ever, little Cat. Pardon me—Lady Fraser. There are moments when your birth shows through the veneer of civility you have acquired. But, more to the point, it was not my act that precipitated Glencoe's downfall, but that of MacIan. And of course, the Master of Stair was left with little option but to retaliate against such insolence and rebellion. The good of all Scotland lies in the hands of men with foresight and enough resolve to pursue eventual consolidation with England. It is too bad that men like Dallas Fraser cannot see past their own ambitions to the good of all.''

Carefully placing the sherry glass on the table next to her chair, Catriona rose to her feet, struggling for enough self-control not to lash out at Campbell. ''If you knew how my husband longs for Scotland to enjoy prosperity and peace, you would realize that his ambitions are dear to the welfare of our country.''

''Certainly, he wishes others to view his position in that light, but I find it difficult to countenance a man who swears loyalty to two different kings at the same time.''

''Dallas did no such thing!'' She drew in a sharp breath when Campbell's mouth twitched with satisfaction at her outburst. ''He is a mediator, and you know it. It is his task to negotiate between James and William, to bring about an equitable peace as quickly and quietly as possible. Not once has he declared for either man.''

''But he certainly has his partiality, I am convinced. Is it not James who has his loyalty at this moment? His troops and his monies? I think so, for 'tis certain that William has no Fraser gold in his coffers.''

Catriona knotted her hands together and managed a casual shrug. ''If you are attempting to get me to betray my husband in any way, my lord, I must disappoint you. I am quite uninformed about pertinent political matters.''

''My dear Lady Fraser,'' Breadalbane said dryly, ''I find it difficult to believe that you would long remain uninformed about anything at all. But then, that is why you are here, is it not? To gather information about your daughter and kin?''

''Yes. You are the one man to whom I could come and learn the complete truth, for if you know it, you will tell me.''

It was a simple statement of fact. Vengeance, if that is what he wished, would be stale if he was unable to claim responsibility for it. And now she saw in his eyes that he had been well aware Lianna was in Glencoe, and had gained great pleasure from it. Satisfaction gleamed in those hooded eyes, and curled his mouth. *He already knew* . . . Damn him—he was toying with her, like a cat with a mouse. He knew if Lianna was alive.

No doubt, he had hoped she would come to him like this, hoped to be able to tell her that her daughter was dead.

Catriona reeled slightly, but when the steward returned with a sheaf of papers, she remained still and quiet, waiting for the terrible news. Campbell took his time perusing the papers atop his desk, and when he finally looked up, she braced herself.

"You will be happy to hear that your daughter is alive, I am certain, but it has been reported that she was abducted by an outlaw. They have been seen, but my soldiers have not been able to seize them."

Catriona stared at him. "An outlaw?"

"Cameron MacKenzie. A young man named Calum reported that he gave aid to two young women, and one of them was last seen in the company of this MacKenzie. I rather fear that if this is true, she is in great danger."

"Danger?" The word came out in an odd croak. "What kind of danger?"

Shrugging, Breadalbane said, "MacKenzie is a rather ruthless individual. I have been after him myself for almost two years, and only recently was able to take his brother prisoner for offenses against the crown. Unfortunately, he abandoned his brother without a qualm, and escaped my men. Your daughter is in much greater danger with him than she would be with my soldiers, I assure you. Of course, if you hear of their whereabouts, you must tell me at once so that I can send my men after them. I will do what I can to help her, and would take great pleasure in bringing MacKenzie to justice."

Catriona wasn't fooled. Apparently Breadalbane wanted this Cameron MacKenzie taken. If Lianna was with him, he would arrest her as well, or he might be cautious enough not to earn the enmity of a powerful man like Dallas Fraser. But did she want to take that chance?

Rising, she smiled tightly. "I will give you any information I can discover, my lord. I ask that you do the same for me. Where were they last seen?"

"Rannoch Moor. That was only a week ago. By now, they could be anywhere. MacKenzie is clever, and has managed to elude me for some time. He is a deserter, and will be hung for his crimes when I catch him, so he is considered very dangerous. But I am certain your husband can manage to overcome him. I only hope MacKenzie doesn't manage to kill him first.''

"Yes, I am quite sure you would like tha' very much.'' She tugged on her fur-lined gloves and turned away.

When she reached the door, Breadalbane said softly, ''I wish you good fortune in finding your daughter alive, Lady Fraser. You will need it.''

"You could have listened to me, you know.''

Cameron's bitter complaint was hardly reassuring, and Lianna spared a glance at the men surrounding them. A motley group crowded into the bothie, garbed roughly and all bearing weapons, and not a civil tongue among them. She was terrified, too terrified to even care that Cameron was regarding her with well-deserved condemnation, but offered a lame explanation.

"I thought . . . when I saw the heather in their bonnets—''

"All MacDonalds are noble and pure. I know.''

There was nothing to say to that. It was obvious these particular MacDonalds were less than noble.

"May I introduce our rude visitors?'' Cameron indicated one of the men with a jerk of his head. "Hugh MacDonald— of the Glengarry MacDonalds. Gallant chap, d'you think?''

"Enough of tha','' the man named Hugh growled, jabbing at Cameron with the muzzle of his musket. He scowled, eyes boring into Cameron. "I dinna mind yer face, but we ha' met before.''

"Under more pleasant circumstances.'' Cameron edged to one side, but the jab of the musket halted him quickly. He shrugged. "I seem to have forgotten the moment. Pardon me.''

"Aye, ye would forget if ye could, I vow.'' Hugh grinned widely. "But I mind ye now—Cameron MacKenzie, by God— and we ha' ye at last.''

"MacKenzie?'' Another man pressed forward. "No' the same MacKenzie as made away with our cattle no' so long ago?''

"Aye, Dugald, 'tis the same. I would never forget how he

beat us so soundly in battle with the odds a'gin him." Hugh's muzzle jabbed again, and Cameron grunted with pain. "Now we can settle yer debt, MacKenzie."

Lianna listened numbly. Was this the real reason Cameron had not wanted to take her to the Glengarry MacDonalds? Perhaps it had nothing to do with being so far away and everything to do with having earned their enmity. It would be just like him to mask the real reason, the rogue.

Hugh was looking at her closely, and when he reached out to lift her face to the light, Cameron surged forward to come between them.

"Leave her out of this."

A beefy hand grabbed Cameron by the collar and swung him around, and another man held his arms behind him. When they struck him, Lianna cried out for them to stop, but Hugh MacDonald took her chin again and squeezed tightly.

"Ye're a fugitive, I warrant, from the king's justice. Else ye would no' be with MacKenzie. But yer no Highland lass. Yer accent is Lowland, and ye dinna know the Gaelic."

"She's not a fugitive," Cameron began, but was cuffed for his effort. He subsided, looking resigned and resentful.

Hugh MacDonald laughed. "Aye, ye're no' looking so smart now, for a man wha' went to university, are ye? All tha' readin' and lecturin' dinna seem to help ye when it comes down to it, now does it?"

Cameron stared back at him, a brow lifted. "That depends upon your point of view, I suppose."

"Aye, and my point of view is tha' ye've lost all, Cameron MacKenzie. Yer lands, yer name, even yer life once th' earl gets his hands on ye a'gin. Ye're outlawed now. And for wha'?"

"Principles. But that is something you would hardly understand."

"Tell tha' to yer brother afore they hang him. See how well he understands tha' he is to die for yer principles."

"I find that more palatable than dying for lack of principles, but again—you would not understand."

Lianna studied Cameron's face. He didn't look at her, wouldn't look at her, and she had the thought that she had not known him at all. Bewildered, she looked away from him to the armed men holding them.

"Look here," Dugald MacDonald was saying roughly to her, "tell us wha' we want to know and it'll go better for ye."

Confused, she blinked. She wanted to look at Cameron but did not dare. She nodded. "I was at Glencoe, if that is what you mean."

"Nay, 'tis no' wha' I mean at all, doxy."

"Isn't doxy a thought strong?" Cameron asked, then dodged a blow from the man holding his arms behind his back. Blood smeared his upper lip. "Jesus, Rogan, you don't need to be so rough. You already took my dirk and sword, didn't you? I can hardly put up much of a fight."

"Tha' ain't wha' worries me," Hugh snarled. " 'Tis said the earl would pay dearly to ha' ye at hand, bruised or no'."

"While that may be true, the *lady*—" Cameron stressed the word—"is a MacDonald from Glencoe as she claims, not a fugitive of any kind."

"And would double our purse if we gave her to the earl as well, I think," Rogan put in with a grin. "Aye, 'tis a handsome way to fill our craws." He poked Cameron with the muzzle of his pistol. "Who is she? An' if ye think to whid, ye needs think a'gin. I'll ha' the truth of ye, or else outa the *lady.*"

"No whiddling from me," Cameron muttered. "And what she knows would not fill a thimble. Ask away, gentlemen."

"Tha' is more like it," Hugh said with a grin that made Lianna shudder. He slapped a thick stave against his open palm, studying Cameron for a long moment.

Across the room of the stuffy hut, a fire burned on the hearth, lending heavy smoke to the air. She wished she had not invited them in, wished she had listened to Cameron. There was nothing for it: She would tell them who she was.

"Sirs, please—I can explain everything if you will only listen to me a moment. You might find it useful to—"

Cameron turned to her, slanting her a fierce glance and hissing, "Shut up, beauty. These gentlemen want the truth, not more lies. Leave it to me."

She nodded mutely, warned by the glint in his eye and his

taut expression that she might very well endanger them even
more with an unwise remark. Still, it was hard to watch as they
dragged him close to the fire kindled on the stone hearth, leaving
one man to guard her while they began the interrogation. She
wanted to close her eyes, wanted to cover her ears and blot it
all out, but refused to exhibit her cowardice so openly. If
Cameron could withstand it, she would as well.

The dialogue that followed was in Gaelic, and Lianna could
only judge by Cameron's expression how bad their situation
was liable to become. On occasion, one of the men hit Cameron,
apparently misliking a reply, and another would jerk him
upright again. Cameron's hands were tied behind his back, his
weapons taken, so that he could only submit. Oh God, it was
her fault, all her fault, and she bit her lower lip to keep from
crying out when he was struck yet again.

At last she recognized their mortal danger. It wasn't just
hostages against their own capture these men wanted, it was
money and pawns. To dangle Cameron as a prize would earn
them Breadalbane's favor, and if they discovered who her father
was, they would be able to draw him into the affair and perhaps
endanger them all. Oh God, she really was a fool.

It seemed an eternity before they left off questioning him.
Dugald half dragged him toward her, and flung him to the floor
with a snarled command in Gaelic that needed no interpretation.
Lianna sat still and huddled in misery. She watched silently
while the men sat in front of the fire, passing a jug and talking
among themselves.

"I hope you weren't planning on confessing your name,
angel." Cameron's low voice was rough and grating, broken
by a sudden cough.

Hugging her knees against her chest, she slanted him a quick
glance. His hands were tied behind him, his face bruised. Oh,
if only she had not insisted, had listened to him when he'd said
he did not like the looks of the approaching men. But she had
not. It would hardly help to express regret now, and she had
no desire to invite any more criticisms.

"Nothing to say to that, I see," Cameron muttered, and
leaned his head back against the wall. His eyes closed. The

only indication that he remained alert was a splinter of silver light beneath his lashes.

Lianna drew in a shaky breath, then let it out again. "Why are they doing this, Cameron?"

"It's called getting the upper hand." His lashes lifted slightly on the silver gleam. "A trade, a bargain with the devil, so to speak. Not a bad idea, actually, but deuced awkward for us."

"Must you make light of it?"

"Light? I think it an accurate description of our circumstances."

"What are you going to do now?" He was silent. When she looked at him his eyes were closed again, and his mouth turned down in a bitter slant. "Well?" she prompted.

Blindly, softly, he replied, "Not a damned thing."

"How can you say that?" She shivered, hugging her knees more tightly to her chest, wishing he would not provoke her like this. "Cameron, we cannot just allow them to turn us over to Breadalbane."

"Then revolt, m'dear. It seems to be the favorite theme in Scotland these days anyway. Foment a revolution among the prisoners."

"We are the only prisoners, you dolt."

"Excellent point. This dolt finds himself too sore and weary to be involved in an insurrection that can have only one result."

"Cameron, blast you—must you be so stubborn? Do you want to hear me apologize? Is that it? Must I admit how wrong I was about them before you will think of a way out of this?"

His eyes opened at that, and the bitter slant of his mouth curved into a faint smile. "I would like to hear an admission that I was right, yes."

She glared at him. "Very well, if it will rouse you from your indulgence in a fit of the sulks, I will be quite happy to admit I am wrong. You are right, Cameron. Not all men with the name of MacDonald are fair and just, nor are all men with the name of Campbell evil. I should have stayed with the Campbells, and allowed you to leave. There. Are you satisfied?"

"Somewhat." He closed his eyes again, shifting against the

wall to settle his shoulders into a more comfortable position. "Unfortunately, it doesn't change anything."

"How can you say that?"

"Because, blast you, it's true. And if you don't lower your voice, we may very well have the opportunity to enjoy more of their company, for Hugh MacDonald is just itching to have at me again."

Lianna subsided into silence, glancing toward the men by the fire.

"I'll do what I can to help, you know," she whispered, keeping an eye on the men across the room. "Just tell me what I should do."

A heavy sigh lifted his chest, and his eyes opened to stare at her dubiously. "No doubt. I'm not at all certain that any more of your help will be useful, however. It could very well propel us to early graves."

"Yes, I know I was wrong. I said it, didn't I? Stop being so stubborn."

"If you will recall, angel, I did my best to convince you that one cannot judge a man by his name, or any other superficial and accidental virtues. Blow me, here we are caught neat as netted trout, and now you come all helpful. A little late, unfortunately."

Lianna couldn't help the small break in her voice: "I did think they would be agreeable to helping us, or at the least . . . helping me get home."

Silence greeted this last comment, then he groaned. "Naïve little goose."

"So it seems." She glanced fearfully toward the men by the fire and shuddered. There were four of them. All big, brawny men, rough and apparently with little remorse about turning over Cameron. "Did you really steal their cattle?"

"Aye. It was a lively fight in Glengarry Forest, I can tell you that, for when I looked around, the men who were supposed to be with me, had disappeared. There I was, facing five angry men whose cattle were vanishing over the far hill. A most illuminating moment in my life." He said it calmly, but there was the ever-present bitterness in his voice.

"What happened, Cameron?"

"Oh, I laid about me with my sword and pistol, and managed by some vagrant whim of the gods to escape with my life. It would have been too kind to kill me outright."

"Why did your men leave you behind?"

His head tilted forward. He looked thoughtful. "Because they were told to. Compliments of the earl, I think, though I cannot prove it. It's beginning to be a habit, for it seems that in times of great hazard, I usually find myself alone. Just as well. I'm not at all certain I'd know how to act if I found myself with support in dire times."

She lapsed into silence again, and bent to rest her forehead on crossed arms braced atop her knees. Perhaps he would not be able to extricate them from this situation. What would she do then? There was always the possibility the earl of Breadalbane would hold her hostage against Papa's paying ransom, but what about Cameron? What would happen to him? The earl held his brother, and apparently wanted him as well. But why? What had he done that was so bad Breadalbane wanted to kill him for it?

Beside her, Cameron shifted, and she heard his hoarse grunt of pain. Escape seemed impossible. She didn't want to admit what a coward she was, but what if they interrogated her as they had him? And what had he told them?

Looking up, she found his gaze on her. "What did you tell them?"

"About me? Anything I thought would help. You, however, are my poor little hostage. Try to remember that."

"I hardly see how being your hostage will help the situation," she said tartly, and he grimaced.

"Fine. Tell them your father is the one man who can be used by both sides in this damnable tangle they call Scottish politics, and see where that gets you."

He sounded angry, and kept his eyes fixed on the men by the fire. After a moment, she said softly, "I still don't see how it will help for them to think I'm your hostage. Won't they assume I must be worth something? Won't that make it worse for me?"

His head turned, and in the shadowy light she saw the mocking gleam in his eyes. "It might, if I had informed them you were that kind of hostage, m'dear. However, as I sensed they might turn up greedy, I thought it best for them to assume my passions overtook my common sense. It is much easier for these men to understand a man taking a woman against her will for pleasurable pursuits, than it would be for any kind of misplaced sense of charity."

She flushed. "Then they think—"

"Precisely. And as you are supposed to be abducted, have the decency to continue railing at me like any self-respecting hostage, if you don't mind."

"Really, Cameron, you say the most incredible things." She looked away from him, frowning.

"It's a talent." He shifted, looked at her again, his voice kinder this time. "Better to be thought my unwilling lover than an important hostage, don't you think?"

A faint smile pressed at the corners of her mouth, and she pushed a heavy strand of hair from her eyes with one hand. "Why be unwilling?"

Amusement danced in his eyes. "Aye, you would make this difficult, you little tart. And don't contradict my story, if you please. If they think you are willing to be with a rogue as wicked as me, you won't be treated quite so nicely."

She laughed at that, a low sound, then glanced at the Mac-Donalds. "Yes, I see your point. What do you think they intend to do next?"

"It boggles the mind." Cameron leaned forward, with a clumsy motion because of his bound hands, and his voice was so low that she had to strain to hear. "But I do have an idea if you would care to hear it. . . ."

She glanced up at him, and her heart lurched. "What is it?"

"In my right boot—my *sgian dhu*—they forgot to take it when they took my other weapons. Be so good as to remove it, if you please. Slowly, so as not to attract their attention. Perhaps—an argument will suffice. They think you hate me anyway, do they not? Create some kind of disturbance after you cut the ties on my wrists, and I will take it from there."

With agonizing slowness, Lianna complied, afraid that at any moment one of the men would glance over at them and see what she was doing. Cameron had crossed his legs at the ankles, presenting his right boot casually, but she had to reach across him to slide her hand beneath the turned-down leather cuff. To disguise her action, she pretended to curl up as if going to sleep, her hair tossed carelessly over him while she slipped her fingers along his leg and under the cuff. Her fingers grazed the dirk's hilt, and she palmed it and sat up, pushing the hair from her eyes with feigned annoyance.

Constantly aware of their captors before the fire, she eased back to lean against the wall, arranging her skirts to hide the movements of her hands, and slipped one arm behind Cameron to saw at the leather strips binding his wrists. It was more difficult than she had imagined it would be, though the blade was razor sharp. It took a moment of fumbling before she could angle to cut only leather and not skin. Then she did it, felt the blade move freely as the leather parted, and heard Cameron's soft mutter to be careful, by God.

She left the dirk by his hands and sat up straight to look at him. He nodded at her, a faint smile on his mouth. In the shadows, with only pale light to define his features, he looked saturnine and expectant, the familiar mockery and casual amusement lurking behind his eyes. Somehow, that gave her courage.

Surging to her knees, she slapped him across the face, a resounding blow that sounded much too loud in the stuffy hut. There was a swift shaft of outrage and shock in his gaze when he stared up at her, but she ignored it as she raised her voice. "How dare you! I hope they hang you, you thieving rascal! Taking me as you did—I hope the earl gives you what you deserve. . . ."

Her outburst brought the men to their feet; Hugh swaggered toward them, grinning. Just behind him, Dugald MacDonald laughed loudly. "Aye, he's a rogue, he is for a fact. Dinna fash aboot his fate, for the earl will give him his reward, I'm thinking."

Cameron's upward glance through his lashes was dark, and

his mouth twisted in a grimace. "No doubt you will both get
your wish soon enough. Though I hardly think it will matter
to either of you, for the earl is notoriously laggard when it
comes to proper appreciation for expended effort on his behalf.
I should know well enough." He leaned his head back against
the wall, his gaze mocking as he regarded Hugh MacDonald.
"You, especially, should be wary, for if you think to get other
than lead shot for your pains, you're a fool. Not that I've
thought any differently about you."

While he talked, he drew up one leg, and when Hugh came
closer to glare down at him, Cameron tensed. Lianna heard the
swift intake of his breath before he kicked up and outward,
catching Hugh MacDonald square in the chest. In a move as
agile as a striking snake, Cameron surged up as MacDonald
went down with a choked sound. The dirk in Cameron's hand
flashed with quick light as he straddled Hugh.

"Oh no," Cameron said to the other men leaping toward
him, "if you think I won't slice his throat, remember that I've
little to lose. That's better, gentlemen. Now, throw down your
weapons, if you please, and be quick about it. My hands are
still numb from being tied so tightly, and might slip and cut
his throat anyway."

Cursing, the men complied, and there was the metallic clatter
of weapons against the hard dirt floor. Holding MacDonald
with the dirk pressed against his throat, Cameron said over his
shoulder, "Get Hugh's sword and pistol first, Lianna. Quickly
now, or I might leave you with these kind gentlemen."

Her hands shaking, she complied, then moved to gather the
other weapons while Cameron dragged MacDonald to his feet
and held him in front of him like a shield. Firelight cast a
dancing glow in the room, and smoke wisps drifted in shifting
currents as Lianna collected all the weapons and tossed them
out the door. A cold wind swept into the hut, and she shivered.

"What do I do now?"

Cameron's mouth quirked up at one corner. "Shut the door.
It's deuced cold. Then, I must ask you to donate strips of your
shift, if you will be so kind. Necessary, you understand, to help
these gentlemen adjust to their new situation. Gentlemen, the

first unwise move one of you makes while my lovely assistant binds you, will cost poor Hugh his life. Keep that in mind, if you will.''

Quickly, she tore several strips from her shift, and followed his instructions in binding the men. Doubling the strips to make them stronger, she took so long tying them that Cameron began to grumble.

"For God's sake, they're not Christmas geese being trussed for roasting, Lianna. Just make certain they're tied tightly, will you? It doesn't have to be pretty."

"I'm doing my best, blast you."

When all the men were tied except Hugh, Cameron beckoned her to him. "Now be so good as to open the door and precede me outside, beauty."

"Ye'll no' get away, MacKenzie," Hugh snarled, but his threats were quickly choked to silence by Cameron.

"Ah, Hugh, Hugh, you challenge me to new heights of creativity." Cameron shifted the dirk so that the tip grazed just beneath MacDonald's jaw. "I've heard that men make a most peculiar whistling noise when there is a hole in their throat. Have you heard that?"

Hugh swallowed. His face was pale and beads of sweat dotted his forehead and upper lip. He did not move, but stood stiffly still in Cameron's hold. "Aye." It came out a faint whisper.

"We can always test that theory if you prove bothersome in any way. Yours would not be the first throat I've cut, though it might be the most well-deserved."

"MacKenzie . . . ha' mercy. . . ."

"Mercy is not one of my virtues, you bleeding sod. I'd as soon slit your gullet as I would not, and may do it if you say or do one thing I don't like." He jerked him back a step, the dirk pressing against Hugh's throat hard enough to draw a drop of blood.

Lianna paused in the open door and stared at him. This was not the Cameron she knew, the teasing, mocking rogue who preferred sarcasm to actual battle. This Cameron had a savage light in his eyes, and a grim purpose to his actions that was frightening. For the first time, she could visualize him as a soldier, though that term was not as appropriate as she would have liked. Outlaw, perhaps. Villain. Brigand. Those fit better as he ruthlessly dragged Hugh MacDonald to the door and outside.

Cold wind whipped at her skirts, but it was not the chill that made her shiver as Cameron drew MacDonald over the rough ground heedless of his pleas for mercy. Light from the open doorway cast a blurred rectangle across the ground in front of the hut. It glinted on the scattered muskets and swords she had taken from the others, played over Cameron as he shoved Hugh to the ground with a disgusted mutter.

"I should gut you where you stand, MacDonald, but I won't. It would be too easy."

Hugh staggered from his knees to his feet. He stood swaying a moment, wiping at his mouth with the back of one hand. "Then wha' d'ye intend?"

"You'd only slow us down. But I rather fancy the notion of seeing you tied to a tree for the wolves to find." He gestured with the dirk. "Take off your belt, then your boots."

Slowly, MacDonald began to comply, his eyes darting about restlessly. The leather belt dropped to the ground, and he knelt to pick it up. Then, in a swift motion, he lunged forward and scooped up one of the discarded swords, rolling to his feet to face Cameron with a wicked grin. The sword flashed competently in his fist.

"Ye're quick enou' with words like a woman, MacKenzie. How d'ye be with a man's sword in yer hand?"

Eyes narrowing warily, Cameron stepped back and picked up a sword. "Well enough, as you certainly should recall. All right, you pawkie bastard, another test. See how well you do when no one is holding my arms or my hands aren't tied."

Cameron hefted the sword from one hand to the other, grinning like a devil in the dim light. Lianna cried out in horror.

"No! Oh God, Cameron, what are you doing?"

He ignored her. There was a feral gleam in his eyes, and his chest rose and fell with harsh movements. He gestured, and the sword in his hand caught the light with a lethal glitter.

Hugh MacDonald grinned. He hefted the sword with an expert motion. "Aye, come to the killing, MacKenzie."

Panic welled in her, and terror that Cameron would be killed, but she could only watch, spine pressed against the stone wall of the hut and her hands over her mouth. She wanted no distractions to hinder him.

In the pale shimmering light from hut and setting sun, she watched as Hugh and Cameron slowly circled on the balls of their feet for a moment, gauging the other. Suddenly Hugh was no longer waiting, but his sword glittered briefly in a downward arc that Cameron met with his own blade. There was a peculiar, deadly grace to their movements as they fought. The clash of metal against metal made a deafening ringing in her ears. Yet she could not look away, was paralyzed with fear and dread.

It was quickly apparent that Cameron outstripped his opponent in skill, his movements sparse and efficient, each thrust drawing blood while Hugh's blows were easily parried. They feinted, met, closed, then Cameron sprang back and turned in a complete circle; his blade slashed down in a deadly swing that caught Hugh MacDonald deeply across his chest. A wide gash ruptured across his shirt and plaid, spurting blood.

An expression of shock creased Hugh's face as he stumbled forward a step, his sword slowly tilting down, then he dropped to the ground. He lay still, and Cameron went to him and rolled him over with the toe of his boot. Hugh's arm flopped limply, and his eyes were already glazing in death.

Cameron glanced up at Lianna, the feral light still in his eyes, and his breath coming harshly between his teeth. "That's one less pawkie bastard in the world."

Lianna could not reply. The edges of her vision blurred, and she clung to the cottage stones with both hands behind her to keep from sinking to the ground. No, this was not at all the Cameron MacKenzie she knew.

Chapter 15

Dallas Fraser stared stonily at his wife. "I thought you had better sense than to do such a thing, Cat."

She shrugged, one of those careless gestures that could bring him to the point of anger even when he was in a good mood—which he was certainly not at this moment.

"I told you I intend to do everything I can to find her, Dallas. And I was not fool enough to go alone. I took Duncan with me as guard."

"Old Duncan?" Dallas snorted. "What could he have done to help? Not much, I'll tell you. Dammit, Cat what could Breadalbane know that would be worth the risk you took?"

"Where our daughter is, for one thing." She shrugged calmly out of her traveling cloak and met his eyes steadily.

With great restraint, he turned back to gaze out the window of the inn tucked into the Highland mountains. The serene waters of Loch Leven glittered in the thin sunlight. Mist hovered above the loch and shrouded reeds and rocks in a hazy veil. It would soon be spring. Six weeks since the massacre, six weeks since his daughter had been sent into the very teeth of a blizzard, fleeing for her life. His hand curled into a fist atop the window ledge, and he turned back to look at his wife.

"All right. What did Breadalbane have to say? It better be important enough for you to have risked so much to hear it."

"It was quite important." Catriona looked up at him through her lashes, and he saw the anxiety in her green eyes as she blurted, "Lianna was taken by an outlaw, if the earl is to be believed."

"Aye, if the earl is to be believed." He studied her, frowning. "Who is this outlaw?"

"A man named Cameron MacKenzie. Oh Dallas, I'm so afraid for her. Even if Campbell is exaggerating, or outright lying, she must be terrified. Why hasn't she gone to a village and sent us word? You know if she was able, she would have done so. She must know how we're worrying about her. If she was able, I know she would—she must be so scared."

"Aye, she must." Cat was quivering, and there was a little catch in her voice that made his mouth tighten with anger at Breadalbane as well as MacKenzie. He put a hand on her shoulder, then drew her to him. Her hair smelled of wind, rain, and smoke as she leaned against his chest. "Cat, if she is with this MacKenzie, we'll find her. I've posted a reward for her, and will post one for him as well. Believe me, if anyone has seen them or does see them, we will soon know about it. A thousand pounds is enough to make some men betray their own brother."

"Aye," Catriona said against his shirt, her words muffled. " 'Tis enough to tempt even me."

Dallas laughed softly. "You minx. You would never betray anyone. It's not in your nature. You're too bloody honest."

"You once said I was too bloody lazy to try and remember to lie," she said, tilting her head back to look up at him. Tears clumped her black lashes into spikes, and he brushed them away with a gentle hand.

"Aye, so I did. It's the truth. It amazes me that you managed to visit Breadalbane without telling him what you think of him. The bastard. He still holds a grudge for what happened so long ago. Not that I blame him. After all, I wanted you the moment I saw you, and he was much younger then, too—not as adept at getting what he wanted. Thank God. When I think I could have lost you to him—''

''Never.'' She sounded fierce. ''I detested him, and told him so. I would never have gone with him, even if you had not survived his schemes and traps.''

''I wonder that you did not tell him what you think of him, this time as well.''

''I could not, though I wanted to. And it was difficult, I can tell ye tha'.'' Her voice slipped into the Highland burr, a certain sign that she was strained. ''If no' for Lianna . . .''

''We will find her, Cat. I have Logan and Morgan out now putting up bills for her return. I'll have more made up about MacKenzie, then post them as well. By God, we will find her if I have to tear all of Scotland apart. And at least we know she is alive.''

''Aye, alive, but at wha' cost? I am afraid for her. Wha' if this MacKenzie harms her?''

''Then he will certainly pray for death long before I grant it to him,'' Dallas said softly, and there was such menace in his words that she looked up at him with anxious eyes.

''Dallas—ye willna kill him until ye find her?''

''I think I'm intelligent enough to hold my hand that long, Cat. God. Haven't you known me long enough to realize that if there is anything I am expert at managing, it's holding my tongue and my hand? If not, you would have lost *your* tongue long ago, I assure you.''

A faint smile curved her mouth. ''I suppose I do know that. I forget at times that I'm the only one who can make you forget how expert you are at holding your tongue.''

Putting his arms around her, Dallas drew her close to him, one hand under her chin to tilt her face up for his kiss. She still had the power to arouse him, this headstrong, irritating, desirable wife of his. There were times it seemed as if it had been only the week before he had seen her bathing in a woodland pool and decided he must have her, instead of twenty-five years ago. The impetuosity of youth had waned with time. But time had not dimmed her beauty, or his need for her. And he had finally learned not to try to settle every argument with angry words, just as he had learned compromise instead of outright defiance when it came to politics. It had been a harsh lesson in both circumstances, but one well studied.

He broke off the kiss and rubbed his thumb across her lips until her eyes opened. "Cat, do you ever regret the way we met?"

Her eyes widened. "Regret it? Ah, no, my fine braw callant, how could any woman long resist a man who sweeps her off her feet and carries her naked through the woods?"

"You gave an excellent imitation of resistance, if I remember correctly," he said dryly.

"Aye, but that was only so you would not lose interest too quickly." She smiled slyly. "I thought you the most handsome man I had ever seen, and I had not one moment's regret, no matter what I may have said to you."

"Good." He kissed her again, hard and briskly, then set her back. "Let's hope this MacKenzie has not abducted our daughter for the same reason. I greatly fear that he may not be as even-tempered as I am."

Catriona's eyes widened with anxiety. "Oh God—I had not thought of that, only that he might want to ransom her. Dallas— we must find her quickly!"

He nodded. "I know, Cat. I know."

Cameron glanced back at Lianna when she wasn't looking. She was only a vague shadow among darker shadows as they trod the mountain path, her bright hair a dim beacon in the moonlight. She had barely looked at him since leaving the bothie behind. He had frightened her, and he knew it. It had been unavoidable. He had no regrets about killing Hugh MacDonald.

Wryly, he thought that Lianna must have lost any illusions she had about him. If, indeed, she'd had any left. He had seen the horror in her eyes when he stood there with bloodied sword and the killing fever on him; that old, mindless blur had wiped out everything but the need to survive. He'd thought perhaps he had grown more civilized in the past months, but obviously he was wrong. Facing Hugh MacDonald, he had felt it again, the wild, savage lust to conquer and destroy. God, he had degenerated to the savage level he so deplored, had relished the feel of the sword in his hands, the dawning realization in MacDonald's eyes that he had lost.

And now Lianna shied away from him, regarding him as if he still had blood on his hands, and he could have told her that it would never go away. Blood stained more than his hands or his clothes, it had seeped into his soul that day at Killiecrankie, leaving him changed. But not even the carnage at Killiecrankie had affected him as Glencoe had done.

But now there was a growing sense of urgency. He must get Lianna to safety, must get to Fort William to talk to Hill in an effort to save Jamie. It had been too long since he had seen him, too long since Jamie had been taken as a prisoner. If Breadalbane discovered Cameron was still alive . . . aye, he would use Jamie badly, that much was certain.

Christ. Hugh MacDonald's kin would be looking for them more quickly than he liked, as well. It was too bad he had left them free, but at least they were tied and would take time to free themselves. That might gain them a little time, but, God knew, it would not be much. If the MacDonalds reached Fort William or Breadalbane . . .

"Cameron . . ." Lianna's faint whimper stopped him, and he halted on the rocky ledge to wait for her. Wind tugged fiercely at his hair and clothes, chapping his face.

"Come along, now. It's wide here, but watch your step."

"When will we . . . stop? It's late, dark, and I'm so tired. Can we stop soon?"

"Soon. When we get to Loch Treig."

"Loch Treig . . . dear God. That's so far away."

She sounded exhausted. How much longer would her strength hold out? She'd been through so much, but they had to go on, had to get to safety before the hue and cry went up. It was bad enough being hunted for crimes he had not done, but now he was guilty of killing a man outside of battle. No doubt, Breadalbane would be quick to seize on that fact to nail him to a wall somewhere.

He surveyed her carefully. In the thin moonlight her face

looked so pale and wan beneath the wind-tangled mass of her hair. There was still that wary look in her eyes, and he sighed.

"Lianna, let me carry you."

"Carry me!" She stared at him. Then she pushed the straggling hair from her eyes and laughed softly. "You dolt. How far would we get if you exhausted yourself carrying me? I'm not helpless, just tired."

"Yes, so you should be." He looked at her more closely. Was the wariness still there? The doubt and revulsion he had seen in her face outside the hut? "About . . . back there. You know I had to—"

"Yes. I know. You needn't explain. I can't say it was pleasant to watch, but . . . but oh God, Cameron, I was so afraid for you! I thought that at any moment you would be killed. And I knew I wouldn't be able to go on, wouldn't want to go on without you. I was terrified for you. . . ."

Relieved, he smiled wryly. "You would have made it fine without me. You would have told them what a thorough bastard I was and convinced them you had been taken against your will, of course. It would be the only sensible thing to do."

"It's not at all what I mean, you lackwit. Don't you understand? I was scared *for you*."

"Come here, girl." Reaching out, he pulled her to him, and closed his eyes when she came willingly. The fear in her eyes had been for him and not against him. Silly little goose. "Don't you know I wouldn't let anything happen to me as long as you're with me?" he murmured against her hair. It smelled of peat smoke and mist. He crushed it in his fist, and rubbed the damp, silky strands against his cheek. Her arms came around him and he held her more tightly. After a moment, he pushed her back a step, tilted her face upward and kissed her soundly. "Better now?" he asked when he released her again.

"Much better. But still tired."

"Yes . . . well. Sorry. MacDonald's men could catch up if we don't hurry."

She rubbed her face against his chest, then nodded. "I know. I'll go on."

"My brave little goose." He gave her a quick, fierce hug,

and was surprised at the surge of emotion he felt. There was something so touching about her, with her shaky courage and determination, her fear for him that no one had ever felt before. He'd had men fear him, and even a woman or two on one of those awkward occasions when he'd been caught up in the depredation of war before he could stop the others. But never could he recall someone actually being afraid *for* him. It was a novelty, and he rather liked it, which only went to show how far he'd sunk to be wanting something he knew would never happen.

"I'm not a goose, thank you." She cuffed him lightly, then stepped back. "I'll keep up as best I can."

Cameron couldn't speak. Mixed with the relief and sudden revelation that someone cared about him, was the bitter knowledge that he could never really have her. This was all an illusion, a fantasy just out of his reach. But he was damned if he intended to forgo this brief pleasure for the time he had to enjoy it.

So he tucked her close to him on the rocky road down the mountain, relishing the feel of her next to him, and the sweet awareness that she cared. He dreaded parting from her.

"I hate to be the one to tell you this, MacKenzie, but there's a price on your head tha' would choke a horse." Rory Mac-Donald, laird of the small clachan near the banks of Loch Treig, sounded regretful but much too certain of his facts.

Lianna glanced at Cameron. His face was carefully blank. Then he shrugged, glanced warily around the small village with its neat stone cottages and said, "I see. Then it will do me no good to go to Fort William, I suppose."

"No' unless you want to lose your head."

Rory MacDonald gazed at him with sympathy. A brisk wind blew over the sun-lit haugh, ruffling his gray hair as he turned to look at Lianna. "And there is a price for you too, lass, though no' for the same reason, I ken."

"For me?"

"Aye. Put up by Dallas Fraser."

"Oh, poor Papa. But who has put the price on Cameron's head?"

Rory scratched his jaw, and looked at the ground. A dog barked, and two children ran laughing by. "The same."

"Papa? *Papa* has a price on Cameron's head? Oh no, that can't be."

"I'm sorry, lass. 'Twas your own kin who told me of it, Alex and Iain, who brought the news from Kinlochleven last week. Handbills have been posted."

"My cousins are alive then—are they here? Do Alex and Iain know—?"

Rory nodded. "Aye, lass. They know about wha' happened to their father and sister. They have gone to bury them, like others who are creeping back to Glencoe one at a time."

Tears stung her eyes, and she looked away, staring down at her fisted hand. "And my aunt?"

"She has no' been seen, but they hope to find her." Rory's voice was gentle and sad. A mist hung over Loch Treig, dampening Lianna's hair and cheeks, and she wiped her hand across her face.

"I should have found her."

"From wha' has been said, you were lucky to get out alive, lass. Dinna fret. There are so many dead, so many missing . . . there is much to answer for in this affair, tha' much is certain." He glanced at Cameron. "Fraser willna rest until he has you, but he wants you taken alive. There is a thousand pounds on your head, enough to make a man rich."

Cameron made a disgusted sound. "I knew it."

"And tha' is no' all, Cameron," Rory said with a shake of his head. "Breadalbane has put it out tha' you are outlawed. Any man who gives you shelter is at risk. He doesna care if you are taken dead or alive."

"I can't say I'm surprised. Here, Rory, do me the favor of seeing that Miss Fraser is escorted to her father, will you? I won't endanger you by staying here, but she—"

"No." Lianna grabbed Cameron's arm. "I won't leave you. You heard what he just said—Breadalbane would prefer you dead. If I am with you, you have a chance."

"Beauty, if you are with me, you are likely to end up dead or treated quite roughly, at the least. Breadalbane's men have a history of being less than gentle with women, in case you have forgotten."

Her mouth tightened. "I have not forgotten for a moment, but I refuse to allow you to be killed without a trial or hearing in front of a justice."

Cameron looked at her oddly, then glanced away. The fine white scar at the corner of his mouth tightened. "It's not that I don't appreciate your concern or effort, but it's quite useless. And I'm not a bad hand at survival, you might note. I'm still here, after all."

"Yes, but with the amount of money being offered for your capture or death, you won't be alive long." Her throat grew tight with suppressed fear and fury, and she swallowed hard before saying softly, "Cameron, please."

"Jesus."

"Papa can help you free your brother. I'll ask him. You know if anyone can manage it, he can. And now you can't even show your face at Fort William, or anywhere else for that matter. You can do nothing on your own, Cameron, but if you let me help you, perhaps together we can manage it."

His jaw clenched. The bruises on his face gave him a villainous appearance, and the beard stubble on his chin and cheeks had grown quite dark and thick. The look he gave her seared to the soul, and then he shrugged. "I suppose I'll burn for this, but—I'll take you to your parents. That is as far as I will go."

"You won't regret it."

"Oh aye, beauty. I already regret it. If anything happens to you, I won't be fit to bury." He reached out to slide his fingers through her hair, looping a curl around his finger with a faint smile.

She caught her breath at the light in his eyes, and felt Rory MacDonald's wide stare on them. But she didn't care. For a moment she could not force any words past her frozen lips, could only gaze up at Cameron with a thick lump in her throat that defied the effort. He loved her. He hadn't said the words, but he loved her.

And God help her, she loved him too.

"Nothing will happen to me, Cameron. Nothing can, now that I'm with you."

His hand fisted in her hair, and he leaned forward so that his forehead pressed against hers. "I hope to God you're right, angel. It looks like we'll find that out soon enough."

Rory cleared his throat, looking embarrassed. "If I might offer my aid, to ye, Cameron—I know of a place to go where ye'll be safe for a time, while I get word to Dallas Fraser tha' ye would like to see him. D'ye trust me?"

Lianna held her breath, uncertain and afraid, yet not knowing if she should voice her reservations. Perhaps Rory could help them—but would Cameron trust him? And would Cameron agree to more delay before going to his brother's aid? It was an agonizing decision for him to make.

Mist hung over the valley below, but the sun shed fading light on the mountain crags tucked between two rocky promontories. Lianna watched the sun sink lower, spreading a diminishing glow in shades of rose, purple, and deep blue that leached into corries and woodlands with silent beauty.

Below on the rocky trail that led to the summit of Stob Choire Claurigh, she could see Cameron deep in conversation with Rory MacDonald. The old laird had brought them into the mountains above Loch Treig to a hut very few knew about. They were to remain here while he got word to Lianna's parents, and discovered what he could about Jamie.

She wasn't as distressed as she might once have been to find herself in hiding again. Indeed, she was glad for a chance to be alone with Cameron, grateful that circumstances had rendered it impossible for him to leave her behind. She wanted to be with him, even at the risk of being caught by Breadalbane. And surely Papa would protect him once everything was explained to him.

But—would Papa listen before he acted?

Papa had a history of being quick to action, forming opinions and acting upon them swiftly and efficiently. It was one of the traits that made him such a renowned hero, that ability to react deftly to any situation. Yet if he was convinced that Cameron was guilty of abduction or even worse—well, she would just have to get to Papa first, that was all. Or even better, get to her mother first. Mama always knew how to handle Papa, even when he was angry.

But for now, tucked into a cozy hut nestled in a thick grove of pines and cedars, she was content to stay where she was. Rory MacDonald had promised to let her parents know she was alive and well, had promised to tell them she was with Cameron of her own free will. All they had to do was wait until enough time had passed for Papa to get the message.

Cameron had tried to convince her to allow someone to escort her to Fort William or Inverlochy, but she feared for him if she left his side. Without her as protection—or hostage— he may very well be shot on sight. This way, he had a chance, if only he would admit it.

And the mountains were beautiful, but brutal in their unforgiving preserve. Snow still lay thick on the crags and in the corries at this altitude. It was cold, with the wind a constant, keening presence, whistling around them in gusts so loud it was hard to hear anything else, and at other times, falling off to a soft, mournful wail.

Huddled into the warm folds of her cloak, Lianna watched Rory MacDonald depart, trudging down the narrow, rocky trail to disappear around an outcropping of boulders. Cameron glanced up, and even at a distance, she could see the strain in his face as he climbed the trail toward her.

When he reached her, he sat down on a flat rock beside her, saying nothing for several moments. His hair was wind-ruffled and tangled, falling over his forehead and into his eyes, and his mouth twisted in a slight grimace.

"It seems that we are destined to spend our lives in the rocks, angel. Oddly, I'm beginning to grow accustomed to sleeping on rocks. I would consider the life of a recluse if it wasn't so deuced uncomfortable."

"A recluse? Aren't they reputed to live alone in solitary existence?"

''A semi-recluse then.'' He slid an arm around her shoulders and pulled her hard against him. ''I cannot think what I would do if you were not here.''

She turned to press her face against his chest. ''Nor I. You make any circumstances wonderful, but I suppose you know that.''

''Do I? No, it had not occurred to me that you were so witless. Or easily pleased. No point in trying to impress you with jewels or other baubles, I see. Not if you are content hiding in the rocks with an outlawed villain. However, I must question your judgement. And I'm not at all certain I am easy about a woman with so little proper respect for danger. Or the proprieties. Scandalous creature. Why on earth would you be content living with a felon?''

Laughing, she tilted her head back to look up at him. The wind quickened, almost drowning out her soft words: ''I think you are much more a proper hero than I had ever considered, Cameron MacKenzie.''

He grew quite still. His arm tightened around her, then dropped away, and as he turned his head, she caught a glimpse of his bitter expression. ''Hero. How droll. And here I thought you had a dash of good sense. Not that being a hero is commendable, for most heroes are lying under dirt and laurel wreaths in some churchyard instead of knocking about above ground. *Hero,* angel? Hardly an apt description. You must have been driven mad by our recent travails.''

''Perhaps I did not mean it as a compliment,'' she said, frowning. ''I never have cared much for heroes, you know. In my experience, they are prone to running about inviting more trouble and danger than is necessary, and forever causing no end of grief and worry for those who love them.''

''Ah. If you did not mean it as a compliment, then of course I am quite pacified.'' He turned back to look at her, and this time there was amusement in his eyes. ''Little goose. There are moments I find you completely irresistible, and those are usually your most lunatic. Which only goes to prove how preposterous I am, I suppose.''

"Yes, I suppose so. So here we are—two witless individuals high on a mountaintop, alone with no one around for miles."

"And freezing to death instead of going inside to sit by a warm fire. An excellent example of lunacy." He stood up and put out his hand for her to take. "Come along, angel. I think it's time we set about sprucing up our tidy little hut into something other than the complete shambles it is now."

It had apparently been some time since anyone had inhabited the stone hut, but the roof was still intact and unbroken shutters swung over the two windows. It was one room, with a half-loft at one end, and a wide hearth at the other, cozy and sturdy enough, if not very elaborate. Lianna set about straightening it, while Cameron built a fire on the stone hearth. Soon it was fairly tidy, if a bit sparse in the way of furnishings. A moss-stuffed mattress, wooden stool, and three-legged table made up all the furniture. Discarded candle stubs were scattered about, but there was a lantern that Cameron had to fiddle with for several minutes before the wick would burn. Rory had seen to it they were well supplied with basic foodstuffs, and Cameron was armed with musket and shot for fresh game. They could retreat here for some time without hardship.

Lianna glanced at him where he sat at the rickety table working with the lantern. He looked so intense, involved, and she smiled. He wore only his shirt and trews, the plaid discarded over the foot of the mattress that would serve as a bed. She had pulled the back of her skirt up between her legs as she had seen women in the village do, tucking it into the front of her waistband to form baggy trousers of a kind and give her freedom of movement. Cameron had eyed her bare legs with a raking glance, his mouth curling in amusement, but said nothing. The effort not to comment was most likely exhausting him. Smiling, she set about stacking supplies in the corner.

"I hope you can cook," Cameron murmured when he had the lantern lit, then gave her a resigned look when she bit her lower lip and shook her head. "I see. Our past weeks should have warned me, but I rather thought it was because of lack of supplies instead of skill that held you back. Well, I shall endeavor to train you properly, angel. By the time we leave here, you'll know how to bake, boil and baste as proficiently as any French chef I know, though it's been a while since I've tried my hand at certain dishes.''

"Mary tried to teach me. I tutored her in reading, and she showed me how to boil bannocks.''

Cameron grimaced. "You don't *boil* bannocks, m'dear. Those are cooked on a griddle. I see your education is sadly lacking in even the most elementary skills.''

Heat warmed her cheeks. "Maybe I meant scones.''

"Ah, perhaps not. Bannocks, baps, or scones, I doubt we have the ingredients for all those delicacies anyway. Rory was able to share only so much from his dwindling supply of meager stores. I imagine we'll have to come up with creative methods of preparing porridge. While we may not have milk for it, there's salt. And some treacle, I think.''

"All the comforts of home,'' she quipped, and he turned to look at her with a strange, almost wistful expression.

"Aye. All the comforts of home, angel.''

There was an odd nuance in his words, a soft regret or melancholy strain that made her move across the room to him. "Cameron—I would rather be here with you than anywhere else in the world.''

He looked away from her. Long beautiful lashes hid his eyes, and there was a definite bitter tilt to his mouth. "You have the oddest notions, angel.''

"Yes, but this isn't one of them. Can't you tell? Don't you know? I mean it, Cameron.'' She inhaled a deep breath for courage, and blurted, "I love you.''

His lashes flew up and he regarded her incredulously. Light from the fire played across his face in shifting patterns. She began to think she had made a terrible mistake saying it, but then he drew her to him. He held her in a crushing grip, pressing her face against his chest and groaning.

"God, angel. You don't mean it.''

"Yes,'' she said against his shirt, "I do mean it. I mean it more than anything else I've ever said. I love you, Cameron MacKenzie.'' His heartbeat was rapid beneath her cheek, his arms taut and slightly shaky. She waited, but he did not say the words back, only tightened his arms around her before drawing away.

While he stood staring down at her, she studied his dark features with trepidation, noting distractedly the spare lines of his face, the beard shadow on his lean jaw, and the fine-chiseled cut of his mouth. His black hair was windblown, tousled into careless disarray, and beneath his lashes, his eyes were gray contemplation. He looked at her sideways.

"You don't really know what love is, angel. Not the kind you're talking about."

"Yes, I do. Don't treat me like a child, curse you. I know what love is, and I know what I feel. And I know what you feel, if you were only brave enough to admit it."

"Do you now." His eyes narrowed. "Why do you think you know how I feel?"

"Because of the way you look at me, and the way you hold me, and the things you have done to keep me safe."

"I'd do that for anyone."

"I don't believe you." Daringly, hopefully, she reached up to take him by the collar, holding him when he would have twisted away as she said softly, "You love me, too, Cameron. Say it. It won't hurt to admit it."

"Won't it?" His hands closed over hers, but he did not pull away. "Angel, everything I've ever loved I've managed to hurt in some way, or to lose it. I have no intentions of dooming you by loving you when you have no idea what it is."

For a moment, she was silent. In a way, he was right. Not about now, but when she'd first met him. Then, for a while, she'd thought she was in love. It had made her feel giddy, reckless, wonderful. But these past weeks with him had shown her how shallow that emotion had been, and easily influenced if she'd thought for even a moment he was capable of murdering his friends. The attraction she had felt for him before had flared hot and bright, leaving her breathless and anxious. He had been right when he'd said it was infatuation.

What she felt now was steady, a deep unwavering emotion. Entangled with her admiration for him, was an awareness of his faults, his sterling qualities, and all the complex facets of his character that made him what he was. And he really was, she decided, a hero. Not flamboyant like Papa and Logan and Morgan, but one of those steady, dependable heroes that quietly went about the business of survival with little fanfare, just determined persistence.

And it occurred to her that the Cameron she had first met had been an illusion, a mocking facade that masked the real man beneath. Or perhaps, in the past two months, she had shed the fictions of the perceived image and come to know the truth. Perhaps not all heroes were blindly reckless, but only masked fear with bravado. Perhaps Papa and her brothers were not as foolishly reckless as she'd always thought, but doing what they must in the only way they knew. It was something to think about.

Now, looking up at him, she smiled confidently. "I know what love is, Cameron MacKenzie. And I know how I feel about you. If you're not ready to hear it, fine. I can wait as long as I have to wait."

With a kind of perplexed expression, Cameron bent to kiss her, cupping her chin in his palm. It was a sweet, gentle kiss, and when he drew back, he rubbed his thumb over her cheek to wipe away a single tear.

"You shatter every misconception I've had about you, angel. Maybe—no, that would only be living on borrowed time." He blew out a short breath, then grimaced. "But hell, what else is life but borrowed time? We're here for such a short while . . . ah God, you make me feel and say things I know I shouldn't, but I love you, too. God help me, I love you, Lianna Fraser."

Chapter 16

The last thing he had expected, was an admission of love. His love, especially. Hers, he had suspected for some time, but assiduously avoided broaching the subject even in his most desperate moments.

But now he had gone and done it.

Oh aye, he was a resolute fellow, wasn't he? Staunch to the bitter end, denying it all . . . Christ. He was an idiot and worse. The words had tripped from his tongue as blithely as if he could do anything about loving her, could give her a home and his name, and everything in the world she should have. He should have anticipated his capitulation, but he hadn't. He'd thought himself stronger than he was, obviously, but all her prattle about heroes and love and other idiocy had apparently turned his brain to mush.

And it certainly didn't help that she was looking up at him as if he truly was a hero, with her wide green eyes and dazzling smile, her lips slightly parted and her arms around him. It was too comfortable, too tempting, and if he didn't stop it now, there would be no turning back. Already, there had been too much between them.

That was the stern directive his brain urged, but his body was urging something entirely different. His body urged surrender. Unconditional surrender. No terms. No debate. Just the delicious yielding that waited for his next move; the touch of his hand, a kiss, and she would be his.

Insanity to allow it, yet, even as he thought it, he knew the die had been cast.

"Angel," he muttered, and kissed her. Heat curled in his belly. He deepened the kiss, heard her soft sigh, and knew he was lost. In a dream, a fatal, inevitable dream, he lifted her in his arms and carried her across the room to the straw mattress scattered with blankets. Her weight was slight in his arms, her body a warm pressure against his chest as he laid her down upon the mattress without breaking their kiss. Her arms were around his neck, holding him, and he slid his hands down her sides to her waist, clutching fists full of material.

She pressed upward with a soft moan, and he leaned forward, drawing up her skirts, loosening the hem from her waist band to pull it free. "You know this is insane," he found the presence of mind to say as he loosened the ties to her skirt and slipped it down her thighs. "Crazy . . . God . . . I must . . . stop . . . so sweet . . ." The last word trailed off into a wordless sound of fervor as his hand encountered bare skin. Her blouse and shift joined the skirt on the floor, and he sat back on his bent knees a moment to gaze at her with mute appreciation. A faint glow from the fire illuminated her.

Soft soft skin, velvet and cream, swelling hips and high, firm thrust of her breasts . . . her breasts. The breath caught in his throat, and he reached out to cup them in his hands. Desecration, to put such dark, callused hands on her luscious white skin, the contrast too vivid. He started to pull away and she stopped him, her fingers lightly circling his wrists.

"Cameron . . . do what you always do," she murmured, and her tongue flicked out to wet her lips, a lightning motion that made him ache more fiercely.

He throbbed all over, wanted her with mindless, headless need, and closing his eyes, he teased the taut peaks of her breasts with thumbs and fingers until she was breathing as heavily as he was. She twisted restlessly beneath his hands, and he opened his eyes.

Loose coppery hair spread over the blankets beneath her head, a silken frame for her lovely face. His breath came in shorter pants for air now, and he looked down at her body to watch what his hands were doing.

"Christ, you're beautiful." His voice sounded rusty and thick. He traced a downward path from her breasts to the dip of her navel with one finger. Circling it slowly, he began the inevitable trip lower, over the slight mound of her belly, to the rich crop of red-gold curls at the apex of her thighs. When his fingers stroked the silky mound, he lost direction for a moment.

Lianna moved restlessly again, her hips arching upward, and her hands eagerly caressing his chest, plucking at his shirt impatiently. He looked up at her, a little dazed, wanting her fiercely.

"Lianna—" God, he sounded hoarse—"You'll have to stop me. I . . . I don't think that this time I can restrain myself. It's a wonder . . . I've held out this long."

A dreamy smile curved her mouth. "We're handfasted, aren't we? At least, everyone thinks we are. I see no reason not to do what other handfasted couples do . . . do you?"

"A hundred reasons, and that's only in the space of a few seconds." He shuddered. "Fine time . . . for you to turn up so . . . willing."

He bent, kissed her again, and lost himself in the taste of her, scent of her, feel of her beneath his hands. It was exquisite torture. And it occurred to him that she was right. Couples were handfasted in the Highlands to ensure an heir would be born, a trial marriage of sorts, with only words spoken in front of a witness to bind them for a year and a day. It was another Highland convenience, and simpler than waiting months for a priest or minister to arrive in remote areas to church them. Malcolm MacDonald could verify that words had been spoken in front of a witness, though not quite as meant, with both of them making the vows, but still . . .

"Cameron?" she arched upward, reaching for him, and he lost all track of rational thought. Feverishly, he removed his clothes, then leaned over her, his hands on her thighs. He glanced up, smiled slightly at the bedazzled glow in her eyes. He kissed her again, and lowered his weight between her thighs until he was cradled closely.

Then, in a slow, leisurely glide, he moved forward, still kissing her, whispering her name against her cheek, her ear, muttering endearments in Gaelic and English, as his body slid inside. She was heated satin, closing around him, and he shuddered at the delicious sensation. Tight, so tight and welcoming, urging him deeper and deeper until he met the thin barrier that kept her virgin. He paused, panting from the strain of holding back when his body clamored for fierce release.

"Cameron . . ." His name was a faint moan on her lips, and he lifted his head to look down at her. Her face was flushed, lips parted and eyes shadowed with anxiety.

"Sweeting . . . am I hurting you?"

"A little bit." A weak smile wavered on her lips, then she put her hands behind his neck and drew his face down for a kiss.

He kissed her deeply, prolonging it until she was arching up against him again. His body throbbed, taut and insistent, and while she was arching upward, he thrust deeply. She stiffened at the sudden intrusion, and he remained still to allow her to adjust.

Firelight wavered over the floor, rosy light and dark shadows billowing in waves like ocean currents. The smell of peat was thick in the air, and outside the wind howled around the stone cottage unceasingly.

Lianna locked her fingers behind his neck. Her eyes closed for a moment. Then she drew her fingers lightly down the hot, damp skin of his throat and chest.

"I love you, Cameron." The words came out in a faint whisper, and she managed a little smile. Then, slowly, she arched upward again, and as he came deeper into her, she found that the first sharp pain had been replaced by only a dull ache.

"And I . . . love you. . . ." His breath was heated against her shoulder, his words husky as he moved against her.

Tilting her head back, she gloried in the increased pressure inside her, the overwhelming sensation of fullness and the friction of his rhythm. She began to move beneath him, arms around him and legs folded over his, her hands moving up and down his bare body, reveling in the taut feel of his muscles beneath her questing fingers, relishing his groans as he possessed her with growing fervor.

Burying her face in his shoulder, she responded to his touch with excited little cries, delighting in his kisses, his thrusts, forgetting everything but the sweet power of their love. This was all that mattered, this joining of body and soul, and she knew that no matter what else happened in her life, she would never have another moment as special as this one.

Cameron groaned, his movements growing faster and faster, and everything around her faded into a dim haze as she met his thrusts with her own until at last he shuddered, his taut muscles trembling with strain before he exploded inside her. Shivering, she clung to him, joyous tears stinging her eyes as he moaned, a long, shuddering sound against her ear.

When he relaxed atop her, his arms still around her and his hard body still pinning her, she closed her eyes and held him tightly. He was hers, and now she was his in the ultimate act of love.

It was worth everything. For the first time, she prayed that they would not have to leave the mountains for a long time— maybe never. Up here, they were together and safe, where no one could part them. And she felt as if she had come home at last.

"Come here, Cat." Dallas Fraser beckoned, and his face was so set that Catriona felt a shiver of apprehension as she joined him in the parlor.

Two men she'd never seen before were there, and from the heather sprigs in the bonnets they held in their hands, she knew they were MacDonalds.

One of them nodded briefly in her direction, then looked back at Dallas. "Do I get the money if I tell wha' I know aboot Cameron MacKenzie?"

"If it leads me to him, yes." Dallas crossed his arms over his chest and rubbed his thumb against the underside of his jaw as he usually did when struggling for self-control. His brow lifted, and his cool blue eyes were steely as he pierced the man with a steady stare. "Tell me where you saw them, Mr. . . ."

"MacDonald, o'course, Dugald MacDonald of Glengarry. I come for me thousand pounds, and I willna tell wha' I know until 'tis given me."

"I am not a fool, sir. I will not blithely hand out money to any man who comes to me claiming they've seen MacKenzie. Already, I've had a round half-dozen claimants at my door, all of them swearing they've seen him only an hour before. Unfortunately, no one could describe him or my daughter, and all the supposed sightings were miles apart. So you see, I am naturally cautious about trusting too quickly."

"Aye. So I see."

From the corner in front of the window, Morgan stood up, his tall frame momentarily blocking the light as he strolled across the parlor toward Dugald. A pleasant smile curved his mouth, and blue eyes very much like his father's gazed quite companionably at the informant.

"Come now, sir, you must know how worried we are about my sister. If you know anything, and can take us to him, you shall be handsomely rewarded, I promise you that. After your claim is verified, you will be able to collect the money from the local magistrate where it is being held. Will that satisfy you?"

Catriona almost smiled. Morgan, with his charm and ingenuous manner, could usually entice anyone to say anything. Dallas claimed he was the child most like his mother in that way, using the considerable force of his appeal as a weapon to get what he wanted. And it usually worked.

After a heavy hesitation and quick glance toward his companion, Dugald nodded slowly. "Aye, 'twill satisfy me well enough. We had MacKenzie caught a fortnight ago, up in the hills by Loch Ericht. He killed our leader and managed to get awa' before we could stop him."

"Really." Dallas curled his arms more tightly around his

body. "How did he manage that, if there were several of you
there? And was my daughter harmed in any way?"

"Didn't know 'twas yer daughter then, of course, but she
looked all right. We thought she was wi' him willing, but tha'
was before we knew the truth of it." He raked a hand across
the bridge of his nose, glanced at his silent companion, then
back to Dallas. "He's a canny one. Had a dirk in his boot tha'
we didna find, and pulled it on us. Killed poor Hugh outright,
then made the lass tie us up. If we had no' done wha' he said,
he would ha' cut her throat as well, he said. We dinna want
to see her hurt, of course."

"Of course."

Catriona listened with growing dismay. Lianna with a man
as brutal as that? Dear God—she was so delicate, not at all
capable of surviving extreme hardship . . . that was why she
had agreed to allow her to remain in Scotland rather than endure
the risks in France, why she had—but never mind that.

"Tell me about my daughter," Catriona said firmly, and
Dugald swung his gaze back to her.

"She be fine. He took her wi' him. But she didna look hurt,
or even surprised when he did wha' he did to Hugh. A bit
scared, 'twas all."

"Describe her, if you please." Dallas lifted a brow at
Dugald's scowling surprise. "Just to be certain we're discussing
the same girl. After all, if this MacKenzie is the rogue everyone
says, he could have any girl with him by now."

"Aye. She be aboot medium height, I think, wi' hair the red
color of the lady's here, and slender, though 'twas hard to tell
wi' the heavy cloak she wore. Her eyes looked to be green,
and her skin pale as summer cream. Mind, we didna get a close
look at her, as she kept her head down mostly."

Catriona reeled slightly. "Did you catch her name?"

"Aye. Lianna, he called her, when he wasn't calling her
something else." He grinned suddenly. "They had a spat, and
she struck him acrost his face and screamed at him like a
fishwife, she did. Told him as how she hoped they'd hang him,
and tha' the earl would gi' him wha' he deserved for taking
her as he did."

Silence fell. Morgan's hands clenched into fists, and Logan muttered something under his breath. The fire popped on the hearth, and finally Dallas cleared his throat.

"Can you lead my sons and me to where you last saw him?"

"Aye, but he willna be there."

"Perhaps not, but we must start somewhere. We can follow their likely route, and question those we pass along the way." Dallas looked up at Catriona, and she returned his gaze with agonizing calmness.

It wasn't until the men had gone that she went to him, her throat almost too tight to force out the words. "It is said that MacKenzie abandoned his post during the massacre, taking Lianna. Perhaps he had a change of heart about the killing, and took her to safety."

"Aye, and perhaps he saw his chance to take her for another reason." Dallas drew in a sharp breath and blew it out again, his eyes so pale with rage as to be almost colorless. He glanced toward Morgan and Logan. "We leave at first light. Be ready."

Logan nodded tightly. "When we find him—"

"He will wish for death," Morgan finished softly, and Dallas nodded agreement with his sons.

"Aye. 'Tis my plan. He will rue the day he took my daughter."

"Dallas—" Catriona put a hand on his arm. "Let me see what I can do in other quarters. If he learns that you are after him, he may . . . may hurt her." Fear squeezed her heart, but her voice was steady as she said, "I don't want to endanger her any more than she may already be, do you understand?"

"No. I have sat and waited long enough. I intend to *do* something other than pace the floor like a caged lion, by God. I will find Lianna, and gut this bastard spawn for his troubles, and I will not be delayed!"

His voice had risen with each word, until he was roaring at her. Catriona lifted a brow and waited. In a moment, he quieted, glaring at her. She smiled. "If you are through filling the ears of everyone in Kinlochleven, I will discuss with you my plans, Dallas."

He said something rude, and Logan and Morgan discreetly

withdrew, leaving them alone in the private parlor. Catriona studied her husband. Dallas paced, looking like the caged lion he'd named a moment before, his golden hair and dark countenance as fierce and regal as any noble jungle beast. She smiled to herself. He still thought deliberate force was the only answer at times, despite years of mediating between kings. Had he learned nothing? But then, he didn't usually feel as helpless as he felt now, and she knew that was part of the reason for his desperate drive to action.

"Dallas, send me messages of your progress, if you will." She saw his surprised glance waver, then turn wary.

"Do you yield in your wish to find other methods, then?"

"No. But one of us might as well use our heads." When he scowled furiously at her, she shrugged and moved to the fire. "I think I shall journey to Fort William and visit with Colonel Hill. Didn't you say that Cameron MacKenzie has a brother imprisoned by the earl?"

"Aye." Dallas paused, then grinned. "You scheming vixen. I see what you're about."

She smiled. "Well, I haven't been an intermediary's wife for so long without learning *some*thing. A little word here, a little word there, and if it's to the right people, one can maneuver circumstances to produce the desired results, isn't that what you always say?"

He came across the room to her, pulling her into his arms. "Aye. And I'm ashamed I didn't think of it myself."

"That's because you prefer action in this kind of situation. Just storm in and overcome is an excellent motto on many occasions, but this seems to be a more delicate matter." She sighed, and ran her finger along the line of his clean-shaven jaw. "And besides, negotiation between kings is not nearly as personal as retrieving a daughter."

Dallas's sigh stirred her hair. He sounded bitter when he said, "I have found that I am not as invulnerable as I once considered myself. It's a damned awkward discovery."

"Yes, my love."

"Cat, has it occurred to you that Breadalbane should have

considered using the outlaw's brother as bait to draw him in? With his devious mind, I would think—"

"It doesn't matter what Breadalbane does. I don't trust him not to kill them all, just to be shed of anyone who opposes him. Well? Do you object to my leaving in the morning to go to Fort William?"

"No, my love. Hill is honorable, if a bit ineffective. Let us hope that between us all, we can bring Lianna safely home again."

Chapter 17

"I'm no blasted hero, curse you."

Lianna smiled. She wriggled against him beneath the blankets, her toes inching along his bare leg. "Good. I detest heroes."

"Then stop trying to make me into one." He scowled and stared up at the ceiling, refusing to be jollied out of his sulks. "We've been waiting near a fortnight for Rory. He should have returned by now."

"Perhaps we are supposed to meet him at Loch Treig."

"No. You heard him. He'll get word to us."

"But if something has happened . . ." Her voice trailed into silence. She didn't want this to be over yet. But she knew how Cameron worried about his brother, knew that he fretted constantly that Breadalbane would hang Jamie before he could prevent it. She turned her head to look at him. "The weather is much better now. Do you think we could go down into the village and learn what we can?"

"Aye." He smiled a little when her brows lifted in surprise at his quick agreement. "But I was thinking more along the lines of me going into the village and you remaining up here in our bird nest where you're safe."

She frowned. "Oh no, Cameron MacKenzie. You're not leaving me behind. I go where you go. I have no intention of staying up here alone. Besides, I could go to the market while we're there."

"The market." His lips twisted slightly into a droll smile. "Silly goose. And how utterly female, to think of shopping instead of survival."

"Don't be silly. Shopping is survival." She propped up on one elbow to scowl down at him. "We could use some milk and cheese, you know, and something other than oatmeal."

"Fresh venison and fish aren't enough for you? Greedy goose."

"I have no complaints about your ability to provide for us quite handsomely, Cameron. It's just that . . . that there are a few things I hadn't realized I'd miss." Her voice grew soft as she thought of hot buttered scones, soft white rolls, a dense slab of roasted beef hot off the spit, and green vegetables . . . oh yes, there were elements of civilization that were definitely missed, though she would not trade one of them for this time with Cameron. Having it all would be paradise.

"Such as boiled bannocks, perhaps?" Cameron slanted her a wicked smile, and she couldn't help a laugh.

"You wretch. I admit I should have known a griddlecake is hardly boiled, but you must acknowledge that I have improved a great deal in my cooking efforts."

"Sweeting, your improvement has been duly noted and appreciated. It is all owed to my extensive instruction, of course, but most impressive."

"You are a man of many talents, Cameron." She smiled back at him, gazing at him in the firelight as if she could not get enough of him. And in truth, she could not. There were moments she woke from a sound sleep reaching out for him, afraid that somehow in the night he had disappeared, or been taken from her. And there were the times she had nightmares, of Glencoe and Mary, of the fight between Cameron and Hugh MacDonald, all mixed up and imbued with a red haze of blood that seemed to permeate everything. On those nights, Cameron held her in his arms, stroking her hair back from her forehead

as he would have a small child's, murmuring gentle, soothing
words to her, telling her that she was safe and he would let
nothing happen to her, holding her until she fell asleep again.

And of course, at night before they slept, he gave her instructions in things other than cooking. It still amazed her, that the
body she had been familiar with all these years could produce
such exquisite sensations when he touched her. The heated
hours under the blankets, with the fire a low hiss on the hearth
and the wind howling outside while they were snugly wrapped
around each other, were the most precious she had ever known.
She had discovered in his arms a passion she had not dreamed
existed, an eagerness and joy, and the end of that restless
longing that had once filled her head and heart with empty
dreams.

She was happy. Insane, she knew, but she was deliriously
content in this small hut tucked into barren rocks with the wind
a constant keening in their ears, and the cold seeping through
cracks, and a monotonous diet of oats and unleavened bread.
Never before would she have thought it could happen, but it
had. It was funny now, to think of how she had considered
Glencoe the most primitive of places on earth, with its stone
cottages and unpaved tracks for roads. Yet, amidst this wilder-
ness, was a majestic beauty that Cameron took pains to show
her, taking her up to a high crag to overlook a breathtaking
view on days when the mist lifted. With the wind tugging
fiercely at her skirts and hair, he would hold her against him,
his arms wrapped around her body and his mouth against her
ear as he pointed out distant landmarks. Once, on an especially
clear day, he had shown her the peak of Ben Nevis in the
distance, the tallest mountain in the Highlands. Fort William
lay in its shadow, and as he held her and went quiet, she knew
that he was thinking of his brother.

Yes, perhaps they should risk going into the village to discover what they could. After all, anything could have happened
to delay Rory. While she would be content to stay here forever,
Cameron would never abandon his brother. And she didn't
expect or want it of him. They could not be happy together
until James MacKenzie was released.

Still propped on her elbow, she rested her head against her palm and studied Cameron. His arms were folded behind his head, his chest bare and gleaming gold above the edge of the blanket. Firelight played across him, and his head turned slightly, his eyes reflecting the glow with a rising light that she had come to recognize.

"It has occurred to me that we could go about as bare as Adam and Eve, and no one would be the wiser," he murmured, and shifted to trace his fingers along the edge of the blanket covering her. "In fact, I've come to think it might be the most efficient in terms of wear and tear on our clothing, even if a bit chilly."

She laughed softly, then caught her breath when his hand moved downward, tugging the blanket from her breasts. His thumb raked across her nipple in an idle stroke that sent shivers down her spine. With a little catch in her voice, she said huskily, "Fig . . . leaves."

His hand paused, hovering over her breasts as he glanced up at her through his long lashes. "Beg pardon?"

"Fig leaves. You know. What Adam and Eve wore in the Garden of Eden."

"Ah." His hand resumed its erotic play over her skin, teasing, exploring, until she was shuddering. "Don't need fig leaves. Dashed nuisances to remove."

His hand shifted to cup her breast, and he levered his body forward, tongue moving across the tight bud of her nipple in damp play. She closed her eyes and sighed as his teeth nibbled along her skin and his lips closed over her nipple. After a moment, he worked his way to the other breast, while his hand skimmed over her body beneath the blankets, familiar and arousing, and deliciously seductive. When his hands slipped down, palms cupping her hips, she rocked against the growing evidence of his arousal. Slowly, she swiveled her hips in a tantalizing message, and felt his instant response.

He rose to his knees, pushing her back down into the blankets, spreading her legs with his knees to lie between them. A faint, satisfied smile lifted one corner of his mouth as he gazed down at her. "Lusty wench."

"Yes." She arched upward against him. "Lusty. Wanton. Lascivious. What of you?"

He laughed softly, and bent to swiftly kiss her mouth. "Licentious. Profligate. Immoral."

"No. That's amoral, isn't it?"

"Not anymore. Since I met you, angel, I care deeply about right and wrong. I prefer being immoral, thank you. It is a much more accurate definition."

"Ah." She curled her arms around his neck to draw him down so that she could kiss his mouth, his jaw, the pulse in the hollow of his throat. "Immorality is more interesting, I suppose. But I had hoped you were cured."

"Not," he said feelingly, skimming his hands over her breasts, "as long as we are together. Immorality is only a word conjured up by the terminally respectable to denote anything they don't have the desire to do anyway, in my opinion."

"Another philosophy lesson? Aristotle would be proud that you could concentrate on such noble ideals when I touch you like this . . ." Her hand slid between their bodies, fingers finding and holding him, moving in sensuous strokes that made him close his eyes and shudder.

"Aristotle," he said between clenched teeth, "be damned."

She explored his length with tiny strokes that made him groan, caressing his heated shape in leisurely glides. There was a tense vibration deep in his chest, a faint quiver to the arms he braced against the mattress, and his head was thrown back, eyes closed and throat muscles corded with strain.

"Enough," he finally muttered, long lashes lifting as he lowered his body. "Enough, before I forget myself."

Slowly, he entered her, a long exquisite slide of his body into hers, and she welcomed him with damp heat and arching hips. The powerful friction of him inside her made her lift into his potent thrusts eagerly, and just out of reach was the promise of release . . . waiting, tantalizing anticipation and delicious deliverance. Tonight, as he lost himself in her body and she lost herself in his, she wanted the same abandon of their first night, the sweet joy of unfettered passion. Since that first night, he had not allowed himself the luxury of releasing inside her again, but would only smile wryly and mutter something about *coitus interruptus,* a term that was self-explanatory.

"You don't want a bairn up here alone, and neither do I, angel," he'd said, and she agreed, but still felt cheated each time he withdrew right before climax. Not that he ever left her frustrated, but there was something so special, so right, about thundering toward that sweet release together that she always felt incomplete.

"No, Cameron," she moaned when she felt him stiffen, his shoulder muscles growing taut beneath her hands as his breath rasped against her ear and he slid away from her. "Please don't . . . not tonight."

He shuddered beneath her hands, but shook his head, his face bent so she couldn't see his expression, could only see the taut slope of his shoulders and the dark disarray of his hair. "You know . . . I cannot . . . angel."

She wriggled her hips, holding him, wanting him deep inside her, striving toward that elusive finish. "I don't care. We'll be married soon anyway, as soon as we can be churched . . . I don't care, Cameron . . ."

"Damn you, I do!" He pulled back, violently, sitting back on his haunches to stare at her with angry frustration. "I have no intention of bringing a child into this world, so you can forget it if that's what you have in mind."

She grew still, the flush of pleasure disappearing. "Is it—?"

"It's nothing you think." He looked away from her, his mouth set in a sulky line, his face sullen. After a moment, he looked back at her, sighing. "It's me, angel, not you. I have nothing to give you, don't you see that? I can never make a proper home for you, never even give you my name, because Breadalbane has taken it all away." He raked a hand through his hair, and his voice was almost pleading when he said softly, "Try to understand. It's not that I don't want to give you all those things. I do. But I no longer have them to give."

"Then we'll get them back."

He gave a harsh laugh. "Naïve little goose. It's not as simple as repossessing a stolen horse or a goat. God, if it was—no. This is all we'll have, I'm afraid. A paltry bed of moss and a

hut so high up not even self-respecting birds will nest here.
You deserve more, much more.''

"But I want you." Her mouth set in a stubborn line, and
she grabbed his arm when he swore softly and started to rise
from the bed. "Don't you even think of giving up. I never
thought you were a coward, Cameron MacKenzie, not you."

Moody anger flashed in his gray eyes, and he shrugged
lightly. "Shows how wrong you can be. I'm a coward through
and through."

"You are not. A coward would have given up long ago."

"There's a deuced lot of difference between a coward and
a man too muddle-witted to know when to quit, angel. Don't
give me virtues I don't have."

"You're no coward," she said staunchly. "Muddle-witted
sounds more correct, but not cowardly."

He laughed at that, though it sounded a little hollow. "And
you're my greatest—only—admirer. All right, sweeting. I may
not fear for myself so much, but I certainly do for you. I don't
know what you'd call that form of cowardice, but it's there,
as big and immovable as Ben Nevis."

"That can definitely be solved. Papa will help us, I know
he will."

"Angel, when *Papa* finds us—and I hope to God he doesn't
find me—I have a notion he will not be in any mood to help.
You'd best put all your energies into praying Rory finds him
before he finds us, rather than trying to make babies we don't
need."

She smiled. "I wasn't trying to make a baby, though I think
one would be nice one day. I just like to hear the things you
say when . . . when you . . ."

Her voice trailed into a suddenly embarrassed silence at his
grin and lifted brow. "What a singular creature you are, Lianna
Fraser. A most uncommon mix of innocence and bawdy sophis-
tication at times."

He kissed her, a lingering caress, then lifted his head to muse
wistfully, "It would be too fortunate if your father were to
give me at least the opportunity to plead Jamie's case, and I

don't count on that. My fortunes have never run to the fortu-
itous.''

"Your fortunes changed the day you met me."

"Aye," he said with real feeling, kissing her again, "I have
to agree with that, angel. That's the only time in my life I have
ever had a blessing fall into my arms from the sky. Usually,
what falls from the sky on me is hardly what I would term a
blessing."

"You rogue," she murmured, laughing a little against his
mouth, "comparing me to bird—"

"Hush." He kissed her, fiercely, and she forgot about everything but the moment and the man in her arms.

Colonel John Hill gazed with a mixture of admiration and
trepidation at the exquisite woman sitting in the governor's
room. Lady Fraser was certainly intimidating, but she was one
of the most beautiful women he had ever seen. Her red-gold
hair was pulled back from her face in the stylish French fashion,
smooth on the top and sides, and gathered into long curls atop
her crown and falling to her shoulders. A band of deep green
ruffles that matched her eyes perched saucily atop her crown
of curls, with filmy green gauze draping from it down each
side of her face to tie in a loose knot on her bodice. Her
striped green and gold gown was also of the latest fashion,
with matching overskirt and deep-ruffled sleeves. She looked—
and acted—more like a duchess than a baron's wife.

"How may I help you, Lady Fraser?" Hill regarded her
politely as he took his place behind his desk, preferring the
familiar comfort of an emblem of his authority between them.
He had no illusions that she would discover what she could
about her daughter by any possible means, and he could not
blame her. But whatever could he say?

"You have spoken to my husband recently, I understand."
She smiled, and went on without waiting for a reply. "It has
come to our attention that our daughter is in the company of
a man named Cameron MacKenzie, and that this man has a
brother in government custody. Are these facts correct?"

Nonplussed, Hill nodded. "Yes, but I cannot see how that pertains to—"

"As I am certain you are also aware, the earl of Breadalbane holds the key to the imprisoned man's cell. It seems to me quite extraordinary that no one has thought to put it about that if my daughter is not returned swiftly and unharmed, this young man will be executed without delay. If nothing else, it should certainly bring about her return, do you not think so, Colonel Hill?"

At a loss, Hill stared at her helplessly. "My dear Lady Fraser, while I admit to the veracity of your estimation of the affair, I'm afraid that my hands are tied in the matter. James MacKenzie is not in my jurisdiction, but answerable to the earl. Perhaps if you—"

"But MacKenzie is here at Fort William, is he not?" Sharp green eyes gazed steadily at him, piercing him so that he could not look away and could only nod. "I thought so. Therefore, it would hardly be a viable option to return him to the earl if he is already here."

"My dear Lady Fraser, you must understand . . . the earl sent him here as a prisoner, until the matter of the stolen horse and the other accusations against him are cleared. I do not have the authority to use the prisoner as a lure to draw in Cameron MacKenzie, if indeed, it is even viable. You see, I do not necessarily believe the charges made against either of the Mac-Kenzies."

It was a bitter admission, made more bitter by the fact that he was certain he was right yet had to yield to the earl. Another case of justice gone awry, as in Glencoe.

Catriona Fraser fixed him with a keen stare, and leaned forward, her voice lowering. "I do not suggest you actually carry out the execution, Colonel, of course. Only the threat of it should be enough to bring him in."

"Yes, I realize that, but—what if something should go wrong? I hardly want to be responsible, now."

"Colonel, I believe you are a good man, and a man of shrewd judgement. What do you think of Cameron MacKenzie?"

He hesitated. Danger lurked in admitting too much, and he

was old and tired. But the massacre of Glencoe weighed heavily on his mind and heart, and he longed fiercely for justice to be done in the matter. So many lives had been destroyed or shattered, and now he had the opportunity to lessen the burden for one of the survivors of that terrible tragedy. Could he risk his pension and reputation by telling what he knew?

Finally he said, "Cameron MacKenzie was always a just man, in my opinion. I do not think the charges of treason and abandoning his post are true. There are most likely extenuating circumstances that caused him to desert his company as he did, and I am certain that if he could be found, he would tell the truth of it."

"Yes, yes, but is he the kind of man to abduct a young girl? Perhaps—harm her?"

It did not escape Hill's notice that Lady Fraser's knuckles were white where she gripped a small satin reticule, and he sighed. "It's difficult to know the true nature of a man by only chance meetings, but—no. I do not think him capable of causing harm to innocents, no matter the charges against him. This most recent charge of murdering Hugh MacDonald is a grievous one, however, and until more facts are known, cannot be dismissed out of hand."

"He is hunted far and wide, yet no one has offered information." Lady Fraser shrugged slightly. "Other than those seeking the offered reward, of course, and I am never convinced of the validity of those claims."

"Yes, you are wise to be skeptical." Hill hesitated. "Lady Fraser, forgive me, but—if it happens that your daughter has merely run off with MacKenzie, what—"

"Lianna would never do such a thing." Her eyes flashed angrily. "She cares more about her family than that, and would not leave us in suspense for so long, not knowing if she is alive. No, she must have been taken, but I am glad to hear that you do not consider him a cruel man to women. It does ease my mind and heart. Now." She sat forward. "We must put it out that MacKenzie's brother will hang unless he brings Lianna home at once."

Colonel Hill realized that he was no match for this determined woman, and thought wearily and longingly of the pension being dangled like a cart-horse carrot over his nose. But, Dallas Fraser was a man with great influence, and if he helped him, then there was a chance Fraser would return the favor.

"Very well, Lady Fraser. I will see what I can do."

She smiled. "Excellent. I am certain that my husband will be quite delighted to show his appreciation properly once I tell him how cooperative you have been, Colonel."

"No doubt. I can only hope that I am still alive to properly receive this appreciation."

Catriona laughed softly. "Oh, you will be, sir, I can almost promise. Dallas never fails. Never."

It was a prophetic statement, Catriona thought later as she sat in the small inn room she had rented in nearby Inverlochy. She twisted her hands together, staring at her visitor. She could not recall the last time Dallas had failed in something he set out to do, save for the ongoing wrangle between James and William, and that was hardly something that was in his hands alone. No, he would find Lianna and MacKenzie, as he had said he would, yet she now prayed that he would not succeed.

Rory MacDonald stared at her with distress. "Lady Fraser— och, 'tis hard for my tongue to form tha', as I have always known ye as Catriona, but I will try."

She smiled slightly. "Never mind formalities. Just tell me where you think they are now."

Rory shrugged. "I left them in a bothie high atop Stob Choire Claurigh, but tha' was over a fortnight ago. By now, Cameron may have wearied of waiting and come down to see wha' he can discover on his own." He shook his head, worried creases in his forehead. "Can ye no' stop yer husband from his intention, Catriona?"

"I'd have to find him first, Rory." She surged to her feet, wringing her hands. "I'm glad to know this MacKenzie is a decent man and that Lianna is fine, but are you certain she is safe with him?"

"Aye. He wanted her to be escorted to you, but she refused to leave him, my lady. She said he was safer if she stayed with him, for he might be shot on sight if no'. I canna say she was wrong, and if I had thought she was unsafe wi' him, I would have no' let her go.'' He paused, then said softly, ''I think they care much for one another, and I dinna think he would ever let harm come to her as long as he draws breath.''

''Aye, but how long will he draw breath once Dallas finds him?'' Catriona paced the floor, then whirled around with a horrified cry. ''Oh God! I ha' set a trap for him if he comes to Fort William—if he isna wha' I thought . . .'' She drew in a shaky breath and swallowed hard to regain control. ''I must stop Colonel Hill at once. If I don't—''

Rory's eyes were grave, and he nodded. ''Aye, my lady, if ye dinna stop it, ye may lose them both, for Breadalbane has set his soldiers on the hunt as well. If MacKenzie falls into your trap, the earl willna hesitate to slay either of them if it suits his purpose.''

Catriona gripped her hands tightly together, but did not cry out again. ''Yes. You are right, of course. I must hurry—Rory, do you think you can find them?''

''I will go straightaway to where I left them, my lady, and pray tha' they have no' yet gone. But I canna promise tha' I will make it there before Cameron decides I canna return and comes down to help his brother. If I had been able to find ye sooner, we would have had enough time, but now I dinna know. 'Tis been over a fortnight, and I was to return within a sennight.''

''Godspeed, Rory MacDonald, and do your best. I will go to Colonel Hill first, then find my husband. He is with Dugald MacDonald, and they—''

''Dugald MacDonald of the Glengarry bunch? Oh Lady Fraser, tha' man is no good. I hope yer husband has no' believed anything he may ha' to say.''

She swallowed the lump of apprehension in her throat. ''I am afraid that we both did. Dear God. Pray that we are both in time.''

Lianna reached with a shaky hand for the handbill tacked to the wall of the village marketplace. Her first impulse was to pull the parchment down and tear it up, but she knew she could not. But still, her insides quivered with the awareness that now everything was changed, their idyll ended and reality a harsh intrusion. She took a deep breath.

"Cameron—read this."

He took the handbill she had pulled down, a brow slightly lifted. "Another advertisement for silks or ribbons, sweeting? I see my pockets shall be to let soon if you continue to—"

She stood silently, throat aching as he scanned the handbill. Then he swore softly in Gaelic, crushing the parchment in his hand. For a long moment, he stood on the paving stones of the village street, his throat working. Then he looked up at her, and she knew.

"Cameron—"

"I must go, Lianna. Do not try to stop me. They hang Jamie in a fortnight. I cannot let them, when it is me the earl really wants."

Weakly, half-sobbing, she clung to his shirt heedless of the stares of passersby. Cameron slung his arm around her shoulders and ushered her into the narrow alleyway that ran between two-story shops. She pressed her face against his chest.

"Oh, why must you be a hero? Can't you just—there must be another way, Cameron, there must. If I can just go to Papa—"

"No. Nothing will satisfy Campbell but that I surrender to him. Now that he has definite charges against me, he will not need Jamie as a hostage any longer."

"But why, why does he hate you so?" she wailed, and wiped her eyes on the edge of her cloak. "I don't understand why he would go to such lengths to hurt you."

"It's his nature. Campbell has long had a reputation for thievery and murder. He rids himself of anyone ho has earned his enmity or is an obstacle to what he wants. Once, I was an obstacle—and worse, I discovered something about him that he doesn't want known."

Moaning, she rubbed her face with her cloak. "Cameron, if you will only let me—"

He lifted her face to his, hands gently squeezing each cheek

"No, Lianna. There's no time, and it would be useless anyway. I was only deceiving myself when I entertained even the slightest hope otherwise. Christ, when I think what an idiot I've been, and how much time I've wasted for poor Jamie sitting in that cell wondering if each day is to be his last—but then, if I had given up to Breadalbane long ago, I would never have met you, so I cannot say I regret these past months."

Curling her hands into his shirt, she said fiercely, "I will not let you die, Cameron MacKenzie. I will not! If I have to . . to kill the earl myself, I won't allow it!"

"Vicious little goose," he murmured, and pressed a kiss on the tip of her nose. "I've no time to lose. I must get to Fort William."

She drew back, drying her tears, and nodded. "Yes. I'll do my best to keep up."

"No, angel. Not this time. You must stay here where you're safe."

"They'll kill you if they find you. And who will keep me safe if I'm here alone?" She put a hand on his arm when he scowled. "Cameron—let me come with you."

"We seem to have recurring versions of this same damn argument," he muttered resignedly. "You will be safer in this village. I'll leave word—"

"Curse you, Cameron MacKenzie, if you insist upon being the noble hero, you can let me come with you!"

"Hero? This has nothing to do with heroics, beauty. If it has to do with anything other than responsibility to my brother, it is love and loyalty. Not even kings can regulate those emotions, or at least, they have not yet found a suitable method of regulating them successfully. I think even your father would agree with that, and it is his business to see both sides of the issues." He wiped a hand over his face, and glanced toward the mouth of the alley. "It grows late. I will need to take untraveled roads to get there without being caught, so I've no time for more discussion. For once, do what I ask you and stay here."

She studied his face in the gray light of the alley, and fought the urge to weep again. A feeling of impending doom descended on her, but she had already made her choice. There was no other reply she could give him, but the answer from her heart.

"Cameron, you are my life, my love, and I will go where you go if it costs me everything. Without you, I do not exist."

She said it so quietly he bent his head to hear her, and he made a soft noise in the back of his throat before clasping her to him. His embrace was fierce, his voice tortured. "God, angel, I don't deserve you. Or maybe I do. For it will be sheer torment worrying about you every step of the way."

"Then you'll let me come?"

"Aye. And I pray to God that we both don't regret it."

"We won't, Cameron. I have enough faith for both of us. We will not regret anything that happens as long as we are together."

Chapter 18

The heavy mist that had been hanging over the mountains lifted finally, just before the sun set. Cameron stared at the deep rose, purple, and blue sky without really seeing it for a time, then roused himself. He was only postponing the inevitable, of course. Once they reached Fort William, he would have to deliver Lianna into the protective custody of Colonel Hill until her parents could arrive. It was the best he could do for her, and it gave him precious few hours to spend with her before he had to give her up. By tomorrow noon, they would be at Fort William, and he would lose her.

But he would give Jamie a chance, if he could manage to strike a bargain with Breadalbane. A thin smile curved his mouth. He had one last trick in his bag, and he intended to play it, a last desperate attempt to save everything. He had always known that it would come down to something like this, though he had never guessed it would involve a woman. Once the card was played, the game would be over, and if he was not careful, he would lose it all.

Lianna came toward him, a bunch of flowers in her hand, wild buttercups, sprigs of sweetly scented woodbine, and delicate sprays of spring violets. "Aren't they lovely? Here in the

glen, it's so much warmer than up in the mountains.'' She
buried her nose in the bouquet and breathed deeply. ''It is hard
to think that 'tis already May.''

''Aye. The flowers are almost as lovely as you, angel.''

She laughed. ''I saw my reflection in the river. I know better
I look a fright, with my hair so wild and my skin all chapped
I miss my salve.'' She paused, and her face grew sad. ''Mary
always thought it so pretentious of me to use salve for my face
and hands. She would laugh . . . if she saw me now.''

Cameron recognized the little break in her voice, and put an
arm around her shoulders. ''She would be quite proud of the
calluses you've acquired on your hands, don't you think? They
would rival even Mary's for thickness, though I do think per
haps she would win out for longevity.''

''You always know what to say, though at times, I am sure
you say things for base meanness.''

''I'm wounded, my love, that you would think me so cruel.'
He squeezed her shoulders, and plucked one of the buttercup
from the bouquet to stick into the hair over her ear. ''There
Now no one will notice your chapped skin.''

''Wretch.''

She smiled at him, the reaction he wanted, and he grinned
back at her. No point in going maudlin now. There would be
time enough later for that kind of nonsense.

Ben Nevis towered above them, and it was going to be
deuced grueling walk getting to Fort William by the back way
To go around would take too much time, and he would have
to risk capture if he took the main road that led through Glen
Nevis. So, he chose the little-traveled path, hoping that no one
would look for him this close to Fort William.

''Cameron—look.''

He glanced around, warned by the odd note of strain i
Lianna's voice, groping for his musket and sword. Two men
came through the blue shadows thrown by the mountain, and as
they drew closer, he recognized John and Alasdair MacDonald
MacIan's sons. He went still. No doubt, they would think as
everyone else did that he had betrayed them, but for the life
of him, he could not bear to draw a weapon.

Alasdair spoke first, eying Cameron from the soft gloom of the shadows. "It has been a bitter road since last we met, Cameron MacKenzie."

"Aye. That it has, Sandy." He relaxed slightly. There was no enmity in his eyes or voice, only a great sadness. Lianna remained silent, clutching her bunch of flowers, staring at them, and Cameron reached out to draw her close. "You will remember Lianna Fraser, do you not? Catriona's daughter."

John nodded. "Aye, we remember her. I am glad to see she has survived."

"It was not easy." Cameron did not release his grip on her arm when she shrank back. "Mary died that day, as did Robbie and Colin. Have you heard anything else of her kin?"

"Aye. Morag managed to escape to the Stewarts of Appin, along with several others."

Cameron paused. "What of your mother? Lady Glencoe?"

Sandy spoke when John could not. "She died on the road to Glen Ure, sorely abused by Glenlyon's soldiers."

"It was Barber," Cameron said softly. "I saw them. I was there, Sandy. My face was the last MacIan saw that night, though God help me, I tried to stop it."

For a moment there was taut silence, then Sandy sighed softly. "I am glad that our father's last sight was of a friend's face. Duncan Don told us of what was done to you, Cameron. Near forty perished in the glen that night, and at least that many died fleeing in the blizzard." He paused, swallowed, and shook his head.

John looked up, his face pale. "I should have known, should have suspected—I couldna sleep, you see. I heard something that I know now were the shots that killed my father. But then I didna know. I even dressed and went to Glenlyon, who greeted me cheerfully enough, and said he was off after those of Glengarry. He laughed—*laughed*—and said it was not likely he would lift his hand against his good friends of Glencoe. I went home to bed, and knew naught until my servant woke me an hour later and told me he had seen twenty redcoats with fixed bayonets approaching. I barely escaped to the screes of Meall Mor."

"And there he found me," Alasdair said heavily. "My gillie also woke me, saying he'd seen soldiers with bayonets going toward John's house. I canna say I didna expect it, for I had long dreaded the moment this would come. I hid my family in a place I had already made for them, and took to the hills. We could hear the musket fire below us, could hear the screams and see the flames . . . and when it was done, while the ravens came to finish it all off, I could hear Glenlyon's pipes from the shores of Loch Leven. They played 'The Glen is Mine'. . . ."

His words ended in a bitter whisper, and it was John who said, "It was grim work, but even Glenlyon is said to have tired of it. Captain Drummond did not, but then, he is Breadalbane's henchman. 'Tis said Drummond looked most closely for you, MacKenzie."

"Aye, I've no doubt of that." Cameron managed a wry smile. "The earl wants me dead badly enough."

"So we hear." John exchanged glances with Sandy, then said, "Fort William is not the place for you to go right now."

"I know. But I've no choice. Breadalbane holds my brother."

Both men nodded understanding, but Lianna made a soft sound of distress. To prevent her protests, he asked Sandy, "Are you going to settle elsewhere?"

"No. Glencoe is our home. We have been back, a few of us, to bury the dead and see what can be salvaged."

"Do you intend to return to Glencoe to settle?"

"Aye. We have just come from Fort William, where Colonel Hill has granted protection to us. It was approved by the Scottish Privy Council, but I've been under this government's protection before, so I am not certain I trust in it." He sighed. "But still, we want to go home, to rebuild."

Cameron hesitated, then shrugged. "And while in Fort William, did you hear news of my brother?"

"Aye. But I am thinking you already know he is to be hung a sennight hence."

It felt as if someone was standing on his chest, squeezing all the air out of his lungs, but Cameron managed a casual nod. "Aye. I knew."

"Breadalbane's doing, Cameron."

"I know that, too, Sandy." He looked at Lianna. She could have been made of wax for all the life she displayed, stark still and stiff, still holding those damned flowers in her hand though they had begun to droop. He relented at the numb misery in her face. "But I have a notion the earl will want to hear a scrap or two of beneficial information I have for him before he cuts up too badly."

Lianna looked up at him, blinking. "What is that?"

He squeezed her shoulders. "Nothing that I feel should be shared until the last possible moment, sweeting, but do not despair. I am not without my tricks." There was such a relieved light in her eyes that he felt almost guilty at giving her false hope. He well knew that the moment Breadalbane had those papers in hand, he would not hesitate to rid himself of Cameron. He harbored no illusions about his own fate. But first, he intended to ensure the safety of those he loved.

John and Alasdair stayed with them that night, talking around the fire until far into the night before rolling up in blankets on the hard ground. Cameron held Lianna close to him, savoring the feel of her next to him, the scent of her hair, and the soft sounds she made while she slept. He thought of all he'd done in life, the good and the bad, the necessary and unnecessary, and knew that when it came down to it, the event that would stand out the brightest in his mind as he died would be the day Lianna had tumbled into his arms from heaven. His angel, complete with wobbly wings. His light, his love, and though others might be able to take his life from him, they could never erase the memories.

It was their last morning together, and Cameron woke first, holding her to him briefly before he rose from their blankets and joined John and Sandy by the fire. He was alone when Lianna awoke, stumbling from the blankets to blink at him sleepily as she asked about MacIan's sons.

"They've gone on to Glencoe. Here. Have some bread and cheese while I walk down to the burn to wash up." He grimaced slightly. "A bath is long overdue, I think, and the day promises to be fair enough that I won't freeze."

Smiling at him, Lianna plopped down on a flat rock near the fire. "Shall I come with you to wash your back?"

"Oh no. I'm afraid we'll never get to Fort William if we begin cavorting in the water like fish, my sweet. You have a most enticing way of making a man forget all about his duties."

"I try."

"Aye," he said appreciatively, "and succeed most admirably." He rose to his feet, gazing down at her. "I'll be close enough to hear you if you call out, so don't fret about being in danger."

She tore off a chunk of bread and stuffed it into her mouth, nodding. The seductive tumble of her loose hair around her shoulders and into her sleepy eyes made him almost forget that he needed a bath. It did, however, remind him that icy-cold water would solve the pressing problem of his damnable lust for her. Really. He felt like a schoolboy at times, his body rising to even the suggestion of having her. It was embarrassing, but there it was. And he heard himself proposing that if she really wanted to wash his back, she knew where to find him.

Lianna laughed softly, hugging the blanket more closely around her shoulders as she looked up at him. "Rogue. Do you think I needed an invitation? Besides, I want to bathe as well, and put on the new clothes you bought for me. I might as well look my best when we arrive at Fort William."

"Sweetheart, you never look anything but the best." He bent to scoop up his clothes and a blanket scrap for drying, feeling awkward and damnably young. Incredible, how she could do that to him at times, make him feel strange to himself, like another person instead of the villainous sort he really was. He rather enjoyed it.

Mist lay heavily on the ground, shrouding trees and rocks, a gauzy veil that almost obscured the faint path that led down to the burn. Water channeled through a tumble of rocks, washing over rock and ground in a swift icy current. Cameron shrugged out of his clothes and stepped into the burn, sucking in a sharp breath at the shock of cold water. Trees crowded the bank on one side, and filtered light lit the shallow river; birds fluttered in the branches overhead with noisy abandon.

It was peaceful and quiet, with the only turbulence in his thoughts. If not for Lianna, he would almost welcome the end of the struggle that loomed ahead. But he had little faith that he would be able to bring Breadalbane to heel, for the wily earl always seemed to survive scandal and justice.

This time, the evidence he had against Breadalbane would be used. God knew, he'd managed to keep it from him this long, knowing that there would be a time to use it to save Jamie's life as well as his own. That time had come.

He laid back in the water and closed his eyes for a moment, listening to the rush of the water over rocks, the wind through the intertwined tree branches overhead, and the noisy chatter of birds. Peaceful. He floated, in a rare suspension of time and place, cognizant of his own mortality and vulnerability, yet achingly aware that it would soon cease to matter.

An alien sound intruded into his thoughts, and he tensed before realizing it would be Lianna. Enchanting little creature, all soft skin and delectable curves, inciting him to radical, irrational actions at times. He relaxed again and waited for her to join him, eyes closed, floating blindly in the water, anticipating most delicious moments, final memories to hold on to when the end came.

A splashing sounded near him, muffled by the water in his ears, and he opened his eyes, blinking away water-blur. "Step carefully, Lianna, there's a drop-off near the edge right past—"

"Lianna won't be coming, you bloody sod," a deep voice snarled, and the blurred figure reaching down for him blotted out the trees and sky and light.

Harsh hands grabbed him from the other side, and shaking the water from his eyes and cursing himself for ignoring caution, Cameron braced for the inevitable. Bandits, for God's sake, and—no. No bandit would say *Lianna* so familiarly, as if they knew her.

Then there was no time to wonder about them, as he was thrust beneath the water's surface and held there until he had presence of mind to stop futilely thrashing. When he went limp, he was brought to the surface, and barely had time enough to draw a choking, watery breath before he was ducked again, strong hands holding him down. Bloody hell, they meant to drown him slowly. His lungs hurt from the lack of air, and black spots began to dance before his eyes in a strange, watery pattern. Strangling, his body rejected his brain's order to remain calm and began to struggle for air. His muscles jerked as he twisted into uncontrollable spasms against the hands holding him down, and his lips opened involuntarily. Water gushed in, filling mouth and nose and world, and he thought of Lianna, and hoped that she would find happiness once he was gone from her life. Drowning was said to be a peaceful death, once one gave up the struggle. Maybe it was the easiest way for all of them, after all. Then he thought of Jamie languishing in prison, and his body rebelled of its own volition.

He began to fight. Surging up, he managed to break free of one of them, and struggled to his feet, slipping a little on the river bottom, but at least able to draw in a gurgling breath. Water clogged his lashes and obscured his vision; he struck out blindly, and heard a yelp and a curse. Then he was grabbed again, harshly, hands slipping on his bare wet skin and giving him small advantage. More curses sounded in his ears, breathless and angry, and he lashed out with a fist in the direction of sound and made brutal contact with a body. There was a grunt, then another snarled oath, and he was brought up short by the cold press of steel against his bare belly.

"Move and you'll die right here."

Panting for air, Cameron went still, arms spread out to the sides. He was jerked forward then, one on each side, the dirk a sharp pricking reminder on his ribs.

Peering at his assailants as he was hauled from the water, he had a smeared view of two burly young men with light blond hair and angry faces. Coughing and spitting out water, Cameron wheezed as he was pushed to his knees on the banks, "Fraser, by chance?"

"Aye, you bloody bastard. Lianna's brothers. And there is no use denying you are MacKenzie."

"I wouldn't dream of it." He coughed again, a strangled sound. A shiver contracted his muscles, and he leaned forward, his palms on his spread thighs, shuddering at the cold air and effects of near drowning. He looked up through his wet lashes. "Mind if I dress? It's a bit cool with no clothes."

"You'll be warm enough in hell, MacKenzie."

His mouth twisted. "Right-ho. But I'm not there yet, and if you want vengeance, it would be a sight more effective if I was capable of feeling it."

"Oh, you'll feel it, MacKenzie. You'll feel it."

The tone of his voice was only a brief warning, and Cameron's guts spasmed instinctively as one of the Frasers grabbed his shoulder and drew back a fist to plow it into his belly. All the scant air left his lungs in an explosive gust, and sparks flew in front of his eyes, tiny firefly dots lighting black waves of pain. He couldn't breathe, couldn't see, could only resist the smothering swells of agony that washed over him in suffocating torrents.

Over the throbbing surge of pain, he heard Fraser say, "We'll keep you alive a while, MacKenzie, long enough for you to wish you had never taken our sister."

Cameron wanted to reply, but his body wouldn't cooperate. No words would form properly, and his tongue ached where he must have bitten it. There was the rusty taste of blood in his mouth. Not that words would help anyway. No explanations would satisfy these Frasers. They were the kind of men appeased only by blood. Heroes. Real heroes, not the fraudulent sham that he was, though he'd tried often enough to convince Lianna of the truth. She only thought she didn't want heroes. He knew better. She'd been weaned on them.

Blinking, his vision finally cleared enough that he could see both young men watching him. There was a taut wariness about them, a sense of barely controlled anger, and he could understand their rage. His gaze shifted, and he saw the loosely clasped fist of the tallest Fraser. Briefly wishing he hadn't been so careless, he braced himself for the inevitable.

The young man leaned down, his other hand gripping Cameron's shoulder again. The powerful blow doubled him over, and his muscles contracted in helpless reaction. His entire body burned, a white-hot ache that was compounded by another blow, and another, until he heard faint sounds of misery and realized they were his own. He tried to focus, but everything was a blur, the near-drowning and smashing blows blending together in a painful whirl of impressions that left him floundering for consciousness.

From the depths of the darkness creeping closer, he heard someone say, "Enough, Logan. You'll kill him."

Yes. They would. Strangely, it didn't seem to matter any more.

Lianna whirled around, eyes widening as she recognized the man approaching through the early morning mist. A hazy shaft of sunlight pierced the trees overhead, illuminating pale hair. Tall, blond, with shoulders she had once thought the broadest in the world, he appeared at the ridge of the misty wooded path like a dream—or an apparition.

"Papa?"

"Thank God." Dallas Fraser strode swiftly toward her, almost running the last few steps as Lianna stood hesitantly, and when he reached her, lifted her into his arms and held her tightly. "Are you all right, Lianna?"

As disbelief faded, she hugged him tightly, her voice muffled against his collar and neck, tears stinging her eyes. "Yes, Papa. I'm fine. Oh Papa, I'm so glad to see you! I hoped I would find you, hoped you would come—they're dead, you know. Mary, Robbie, Uncle Colin—all dead. It was horrible . . ." A sob broke into her words, and she quivered as he held her so tightly against him she could barely breathe. "Everyone died, even my kitten, Papa. And for a while, I thought I would die— I didn't know why I was still alive until Cameron came . . . Did you get our message?"

For a moment his embrace tightened, then he released her and let her down slowly, keeping one arm around her shoulders. "So you did try to send a message. We hoped you would find a way, but weren't certain you could manage it."

A tremor of apprehension went through her, and she looked

up at him, smiling a little hopefully. "You did talk to Rory MacDonald, didn't you?"

Dallas shook his head. The relief in his eyes was heartwarming, the slight quiver in his voice betraying. "No, sweetheart. He wasn't able to get any message to me. If not for Hugh MacDonald's cousin, we would not know you were still alive. He—"

"Hugh MacDonald." She fairly spat the name, and shook her head vigorously. "I hope you didn't listen to anything his cousin had to say, or believe any of it."

Dallas frowned. His hand remained on her shoulder, and his fingers tightened. "What do you mean?"

"Just that Hugh MacDonald was going to turn us over to Breadalbane for a ransom, that's all. He was utterly despicable, and I'm glad . . . *glad* that Cameron killed him."

For a moment, Papa was quiet. "Did MacDonald harm you, Lianna? Tell me if he did, and so help me, I'll—"

"No, no. But he would have if Cameron had not killed him, I think. He was . . . wicked. And I was foolish enough to invite him in . . . but I discovered quickly that he meant us harm." She sagged against her father, drawing strength from his strong presence. "I'm so glad you found us. Now you can help Cameron rescue his brother from the earl, and—"

"Do you mean Cameron MacKenzie?" He had stiffened, and she drew back to gaze up at him with growing apprehension.

"Yes. Of course. Oh, I know you have not talked to Rory, but we sent him to find you hoping that you would help."

"I intend to help you."

Lianna smiled with relief. "Oh, Papa, I knew you would! I told Cameron you would help, but he thought you would be too angry that he was with me to want to help him, and—"

"He was right."

A heavy silence fell, and she felt a flutter of fear at her father's cold tone. Anxiously, she put her hands on his chest, noting the pistols in his belt and the sword at his side. "Papa, surely you don't think he meant to harm me, do you?"

Dallas dragged a hand through her loose hair, gently but firmly, patting her head as if to soothe her. "All that matters is that you're safe now, kitten. You don't have to say anything you don't want to say, or make any pretenses. I don't care what he did, you're still my little girl. And I'll kill the first man who dares say anything to you in my presence—''

"Papa." She curled her hands into the leather sword strap across his chest. "Listen to me—Cameron did not hurt me. Do you hear me? He rescued me. He saved me in a blizzard after the massacre, and tried to save Mary, but it was too late for her. He *did not abduct me*. Are you listening?''

Dallas's eyes were cold and flinty, and she saw that he had already dismissed her protests as fear or humiliation. Desperation tinged her voice, and she gave him a little shake, though it was like trying to shake an oak. "Cameron rescued me, Papa. I would have died if he had not found me. Do you hear?''

"I hear, kitten." His old pet name for her—Cat's kitten, he'd always teased—sounded stiff on his lips, and she stared up at him helplessly as he said, "You don't have to defend him anymore. I intend to see him punished for what he's done, and you don't have to say a thing. I'll take care of it.''

"No, no . . ." The words came out in a moan. "You don't understand. Where is Mama? She'll listen . . . she'll believe me. Where is my mother?''

Clumsily patting her head, fingers raking through her hair, Dallas said softly, "She's waiting for you at Fort William. I'll take you to your mother, kitten, as soon as I have dealt with Cameron MacKenzie. I see no need for a trial, not since even Breadalbane has put a price on his head dead or alive.''

Clenching her hands into fists, she beat on her father's chest furiously, startling him as she screamed, "I won't let you hurt him! You've got to listen to me, got to help us . . . oh, he was right and I should have known it . . . he has been right about everything when I thought he was only being cynical and suspicious . . . I should have listened, should have listened. . . .''

Sobbing, she barely noticed when her father curled his hands around her wrists to still her frantic pounding against him. She sagged against him, whimpering that he had to listen.

And then she heard curses behind her and pushed away from her father, turning to see Logan and Morgan approaching from the direction of the river. They were half-dragging something, and it wasn't until they emerged from the mist that still clung to the woodland path and into the clearing that she recognized Cameron. His dark hair was wet and plastered to his head, and he wore only his trews. Bruises marked his face, and blood from cuts smeared his jaw and mouth. He could barely walk, and only stumbled between them, his breath a harsh rasping sound in his throat. She cried out in horror, and would have run to him but her father grabbed her by the arm and held tightly.

"Stay here, Lianna."

There was a cold finality in his words, but she turned on him fiercely. "I will not! How dare you! Look at him—what have they done to his face? He's so bruised and bloody and there's no reason for it, if you'd only listen to me."

"I have listened to you, and I understand why you are saying these things, but it doesn't change anything." Dallas looked up when Logan and Morgan flung Cameron to the ground. "Tie him to that tree, then take your sister back down to the river and let her wash her face."

Cold terror seeped through her. Cameron looked up, a knowing twist to his mouth. She stared at him, and he managed a faint smile for her. "It's . . . all right . . . angel." His voice was a painful grating whisper, but she heard the love in it and wanted to fling herself on the ground beside him.

No. It wasn't all right. Papa intended to kill him the moment she was taken out of sight. God, what could she do? She knew her father well enough to know that he was convinced he was doing the right thing, and he would never retreat unless— unless she could force him to wait long enough to prove to him that he was wrong.

Whirling around, shaking Morgan's restraining hands loose as he tried to grab her, Lianna threw herself to the ground in front of Cameron. On her knees, with her chin tilted defiantly as she faced her father, she said in a loud, clear voice, "You cannot kill my unborn child's father."

Chapter 19

Stunned silence followed her wild announcement. Cameron blinked. The beating had affected his hearing. His eyes were still cloudy with water and pain as he studied her. Even in the skirt and blouse she looked as healthy as ever. How would she know if she was pregnant? It had been only a fortnight since . . . the little minx. She couldn't possibly know. It was a ruse, and a damnably clever one, given the circumstances and shock. But he could not allow her to risk herself for him this way, not even to save his life.

Lianna glanced at him quickly, frowning when he tried to speak, and put a hand on his arm. "I have to tell, Cameron. After all—you want to be alive to save your brother, don't you?"

Of course he did. God, his head hurt. His mouth hurt, his belly hurt—even his toenails hurt. He couldn't think. He wanted to deny her words, but then, she might very well be pregnant, after all. He'd tried to be careful, but that last night in the bothie, she had made him forget everything but possessing her, all common sense and good intentions out the window like smoke.

"Lianna—God." Dallas Fraser stared at his daughter with

obvious pain and disbelief and rage, and Cameron couldn't really blame him. "I'll kill him," Fraser snarled, starting forward, but one of his sons spoke up quickly.

"And shame her with no father for her bairn? Let's think about it first."

Heavy silence descended again, and Cameron tried not to shiver too noticeably, preferring to be forgotten in this little family discussion. He should focus on what was really important, such as breathing. Her brothers seemed well acquainted with methods of inflicting great pain in a short time, and had been too enthusiastic about it, in his opinion. But then, maybe he couldn't blame them. It was obvious they thought he had abducted her, and just as obvious that it made no difference to them that he had not. They wanted their pound of flesh, and weren't particular about how they got it.

If it hadn't been for his brother, locked in some dank dismal cell somewhere in Fort William, he would have been quite willing to forget the whole thing. Let them take her home with them, and let him just die quietly under some tree. But there was Jamie, and he was his only hope. So he waited, shivering, while Lianna argued with her father and brothers in a way he had never thought to hear. She really was quite a vociferous little thing, and stubborn, to boot.

"I mean it, Papa," she was saying, her voice growing more quiet as Dallas Fraser's face darkened to a thunderous scowl. "I will never forgive you if you harm my baby's father. If you touch him again, I swear I will hate you the rest of my life—and you two as well, Logan. Morgan. One more bruise—one more threat to him—and you might as well say your farewells to me now, for I will leave and not return."

"You don't mean that, Lianna. You're just upset." Dallas stared at her with hard, narrowed eyes; his icy gaze shifted to Cameron with mute hatred. "Once you think about it, you will see that I am right."

"Papa—you are talking about killing the man I love, the man who rescued me from certain death, and the man who has given me a child. I know what I mean. And I think you know that I will do what I say." Her voice quivered a little, and her chin trembled as she said softly, "I have always been an obedient daughter. I have adored and admired you my entire life. You are my father. A hero. But if you do this, I will not be able to bear even the sound of your name." She took a deep breath. "You might as well kill me, too, for without Cameron, I will not want to live."

Fraser actually winced. Logan muttered something under his breath and gave Cameron a baleful look, while Morgan's face reflected only pensive reflection. Cameron waited. At least Fraser was considering his fate before he gave the final order.

Finally Dallas Fraser swore harshly, and gave Cameron a stony stare before looking at his daughter. "Very well, Lianna. I won't kill him, but I have a requirement that must be met."

Lianna gazed at him, not leaving Cameron's side. "What is the requirement?"

"That he wed you in a church. I will not have a bastard born to my only daughter. If you are to bear a child, then that child will be recognized, even if it is sired by a man like MacKenzie."

A flush stained Lianna's cheeks, and indignation sparked in her eyes at the contempt in her father's tone and words, and Cameron wanted to tell her not to bother. He'd heard it all before, and had discovered that words alone had no power of destruction. The intent behind them, and the person using them carried all the responsibility and weight.

Lianna stood up, tossing the hair from her eyes as she faced her father. "You are talking about my child's father, and I do not appreciate your tone or your words. However, it seems like a fair bargain, and I am certain Cameron will agree. After all, we are already handfasted."

Fraser's eyes narrowed at that, and a scornful smile curled his lips. "Aye, 'tis easy enough to be a temporary husband, I suppose."

She gave him an odd look. "Perhaps you would know the answer to that better than I do, Papa."

To Cameron's astonishment, Dallas Fraser flushed a bright red that made his blue eyes vivid. He looked away, and said in a growl, "If he agrees, I'll take you to the kirk myself."

When Lianna turned to him, Cameron managed a painful wheeze that turned into agonizing, damp coughs. His body was racked with them, and one of her brothers pounded him helpfully on the back, sending sharp spears of pain through his entire body. When the convulsive coughing ended, he managed to look up at her. "Good . . . idea . . . angel."

She knelt beside him, and pushed back the wet hair from his eyes. "Oh God, what have they done to you? My poor love. Morgan, give him his shirt before he freezes to death and I have no husband at all."

After a startled instant, Morgan obeyed, and brought a shirt from the pack by their dead fire. He started to put it around him, but Lianna snatched it away, glaring at her brother. "You should be ashamed, two of you against one."

Logan said sullenly, "It wasn't that easy, so don't waste your sympathy on him. He busted my lip and gave me a black eye, so I wouldn't think him too bloody defenseless."

Cameron tried to rise to his feet, but found to his vague dismay that his legs were not working properly. He lurched forward a little, and lost his precarious balance. Morgan grabbed him, causing another sharp pain, but stood him on his feet. Swaying a little, Cameron managed to look up at Dallas Fraser, who was watching them with a forbidding expression.

"If you are ready, MacKenzie, I know of a church nearby with a priest to read the vows."

It would be too much effort to speak, so he only nodded, but that movement almost made him lose his balance again. Logan and Morgan stood on each side of him, while Lianna gathered up their few belongings and stuffed them into the leather pack.

As they started up the road toward Fort William, Cameron had the wry thought that he'd never considered he would be a married man, a father, and a corpse, all in one day. For it was as plain to him as the bloody nose on his face that Dallas Fraser had very carefully avoided clemency in his agreement to let him live, but only postponed the reckoning. It would be interesting to see what direction his form of justice would take.

* * *

The rotund priest of the stone kirk set beneath a grove of cedars looked nervous as he escorted the newly married couple down the narrow path, glancing from Dallas to his sons and back. The ceremony had been swift and grim, held on the church steps, and Cameron thought wearily that it was just as well. He did not think he could have managed a longer service.

A soft wind blew, but up on the peak of Ben Nevis, snow and clouds wreathed the high crags. Lianna looked relieved, but as nervous as the priest, and launched into a defensive monologue. "I am so sorry, Father, that we are not better dressed, but this is all the clothing we have left to us. We were set upon by brigands a few weeks ago, and lost everything."

The priest looked uncertainly at Cameron's battered face. "Your husband has taken a long time to heal, it seems."

Lianna bit her lower lip. "Those hurts are more recent, I fear."

After a moment, the priest nodded, and said in a kind voice, "My children, even if this marriage has started out under strife, trust in the Lord and all will be well."

"Yes, Father. Thank you, Father." Lianna glanced at Cameron flanked by her brothers, and managed a smile. "I love him very much."

"And the Lord loves you as well, child."

She looked momentarily startled, then nodded. "Yes, Father."

Dallas cleared his throat. He held out a small cloth pouch to the rector. It jangled slightly as he placed it in his open palm. "Father, we appreciate your indulgence in accommodating us today."

"My blessings on all of you, my son." The priest smiled as he weighed the bag in his hand, then blessed them all with the sign of the cross, and turned back up the path to the kirk.

Sunlight filtered down through thick cedar branches, swaying over Fraser's face in patches, and Cameron saw in his eyes a faint flash of satisfaction. He braced himself, and wasn't at all

surprised when Fraser nodded at his sons and they each took
one of Cameron's arms.

Lianna frowned, and turned to her father. "What are you
doing?"

"You are churched now, and the bairn will have a name. I
promised you I would not kill MacKenzie, and I won't, but I
made no promises about turning him over to the government.
We take him to Fort William, and I will hear no words against
it."

All the color leached from her face, but Cameron felt only
numb. He had expected it, really. Dallas Fraser was not the
kind of man to make idle threats, or take lightly an insult to
his honor. And it was obvious he felt his honor had been
insulted by Cameron MacKenzie.

Lianna railed and wept, but Fraser was adamant. By night's
fall, they would be at Fort William.

Catriona paced impatiently. Where were they? Had Rory not
found them by now? Oh God, everything had gone wrong. The
word had already gone out that Cameron MacKenzie's brother
was to be hanged, Duncan had not found Dallas, and now Rory
had not returned. She had visited Hill again, and learned things
about MacKenzie that made her almost positive he was not the
kind of man who would murder another in cold blood. Dugald
MacDonald had lied. No doubt that Breadalbane had lied, of
course, and now—now, she would have to convince Dallas.
Oh God, she didn't want Dallas killing another man for things
he had not done, especially as her nephews had come to her
and told her how MacKenzie had tried to help when the soldiers
attacked Glencoe.

Alex and Iain had no reason to lie, and they had the truth
from someone who had been there that terrible night, as well
as in the bothie when Mary died. Little by little, the story was
being pieced together, and whatever else might be true, it was
not true that Cameron MacKenzie had any part in the betrayal.
She felt sick.

If it was true that MacKenzie had not harmed Lianna, as it

certainly seemed to be, then Dallas would be guilty of murder if he killed him outright. Not that Breadalbane would protest, but it might one day return to haunt him. And if what Alex claimed was true, Lianna was exceedingly fond of Cameron MacKenzie, and would not forgive her father's brutal killing of him easily.

"*Ohon ohonari,*" she moaned, putting a hand over her face, and lapsing into her native speech. "What will I do?"

That question was answered more quickly than she had even hoped for, when at night's fall, she heard a shout come up from below and ran to the window to throw up the sash. It was Morgan, and his face was set into worried lines that she knew well. She met him halfway down the stairs, and took him immediately into the small inn parlor.

"Morgan, what is about?" He put a hand on her shoulder, and his grave expression made her heart leap. "Oh God—your father—"

"Is well and hale. We have Lianna. No, wait—she is well, but there are circumstances . . .''

He paused, and Catriona stared at him. Rarely did Morgan lose his power of concise speech. Now, he seemed flustered, and she grabbed his arm and shook him as if he were a small boy again.

"Tell me what you must, Morgan, but do it quickly before I run to see for myself!"

"Lianna is overwrought that Papa has turned MacKenzie over to Colonel Hill. He is imprisoned, and Lianna will not leave, but swears to hate us all until he is free again." He looked miserable. "I tried to talk to him, but you know how Papa can be when his mind is set. There is a great uproar, and I was sent to tell you to stay here and not to interfere."

Her eyes narrowed angrily, and Morgan rolled his eyes. She put up a hand. "No, do not fear that I will make a scene here in the inn for everyone to mock later. But your father will rue the day he thought to keep me from my daughter and ignorant of her troubles. Fetch my cloak, Morgan."

He stood still. She glared at him, and he looked away from her. "I swore I would not take you to them."

"Then don't. Did you swear you would not tell me where to find them?"

He smiled a little. "No."

"Excellent. Where are they?"

"In the governor's room at the fort—Mama. There is something else I must tell you."

Pausing, she turned back to look at him. He stood facing her, his hands clasped behind his back, misery in his face. "Lianna bears MacKenzie's child. They were churched earlier today."

"Married and pregnant?"

"Aye." He shrugged. "Papa was set to kill him for taking her, but when Lianna told him she carries MacKenzie's bairn, he wed her to him instead." Morgan laughed hollowly. "She will soon be a widow if justice is to be done."

"Not if I can help it, not if she wants him." Catriona stared at her son, thinking furiously that there were times Dallas Fraser far outdid himself in idiocy. Poor Lianna. She must be so distraught. And Dallas would be no help, she was certain, blustering and making threats—"Your father is a pigheaded, stubborn smaik, Morgan. Where is Dugald MacDonald?"

Morgan looked a little uneasy. "He left us in the glen before we found them, saying it would be best if MacKenzie did not see him again. The man is a coward, I think."

"A liar, would best describe him." She shook her head angrily. "I suppose your father believes him now?"

"Well . . . he has given us no reason not to believe him. And MacKenzie offered no defense."

"Was he given the chance? No, I didn't think so. 'Tis a miracle he wasn't beaten bloody but that would be just like Dallas Fraser to forget all the years it has taken him to learn—" She halted abruptly. Morgan looked embarrassed and ashamed. "You didna kill MacKenzie? Tell me you didna—"

"No, no, of course not. But when we found him, I'm afraid that we may have reacted a bit more strongly than we should have."

"Oh aye, 'tis easy for me to see what has happened now.

The poor man is likely beat to a bloody mess, and my daughter is frantic, am I right?''

''Nearly.''

She glared at Morgan, who was gazing at her with unhappy resignation. ''A willful man must have his way. But I am about to convince your father that his will is contrary to what is best.''

''I wish you good fortune in that attempt.''

Catriona was almost out the door, but she said over her shoulder, ''I shall not need good fortune, only a few minutes alone with the man.''

But it was not as easy as she had thought it would be, when she burst into the governor's room and saw Dallas leaning against the wall with arms crossed over his chest, a thunderous scowl on his face, and Lianna railing at him while poor Colonel Hill cowered behind his desk.

It was the latter who looked up hopefully when he saw her, and surged to his feet. ''Lady Fraser. Thank God you've come at last. I had begun to lose hope—talk to your daughter.''

''I intend to talk to my husband, Colonel,'' Catriona said flatly as she crossed the room, and saw the upward flash of Dallas's eyes in her direction. His eyes cooled, and he pushed away from the wall.

''I should have known you would come anyway, Cat. Go home. This is none of your affair, and I will not relent.''

''How do you know I intend to ask you to relent?'' She slid back the hood of her cloak, and unfastened the throat laces to slide free of the garment. ''Perhaps I came to advocate your decision to have my daughter's new husband killed, not oppose it.''

Dallas's brows lowered. His mouth thinned into a taut slash, and he muttered something under his breath. Now Lianna turned to her, eyes awash with tears, her pretty mouth trembling with grief and despair.

''Mama—please help me.''

It was a plea guaranteed to go straight to a mother's heart, and even if Catriona had not known MacKenzie was innocent of some of the charges against him, she would have had to champion her daughter's cause. Tugging her gloves free of her hands finger by finger, she smiled reassuringly at Lianna.

"My pet, perhaps you should listen to your father. You know he is always right. Surely, this man must be a vile scoundrel indeed, or why else would he be charged with all these crimes?" Her gaze flicked up to Colonel Hill. "Is that not correct, sir?"

Colonel Hill coughed politely, and turned a miserable face to Dallas before shaking his head. "That is not up to me to decide, Lady Fraser. A magistrate will make that decision."

"Ah, and magistrates are infallible, are they not?" She smiled again, and dropped her gloves atop the colonel's desk. Crossing to Lianna, who sat huddled on a stool near the fire, she knelt beside her, and cupped a palm beneath her chin. Tear streaks stained Lianna's pale face, and the quiver of her lips was echoed in the tremble of her slender body. She patted Lianna's cheek gently. "Listen to me, my pretty. Go to the inn on the corner by the market, and there you will find your brother Morgan. He will tend you. No, do not argue now. I will make everything as right as I can."

For a long moment, Lianna gazed at her with wet eyes and spiky lashes, then she nodded. "I love him, Mama."

It was all she said, but it was enough for Catriona. She stood up, pulling Lianna with her, and gave her a quick hug before bundling her in her own cloak and escorting her to the door. She was well aware of Dallas's dark gaze on her, his rigid anger and the unyielding set of his mouth, but did not acknowledge him in any way. Let him stew a bit longer, while she tried to think what to say.

When the door shut behind Lianna, Catriona turned to face her husband. Dallas had not moved or spoken, and Colonel Hill stood fidgeting by the fire. She walked to the hearth and held out her hands to the blaze.

"What has been done with MacKenzie, Colonel?"

Hill swallowed and looked away. "He is in custody."

"May I see him?"

"No." It was Dallas who answered. He pushed away from the wall, his movements angry and impatient. "What's done is done. Let it be, Cat. The earl will deal with him."

"When did you become such a proponent of Breadalbane, may I ask?" Her brow arched at his soft curse. "I see. Then he is to be used when it is convenient to what you wish, and reviled when it is not. Is that what you have learned in these past twenty-five years, Dallas Fraser? To use men as willfully and carelessly as Breadalbane used us so long ago?"

Colonel Hill made a small, helpless sound and edged toward the door. "Excuse me—feel free to use my quarters for the moment."

Neither of them turned when he slipped through the door and closed it behind him with a solid thud. Dallas glared down at her, using his height as intimidation, though it had never worked in all the years they had been together. Her chin lifted, and she held his angry gaze steadily.

Finally he exploded. "Curse you, Cat, the man deserves what he will get. He dishonored our daughter, by God, and for that he should pay!"

"Has he?" She whirled to face him, angry now herself. "Do you not remember my own father's anger when I was taken from my home? He came after you then, did he not? And swore revenge, your head on a pike and your hide on a wall—but I stood for you, just as Lianna has stood for her man. Is that any different, Dallas? Is it? I was truly abducted, not just rescued from the cruelty of others, but stolen away with no regard for my family's grief." Her voice softened at the tautness in his face. "But I fell in love with my captor, as our daughter has fallen in love with this MacKenzie. If she loves him, then so shall I, and if you do not help him, I will feel the same anger and grief that she feels."

Dallas was silent for a long time. Peat smoke curled around them from the fire. Then he said heavily, "I was not a wanted outlaw, Cat. MacKenzie is a hunted man. If she stays with him, she will be hunted as well."

"Not if you help them."

"Christ! You want me to help a man I detest?"

"Yes." She smiled slightly at his oath.

Dallas folded his arms across his chest. "When we were in

Kinlochleven you were quite willing for MacKenzie to be taken into custody, and even hung.''

"Aye.'' She nodded. "But that was before I knew that he had no part in the massacre, indeed, did his best to help the survivors at great risk.''

Dallas snorted. "And who told you such foolishness?''

"My nephews, Alex and Iain, and Rory MacDonald, whom I have known since I was a child, and—''

He put up a hand. "Wait. Start over. From the beginning, please, and tell me what you have heard. I will listen, but I make no other promises.''

She took his hand and pressed it to her cheek. "You are a just man, Dallas. When you hear the truth, you will help. A less honorable man than MacKenzie would not have risked his own life or his brother's for our daughter unless he really loves her. I think you will see the truth.''

"Whatever the truth is, I will have to believe in MacKenzie's innocence before I give him aid.''

She smiled. "You will. God help me, I condemned him myself before I learned the truth. He is not the kind of man to kill without provocation, and 'tis my belief that Hugh MacDonald provoked him. Talk to Hugh's cousins, not just Dugald—whom you didn't like anyway—but the others who were there. Talk to them, Dallas, please. If you know the truth, you will help him, I just know it.''

"All right.'' He blew out an exasperated breath. "I'll talk to Dugald again, and to the others who were there. I'll do my own investigations, and if there is enough doubt in my mind, I'll do what I can to help him. But for God's sake, Cat, stop talking to everyone about it. He's already been charged with murder, and the less said, the better for him until we decide what is truth and what is fiction. And do not look at me like that. It wasn't me who leveled the charges, but Colonel Hill. He had to. Dugald MacDonald went to Breadalbane as well after he left me in the glen. I suppose he hopes to get reward money from both of us, for his part in this affair, and if he wasn't such a damnable onerous man, I might not believe this ridiculous tale of false charges and evil designs. But then, I know Breadalbane and his capabilities, so I cannot say I disbelieve it, either.'' He smiled slightly, shaking his head. ''If the MacKenzie's claims are true, I'll do what I can. But if they are not—I will help to put him on the gallows.''

Chapter 20

"Cameron . . ." Lianna choked a little, saying his name, and he drew her into his arms, managing a wry smile against the sweetly scented mass of her hair.

"Don't. I'm all right, if you ignore the rather grim surroundings. Which I try to most of the time, I assure you."

"Must you joke?" She drew back, sniffing a little, and even in the dim light of his dank cell he could see the silver glitter of tears in her eyes and on her cheeks.

"Why not joke, angel? It's better than crying, and I don't look half as pretty as you do with red eyes and a stuffy nose." He cradled her chin in his palm, thumb stroking across the trembling curve of her lips. "Besides, we don't have much time, and I'd much rather spend it kissing you than weeping into your neck."

She gave him an exasperated look. "There are moments when I think you must be quite mad."

"As a March hare, sweeting. Come here. Sit in my lap like this . . . that's right. See? Isn't a cuddle better than crying?"

"Cameron . . ." She paused, sighed, and half turned on his knee to look at him. Bars of light from a high window across the cell striped her face, and she blinked against the hazy shaft.

"Cameron, listen to me. Papa has gone to see a friend and distant kinsman, Sir Simon Fraser, 11th Lord Lovat. He is William's ally, but Papa has some influence with him."

"Good God—isn't that a bit much just to get me hung more quickly?"

"No, no, you misunderstand." She took his face between her hands, and held tightly even when he turned to kiss the soft little mounds on her palm. "Cameron, pay close attention, please. This is very important and I don't know how long they will let me visit. Papa has gone to get you a pardon."

Cameron paused in the midst of kissing the heel of her palm and her wrist, his mouth hovering over the blue-veined cream of her skin. "A pardon?"

"Yes. And for your brother as well. But we must know— you once said you had information that would enable you to work the earl of Breadalbane to your benefit—is that true?"

He pressed kisses along her arm up to her elbow, pushing aside the draping lace cuff, then glanced up at her with his lips still pressed into the crook of her arm. "Yes." He lifted his head, and pulled her closer against him. "Unfortunately, you're the first person except for my charming jailor that I have seen since being cast into this dingy hole, so I doubt very much there is enough time to do anything with my information. I'm already condemned for murder. However, if you would be so good as to contact barristers Locke, Legget, and Larson, on Princes Street in Glasgow, you might be able to save Jamie for me."

"Locke, Legget, and Larson. Very well. How can they help?"

"They are holding a packet of letters that fell into my possession quite unexpectedly last year. A fluke, for I certainly had no idea what they were at first. A courier, you see, met with a rather gory accident, and the packet was lost under the bridge where I happened to be taking refuge at the time." He smiled slightly. "My curiosity has always gotten the better of me at the most inconvenient moments, but that time, it paid well. Inside that packet were most incriminating letters from Breadalbane to a confederate, concerning the Jacobite rebellion. The earl had been very careful not to leave any betraying evidence that he was promoting James, you see, but these letters are in his handwriting, sealed with his mark, and quite explicit in detail. It has been my salvation and my undoing, for when Breadalbane discovered that I had these indicting letters, he set out to ruin and destroy me. All I could do was leave the sealed packet with my barristers, to be opened only in the event of my death. No other method would secure my life or Jamie's, I thought, but Breadalbane has done everything short of murdering us to get them. Not that he quibbles with murder, but I was quite careful to inform him that in the case of my . . . unnatural . . . death, the letters are to be sent immediately to William's court. Taking Jamie is his way of coaxing me into relinquishing the letters, but of course, once I do, he can just forget to tell the hangman to halt.''

Lianna sat quietly. Then, in a small voice, she said, ''Then a pardon will only be a temporary measure. The earl will not stop until you are dead.''

''You are very perceptive, angel.'' He nuzzled her neck. ''I do not foresee a long life span for myself, which is why I rather regret your being forced to wed me—which also brings to mind a question burning in my mind—are you with child?''

''Would you mind if I was?''

''Do not answer a question with a question, goose. Tell me.''

''I might be.''

''Just as I thought. Lying to your father like that. You should be ashamed.''

She flounced around to grip his shirt collar in both her hands. ''Ashamed of what? Saving your life? Saying what I could to keep Papa from killing you? It was bad enough that Logan and Morgan battered your beautiful face so brutally, but Papa would have shot you, Cameron!''

''I realized that. It was an illuminating moment, of which there have been many since I've met you.'' He pulled her hard against him, fiercely protective. ''Do not risk yourself, Lianna. It won't change anything, and I could not die peacefully if I thought you would be in danger. Your father may have powerful connections, but so does the earl. Stay out of my affairs, if you please.''

She pressed her forehead against his so closely her eyelashes almost tangled with his as she said softly, ''No.''

He groaned. ''Lianna . . . God, angel, please don't do this. Can't you see it won't make any difference? Whether it's this week or next year, the end will be the same.''

''No, it will not. And how can you possibly give up so easily? Think of your brother, if you won't think of yourself, and think of me—it is entirely possible that I am with child, you know, as we weren't very careful the last time.''

''To my chagrin.'' He jerked his head back, and leaned against the damp wall. Moisture seeped from the stones into his shirt, chilling him, but he was too afraid for her to take much notice of it. The fear was almost tangible, rather like that a man sometimes felt in battle. The beast could be crippling if he didn't ignore it and go on, moving and thrusting, always thinking and not feeling, for if he stopped to feel, he was doomed. Compassion would be suicide, and he had found that out to his horror and self-disgust in his first real battle, when men crumpled before sword and musket fire, screaming and sometimes crying, sometimes just a whimper like a child's . . . God, when he thought of it, let himself remember, it was as if it had all happened to someone else. But Lianna was real. She was solid substance and warm acceptance, her skin soft, her hair wild and scented, her body a sensual delight. If Breadalbane won, would Dallas Fraser be able to protect her from the earl? Would he realize just how devious John Campbell could be? Because if he didn't give the devil his due, the devil would win.

He looked up at her, blinking a little as he realized she'd been talking to him. ''Sorry. If I thought it would help—''

''It will. I'll tell Mama. She has connections of her own, you know, though not the same way Papa does.''

''Excuse me—what are we talking about now?''

''I knew you weren't paying attention.'' She pushed away from his lap and stood up, fumbling with a pouch at her waist.

"The jailor is returning—take this. It should help for now, and I will try to send more later."

He studied her face without reaching for the pouch she held out. "Lianna—"

"Don't worry." She lifted his hand and pressed the pouch into his palm. "I bought them. And I sent a pouch to your brother as well. He's here too, you know." She leaned forward to kiss him quickly as keys grated in the lock with a heavy metallic rasp, and the jailor announced that their time was up. Then she released his hand and the pouch, and stepped back, her face wistful, her eyes shiny again with unshed tears. She managed a bright, reassuring smile that fell a bit flat. "I love you, Cameron. And don't worry. Papa never fails."

It was a long time after she left that he remembered the pouch, and when he opened it, he found two thick meat pies— and some bannocks. He laughed softly.

Dallas smiled slightly. "You will not regret this, Sir Simon."

"No?" Sir Simon Lovat arched a brow. "I trust not. It is most unusual, is it not, for you to intervene in these matters? Your talents are more usually utilized by kings instead of outlaws."

For a moment, Dallas toyed with the sealed, beribboned document. It had occurred to him that neither king was very ethical in their dealings, but after the disastrous affair at Glencoe, he had begun to reevaluate his opinions of King William. To be fair, the monarch was too busy fighting Flanders to be concerned with squabbling Highlanders, but decency demanded he bear some of the blame. He looked up at Sir Simon, and managed a diplomatic smile.

"Usually, I am too busy, yes. But this particular outlaw is wed to my only daughter. More important—he is innocent of the charges. I've had dealings with Breadalbane in the past, and I know the man's reputation."

Lovat leaned forward. "The papers you mentioned earlier— have they been verified as authentic?"

"No, but they are currently under proper scrutiny. If they

prove to be genuine, then Breadalbane can be proven to have lied about his involvement with the Jacobite cause, and you will have him just where you want him." The smile deepened. "Not that I will object to that, of course. We have a history, John Campbell and I."

"So I understand. Breadalbane is the most distrusted man in all of Scotland. The Master of Stair is using him, of course, but no one has any illusions about his past deeds of chicanery and violence. If we can prove that he was involved in last summer's intrigue with the Highland chiefs on James's behalf, then we can prove treason. I, for one, will be glad to see him fall. The man is far too powerful for my liking. The fool—he must know that William can offer him more than James, for if the Stuarts return to power in Scotland it will be Glengarry, Sleat, and Clanranald who will curry the king's favor, not Breadalbane, despite any of his efforts to earn James's favor." Sir Simon leaned forward, and his chair creaked loudly. "You will send me the evidence as soon as it is in your hands, I trust. A bargain is a bargain, and MacKenzie's possession of those documents has purchased his and his brother's life."

"I counted on that, Sir Simon." Dallas grinned, and rose to his feet. "I will leave at once to see that this pardon arrives at Fort William in time."

Sir Simon waved a hand. "No, no, there is more we need to discuss while you are here. I will send my swiftest courier. He will make it there in time, I assure you."

Dallas hesitated. Sir Simon was gazing at him with a lifted brow, and he had no desire to offend him. So he relented, and handed over the pardon to the courier that was called into the room.

"Walter, go swiftly," Lovat commanded, "and take this to Colonel Hill at Fort William. It is urgent business." As the courier took the pardon and departed, Lovat turned to Dallas. "Now, we need to see what we can do about this latest news from France. How do we manage James?"

"Ah, I am not at all certain James needs to be managed, Sir Simon." Dallas smiled his most diplomatic smile. "What is needed, is more understanding between the Scottish Privy Council and Parliament. Let's discuss that instead. . . ."

"No word yet?"

Lianna shook her head miserably. It was dawn, and she was still awake, too fretful to sleep. The morning sun was just brightening the sky outside, a respite from the rain of the past days. She looked up, and caught a glimpse of exchanged glances between Logan and Morgan. Her heart gave a lurch. "What is it? Do you know something?"

It seemed an eternity before Morgan replied, coming to her to take both her hands in his, his face solemn. "Lianna, the execution is set for tomorrow at noon. Hill cannot delay any longer. If Papa does not return with a pardon . . ."

There was no need for him to complete the thought. The edges of her vision blurred, and she swayed slightly but kept her balance. Someone grabbed her, and she turned blindly as her mother's arms went around her.

"He will get here, Lianna, your father will arrive in time. We have a day and a half, and he has never failed us yet. He will come in time."

A shudder ran through her, and she nodded mutely. It was so easy to retreat into her mother's arms, but it would not help Cameron. She had to be strong, had to remain calm and collected, or he would die. She drew back, wiped her eyes and looked at her mother.

"We have to do something. There must be some way to delay the execution until Papa arrives."

Logan made a noise, and when she turned to look at him, he shrugged. "We don't even know if he was able to get a pardon, Lianna. Be practical. There may be nothing we can do to help him."

"I will find something," she said fiercely, and did not realize her hands were curled into fists until her palms began to throb. She opened her hands, and saw deep, bluish marks where her nails had cut the skin. Drawing in a shuddering breath, she let it out again slowly. Logan was looking at her warily, and Mama had a small frown on her face. She glanced at Morgan, and he managed a faint smile.

"Courage, little sister. Remember your history."

She stared blankly at Morgan. "History?"

"Yes. Who was your favorite heroine when you were twelve, do you recall?"

She frowned a moment, then remembered. "The martyred Joan of Arc—Yes. I see. . . ."

"What on earth are you talking about, Morgan?" Mama sounded irritable, but beneath the peevish treble was a current of anxiety. She was worried as well, and it showed.

"Joan of Arc." Morgan turned to look at her. "She was young and female, but fought for what she believed was right, didn't she? Why not take a lesson from her fine example?"

Logan hooted. "Are you suggesting that Lianna put on armor and take up a sword like some French girl once did, Morgan? You are daft."

"I'm not suggesting anything of the kind." Morgan remained cool, but gave his brother a narrow look. "There are different ways to wage battle, Logan, though you do not seem to know any. Your only method is slash and burn. That is the attitude of a foot soldier, not a commander."

"A lot you would know—"

"Enough!" Catriona's voice was sharp, and she stepped between her sons with an angry flourish. "You're not helping the matter. But Morgan, you have a valid point, I think. Do you know of another way to do this?"

"No, but if we combine our resources, I am certain we can come up with something. If we don't, he'll die."

Lianna thought miserably of Cameron's face when he had so tenderly cared for her, and then she recalled how he had fought Hugh MacDonald to save them. There had been a fierce, ruthless light in his eyes as he fought Hugh, and she had felt so guilty that it was all her fault for trusting the Glengarry MacDonalds. He'd been right so many times, right about the fact that a name did not make a man, the man made the name. But she hadn't listened. No, she had stubbornly resisted it, clinging to the safe, familiar belief that all MacDonalds were right and all Campbells wrong. It had taken a near disaster to prove to her how wrong she was, and now the man she loved was to be executed for something she had caused with her stubborn refusal to believe.

All her life she had listened to Papa's convictions that Scotland and England could live in peace. Cameron was saying the same thing. Battle between rival clans was common, and the conflict with England a familiar prejudice. It did not have to be this way, did it?

"What do you want us to do," Logan was muttering irritably, "call up the clans to battle for him? That would be a bloody mess. Let Providence decide MacKenzie's fate."

Morgan snapped, "Providence is always on the side of the big battalions, in case you haven't noticed."

"That's it." Lianna wheeled on her brother. "That is it, Morgan."

"What is it? What are you talking about?"

"Battalions . . . Providence—we can rescue him ourselves, and when Papa comes—"

"She's gone mad." Logan sounded disgusted. "Someone tie her to the bed before she runs into the street babbling daft frummery that's liable to get us thrown into prison as well."

Lianna stared at her brothers. She was no Joan of Arc, but she certainly had a mission, though perhaps not as holy as Joan's had been. But to save two innocent lives—wasn't that as important? It certainly was to her.

Numbing grief was replaced with fiery conviction as she said clearly, "I have a plan."

Late May in the Scottish Highlands was always beautiful. Cameron had almost forgotten how beautiful it could be, when the sun was shining bright overhead and the wind was soft. His chains clanked loudly as he was taken across the grounds, his first time outside since being brought to Fort William. He drew in a deep breath of air untainted by dank stone walls and foul straw, detecting the salty scent of the sea and River Lochy on the currents. His guard jostled him forward, growling at him to step lively, and he thought wryly that the man should hardly expect him to run eagerly to the noose.

Inverlochy Castle cast deep shadows, with the northwest tower known as Comyn's tower shading the level ground that stretched beyond it. A banner flew, snapping in the wind as they passed it by, and in a few moments, Cameron realized that he was being taken to the governor's room of the fort instead of straight to the gallows. There was no sign of Jamie, no sign of Lianna, and he prayed fervently that she would not come to witness his death.

That would be unbearable.

Colonel Hill paced the floor of the governor's room, and looked up when Cameron was escorted inside. "Leave us," he said to the guard, then added with a wry glance at Cameron, "He is in chains enough that I do not fear for my safety."

After the door had closed, Hill regarded his prisoner silently for a moment. Finally he said softly. " 'Tis a grim day, Cameron MacKenzie."

"At least the weather is fair. It would be the extreme insult to die on a day that was pissing rain." He managed to sound careless, though the effort was not as casual as he'd wanted.

Hill stared at him. "It will sound very unusual when I ask you this, but were you expecting correspondence?"

"I had rather hoped for a last minute reprieve from the king, of course. Either king would do." Cameron studied Hill. "I take it there has been no pardon."

"No. I am sorry for that, for I do not believe you guilty of the charges levied against you by Dugald MacDonald and Breadalbane. Both men have bloody axes to grind."

Cameron nodded calmly. "I thought not. And I suppose there has been no other correspondence for me."

"No." Hill hesitated. "A courier was brought to the fort this morning, however, raving and out of his head, his garments rent so badly and his mind so addled that no one can tell whence he came, only his name. Walter. Indeed, he would not have been known as a courier if not for the pouch he carried." Hill's eyes met his. "Empty, I am afraid."

He should have been surprised, angry, outraged, afraid, but he was none of those things, only numbly indifferent.

Hill spread his arms out in a gesture of helpless surrender. "Breadalbane is here. He demands the sentence be carried out at once, and I have no authority to countermand him. Without a pardon, or any other evidence—do you have anything that could help your case, MacKenzie?"

"No. But I would like to remind you that I was given only a five-minute trial in front of Breadalbane's magistrate, and that my brother has done nothing that deserves hanging. There are no grounds for the charges of stealing Glenlyon's horse, no witnesses left to accuse him. At least spare Jamie, for God's sake."

He hadn't meant to sound so desperate, but it was difficult not to be emotional when he knew this day was to be his last. And Jamie was so young—impetuous, but good-hearted, and honest for all his brash ways.

Hill seemed to crumble before his eyes, and Cameron knew with sick certainty that it was no use. He bent his head and shifted, and the chains dragged noisily across the floor.

"Here." Hill pushed away from his desk, a weary old man, his eyes red-rimmed and bleary. "The least I can do is ease your discomfort. Ropes would be more comfortable than those heavy chains, and you are not likely to escape an entire garrison of soldiers."

"It had not crossed my mind to try." Cameron stood still, and when the manacles were unlocked and removed, he rubbed at his bleeding, chafed wrists gratefully. He looked up at Hill. "My thanks for your kindness."

Hill looked as if he were about to cry, and Cameron smiled slightly. "If I may, Colonel, I would like to write a small note to my wife, to be delivered after . . . after."

"Of course. And there is to be a child, I understand." Hill went to his desk and opened a drawer. He drew out a sheaf of parchment, and dipped a feathered pen into ink, then held it out to Cameron.

"A child. Yes, I certainly hope—yes." Cameron took the pen. He stared down at the blank sheet of paper for a long, empty moment, his mind blank. What could he say? What would suffice to tell her how she had brightened his last days, made him happier than he had ever been? He didn't have the words; for all his education, his glib speeches and nonchalant assertions that he loved her, he could not find the words to tell her now.

In the end, he wrote a simple quotation from John Barbour, a fourteenth-century poet, across the paper: "For love is of sae mickle might, That it all paines makis light." She would recognize the quotation. It was the best he could do, and he signed it "Your loving husband . . ."

After carefully sanding the ink, he looked up at Hill, who was standing with his back to him, staring out the window. It would be so easy to take advantage of him, to use him as hostage, to wrap the chains around him and drag him outside, threaten to choke him unless he and Jamie were released, but as soon as his mind conjured up the images, they were rejected. It would only prolong the inevitable. There were too many soldiers garrisoned in Fort William, and Breadalbane would not lift a finger to save Hill if it meant MacKenzie would die. He could only hope that Lianna had gotten word to Locke, Legget, and Larson, and they would send on the papers to the proper authorities. That, at least, he could do, though it would avail him little once he was dead.

"I'm ready, Colonel."

Hill started at the sound of his voice, then turned. Outside the window there was the sound of marching, vendors, and the occasional tap of a drum. Apparently, this was to be a festive occasion, with music and refreshments as well as entertainment. He gave the colonel the folded note to Lianna.

"I will see that she gets it." Hill took the letter with a trembling hand, and his voice was bitter. "Dash it, this is a bad business, MacKenzie, and I hope you do not blame me for it. I tried to end it, tried to postpone it, but failed. As I have at so many other things."

"I do not blame you, Colonel. We both know where the blame lies, and one day soon, I hope that all of Scotland, and

England too, know why Breadalbane felt it necessary to hound me to the gallows.''

Hill gazed at him thoughtfully. ''So do I, MacKenzie. So do I.''

Cameron tried to hold to that thought as his wrists were tied with rope and he was taken outside again, put into an open cart and paraded through the crowded street. The cart jerked to a stop beside a tower, and he lurched against the side, cursing as his bruised body smashed into the hard wood. Then he looked up, and his throat tightened.

Jamie.

Always slight, Jamie was thin now, but he looked as cocky as ever, the idiot, brandishing his chains with youthful bravado, even bending once to kiss a young lass who pressed close to throw him a flower. His black hair was matted, but still gleamed in the sunlight as he kissed the girl until soldiers jerked him away. Jamie straightened, grinning, and his gaze lifted toward the cart; his face changed when he saw his brother.

''Cam—you're a sight I dinna think to see again.''

''Enjoy it while you can, you lusty simpleton.''

Jamie laughed. ''Dour hempie. Did you ever think we'd end our days with the wuddy?''

''Always. We were both born to the gallows.'' Cameron leaned back against the cart's side as Jamie was roughly bundled into it, his chains a noisy rattle around his wrists and waist. He lifted his arms, and the long loops clattered loudly.

''The corbies will have a hard time with these, I'll warrant.''

''That's a pleasant image.'' Cameron studied his brother, taking in his thin frame and gaunt face, the pasty whiteness of his complexion that had once glowed with ruddy health. ''You look as if the ravens have already been at you.''

Jamie shrugged. ''I've had better moments than the last months I've spent here.'' He tilted back his head to squint up at the blue bowl of the sky. ''I'd begun to think sky and clouds were just dreams.''

The cart had lurched forward again, making slow progress through the seething crowd. Cameron half expected the usual barrage of rotten fruit and vegetables, taunts and jeers, but there were only a scattered few comments thrown at them, and those he rather thought were made by Lowlanders and soldiers. Bad as it was, he had the thought that this time he was not entirely alone in his travail, but he would have given anything to have been so.

Glancing at Jamie, he said softly, "I tried to free you, or get you a pardon, but I failed."

"I know." Jamie's grin was reckless, and he managed to clumsily catch a tossed flower, this one a sprig of heather. Cameron stared at it as Jamie tucked the sprig into one of the chain links. "As I used to try and tell you, you're not invincible. And you managed to keep me alive longer than anyone ever thought either of us would make it, so I have no complaints."

"You're easily pleased, for a man on his way to the gallows."

"Do I have a choice? No, I dinna think so." Jamie looked down, and when he glanced up again, there was a wistful smile on his face. He held to the cart rail as the vehicle rattled over the rough road, and said softly, "I am to blame for being here, Cam, not you. I lost my temper and behaved like a fool."

"You were used, Jamie. Breadalbane went after you to get to me." The wooden cart rail smacked hard against Cameron's spine as the cart jerked to a stop again. He winced at the sharp pain, and grabbed at the sides to keep from falling. Then he glanced up, and his blood froze.

Above them, gazing down from a dais with a faint smile of satisfaction, stood John Campbell, Earl of Breadalbane. His heavy-lidded eyes were as pitiless as a snake's, and his corpulent frame was bedecked in a velvet coat and lace collar. Cameron's vision blurred with rage and hatred, and at that moment, if he had possessed a weapon, no power on earth could have prevented him using it. No words would form, and he almost choked with fury as he stared up at the earl.

The cart lunged forward again, and Cameron did not look away or lose his balance as it rolled past the dais where Breadalbane stood.

"That must be Breadalbane," Jamie said loudly to be heard over the crowd, and Cameron finally looked away from the earl.

"Yes."

"He looks as I envisioned him, a fat, bleedin' sod with white hands and wickedness sitting on him like a death pall."

"An apt description." Cameron smiled mirthlessly. "You would have made an excellent university student."

Jamie didn't reply, and it occurred to Cameron that much more than a young life was being wasted. Potential worth was being discarded as casually as old clothes.

He looked away from his brother, unable to bear the thought of his wasted life. His gaze skimmed the crowd, and he saw a thick sprig of heather being thrust upward. He smiled slightly. More feminine admiration for Jamie. He must have been a rather lively prisoner to have earned so much attention from the lasses of the garrison.

But as his eyes drifted from the heather to the person holding it into the air, he recognized Duncan Don, who had woken him in the blizzard the night of the Glencoe massacre. He started, then managed a nod in Duncan's direction as the cart slowly wobbled past. Then another heather sprig caught his attention, and another, and familiar MacDonald faces peered from beneath the heather sprigs: John and Alasdair, Rory, Alex and Iain—and to his amazement, Malcolm Campbell, holding up a heather sprig and grinning like an idiot. Then, bobbing among the sea of faces that had gone from an indistinct blur to aching clarity, he saw the one face he had long dreaded seeing this day—Lianna.

She, too, held up a sprig of heather, waving it like a banner, her eyes fastened on his face as if she could draw him into her soul. He stared at her; he couldn't help it. God, she was so beautiful, his precious angel with grass green eyes and copper hair. He wished she were not wearing a hood, so he could see her hair once more, visualize running his hands through it, touching her sweet face, kissing the faint spray of freckles across her nose. An ache like a raw wound pierced his chest. His throat hurt, and for the first time, he felt like crying.

The crowd surged around the cart, pressing so close some of the soldiers began to shout at them, and lay about with the flat of their swords, telling them to retreat. An angry shout erupted, then two men began to scuffle. Blows were struck, more shouts rose, and suddenly the entire sea of people seemed to swell like an ocean wave, washing around the cart and all the way to the foot of the wooden gallows.

Jamie laughed. "Look at that, Cam. Did you ever see the like?"

He was still gazing at Lianna, and shook his head. "No, Jamie, I have never seen the like."

The noise was chaotic, the din deafening as men shouted and women screamed, and above it all the rapid cadence of drums pounding. The cart lurched forward, jerked to a halt, then shuddered under the press of the crowd. Cameron tore his gaze from Lianna as the cart began to tilt, and he grabbed at the sides with his bound hands. Jamie came sliding toward him, unable to keep his footing as the vehicle pitched violently.

There was the sudden, sharp clang of swords, and the tone of the melee abruptly altered. Men roared with the sound of battle, and there was a scattering of musket fire into the crowd. Soldiers crowded around the cart, reaching for the prisoners with rough hands.

Cameron swore softly, and caught a glimpse of Jamie's delighted confusion as they were pulled from the cart. He was shoved forward into the sweating, surging mass, and had a blurred view of the dais above and Breadalbane shouting furious commands. A soldier cuffed Cameron, and he looked around angrily, but had no chance to protest.

A loud, thunderous roar drowned out even the clamor of the crowd, filling the sky with black clouds of smoke and shaking the ground. Debris from the explosion pelted the area, some of it hot, and suddenly Cameron found himself jerked to one side.

"Do you intend to dream, or will you try for your life, MacKenzie?"

Panting, he looked up into the face of Morgan Fraser. A dirk sawed at the ropes binding him, and then his hands were free from aching confinement. Thrusting a pistol into one hand and a sword into the other, Fraser repeated impatiently, "Well, do you try for your life?"

Cameron grinned as he saw that Jamie was being dragged away protesting by Logan Fraser. "I'd best tell my brother we are in good company, before he ruins it all."

"Aye. I don't think Lianna would be at all pleased."

"Good God—is she safely away?"

"She's safely in the midst of a round score of MacDonalds, who would cut off their own—watch it!" Morgan ducked as a man careened into him, and jerked his head for Cameron to follow.

There was no time for conversation, no time for contemplation, as Cameron fought beside Morgan. It was a delirious blur, of slashing swords, the sharp acrid smell of gunpowder, and the excitement of being given a chance to die like a man instead of a bull at the slaughter. So many soldiers, so little chance of success, but incredibly, he found himself standing outside the walls of the fort. A feeling of elation swept over him, and he turned to look for Jamie.

It was only a brief elation, for Logan Fraser came running forward with a brace of saddled mounts, and cast Cameron a cold look as he thrust reins into his hand. "Mount and ride, or we are all done, MacKenzie."

"Where is my brother?"

Logan pointed, and Cameron saw Jamie, chains still flapping from his wrists, mounted atop a skittish bay. He was grinning, his eyes alight with excitement, blazing in his thin pale face.

"Glorious day, Cameron MacKenzie, glorious day!"

Jamie thundered past him, riding down the rocky banks and across the River Lochy, and Cameron swore softly as he swung atop his mount to follow his brother.

They did not take the Loch Linnhe road from Fort William, but used the more difficult West Highland Way, that cut down through Glen Nevis to loop down and around the lower edge of Mamore Forest. There, the MacDonalds left them, fading into the mist like shadows. One by one, they departed, until only Rory MacDonald and Malcolm Campbell were left to make camp with the Frasers and MacKenzies.

Still stunned by the day's events, Cameron studied the others. Morgan Fraser returned his gaze, a faint smile on his face. "It was Lianna's plan that freed you, MacKenzie. I thought perhaps you would want to know."

"Aye." He swallowed hard, staring at Fraser in the moonlight that was near bright as day. He looked up at the silver globe suspended in the sky, then back at Morgan. "You have my gratitude. All of you. I never expected . . ."

He stopped. How could he tell them that no one had ever stood by him before? Not strangers, who had nothing to gain by it. These men had risked all, and for a man they barely knew.

"Don't go maudlin on us, MacKenzie." Logan stood up, stretching, his eyes wary in the pale, silvery light. "We did it for our sister, not you."

"Aye," Rory MacDonald said, "we did it for the lass, but no' a man of us would have bothered if it was for any but Cameron MacKenzie. He stood by us, and deserves like."

Silence fell. Jamie looked up, the chains still on his wrists clanking softly. "I hate to be the one to point this out, especially in light of all this gratitude, but has anyone thought about what Breadalbane will do now?"

Morgan Fraser shrugged. "Aye, but I think that when my father returns to Fort William, he will manage the earl well enough." His gaze met Cameron's. "I understand that he will have some leverage against the earl."

"I hope so." Cameron dug his bootheel into the soft ground beneath the oak sheltering them. "If not, this may all be for nothing."

"Oh no," Malcolm Campbell protested, "I dinna think so. Leave Scotland. Dinna let the earl take ye again. 'Tis better to live free in exile than hunted in yer own country."

It was a grim thought, and Cameron leaned his head back against the oak's trunk. Wind shifted the leaves overhead, and he thought of Lianna. Being hunted would be no life for her, but neither would being in exile. They might enjoy it at first, but to spend the rest of their life away from home and family, wandering like lost souls . . . he could not do that to her.

"MacKenzie." He glanced up to find Morgan looking at him closely. "Let her make that decision."

"Am I that obvious?"

"Aye. But it's a natural concern."

Cameron tried to remind himself of that, even after arriving at the remote bothie high atop Stob Choire Claurigh a few days later. He'd protested the destination at first, not wanting to go back to the place where he'd found such contentment with Lianna, but Rory had sensibly pointed out that it was well hidden and would give him time to decide his next option. Besides, Jamie was weak and in no condition to undertake a grueling flight through Scotland just yet.

But when he was there, and staring at the sturdy stone cottage, he could not help but think of Lianna, visualizing her at the door or the window. The path was so steep the horses had been left behind, and he walked slowly the last few steps to the door, while Rory lagged behind with Jamie. It must be his imagination, but the smell of peat smoke was in the air, along with another scent that eluded his identification.

His hand pressed on the latch, and the door swung open with a suddenness that startled him into reaching for his dirk. Lianna blinked at him, eying the weapon in his hand, then glancing up at his face. She smiled slightly.

"I boiled you some bannocks."

For a moment he could not move, could only stare at her, then he was reaching out for her, laughing at her chiding reminder to put away the dirk before he cut her, and he swung her into his arms and kissed her fiercely.

"Boiled . . ." He kissed her mouth again, ". . . bannocks . . ." He kissed her straight little nose, trying not to miss a single freckle, ". . . are my . . ." He kissed her brows, then the spot below her left ear, ". . . favorite."

She wriggled happily in his arms. "I know."

"Good God," Jamie said behind him, "am I going to have to suffer this tripe for long?"

Cameron did not reply, but stepped inside and slammed shut the door with his boot. A loud banging rattled it.

Lianna laughed softly. "You can't leave him out there."

"It's a fine day. Only a little mist. He'll bear it long enough for me to have a few moments peace with you." His throat hurt, and the ache was back in his chest. He touched her face lightly, fingers skimming over her cheeks. "You shouldn't have done it, angel."

"I had to. They would have hung you."

"I know. But now . . . now you're hunted as well. I won't be able to bear that."

"Not for long." She traced his mouth with her fingertips. "Papa went to get your pardon. And he never fails."

"Perhaps this time—"

"He may be late, but he will come. I know it. Now kiss me, because your brother is banging on the door and we don't have much time."

Closing his eyes, he kissed her.

Chapter 21

"You will note that it is legal, my lord, complete with signatures and seals." Dallas Fraser watched Breadalbane's face with distinct pleasure. The earl was furious. His complexion was a bright red, and his hands curled into fists atop the table.

"This is a forgery, Fraser. And worthless, to boot." Campbell glanced up at him, malice in his eyes. "Sentence was proclaimed. He is outlawed, and will be caught and hung."

"Not for the charges you brought against him." Dallas smiled. He tapped the document atop the table with his fingers. "This is a copy of the pardon that was made at the same time as the one you and Glenlyon stole from Lovat's courier. That is deemed interference with government business, my lord, and punishable by the law."

"So it is." Breadalbane's mouth tightened. "If I was responsible, at worst I would be levied a fine, and that would be the end of it. Nothing you can say will eradicate the charges brought against Cameron MacKenzie and his brother, and I am considering bringing charges against your sons as well. I am certain I saw them in the crowd."

"There were many men in the crowd that day, all come to watch a hanging. Bring a witness that names my sons among

those helping MacKenzie, and I will do what must be done.''
He leaned forward until his face was only inches from the
earl's. ''You will drop all charges against MacKenzie, and
agree not to pursue this matter further, my lord.''

''What makes you think me fool enough to do such a thing?''

Dallas straightened. ''Because I happen to have in my possession some papers that MacKenzie seemed to think were of
some importance to you.''

The earl went still. Not an eyelash flickered as he regarded
Dallas for a long moment, then he inclined his head ever so
slightly. ''Do you. And the nature of these papers?''

''I think you know that answer. To assure you that I have
the right papers, I shall mention the names Achallader and
Dalrymple. Does that verify my claim?''

Breadalbane nodded slowly. ''Quite satisfactorily. I would
like to see them.''

''No doubt. I'm not fool enough to hand them over to you
until I have what I want, my lord. Do not think it. After you
have signed the documents absolving Cameron MacKenzie of
the recent crimes you have attributed to him, I shall give them
to you.'' When the earl's eyes flashed with rage, he added
softly, ''You really have very little choice, my lord. Lord Lovat
is panting for these documents now, and will be very disappointed to hear that they were destroyed. Do we understand
one another?''

''Very well.'' The earl studied him, then reached for pen
and parchment. ''You are a clever bastard, Fraser. If anyone
can manage to mediate between James and William, it must
be you.''

''Kings, as you must know, are a more complex and difficult
matter.'' Dallas took the paper the earl wrote out, read it swiftly,
then nodded. ''Excellent. I trust that whatever you undertake
next, it will not involve Frasers or MacKenzies.'' He waved
the letter to allow the ink to dry, then watched the earl seal it,
smiling a little. ''Even without written proof, I will still be able
to stir up enough trouble for you to rue the day you remembered
we exist.''

''Trust me, Dallas Fraser,'' Breadalbane said as he rose to

take the sealed packet Dallas withdrew from his pouch, "I will be delighted to forget that any of you exist."

The earl went to the fire burning on the hearth, and untied the packet and broke the seals. He scanned the contents briefly, then looked up at Dallas. With a faint smile, he tilted the papers into the flames and watched them burn.

Dallas held Catriona hard against him. She was furious, and turned to glare up at him. "I find it difficult to understand why you allowed him to destroy such damning evidence, Dallas!"

He lifted a brow and said mildly, "Would you have preferred he turn soldiers out after MacKenzie and our daughter? They would be hunted forever. I could not allow that."

Catriona sighed, and shook her head. "What will you tell Sir Simon?"

"I made copies of Breadalbane's letters, but they will be useless as proof. All the copies will do is raise enough questions to hopefully lessen his power and influence."

"I'd like to see him drawn and quartered," she said viciously, and he laughed.

"He sent you his best wishes, Cat."

"The devil he did!" She paused, caught her lower lip between her teeth, then shrugged. "I doubt it."

"Yes, he did. Not in those words of course, but in a pithy way that made me almost reconsider my decision to let him get away without the beating he deserves."

"I can imagine." She laughed now, softly, and turned to put her arms around Dallas. He felt so safe, so strong and secure, and she could forget now her driving fear for him when he had been so late returning to Fort William. Of course, the poor courier would have informed her of his stay with Sir Simon, but the man had been beaten near to death for the pardon he carried to Fort William. No proof of it, of course, for Breadalbane was usually very cautious. It was extremely doubtful that he would ever be so careless again as to leave behind incriminating evidence against him, and thus a dreadful shame it had been destroyed.

''If it's any consolation,'' Dallas said against her ear, ''the earl is furious and practically gnashing his teeth that he is powerless to exact vengeance now.''

''Do they know? Lianna and MacKenzie?''

''No.'' Dallas lifted a strand of her hair in his hand, then let it slide through his palm. ''Morgan will know where to find them. Write a letter. And tell Cameron that Colonel Hill has refused to file charges against him or his brother for any part in the riot. He feels guilty enough about the massacre at Glencoe as it is.''

''You should write the letter. You're much better at that than I am. After all, you're the educated member of the family, and—''

''Rubbish.'' He tilted up her face for a kiss. ''You can read and write, and know more than most men. It's a vital necessity in today's world. Education is the cornerstone of civilization, which is why I insisted Lianna attend classes at the university. Not that she protested.''

Catriona smiled. ''No, she enjoyed them very much. I had hoped . . .'' Her voice trailed into silence, and he gave her a squeeze.

''Perhaps after the baby is born, she can continue her studies.''

''Yes.'' She smiled against his chest. ''That may be a long while from now.''

''Not unless the rules have changed since our last bairn was born.''

''Dallas.'' She tilted back her head to look up at him. ''Have you changed your mind about MacKenzie?''

''If I had not, I would not have gone to Sir Simon as I did. Why do you ask?''

''Just curious. I was hoping—Lianna told me he attended a Paris university, and perhaps one day, he could be of some use to you.''

''Yes.'' Dallas sounded thoughtful. ''That's always a possibility. Perhaps I'll add something to the letter when you finish it.''

* * *

Lianna sat impatiently on a stool before the hearth, her eyes closed. "Well? Are you done yet?"

"There are times you are as restless as a child. Not yet. Let me—" Cameron broke off, muttered something under his breath, then there was the scrabbling sound of activity before he said, "Here. Your surprise, my lovely lady."

She put out her hands, eyes closed as he'd commanded, and gave a soft squeal as she felt the unmistakable outlines of fur and feline. "A kitten! Oh Cameron—" She opened her eyes, and the tiny black and white creature in her palms batted enthusiastically at her nose. Gold eyes gazed at her with interest, and a loud purr rattled the small frame. "Oh, Cameron, she's just precious."

"Glad you like her. Maybe she'll rid the cottage of mice."

"We don't have any mice that I've seen." Lianna rubbed her face against the kitten's whiskers, and was rewarded with a loud squeak of protest. She laughed at the noise coming from such a small creature. "Isn't she precious?"

"Yes. Precious. Here. Morgan brought a letter from your mother."

She looked up, some of her contentment fading. What if it was bad news? Cameron's face reflected nothing, and she looked back down at the kitten in her lap. After a moment, she set it on the floor, and watched it scamper under her skirts, batting at hems and ankles indiscriminately. With slightly shaking hands, she broke the seal on the letter, and unfolded it.

With Cameron watching, she read the letter once, then twice, scarcely able to believe the news. Then she looked up at him, relief and amusement and disbelief making her voice shake.

"Cameron . . . you have your pardon. You and Jamie are no longer outlawed."

He stared at her. Beneath his lashes, his eyes were guarded, gazing at her as if he would say it was a mistake. Peat smoke drifted out the open door and window, and in the clearing beyond the cottage, she could hear Jamie playing the pipes, a wild, keening melody that filled the air.

Cameron turned on his heel, and walked to the open window to stare out. She waited, and after a moment, he turned back to her.

"It's true?"

"Yes." She held up the letter. "Mama has written in great detail all the reasons and explanations, if you would care to read it yourself."

He walked slowly toward her, and she held up the letter, assuming he meant to read it. Instead, he dropped slowly to his knees, and buried his face in her lap. Surprised, she put a hand on his head, fingers stroking his lustrous black hair with long strokes. His broad shoulders were taut, his muscles quivering slightly, and when he looked up at last, a faint smile tucked in one corner of his mouth.

"Your precious kitten is chewing on my knee."

"Poor Precious."

"Poor Precious needs to be relocated." He lifted the hem of her skirt, and there was a loud shriek as he found the kitten and dislodged it from the material. The kitten, blinking owlishly as he held it up, opened its mouth again, pink tongue a vivid contrast to the white and black fur, and emitted another yowl as if being skinned. Cameron cocked a brow. "I know just how she feels."

Lianna laughed. Cameron was smiling at her, sitting back on his heels, his hand atop her knee for balance. He gently set down the kitten, and it immediately scampered across the floor to assault a ball of wool yarn. Cameron put both hands on her knees now, his fingers kneading softly.

"What else does the letter say?"

She caught her breath when his palms left her knees and skimmed up her thighs, but opened the letter again and tried to focus. "Let's see . . . Papa has extended an invitation to us to join them in Edinburgh. If you . . . like. . . ." She faltered when his fingers grazed her rib cage, then continued, "as he says he could use a man in Scotland who is knowledgeable about politics . . . and . . . and capable of seeing both sides of an issue . . . at once. Cameron."

"Yes, my love?"

"You . . . your brother—"

"Will stay outside playing those pipes for your brother until the sun sets." His hands cupped her breasts, fingers teasing them into hard, throbbing points. "Didn't you tell your father that you are with child?"

"Yes. . . ."

"Do you really think we should disappoint him?"

She had trouble focusing on what he was saying. His steady caresses and teasing hands made the world around her blur, and it took a moment for his words to sink in. Then she jerked her gaze to his face.

"Are you saying you want to make an honest woman of me?"

"I thought I'd already done that, angel." He leaned forward to kiss her lips, her chin, her earlobe. She shivered, and he blew softly in her ear until she twisted away.

"Yes. So you have. Well then." She braced her palms against his shoulders to lever him slightly away from her, and as he glanced up from beneath his lashes, she said softly, "Bar the door." When he hesitated, she lifted a brow. "Unless you have objections to a bairn?"

"Oh no, my love." He grinned, and rose to his feet in a lithe glide. "No objections at all. This is one time I have no dispute with being a hero."

"I detest heroes."

He barred the door and turned back to her, and there was such love in his eyes that all the worry, the fear of the past months faded into memory. Lianna lifted her arms to him, and as he swept her into his embrace, he said, "I love you, angel. Now and forever. No matter what happens, whether good or ill, I will love you."

" 'For love is of sae mickle might, That it all paines makis light,' " she quoted, and he lifted his head to look down at her.

"Aye, my angel. All pains are made light with love."

It was true, and she didn't need a fourteenth-century poet to tell her that. All she needed was Cameron.

AUTHOR'S NOTE

While Cameron MacKenzie and Lianna Fraser and their families are purely products of my imagination, Colonel Hill, Breadalbane, Glenlyon, Drummond, the Lindsays, and Sergeant Barber are actual historical characters. Their actions as recorded by some of their contemporaries are reported here, with creative license taken only as it pertains to Cameron, Lianna, and their families. I have also reported MacIan MacDonald's actions as they were recorded in a contemporary account, and some of the atrocities committed upon the people of Glencoe as well.

When dealing with history, I try to portray it objectively, but of course, the fictional characters involved will not be unbiased. They would, naturally, view the situation from their own perspective. That there was barbaric injustice done in Glencoe is historical fact.

It would be nice to be able to assure my reader that the perpetrators of the massacre met vile ends, but unfortunately, real life is not always just. In this case, it is certainly not, as proven by the following:

Master of Stair was publicly hated, and outcry forced his removal from the Scottish Secretaryship. Yet he was soon afterward exonerated by King William and granted the regality of Glenluce in his own country of Galloway.

Hamilton was punished and disappeared from history with only a minor footnote. No punishment at all fell upon the three Lowlanders guilty of the worst atrocities—Drummond, Lindsay, and Barber. Colonel Hill received his knighthood and pension—not completely unfair to my mind, for he was caught in the middle. Glenlyon rose to the rank of colonel before dying at Bruges in 1696, only four years after Glencoe.

Breadalbane was arrested and sent to Edinburgh Castle—

not for his shameful part in the massacre, but for the treasonable secret clauses arranged at Achallader in June 1691 when he had his quarrel with MacIan. He defended himself with the excuse that he only arranged the clauses to discover the Jacobite plots, and was shortly released. He continued with nefarious plots, and died at a ripe old age.

King William, though certainly to blame for his part, marched through life with grim resolution of purpose, until February of 1702, his horse stumbled over a molehill at Hampton Court and he was injured. He died on March 8, a few months after the exiled James died, but the Jacobites long drank hearty toasts to the "little gentleman in black velvet"—the mole—who had caused William's death.

As for Glencoe, though the Parliament of Scotland recommended that the survivors should have reparations, none, of course, were ever made. I do not imagine that the MacDonalds really expected such a recompense, and in any case, it would hardly bring back those they had lost. In time, the small clan struggled back to some stability. John, now laird, built a new house at Carnoch, and his successor was Alasdair, his two-year old son carried into the blizzard by his nurse that dreadful February morning. When John died, Alasdair became chief. He and his twin brothers rose in the 'Forty-five for Bonnie Prince Charlie, bringing with them one hundred and twenty fighting men. Apparently the little clan had prospered. The MacIan's grandson was a member of the Prince's Council and fought in all his battles. After the defeat at Culloden, Alasdair languished some years in prison, but was alive and living in the glen in 1773.

Finally, I think it is a fitting footnote that when Prince Charlie's army occupied Linlithgow, it was Alasdair and the men of Glencoe who held Newliston, a Stair property that the Master had gained from his wife. Alasdair demanded the honor of guarding this dwelling, announcing as his reason that the men of Glencoe wanted to prove to the world that the cause for which they fought was pure and unsmirched by the "villainy of hate."

A most noble sentiment.

ROMANCE FROM JANELLE TAYLOR

PASSIONATE ROMANCE
FROM BETINA KRAHN!

HIDDEN FIRES   (0-8217-4953-6, $4.99)

LOVE'S BRAZEN FIRE   (0-8217-5691-5, $5.99)

MIDNIGHT MAGIC   (0-8217-4994-3, $4.99)

PASSION'S RANSOM   (0-8217-5130-1, $5.99)

REBEL PASSION   (0-8217-5526-9, $5.99)